I0606769

MINDROGUE

BLACKWING PIRATES, BOOK 3

CONNIE SUTTLE

Subtle demon
Connie Suttle
subtledemon.com

Copyright © 2017, by Connie Suttle
All Rights Reserved

ISBN: 1-63478-006-X
ISBN-13: 978-1-63478-006-3

This book is a work of fiction. Names, characters and incidents portrayed within its pages are purely fictitious and a product of the author's imagination. Any resemblance to actual persons, living or dead, is purely coincidental.

This book, whole or in part, MAY NOT be copied or reproduced by electronic or mechanical means (including photocopying or the implementation of any type of storage or retrieval system) without the express written permission of the author, except where permitted by law.

Published by:
SubtleDemon Publishing, LLC
PO Box 95696
Oklahoma City, OK 73143

Cover art by Renee Barratt @ The Cover Counts

For Vickie Torres, who suffered an unimaginable loss.
And for Lindsay Torres, who was taken from this life far too soon.
Arms are empty,
Hearts are full.
A mother's love is forever.

To Walter, Joe, Larry, Lee, Dianne, Sarah and Mark. Thank you.

ACKNOWLEDGMENTS

As always, this book is the result of collaboration. If it weren't for the support of my editor, my cover artist and my beta readers, it would be less than it is. All mistakes, as usual, are mine and no other's.

About the Author:
Connie Suttle lives in Oklahoma with her husband and a conglomerate of cats. They have finally banded together to make their demands, which has proven disconcerting to all humans involved.

You may find Connie in the following ways:
Facebook: Connie Suttle Author
Twitter: @subtledemon
Website and Blog: subtledemon.com

ALSO BY CONNIE SUTTLE

Blood Destiny Series:
Blood Wager

Blood Passage

Blood Sense

Blood Domination

Blood Royal

Blood Queen

Blood Rebellion

Blood War

Blood Redemption

Blood Reunion

Blood Recall*

Legend of the Ir'Indicti Series:
Bumble

Shadowed

Target

Vendetta

Destroyer

High Demon Series:
Demon Lost

Demon Revealed

Demon's King

Demon's Quest

Demon's Revenge

Demon's Dream

God Wars Series:

Blood Double

Blood Trouble

Blood Revolution

Blood Love

Blood Finale

~

Saa Thalarr Series:

Hope and Vengeance

Wyvern and Company

Observe and Protect*

~

First Ordinance Series:

Finder

Keeper

BlackWing

SpellBreaker

WhiteWing

~

R-D Series:

Cloud Dust

Cloud Invasion

Cloud Rebel

~

Latter Day Demons Series:

Hot Demon in the City

A Demon's Work is Never Done

A Demon's Due

~

Seattle Elementals Series:

Your Money's Worth

Worth Your While*

~

BlackWing Pirates Series

MindSighted

MindMage

MindRogue

~

Black Rose Sorceress Series

The Rose Mark

Rose and Thorn

Black Rose Queen

Queen of Thorns and Roses*

~

Other Titles from SubtleDemon Publishing:

Malefactor

Transgressor*

by Joe Scholes

*Forthcoming

CHAPTER 1

*F*ren'Ell
    Randl Gage, Commander
BlackWing Pirates

"Are you sure?" I turned toward Charla, who held a whining, wriggling Barkins in her arms. The poor dog didn't like Jewl Yarro's favorite mansion in Calezia, Fren'Ell's capital city. Vik, David and I were still stumped at how Jewl managed to keep a house and a good reputation—under an alias, of course—on a Reth Alliance world.

Charla did the same thing on Campiaa, I reminded myself. She was the daughter of one of the most dangerous criminals in either Alliance, and had operated under Jewl's thumb on the Campiaan Alliance Founder's homeworld.

Jewl despised her child and mistreated her as often as possible to get what she wanted, which was a stake in the criminal activity on Campiaa. Jewl was currently locked away in a cell in Queen Lissa's dungeon on Le-Ath Veronis; Charla didn't care and hadn't asked once how her mother was doing. I can't say I blamed her. With an abusive mother like that, I'd want to separate myself from her, too.

"I don't want any of it," Charla mumbled, before turning her attention to Barkins.

1

"That wood desk is worth a hundred thousand, easy," Vik pointed out.

"You can have it. Can I go back to the ship, now?" Charla soothed Barkins, who attempted to bury his nose against her neck.

"I'll take her back," Vik offered. "That desk would look good in the Commander's office," he jerked his head toward the antique behemoth before taking a step toward Charla.

"I'll keep it, then," I said. "The rest is toast."

"Then I'll go back with Vik," David said. He was half as tall as Vik and had no desire to stay while I considered the best way to destroy Jewl's last residence.

I'd destroyed twelve others already—this would be the thirteenth. The destruction I left behind was added as charges to my criminal record—the one issued by the ASD, naming me as one of their most-wanted.

I'd removed a known criminal from ASD clutches, after all.

Nobody knew it was Jewl Yarro, and that she'd been placed in Queen Lissa's dungeon.

Therefore, I was on the ASD's most-wanted list, although not at the top. The one at the top—I was at the top of *his* most-wanted list.

Definitely.

There was a huge reward offered for the Prophet, after he'd destroyed most of Campiaa City and killed thousands.

Kooper Griff, Director of the ASD, was still trying to determine how many more may have been infected with the Prophet's disease—a spreading version of obsession with no known cure.

Anyone affected would bow, scrape and obey the Prophet's slightest whim.

We're back onboard, Vik sent mindspeech.

All right, I replied. *I'll be there, desk in hand, momentarily.* Breathing out a heavy sigh, I looked around at all the wealth I was about to destroy before sending the desk to my office aboard BlackWing XIII and allowing every wall in Jewl Yarro's massive mansion to fall.

And then setting fire to the entire thing and getting the hell away.

~

"It looks nice." Dori studied the huge, antique desk with a critical eye as it occupied the center space of my study aboard ship.

"I could seal it off and fly it to another planet, it's so big," I pointed out. "Not that I want to," I held up a hand as she made a face at me.

"The news vids are carrying the story about the mansion you destroyed in Calezia," Dori said.

"Is that what you came to tell me?" I teased.

"What do you want me to tell you? I took time away from the bridge for this, you know," she sassed. Sassed was her term, not mine, but it fit.

"I was hoping you'd heard from Kooper."

"He'd contact you directly, Commander."

"Okay, what did I do now?" I asked, frowning at her. She never called me that, unless she was pissed—another of her terms.

"Nothing. I just wanted to see if we could have dinner together tonight."

"You know, it helps if you lead off with that," I said.

"Having a spat?" Zanfield walked right through the open door and held out a comp-vid as if he were handing me a royal decree to sign.

"For me? You shouldn't have," I took the comp-vid. "I didn't get you anything," I added.

Zanfield had recently had his eyebrows done to match his hair; yellow at the base, purple at the tips. You really didn't see the yellow until you were quite close and frankly, the first few times I saw it, my eyes crossed.

"Ah, the longed-for message from Director Griff," I sighed after reading the first paragraphs on the comp-vid. "Thank you, Zanfield."

"No worries," he waved a hand and left Dori and me alone in my study.

"David certainly has a way of rubbing off on anyone," Dori shook her head at Zanfield's favorite new colloquialism. "What does Kooper say?"

"Ah, good work in Calezia, the price on my head went up, and what the hell is he supposed to do with all the stuff from Jewl's house in Calezia that I sent to the hidden space station at the last minute?"

I began tapping away on the comp-vid while Dori's mouth dropped open in surprise. "What *is* he supposed to do with it?" she asked after a while.

"Sell it. Donate it. It's money for a charity or a worthy cause somewhere," I mumbled as I tapped my reply to Kooper. "Nobody has to know where it came from, and if anybody can come up with proper papers for all of it, then Kooper can."

"But what if somebody from Jewl's past recognizes some of it?"

"Why in the gods' names would they admit they knew where it came from?" I stopped tapping for a moment and blinked at Dori.

"Good point," she admitted. "Continue with your missive," she gestured with a hand.

"Fancy words," I grinned and pulled her to me. We were kissing when the comp-vid beeped again.

"Live message from Kooper," I pulled away from Dori to answer the call.

"We have a problem," Kooper announced grimly. "Seven hundred people just disappeared from Campiaa."

~

Captain's Cubby

BlackWing X

Captain Travis Tetsuya

"XIII is already on the way," I informed Trent after asking Nathan and James to set a new course for Campiaa.

"Seven hundred people gone," Trent shook his head. "In a blink."

"We know the Prophet's behind it, and he knows we know. We even have the asshole's name," I fumed. "For as much good as that does."

"We have nothing else, though, including his hideout," Trent observed. Susan knocked on the door before entering to set cups of Falchani black in front of both of us.

"Randl's coming, too?" she asked.

"Yeah—Kooper called him first," I replied. "Thanks for the tea."

"Does this mean Charla will be with him?" Susan had a gleam in her eye. Charla was terrified of birds and Susan, a shapeshifting buff orpington hen, had frightened the woman half to death.

"I believe that's so, but I can't say for certain. He may drop her off somewhere." I shrugged. I had a suggestion on where to leave her, in case Randl asked. She wouldn't easily escape from Avii Castle, if she were so-minded. I had the idea that she trusted Randl, however, so perhaps she'd behave herself—and stay away from Susan's hen—that was a given.

"Let me know if I need to dial the hen back," Susan laughed and turned to leave.

"Any word from Wyatt? Are they back, yet?" Trent asked after Susan closed the door behind her.

Wyatt and Jayna had gotten married—quietly—a month after the disaster on Campiaa. They'd waited six months to take a honeymoon, however, choosing to stay on Campiaa to help in the rebuilding process.

Things were coming along well—until seven hundred Campiaan citizens disappeared before dawn.

"I didn't hear from Wyatt. I heard from Dormas," I shrugged. "He said Teeg is busy trying to calm the population. Families have missing kin, with no idea what happened."

"This could blow up in our faces," Trent's voice turned grim.

"That may be part of the Prophet's plan," I pointed out. "I'm worried it could boil down to blackmail and coercion."

"In what way?"

"The Prophet may hold back on—let's call them future disruptions —in exchange for what we have on Randl."

"How is Teeg explaining all this?"

"He's calling it a massive kidnapping—similar to the one that happened at the mountain resort on Pyrik. The news vids are rightfully blaming it on the Prophet; they just don't have relevant details on how or why it was accomplished."

"If word of the Prophet's disease gets out, we're all in trouble. Right now, the people think he's the worst criminal ever. When they find out he's worse than that, well, you can see how that might turn out." Trent's brow furrowed in a deep frown. Neither of us wanted to discuss the population's immediate distrust of both the ASD and CSD, or that both Directors could be forced to resign.

Those calling for their resignations would have no idea that Kooper and Jett were their best chance—along with Randl and the BlackWing Pirates—of ridding the Alliances of the Prophet and his minions.

As for infected citizens—once the Prophet was eliminated, it was likely things would return to normal if they didn't have someone commanding them.

"You think those people he took will be fodder for another mass killing?" Trent asked.

"Probably. I worry that he'll use some of them to make replacements, like he did with the WildTree employees." I wished Randl were here to discuss this with us—his insights would be most welcome.

We missed having him aboard ship—David, too. We'd had to find a replacement engineer; one who wasn't nearly as funny. Trent called Harlee humorless, but I was still holding out hope that he'd change once he felt comfortable. For now, we still didn't have a replacement for Jayna—Kooper asked us to hold her position open, in case she wanted to return.

"X just isn't the same, is it?" Trent asked. He and I were on the same wavelength, as usual.

"Yeah. Well, back to work, bro. We'll pull into Campiaa space station at midnight tomorrow. Make sure everybody is fresh and ready to hit the ground when we get there."

~

BlackWing XIII
  Randl

Mak and Jak stood at windows in the galley, watching as Dori and her bridge crew docked XIII at Campiaa's space station.

I'd gotten mindspeech from Wyatt already—he and Jayna were waiting in the VIP suite for our arrival.

We had our choice—to either stay at Teeg San Gerxon's palace in Campiaa City, or go to the mountain cabin we'd used before.

Dori wanted the cabin, so we'd stay there. Mak and Jak wanted the privacy, too; two four-armed Blevakians wandering around always caused a stir, and they hated the stares and whispers.

Charla was all for taking Barkins back to the cabin—it was a familiar place for both after their ordeal at the hands of the Prophet's kidnappers. She'd started helping in the galley, and with Gerrett's help, they were turning out amazing meals.

Gerrett was Sirenali. Zaria sent him to me, not just because he was a hell of a cook, but he could also render XIII invisible to those with power. With my shields covering the ship, it was also invisible to the naked eye and to mundane instruments.

Only a few might find us, and I figured Zaria was near the top of that list. Placing a hand on my chest where the medallion she'd given me rested beneath my shirt, I pondered her willingness to protect me and many others.

"Ready, Commander?" Vik now stood beside me—he'd skipped in to let me know the docking was complete and we could disembark.

"Ready," I said.

Mak and Jak fell in beside me as Vik led us toward the gangway.

~

"Good to see you," Wyatt grinned as he and Jayna greeted us in the VIP suite. I'd changed my outward appearance to all except the crew and those I could trust. Wyatt and Jayna fell in the latter category.

"We have a meal waiting for all of you at the palace," Jayna said as she hugged Dori. "You can go to the cabin afterward, if you want. Tomorrow, we have interviews with family members—the ones who actually saw their loved ones disappear."

Dori blinked at me—this was something new. Last time, the Prophet pulled people away in the middle of the night, and nobody knew until morning.

"This bears thinking about," I said. "Talking to those people is a good idea. I'd like to see whether any of them have been infected through the secondary method."

Wyatt knew what I meant—others could become infected with the Prophet's disease by having sex with someone already infected. For now, the Prophet was likely unaware of that possibility, and we wanted to keep it that way.

"X will be here at midnight," Wyatt said. "We've arranged for interviews to start at ten bells tomorrow morning, so they can get some sleep tonight."

"Good. I'll consider this while we eat," I said. "Do you have records and images of those we'll interview?"

"Most of them, yes," Jayna answered. "Teeg has those ready for you in his study."

"Good—thank you. I'll look at them after dinner."

"Dad wants a conference after dinner, so that would work perfectly."

"Who needs to be there?" Vik asked. He and David had made their way toward us, and now stood beside Mak and Jak, my self-appointed bodyguards.

"Teeg asked for you, too," Wyatt nodded at Vik. "David and Chief Markus, if they want to come. Mak and Jak can guard the door if they want, and Dori, of course," Wyatt grinned at Dori. "The others can stay at the palace or go to the cabin."

I didn't tell Wyatt that Mak and Jak would guard the door whether Teeg wanted it or not, but that could wait for later. Those two took their work seriously.

"Is everyone ready?" I turned to ask my crew.

With no objections, I folded all of us to Teeg's palace.

❦

"There are twenty-seven who witnessed the disappearances of family members or friends," Teeg handed a comp-vid to me.

Dori sat next to me inside Teeg's private study—Vik and David sat nearby, and Wyatt, Jayna and Markus took up a sofa against a wall.

I began flipping through images—of both the missing and their relative or friend who'd watch them evaporate from the planet.

My hand—and my breath—stopped at the ninth one.

Missing was Mae'Sandar Keel. The one who'd seen her vanish was her brother, Miz'Sandar Keel.

"I need to talk to this one, first," I handed the comp-vid back to Teeg. "A lot depends on it."

"Can you expand on that?" Teeg asked. His brow furrowed as he studied the images on the comp-vid. "Says here he's an engineer and technical advisor for the major comp-vid distribution concern here on Campiaa."

"I wouldn't care if he owned the company," I said. "Because that's not all he is—or all his sister is, either."

"Can you explain that?"

I pulled in a deep, steadying breath before telling those in the room what I knew about Miz'Sandar and his sister.

"They're shapeshifters," I let the breath out. "And not just any shapeshifters. They're Or'myr. Does anyone know what that means?"

In less than ten minutes, we had Travis and his father, Drake, in the room with us. They'd brought Drake's father, Dragon, with them, too.

"They're a race of rare dragons, and nearly extinct," Dragon said flatly. "A female to them is the salvation of the race. This will kill them all."

"You'd call them ampithere-wyrm hybrids on Earth," Drake explained to Dori. "Long and serpent-like, with forefeet that serve as arms and hands, for lack of a better term. And wings, of course. The Larentii say they're beautiful when they fly, because they curl and ripple as they sail along."

"Trent will bring the ship in—I think I'll stay and discuss this further with Randl, if that's all right," Travis said.

"Fine by me," I shrugged. "We just—we *have* to get this one back. As for the Prophet, he doesn't need to know what he has in his possession, either."

"They're a secretive race," Dragon began.

"And that's why I'll be honest and straightforward with Miz'Sandar Keel from the start."

"I'm not sure he has to know everything about the Prophet," Teeg began.

"He needs to know. He can keep secrets, and I think I can ensure that."

"How?"

"Because I'll help," Zaria appeared in our midst. "I have this for him," Zaria held up a box, which likely contained a medallion for Miz'Sandar. "I have one for our Chief of Security, too," she turned and smiled at Markus before floating a second box in his direction.

"Does this mean that Miz'Sandar will be joining my crew?" I asked as Markus snatched the box from midair and had the medallion over his head in record time.

"That's exactly what it means. I doubt you'll find him a burden." Zaria disappeared while I contemplated berth assignments.

~

"Zanfield." I nodded as I walked past him in the cabin's kitchen. He sat alone at the island, having a glass of wine.

"Commander, want a glass?" Zanfield lifted a yellow/purple eyebrow.

"Sure." I pulled out a barstool and sat while Zanfield retrieved a glass from the cabinet and poured from the bottle he'd selected for himself.

"David says you may be adding to the crew."

"That's true. Don't worry, Zaria says he won't be a burden."

"What will his position be?"

"I think it'll have to be as a special advisor—temporary, of course."

"Ah."

"Zanfield, stop worrying about your job," I said. "It's yours and nobody else's."

"Well, it's difficult not to—since I've never had one before."

"You poor, sad trillionaire," Vik walked into the kitchen and slapped Zanfield on the back.

"With coworkers like you, who needs detractors?" Zanfield sniped good-naturedly.

"Zanfield, I need you to come with me tomorrow morning, to meet with a victim's brother."

"I'll come, but why me?" he asked, pouring more wine in his glass.

"Because he'll recognize you. He won't know any of the rest of us. He still won't trust any of us—not right away, but we have to start somewhere."

"Other than seeing me on the vids, how does that help?" Zanfield asked.

"You're one of his customers—he custom-builds your comp-vids for you, when you order special features," I said. "You just thought those things magically appeared, didn't you?" I teased.

"I thought a bot was doing that," Zanfield considered my words for a moment.

"Some of your quirks are highly specialized," I said. "It requires individual handling, to set up all the exclusive security features you ask for. Once you've reset your passcodes, he no longer has access." I could tell Zanfield was getting worried that his comp-vid security could be compromised.

"You're sure?"

"Absolutely. He isn't the type to do that, anyway. He's quite secretive himself, so he understands your needs perfectly."

"Perhaps I should hire him," Zanfield began.

"Hold your horses," I held up a hand. "We have to rescue his sister, first, because she's in the Prophet's clutches."

"Oh, no." Zanfield's expression turned grim. "Please say we'll find her before it's too late."

"Zanfield, this is the worst part of your new job," I pointed out. "You wanted to wear the uniform. The bad stuff goes with it, too."

"I'm learning." I watched his shoulders sag.

"Be ready at eight bells tomorrow morning. We'll have our meeting at the local CSD Headquarters."

"All right."

"Zanfield," I said when I rose from my seat.

"What?" He lifted his eyes to me.

"You're a good man to work with," I said as I turned to walk away.

"What are you thinking about?" Dori asked when I slid onto the bed beside her.

"About bait," I sighed and pulled her close. Planting a kiss on her bare shoulder, I considered what Kooper and I intended to do initially, and understood that the stakes had just been ramped up in the Prophet's favor.

"I'm not even going to ask," Dori said, turning in my arms. "Just kiss me and forget about it for a while."

I did.

CHAPTER 2

SD Headquarters, Campiaa City
Miz'Sandar Keel

They'd moved up my appointment to speak with CSD authorities about my sister's disappearance.

Outwardly, I was as calm as any of my race should be in the face of danger.

Inwardly, I was terrified for Mae'Sandar. None of the families knew anything about where the victims were or why they'd been taken. I'd used every asset I had and hacked as many official sites as I could, trying to find that information. There was nothing to be found, other than what was readily available to the public.

Some of that hacking could get me arrested if anyone found out. I worried that this was why my interview time had changed—that the CSD knew and were prepared to arrest me.

I couldn't be imprisoned—not while my sister was missing. I felt helpless, too. If the one responsible for her disappearance were someone I could put my hands on, they'd die a swift death, no matter the consequences to me.

Mae'Sandar *had* to be alive. *I* had to find her.

Had. To.

"Mr. Keel, come with me," a receptionist met me at the door of CSD Headquarters. "Your appointment will be held in the basement." She led me toward a trans-vator, and tapped the proper button once we were inside.

The basement. A harder place to escape from, should it become necessary. I was determined not to be arrested, because I had to do whatever I could to find my sister.

"What is this?" I asked, when we departed the trans-vator and entered a cavernous room.

"Normally, it's the exercise facility and shooting range," the woman shrugged. "But we cleared all that out this morning, so your interview could take place."

I went still when several chairs appeared from nothing near the center of the empty floor.

"Everything disappeared the same way, or so I hear," her words were dry. "Good luck, Mr. Keel. Commander Gage will be here momentarily."

I almost called out for her to stay as she boarded the trans-vator. The doors closed and she was gone.

Warily turning back toward the chairs, I found a desk occupying a space behind them, now.

What in the name of the first bloody serpent was going on?

"You know warlocks can accomplish these things, surely?" A man appeared behind the desk, while a chair materialized behind him and he sat. "Come closer, Miz'Sandar Keel. I need to have a very serious discussion with you."

My eyesight is exceptional. From the distance between us, I could see the whiteness of his eyes.

He was blind.

Commander Gage, if this were he, was blind as a night-crawler.

"I don't need them," he shrugged. "My eyes. I see everything anyway."

He'd just pulled the thoughts from my head. My worry increased.

"What—are you?" I asked, refusing to move.

"He's Commander Gage, and my friend." Someone slapped my shoulder as he passed me, making his way toward the waiting chairs.

I froze.

Zanfield Staggs was here. As part of my job, I reconfigured his comp-vids to suit his specifications. *Why* was he here? He was dressed in an ASD uniform, but that was nothing out of the ordinary—it was one of his favorite costumes.

"It's not a costume," Commander Gage called out. "Zanfield works for me."

"I'm meeting with the CSD," I argued. "Not the ASD."

"Ah, but you want your sister back, don't you?" Zanfield turned to blink at me. "If anybody can do it, Randl Gage can."

Cautiously I stepped forward while Zanfield sat on one of the chairs. There were still six others. One for me, I assumed, but the other five?

"Bekzi," the second man—short and wiry, appeared.

"This is Travis Tetsuya." A third man arrived. He looked Falchani, with the traditional, long, dark braid down his back.

"This is Vik Roth," the fourth man appeared.

"Dori Anderson," the fifth—a woman, appeared.

"Susan Plume," the sixth—another woman—appeared. "Come. Sit. We have plenty to talk about."

I jumped when two more appeared to flank Commander Gage. Both folded four arms across each chest and glared at me as if I were intending to attack everyone here.

Blevakians.

Where the hell did he get them?

"They're my bodyguards," Gage shrugged. "Come on—every moment we waste is a moment we could be looking for Mae'Sandar."

The center chair had been left empty. Drawing in a deep breath, I prepared myself mentally before striding forward and sitting in the designated place.

"Allow me to make introductions," Randl Gage said first. "Everyone, this is Miz'Sandar Keel. His sister is missing and we have to get her back—it's important. Miz'Sandar—this is Mak and this is Jak," he pointed to the Blevakians standing behind him.

"I've already told you the others' names, but that doesn't mean you know everything about them, or me, or what we do, or how we do it. Rest assured, the ASD and CSD are fully aware of our existence, because we work for and with them. Understood?"

"I wish I did," I snorted.

"Except for Travis, there," he indicated the Falchani, "I and the others work aboard BlackWing XIII. Travis captains BlackWing X half the time."

It took a moment for the information to soak into my brain. BlackWing ships.

BlackWing Pirates.

The scourge of the shipping lanes.

Commander Gage laughed.

"That's exactly what you're supposed to think," Travis Tetsuya remarked. "That we're among the worst criminals in either Alliance. Nothing is further from the truth."

"Then what?" I stuttered. I was a master scholar of my race, and I knew nothing of any of this.

"I think what Randl is trying to say is that we're all different, here. You're not alone," Vik said. "To show you, I'll go first."

"What is he talking about?" I asked as Vik rose from his chair and walked to a large, empty space.

When the creature burst into view, enormous, tall, black-scaled and breathing smoke, I scooted my chair back in alarm before my brain informed me that he was High Demon.

One by one, the others changed, too.

A large cat, that Gage told me was an ocelot. A hen, that hopped onto Gage's desk and clucked at me. A dangerous lion snake.

Last of all, the sapphire-blue *dragon.*

I held my breath as the Falchani turned to his dragon.

"We know what you are, Miz'Sandar," Commander Gage said.

"Nobody knows," I snapped at him.

"That's how I'm different," he said. "Remember when I said I see everything anyway? Someone who calls himself the Prophet has your sister, and he isn't known for his kindness and charitable works. I've only seen him twice, because he hides himself from even the most powerful. We have to find him—and your sister. I know how important she is."

"We want to take you with us—to look for her," Zanfield said. "Don't worry, your job will be secured until you return—Teeg San Gerxon will see to it."

"My father guarantees it," another man appeared. I recognized him, too—Wyatt San Gerxon, the Founder's only son.

"You really do work for the ASD?" I turned back to Commander Gage.

"He does—and the CSD, too, as often as we can convince him to do so," Wyatt held out his hand to me. "Welcome to the BlackWing fleet, Mr. Keel."

I took the offered hand, feeling numb.

◦

Randl

"This cabin belongs to the King of Karathia," Vik informed Miz'Sandar. "He's ah, close with the Founder."

"It's huge," Miz'Sandar studied the steep, snow-covered mountains surrounding the cabin with interest. "Call me Miz—that's how they shorten my name at work."

"Sounds good—if you're hungry, we can probably find you something to eat," Vik said, leading the way onto the porch. "Or tea or coffee."

"When will we leave?" Miz turned to me.

"Tonight. I need to check through some information before we go —to make sure we haven't missed anything. And, I want you to tell me exactly what you saw when your sister disappeared. Even the smallest detail might help."

"All right. I'd take tea, and we can discuss that."

Later, he and I sat in the man cave, having tea with Travis, Chief Markus, Vik and David.

"Mae and I were—going over information," Miz sighed. "One of the records had conflicting information, so Mae and I were trying to sort it out. Suddenly, she gasped as if she couldn't draw a breath—then clutched at her throat. She was just—gone, then. From one moment to the next."

"That's scary," David mumbled.

"How does this happen? Do you know?" Miz asked.

"It's not a pretty story," I released a sigh. "The crux of the matter is this—your sister, and all the others who disappeared, have contracted what we call the Prophet's disease. You know about compulsion, correct?"

"What the vampires can do?"

"Yes. Have you heard of obsession?" I could see Miz's eyes unfocusing, as he searched for the information in his mind.

"Only a standard definition," he focused on me again.

"Obsession is something the Sirenali do," Travis explained. "Do you have information regarding that race?"

Again, I watched as he shuffled his mental catalog. "Yes. An extinct race."

"Not so extinct," Travis snorted. "There are a few out there with less than altruistic motives. They can conceal themselves from even the most powerful, and that's how the Prophet is hiding from us. Somehow, too, he has the ability to inject an infective sort of obsession, that can then be passed from one to another. That's what happened to your sister. When Campiaa was attacked, it was the Prophet's doing. He arranged to infect any residents who were in the wrong place at the wrong time."

"That fucking parade."

"Yes. Precisely," I agreed. "We were there, fighting them off."

"Did any of your crew become infected?"

It was a logical question.

"We have some help in that area," I said. "That's why I have this for you." I *Pulled* the medallion Zaria left for him into my hand.

"So, you don't just see things, eh?" Miz studied me as if I'd become a completely new topic for research.

"How do you think the basement at CSD Headquarters got cleared out?" David grinned. "Randl did it in two blinks."

"I was hoping you'd turn, too—it's why we did," Travis said. "That'll have to wait, I suppose."

"Wear this always," I handed the medallion box to him. "Never take it off, even in the shower. I can't explain everything it does, because I don't know. Everybody here has one, though, and there's no way we'd take the thing off."

"It comes from the Larentii," Vik whispered with a grin.

"*A* Larentii," I corrected.

"I've never seen a Larentii," he confessed. "Although we do have some information, it is far from complete."

"You may have seen one, you just didn't realize it," Travis said. "The chances in your case are very good, as you're from such a small race, number-wise. They have a habit of studying those races."

"That's frightening, to think a Larentii may be watching you in the bathroom," David sniffed.

"Stop it," Vik smacked David's arm.

"He hit me," David whined.

Travis suppressed a snicker; laughter boomed from Miz's throat.

"Miz, do you know this person?" I handed a comp-vid to him later, after going through all available images of those who'd disappeared. I'd found images recorded just as the parade was beginning—before the casino recording it exploded.

I was grateful the casino had the foresight to transmit recorded data to a secondary location in real time, so there'd be more than one copy if the first were compromised.

He frowned at the image of his sister, standing next to a man who was speaking to her at the time.

"Le'Vestar Limn," a growl rumbled in Miz's throat. "What's he doing there?"

"I think he was taken, too," I said. "Miz, this isn't the time to delve into Or'myr politics; we have to get your sister back. What I really want is this—that Le'Vestar thinks quickly on his feet."

"If I find him, he's a dead Or'myr," Miz wasn't holding back. Long, well-shaped fingers clenched into fists as he glared at the image before him.

"I can't tell you everything I see in this image—not yet," I told him. "But right now, whether you like it or not, I hope Le'Vestar is with her and doing his best to get both of them away from the Prophet."

When he turned his eyes toward me, they looked feral—as if he were considering the turn to his alter ego. "You'll have uniforms by the end of the day, Special Agent Keel," I said, snapping him out of his mood. "We'll be underway shortly after that, and I'll have Chief Markus teach you how to use weapons during our travels."

"What are you going to do in the meantime?" he asked as I pulled the comp-vid away and tapped off the power.

"I need to have a conversation or three with Teeg San Gerxon, Jett Riffler and Kooper Griff."

"I wish I could go with you," he began.

"I'm sorry, but that won't happen," I held up a hand. "I know you want every scrap of information you can gather to get your sister back, but in this case, it's not just about her. Practice patience, all right?"

I folded space, leaving him with a stunned expression on his face.

I'd just handed his deceased father's words to him—*practice patience*. They were all I had at the moment to calm him.

~

"What do you have?" Teeg asked after I'd greeted Jett and Kooper, then taken a seat in his private study.

"Hope, mostly," I said. "For the Or'myr involved, and for some of the others."

"What sort of hope is that?" Jett asked.

"We destroyed many of the Prophet's soldiers, and I'll wager that some of them were more than just expendable grunts. I think he needs engineers, information specialists, technicians—all kinds of people. He may sort through this latest batch, to keep what he needs before ah, destroying the others."

"Mae'Sandar is a technical engineer," Teeg nodded as he digested that information.

"The one she was with—the other Or'myr at the parade who shouldn't have been with her—is an engineer and a weapons expert, who worked at one time for Ruther Kend."

"So, we have obsessed experts who, if allowed to live, will do anything the Prophet tells them to do?" Kooper asked.

"I hope not," I said. "Yes, they're infected with the Prophet's disease, but their physiology is different from humanoids, as you may have guessed already. Their brains are capable of partitioning and compressing information, and I'm hoping they can partition the disease, too. That ability makes them excellent scholars—they have the best and most powerful memories in all the shapeshifters I've ever met."

"What are you hoping for, then?" Jett asked.

"That they'll have enough sense to cooperate to save their lives, while keeping their secrets safe from the Prophet. If that isn't the case and things turn sour, well, then you have to offer a trade."

"A trade?"

"He's already looking for me—you know that," I pointed out. "He recently upped the reward. This may require a great deal of thought on our part, but we can offer a trade—through the Or'myr. They won't like it I'm sure; it will be outing a very secretive race. But, to get their future Queen back, I think they'll try anything."

"Then let's hope it won't come to that," Kooper grumbled. "When are you under way?"

"At midnight," I said. "I have a few loose ends to tie up before then."

"What loose ends?"

"I've gotten DNA samples from all the ones interviewed," I said.

"Standard procedure—you accomplished all that for me, for identification purposes," I nodded to Jett. "I just took part of what you have. Between now and midnight, I have to devise a recognition spell combined with DNA codes and load it onto everybody's comp-vid."

"I don't understand," Teeg frowned.

"I think the Prophet will send his lackeys to gather food and supplies—as he usually does," I said. "Once I load my altered program into ASD and CSD comp-vids, should any of the Prophet's newest slaves take a ship or appear on any Alliance world, then a monitor may pick them up and send an alert to all of you. It's a spell, combined with the technology we have. We detain the ones the computer recognizes, and then DNA codes can confirm it, once they're in custody."

"I'll take anything at this point," Kooper said. "It sounds quite useful, if you can get it to work."

"I'll do my best," I said. "I'll need uninterrupted time to do it."

"Whatever and wherever you need," Teeg waved a hand.

∾

Vik

"He's working on something special," Dori told us as we sat at a long table inside the San Gerxon Casino. It had been rebuilt, and in record time, too.

We'd been given a private room for dinner, so we could meet with X's crew and talk.

"Can you tell us what it is?" Zanfield asked.

"No. I don't understand it myself. He only said it was a combination of power and technology. That's all I know, other than it's supposed to help if any of the missing are seen by Alliance vid cams."

"From a logical standpoint," Miz began, "That's not possible."

"Most of what Randl does isn't possible—from a logical standpoint," Travis pointed with his fork. "He sees everything with his mind, not his eyes."

"The first time I saw Randl," Chief Markus said, "He accomplished more from questioning an informant than anyone I've ever seen. I was shocked and pleased enough to send in a request; I wanted to offer him a position with my department. You see how I'm working for Randl, now, don't you?"

"Has he always been physically blind?" Miz asked.

"Born that way," Trent replied. "Didn't stop him, though."

"Do you know where we're headed, once we leave Campiaa?" Miz wasn't finished asking questions.

"Randl hasn't said, yet," Dori replied.

"She's the Captain," David jerked his head at Dori. "If she doesn't know, then nobody knows."

"We're going to make a stop at Le-Ath Veronis, first," Randl said, appearing behind Dori and placing hands on her shoulders to give her a massage. "There are a couple of things we need to take with us."

"What things?" Zanfield asked.

"A couple of dead people who used to work for the Prophet," Randl shrugged.

~

Randl

Food was brought and set in front of me. I waited until the server left before answering unspoken questions.

"What do you want with Akrinn and Lorvis?" Sabrina's question came first.

"I want to know how the Prophet finds those infected with his disease," I said. "I'm also waiting to see whether those two twitch, once we remove them from Queen Lissa's dungeon."

"To see if they were zombified?" David grimaced. "Sounds spooky."

"The Prophet is a necromancer," Chief Markus informed Miz, who gaped at David's words.

"Among other things," I agreed.

"You haven't seen anything until you've seen an army of the undead marching down the street," David offered.

"Those vids are hidden—for a reason," Dori explained. "That's how your sister was ah—infected."

"Much of the Prophet's living army died in a battle off-planet," I said. "They'd taken a fleet of ships belonging to two well-known criminals, and thought to beat back the ships and crews of the ASD and CSD. We'd called in extra ships because we worried they'd strike that way, and it was fortunate we did. We took out a lot of his soldiers that day."

"This is classified information, isn't it?" Miz asked.

"Yes. Remember that, please, as you currently work for the ASD."

"It will go no further," Miz dropped his eyes to his plate. "I've never been to Le-Ath Veronis."

"Then it's time you paid the Queen a visit," Vik said.

He wanted to see his mother—I understood that. He also didn't want to point that out, so I stayed silent on the matter. "Did Charla stay at the cabin?" I asked, changing the subject.

"She didn't want to leave," Dori said. "I tried telling her we had a private room, but she wouldn't budge. I ordered food for her and Vik picked it up."

"I think she probably needs more help that we can offer," I sighed. "I'll see if Quin can take her in while we're off across the Alliances and beyond."

"Quin has wings," Susan pointed out. "You know—like a bird's wings?"

"I know. I'm hoping to get Charla past that. Quin can be quite convincing."

"Charla has ornithophobia," Chief Markus struggled to hide a grin as he described Charla's troubles to Miz. "Susan's hen got all sorts of information out of her, when we needed it."

"Kooper said he'd never used a chicken as a threat before. It was epic," David snickered.

"You sound as if Charla's a criminal," Miz stated.

"Hmmm," David cleared his throat.

"You may as well know," I told him. "Charla is Jewl Yarro's daughter. I assume you know who Jewl is?"

"One of the Big Three?"

"Exactly. We had to find Jewl before the Prophet did, and we were forced to use Charla to do it. Susan's hen attacked, and here we are," I held out my hands.

"Where is Jewl now?"

"Ah—that's really classified," Vik's laughter rumbled.

"Really, really classified," Trent grinned.

"Above your pay grade," Travis agreed.

"It's a long story," I said. "One I can't tell you for now. I will say this, though—I have an antique desk in my study aboard XIII that used to belong to Jewl. It's quite voluminous."

"There's pay?"

"Yes—as much as you're making at your current job—it's the least we can do," I answered Miz's question. "You can report to David, our engineer, if you want to keep your mind and hands busy during our voyages."

"X will be flanking XIII on this journey," Travis said. "If you'd like to work alongside Sabrina, that can be arranged."

"Sabrina?"

"Sabrina," Travis pointed toward her—she sat between Travis and Trent.

"Sabrina *Kend*," I added as Miz appeared to be confused. "Ruther Kend's daughter."

Miz's indrawn breath was unmistakable, and anticipation bloomed in his eyes.

"Looks like you may have to take him back and forth," I told Travis. "After Chief Markus teaches him to handle weapons."

At ten before midnight, we were loaded aboard our respective ships and waiting on the station's permission to depart. X was given permission first, so we waited for it to clear Campiaa's orbit before we received the go-ahead.

"Have you done much space travel?" David asked Miz as we stood at the windows in the galley and mess, watching as the dock receded from view.

"Some," Miz admitted. "I've gotten used to it."

"It'll take two days to reach Le-Ath Veronis," I said. "We'll arrive late at night, so you have permission to keep sleeping if you want, or unload with some of the others. Beds will be waiting, if you choose that option."

"I'll disembark," Miz said right away.

"That's the spirit," David grinned. "We can stay at the Queen's palace, light or dark side, or at Avii Castle if you want."

"Avii Castle?" Miz was interested immediately.

"I think we have a winner," Vik laughed.

"I'd like to meet with Zaria, there," I said. She was Quin's adoptive mother, and could be easier to find through the Avii Queen. Plus, sending mindspeech to her directly felt uncouth.

"We're clear of Campiaa's orbit. Course and acceleration engaged," Dori announced to the crew ten minutes after we got underway.

"Get to bed," I advised those not manning the bridge. "Breakfast is at seven bells."

"What about you?" Dori lifted an eyebrow at me.

"What about me? You staying up or coming to bed?" I asked.

"I think I can get a short nap in," she grinned.

CHAPTER 3

*L*e-Ath Veronis
> *Randl*

I wasn't surprised to find Drake and Drew, Travis and Trent's fathers, at the space station to greet X and XIII when we docked. They'd transport us to the Queen's palace, where we'd meet with Lissa.

I wanted to ask her in person before taking Akrinn and Lorvis' bodies with us—we had to make sure they were in a sealed and shielded transport container before loading them onto the ship.

Too many things could go wrong if we didn't.

"Are they dragons too?" Miz asked, his voice soft as he stared at Drake and Drew.

"Yes. They're two of Queen Lissa's mates. Travis and Trent are her sons. Their father, Dragon, was the Dragon Warlord on Falchan."

"That was thousands of years ago," Miz sounded stunned—and suddenly quite interested. "His name is held in such high honor that no other warlord is allowed to take it as his own."

"Very true," I agreed. "Ask Travis and Trent to introduce you to their grandfather, someday. Perhaps, if you're lucky enough, they'll introduce you to their step-grandmother, Grace. She's the lace-feathered eagle that women warriors on Falchan hold in the highest esteem."

"I feel as if I've walked inside legends," Miz breathed.

"You may become part of those legends, unless I miss my guess," I turned to give him a smile.

"Will I survive it?"

"No idea."

~

We were delivered to the palace library, where Lissa waited for us, accompanied by Winkler and the twins' nurse, Sandra.

"I'll take them," Sandra offered. She already held one child on her hip, and expertly took the other onto the opposite hip when Winkler handed his small daughter over.

Sandra L'Thorpe, one of those ageless women who would always remain calm, steady and beautiful, walked out of the library before anyone began discussing bodies and current events on Campiaa.

The nurse made me smile—she already knew far more than anyone suspected, and accepted it with grace and aplomb.

"I hear you want Lorvis and Akrinn," Lissa got right to business.

"As a barometer," I shrugged. "Those two, even dead, may have a final use that will benefit us."

"I think we can shield them well enough, and provide proper containment," Lissa agreed. "Erland offered to create some of the shielding."

"I will be grateful for Lord Morphis' assistance," I said. Erland Morphis was King Rylend's father and a powerful warlock, in addition to belonging to the Hierarchy.

"When do you plan to get underway?" Winkler asked.

"Tomorrow," I replied. "Dori and I will be working out our course while we're docked."

"How's your father?" Lissa asked. He now resided on Campiaa, with his identity hidden so the Prophet wouldn't make him a target again.

"He's fine. He's wondering when things will go back to normal. I don't have a good answer for him."

"Nobody does," Lissa huffed. Her eyes lost focus, as if she were looking into a distance no other could see.

I recognized that look, as I often had it myself.

"I suppose you'll be visiting Avii Castle while you're here?" Winkler's grin lit his face.

"That's part of our plan," I smiled back at the werewolf. "I want to see Quin, and I hope Zaria will come—I'd like to speak with her."

Lissa didn't ask about what—she merely nodded. "There are beds here, and Quin has more than enough room. You'll be welcome either place," she said. "Make yourselves at home," she added.

"Miz hasn't been to Le-Ath Veronis before," Chief Markus spoke up. "With your permission, Captain, I'd like to show him around."

"It's your shore leave," I waved a hand. "Just stay out of trouble."

"He thinks we're young and stupid," Markus grinned at Miz.

"When we're old and stupid, instead," Miz laughed. Lissa hid a smile.

~

Avii Castle

Quin

"I think X's crew will be staying at the palace," Randl said. "XIII's will be staying here, with your permission."

"You're more than welcome," I smiled at Randl. "It's good to see you. Zaria says she'll be at dinner tonight if you want to talk."

"I do." He almost let his shoulders sag in relief. Zaria was someone Randl couldn't predict—or read. She was also someone he trusted completely.

"What will you do if Akrinn and Lorvis are reanimated?" I asked, motioning for him to sit on a bench on Justis' and my private balcony. We were at the highest level of Avii Castle, and far below, I could see the small dots that were tourist boats floating in the water. Visitors would be recording images of the massive, glass castle where the Avii lived.

Too bad nobody could give them an accurate history of who'd built it and why—rogue gods were never a topic of discussion on the tour boats.

"Zaria killed him, you know," I released a measured sigh.

"Killed who?" Randl took a seat on the bench and leaned against the back. Lifting his face, he closed his eyes and soaked in the sunlight of a beautiful day.

"Liron. The rogue god, not Justis' nephew," I explained. "Young Liron doesn't know he's named after a rogue. So many people still believe Liron to be benevolent, when he was anything but."

"Zaria killed a rogue god?" Randl was interested immediately.

"After saving my life by disconnecting my fate from his."

"You may have to tell me this tale in full, sometime."

"If I don't, perhaps Zaria will. There may be written records in the Larentii Archives, too, but Nefrigar has never offered them to anyone."

"I'm sure there are many such records," Randl conceded, closing his eyes again to soak up the sun's warmth.

"I agree. The Larentii are a wise race, and there are things that most of us don't need to know. Have you ever seen Zaria as the winged Larentii she is?"

"No. Is it amazing?"

"Yes."

"Can you imagine a race that knows the truth in every political argument, every court case, every war and every planet's history?" A smile curved Randl's mouth as he enjoyed the day at the top of Avii Castle.

"Some of that, you and I can see," I pointed out to him.

"True. Not that I want to know all of it," he said. "It's just good to know there are accurate records somewhere."

"I agree," I said, leaning back on the bench and closing my eyes. "What a beautiful day," I whispered. His soft snore almost made me giggle.

~

Randl

Quin let me sleep for nearly an hour, allowing me to wake on my own. I hadn't intended to take a nap, but I didn't regret it, either.

Dori had gone shopping with Susan, Sabrina and a few others, so there wasn't anything to feel guilty about except lost time.

It wasn't until later that I received mindspeech from Kooper Griff, asking me to meet him at Lissa's palace. *Unusual news*, he'd said, without expanding on that.

I folded space immediately.

~

Blood was everywhere, including the ceiling of a family dining room. "Only the baby survived, because she was asleep at the time," Kooper flipped through more images on his comp-vid while I studied them.

A large family dining room was depicted in every image, where nine members of the entire family of ten—a husband, three wives and five children, looked as if they'd waged war against one another before killing each other or themselves. That last part would be the most difficult to determine—without my help.

"Where is the baby now?" I asked after tapping the comp-vid to view the next set of images.

"In protective custody—it's routine," Kooper shrugged.

"How old?"

"Six months, as they measure time on Lordinus."

"Any unusual behavior?"

"None noted," Kooper narrowed his eyes as he studied me. "You suspect something, don't you?"

"I think the Prophet is expanding his talents in some way," I said. "Can you get me into the crime scene?"

"Yes."

"Good. Keep your shields up, Director Griff, if you intend to stay with me."

~

The dining room looked much like the images I'd seen, except the bodies had been removed and some of the evidence collected and taken away for further examination. Tables, chairs, walls, everything else remained, still covered in a family's blood.

It wasn't wise to touch anything, but I didn't need to—the stink of the Prophet was everywhere in the room.

"He targeted them, somehow," I turned to Kooper. "I'd suggest you have everyone watched who came into the room without protective gear."

"That didn't happen—our forensics teams follow strict guidelines so the scene won't be contaminated," Kooper said.

"Keep an eye on them anyway, and keep me informed, if you don't mind," I said. "I'm very interested in how this turns out."

"Why target this family?" Kooper asked. "Can you get anything on that?"

"No idea," I said. "Do you have images you can provide to Quin and me—from before this happened?"

"I'll put something together," Kooper agreed. "This confuses me. There's nothing in this family's records to indicate why they were made a target."

"Maybe something will turn up in the information," I said, grimacing at the bloody handprint left by the next-youngest child on the carved, wooden dining table. That child was six, according to the records Kooper shared earlier.

"I don't really know what to put in the official records, if this is the Prophet's work," Kooper grimaced. "Practically an entire family," he added, shaking his head.

"We've already seen that he has no sympathy—only ambition, as far as his own goals and desires go," I said. In my mind, this was just as horrifying and more than similar to driving crowds of people into deep holes filled with concrete, so they'd drown.

At least those people hadn't turned on one another at the end, so this was a relatively new twist. "I assume the food was removed for analysis?" I asked.

"Yes. To ensure it wasn't anything they'd eaten to cause this. At least there were no servants involved—the wives took care of the house and cooking chores. The husband owned an accounting firm, with several large banks as clients. You can see for yourself that they were fairly well off." Kooper swept out a hand, encompassing the well-appointed dining room and an adjoining kitchen. The floors were covered in natural stone, the furniture natural wood, countertops natural granite. All signs of being among the wealthier of Lordinus' residents.

"I assume they've gone through the rest of the house?"

"Yes. That's how they found the baby. Somebody here triggered the alarm system, or we wouldn't have found this for another day or so."

"All right. I'm done here for now," I said. "Can you take me to the baby, so I can look at her?"

"Let's go," Kooper said and folded us to the facility where the baby was now sequestered and cared for by suited and protected caregivers.

I stared at the wailing infant for several seconds, as a caregiver, covered in what the baby saw as a terrifying, gloved suit, attempted to feed her.

"There's nothing," I shook my head. "Not even a hint of taint. Tell them to take the suits off and hold the baby, instead of trying to scare her to death dressed like that."

"Are you sure?"

"As sure as I'm breathing."

"There's no need for the protective gear," Kooper tapped the button on the wall communicator and spoke to the attendant. "I have it on good authority that you're scaring the baby dressed like that."

The caregiver nodded and removed the headgear, revealing a woman beneath. She nodded toward us as we stood at the observation window outside. Once the rest of the suit came off and the baby was lifted in a warm embrace, she quieted and fed.

"I'll get those records and images you requested to you in an hour,"

Kooper said. "This—defies logic." With one last look and a shake of his head at the baby, who'd come away from a bloodbath unscathed, he folded both of us back to Lissa's palace.

~

Kooper sent the same information to Quin and me, so we sat at a table in Master Librarian Gurnil's Library, going over it together before dinner.

Dori and the others had returned from their shopping trip; Dena and a few others were showing them the massive bowl at the center of Avii Castle, so Quin and I could work.

"There's really nothing," Quin sighed, setting her comp-vid on the table.

"I agree," I told her. "There's nothing here, except a normal family. I can see a slight rivalry between the wives and children, but nothing out of the ordinary."

"It's too bad there aren't any recent images," Quin said. "We might have a better feel for it."

"Do you think we should ask to see the bodies?"

"It may be the only way," she nodded. "If you'll keep us shielded. I don't want any part of the Prophet or his sick fantasies."

I felt the same, I just refused to say it. The Prophet, in my mind, was more than sick. He was twisted—a mutation that should never have been birthed.

Did he know that about himself? Was he making the rest of us pay for things we couldn't control regarding his existence?

I turned back to the thought of his parentage—who his mother and father might be. I still had the gold coin he'd handled, but information I'd gotten regarding my mother's memory within it had been unnerving to me.

I was reluctant to test its knowledge again for that very reason. Still, I was curious how the Prophet had ended up with the thing— was it theft, or had my mother spent it for food or other necessities, before it fell into the Prophet's hands?

"So many questions," I breathed, setting my comp-vid down.

"I'll go with you—to see the bodies," Quin's voice was soft. "I won't rest until we know whether they can still tell us anything."

"I'll send mindspeech to Kooper."

~

"We're going tomorrow morning, to see the bodies," Quin told Justis as we sat around the long dining table in the royal suite that evening.

"You'll be safe?" Justis lifted a dark eyebrow at Quin.

"I'll be shielding us," I said. "Nothing will harm her."

"Good." Justis thanked the servant who set a plate of food in front of him. The rest of us waited until the table was served and Justis lifted his fork.

Miz, sitting next to Chief Markus, was enthralled to be at the Avii King's table. He was fascinated by the massive, red wings Justis folded at his back, and by Quin's red wings, banded at feathers' ends by gold, copper and silver.

"Is there room for another?" Zaria appeared, making Quin smile.

A place was set quickly, and Zaria settled on her chair to eat with us. Mak and Jak, still somewhat miffed that I'd gone to the Queen's palace and then to Lordinus without them, framed Dori and me at the table, faces drawn in similar frowns.

You can go with me tomorrow, I promised them in mindspeech. Both visibly relaxed.

Ever since I'd given them money to pay off family debts on Blevakia, and then set their current wages at a fair rate for bodyguards, they'd become even more fierce about protecting me. I had the feeling that if I hadn't done it, Zanfield would have quietly paid their debts anonymously.

Zanfield had never really had family. His parents had farmed him out to nannies and tutors when he was young and later, when they'd died in a kidnapping gone awry, he'd inherited their wealth and increased it many times over, while learning to protect himself and his empire.

Zanfield, as eccentric as everyone knew him to be, was also smarter than anyone suspected.

Much smarter. And, as a member of XIII's crew, was now happier than he'd ever been in his life. Secretly, he was giving away his earnings as a member of the crew to charities formed to help the Prophet's victims.

Now that he knew what the Prophet was capable of doing.

Zanfield, watching Justis and Quin initially, now included Zaria in his intense scrutiny. He knew Zaria had provided the medallion he wore. He was very curious about it—and her.

Vik and David sat together, next to Zanfield. Vik had considered staying at his mother's palace, before choosing to come to Avii Castle with the rest of us. He owed his continued-if-altered existence to Zaria and Quin.

At least his mother knew he was alive; I'd watched her watching him in our meeting earlier in the day.

Gerrett, Susan and Charla sat together at one end of the table; Susan and Gerrett had taken Charla under their wing—physically and figuratively. Charla was fine with Susan—as long as Susan looked humanoid.

Gerrett, though—I caught him winking at Zaria.

I knew her before she was Zaria, he informed me in mindspeech. No other explanation was offered, and I didn't ask. Perhaps he'd tell me her name from before—someday. Unless I was badly mistaken, though, I figured Zaria had saved him, too.

He was a slave to others, Zaria said. *Gerrett is his own person, now, as it should have always been. He loves to cook, because he was starved. He is a brother to Terrett, one of Quin's mates, and to Morrett, your friend. I recently gave him the gift of speech, although he rarely uses it.*

Gerrett and his brothers had been mute most of their lives, after having their tongues removed at a very young age. *So many things are complicated, aren't they?* I responded in mindspeech.

More than you know, she replied.

Her words had an ominous ring to them; I had to force myself not to ask further questions. The fear of what I'd learn was too great.

"Leaving tomorrow, then?" Justis' question broke the silence.

"Early," Dori answered. She sat beside me, carefully collecting salad onto a fork before eating it.

I could see easily that Justis was grateful Quin wouldn't be pulled too far into this mission. He had doubts and misgivings about our willingness to search so aggressively for the Prophet, and worried we wouldn't survive.

He hadn't seen a bloody dining room where a family had turned on itself and killed one another, for reasons only known to the Prophet.

V'dar. Yes, I could use the Prophet's name, but it troubled me too much—to put a name and a face together. As if it made him better than he would ever be. He'd had a mother. And a father. What would they think of their son, now?

My father loved me and was proud of what I'd become. I hoped I wouldn't disappoint him before all this was over. He, like Justis, worried about my survival.

As did I.

The Prophet wanted me more than anything, I figured. In order to preserve future lives, I considered that I could be forced to give him what he wanted.

He should be prepared for the fight that would come his way if that happened, because I refused to go down easily.

"Dinner is excellent," Susan pointed her compliment in Quin's direction. Quin smiled and gave credit to the palace kitchen. Time to focus on the meal and leave my thoughts behind.

~

Queen's Palace, Le-Ath Veronis

Sabrina

I saw him for the first time—Roff, the Queen's winged vampire mate. He was beautiful—as beautiful as any male could be who wore folded wings at his back.

No feathers for this one, however—his wings looked to be made of the softest, pale-brown leather—like a bat's. They didn't hamper him in any way; he'd become used to them and paid them no mind as he sat with us at dinner.

His clothes were fashioned to fit around his wings, too, in clever ways that left them unhindered if he chose to fly.

I found myself wondering what that could be like. Travis and Trent flew as dragons, but this one didn't have to change to do so. To me, that was more efficient. Something about Roff pulled at me, too, and I couldn't explain that.

"Is something wrong?" Lissa asked softly as I forced my eyes away from Roff.

"I—just felt like I knew Roff—I can't explain it better than that," I shrugged at her. "No offense to either of you," I added.

Lissa's smile was swift and welcome, as was Roff's. "Perhaps you did, child," Roff made a reply. "In a former life."

People said that all the time. Why did I feel this held more weight —more importance? I sighed. "Dinner is lovely," I remarked, changing the subject. Travis, sitting to my right, reached out to rub my back gently.

∾

Lissa

She is lovely, isn't she? I still feel a kinship, although in most ways we are separated by a wide gulf, Roff sent mindspeech.

Not only had Zaria said Sabrina was once Giff, Roff's first-born, but Breanne had confirmed it, too.

I hope she never discovers the full tale of her former life, Roff added. *It could bring so much harm.*

I'll do my best to make sure that doesn't happen, I told him. *She needs a full life this time—not only for herself, but for my boys, too.*

Life—and fate—are strange, are they not?

I remember when I first met you, I replied.

I bless that day every day, he smiled at me.

Have you told Toff?

Perhaps later, Roff said. *He may not be able to hold himself back if he knows his older sister has been reborn. He is grateful enough that Giff's child was reborn to him.*

He certainly loves his son, I agreed with a smile.

We all do.

~

Avii Castle

Randl

"How bad was it?" Dori asked as she and I sat on the balcony outside our borrowed suite. She wanted to know about the crime scene I'd visited with Kooper while she was shopping with the others.

"Bad," I said, pulling her into my arms and resting my cheek against the top of her head. "Had the Prophet's stink all over it."

"You physically smelled it?" She pulled away, blue eyes searching mine for confirmation.

"No, baby," I pulled her against me again. "The psychic scent, I suppose, for lack of a better term."

"So, you're going to see the bodies in the morning?"

"Yes."

"Just be careful."

"I will."

She didn't ask or offer to go with me—she didn't want to see dead, bloodied children any more than I did. I was going out of necessity; I'd tell her later what I discovered about them, if she wanted to know.

"Will you make love to me?" She mumbled against my chest.

"You don't have to ask, my heart," I whispered. Pulling away, I swung her easily into my arms and carried her toward the bed.

~

Travis

Trent and I had discussed the trip to view bodies; he and I felt it was important that one of us go with Randl and Quin.

Sabrina didn't voice her concern that I was the one going; she didn't have to. It was in the worried, downward pull at the corners of her mouth.

"We'll be shielded," I reminded her. "Several times over, in case there's anything lurking in those bodies. Kooper has them quarantined, and nobody's touched them without protective gear."

"So much has changed since the Prophet made his presence known," Sabrina turned away from me and hugged herself. "Nobody examines bodies without first gearing up as if they're going into the worst contagion known to the Alliances."

"Because it may well be that," I soothed. "This is our job, baby. You know that."

"I think I'll work on better ways to shield and protect first responders," she turned back to me, her worried eyes gazing into mine.

"Come here, you," I pulled her against me. "That sounds like a perfect idea," I added, kissing her temple. "If my baby is on the job, we won't have anything to worry about."

"Flatterer," she smacked my ass before stepping away. "I need my comp-vid," she mumbled, looking around the suite she, Trent and I shared at Mom's palace. "I'll make some preliminary drawings," she added. Plans were already forming in her head, I could tell.

"Breakfast first," I told her. "Then I'll go see the bodies while you and Trent discuss what's needed by those first on the scene."

"A little public education could go a long way," she said.

"Then we'll have to word it carefully, and face it, what are we going to say? Watch out for a horrible affliction that no known science can detect?"

"When you put it like that," she conceded.

Breakfast was a quiet affair. Mom wasn't happy that I was going with Randl, but she didn't object. I think she'd prefer to go herself, but she had the babies to consider. Sandra, their nurse, sat at the table with us, and she fed one while Mom fed the other.

I learned Winkler had gone to visit Lukas on Harifa Edus—there was a joint meeting scheduled with New Fyris concerning crops and a dry spell.

Randl and Quin arrived before breakfast was over, so they sat at the table for a cup of tea. Mom wanted to ask questions, directing the first at Randl.

"Kooper tells me the crime scene had the stink of the Prophet all over it," she began.

"It did. It's not a scent, specifically, it's just an overall psychic residue, I suppose. That's the best way I can describe how it feels."

"I wish I could actually take a sniff," she said.

"No," Randl, Trent and I chorused.

"No, Lady Queen," Randl shook his head. "I worry that going into that mess unprotected will not have good results."

"You're really worrying me, now," Mom said. She didn't look at me when she said it, but her concern was meant for me.

I'll be as safe as anyone can be, I told her in mindspeech. *Randl is adept at keeping things shielded.*

Including you?

Mom, he'd sacrifice himself before he'd sacrifice anyone else, I said.

After what the Prophet did to Campiaa, anyone who knows anything about this is scared.

I know.

Honey, what puzzles me is this—why did the Prophet do what he did to this family, instead of pulling them away?

We don't know. Trent and I have discussed that, and it makes no sense. We'll have that conversation with Randl, too, to see what his thoughts are.

With Kooper's permission, I'd like to be informed of what transpires.

I think we can manage that, I gave her a smile.

Good. Make sure those shields and the container are strong around Lorvis and Akrinn, too. Who knows what the Prophet's zombies are capable of doing?

I wanted to say she was worrying too much, except I had the same damn worries. Instead, I gave a slight nod and went back to my food.

❧

Lunar Base Forensics Facility, Lordinus
Randl

The Forensics Facility was located on Lordinus' largest moon. Days there were half as long as they were on the planet itself, but so were the nights. That allowed plenty of sunlight to power the solar collectors to keep the facility running.

A few bodies from unsolved crimes were kept in frozen containers there, in case new evidence showed up.

And then there was the Gant family, the newest arrivals.

Bodies were laid out on cold, metal tables in a refrigerated room, waiting for further tests. The chests of the adults had already been opened and every precaution taken, in case they carried the Prophet's disease.

Already heavily shielded, Quin, Travis and I accompanied Kooper into the chilled room. "Can you hook me up, bro—to see what you do?" Travis asked as we approached the adult male's body.

"Sure." My answer was somewhat distracted—already the Prophet's cloud had dissipated here, as if the bodies had been drained of that evil before they ever left their home.

"I feel very little," Quin observed, echoing my thoughts.

"Same, here," I agreed. "Kooper, I think he pulled whatever it was away from his victims, so we wouldn't feel it," I added.

"It was there in the room yesterday," Kooper began, a frown wrinkling his forehead.

"I know. And it may have been here, too, yesterday. I should have asked to see them then."

"Is there anything you can tell me?" Kooper asked.

"We see the murder scene—clearly," Quin whispered. "Their lives before that, too. Nothing out of the ordinary, Director. I get nothing from them that would indicate otherwise."

"Except for some reason, the Prophet chose them to turn on one another," Kooper shook his head. "I was hoping for more than this."

"I should have come yesterday," I berated myself. "I should have."

"Quin, will you write a report on what you saw in them—for the sealed files, you understand," Kooper asked. "In case something becomes relevant later."

"Of course," Quin nodded. She didn't like the sight of bodies bearing wounds laid out naked before us, with the added indignity of being sliced open by forensic pathologists.

Travis, who stood beside me, had received the same images I'd gotten—of a family fight that had turned deadly and included knives, pots, pans and every other thing that could be turned into a weapon.

The children had died first, as they were the weakest. How strong and murderous was the Prophet that he could turn mother against child?

"I'll have to think about this for a while," I said, disconnecting from Travis. We'd seen as much as we could stand for one day.

"Let's hope it doesn't happen again," Quin said.

"Hmmph," Kooper snorted.

CHAPTER 4

BlackWing XIII
Randl

"It was disturbing," I told Vik. "Somehow, the Prophet drained the malice out of everything by the time we saw the bodies this morning."

Vik and David sat with me in the ship's dining hall, watching stars slip past like streaks of light. We were headed toward another dead planet, where a science team reported unusual activity.

Other ships had been warned away until someone could investigate. *We* would be investigating. Until then, three Alliance gunships patrolled Ca'Lex's orbit.

Ca'Lex. A target for treasure hunters. No humanoids had lived on the planet for a thousand years or more, but that didn't mean there weren't artifacts remaining. If you could survive the insects, wildlife and rampant greenery covering the habitable parts, you could dig to your heart's content for whatever the ground still held.

"How do you kill your own kids?" David was back to our original topic of discussion.

"I don't know, but it happens at times." I sipped my tea absently, thinking I'd rather be drinking beer.

"May I join you?" Zanfield arrived with a cup of tea.

"Have a seat," I pushed out a vacant chair with power. "We were just discussing the Gant family."

"If I had a family, I'd instruct my own bodyguards to shoot me before I harmed them," Zanfield huffed.

He was serious—I could see it easily. Some might say those words, but they wouldn't mean them. Zanfield meant them with every cell in his body.

"Too bad they didn't have bodyguards," David set his mug on the table with a thump.

"We don't know that they wouldn't have been affected, too," Vik pointed out.

"True. This is fucked up," David shook his head.

"I hope it doesn't happen again," I blurted. I still had the images of a murder scene in my mind and the visions refused to leave or be muted.

"How long to reach Ca'Lex?" Zanfield asked.

"Tomorrow," I replied. Frankly, I wanted to fold space with the ship rather than let it stay the normal course—any activity would be welcome, even if it did involve jungle conditions and a hostile planet.

"Want to work out?" Vik asked. "That's what Markus and Miz are doing."

"Sounds like a plan," I agreed. "I'll change clothes and meet you in the workout room."

"Learned from Drake and Drew," Vik panted as we stood apart after a lengthy sparring session, wooden blades pointed at the floor as we worked to even our breathing.

He was good, and his height and longer reach was an advantage in most cases. I was hard-pressed to beat him back.

"Good workout," Vik grinned and held up his fist, knuckles out.

David called it a fist-bump. I complied and grinned back. The sparring session was worth the sweat and exhaustion—the bad memories had finally taken a back seat to the present.

"Only thirty hours to go—as Le-Ath Veronis measures time," Vik turned to grab a towel from a nearby bench. After wiping his wooden practice blades, he hung them on the wall and settled the towel around his neck, using one end to wipe his face.

"Is it time for lunch, yet?" David wandered in. "Damn, you smell like an old gym locker," he made a face at Vik.

"I'll get cleaned up," Vik said. "Want to do my laundry?"

"What the fuck? Me, engineer," David tapped his chest. "You, brawny grunt," he then pointed at Vik. "Brawny grunts do laundry."

"Says who?" Vik sounded skeptical.

"Says every space movie I've ever seen."

"I don't recall anyone doing laundry in any space movie. I've even seen the specs for the *Enterprise*. I didn't see a laundry room in any of that."

"Then you didn't study hard enough," David teased. "It's on deck H. I checked."

"Shouldn't it be on deck L? For laundry?" Vik wasn't going to let it go.

"See, that's just the kind of thinking you'd expect from a grunt."

"Right," Vik countered. "Go wash your hands, engine monkey, I'm hungry."

"I'll be eating before you get out of the shower, and don't call me engine monkey."

"They used to call mechanics grease monkeys," Vik laughed.

"I'm a mechanic?" David roared. "A fucking mechanic? Oh, you'll be sorry for that one, string bean."

"String bean? You're making me hungrier. Are you walking out of here with me, or do you want to be carried?"

"Oh, sure. Start with the short jokes again," David fumed. Both continued to argue as they walked out of the exercise room. "I'll fart on your pillow," came floating back as they wandered along the hall toward their quarters.

I collapsed onto the towel bench and guffawed.

～

Miz'Sandar

Markus arranged for us to be transported aboard BlackWing X, where we met with Captain Trent. Captain Travis was acting Captain for the day, so Trent agreed to talk to both of us about blade fighting.

"Bro and I have put together a few tutorials that you can read on comp-vid," Trent told us, sweeping his long, black braid over a shoulder. "Mostly, it has to do with the types of blades available, how to care for them and such. These," he pointed to the table between us, "are practice blades. Once I hand them to you, you'll give them the respect you'd give a battle blade. The care you take with them can mean life or death on the battlefield."

"You really are Falchani," I said.

"Yes. From a long line of Warriors and Warlords," Trent agreed. "While that high position will never come to us, we do what we can where we are. We've used our own blades many times, in taking down criminals. This isn't an ancient art for sport or display fighting only."

"Randl says the discipline learned can be translated into other fighting arts," Markus nodded.

"He's right. I know who trained Randl, and he's a blademaster who learned from the best."

"I know this is forward, but how long before we will be allowed to pick up our blades to spar?" I asked.

"Not long—when you're able to go through all the exercises, plus the care and cleaning of your blade, you'll be given wooden practice blades. Those, if broken or damaged, are easily replaced and less destructive on wrists and other body parts." He grinned when he said that.

"I wondered at the lack of a cross guard," Markus observed.

"Some are trained initially with a cross guard, but those are done away with after the first few lessons," Trent said. "We were taught without one, from the beginning. Our grandfather says it isn't wise to depend on your sword to protect your hand—your movements and expertise should do that."

"And fighting with two blades helps, I'm sure." Markus said.

"It does. Most of your enemies won't expect a single blade, let alone two. Great-Uncle Crane always says attack with one blade, stab or slice with the other."

"Those of my race have a similar saying," I offered. "Distract with tail, kill with teeth."

"That's very good," Trent's mouth curled into a smile. "I'll remember that. How are the shooting lessons going?" He turned to Markus.

"Really well. Miz has an uncanny ability to focus on his target."

"My eyesight is very keen—as it is with all my people."

"Like a raptor's?" Trent was curious.

"Very much like that," I agreed. "We can see small things from high up or far away—while having an extended field of view. It's how our eyes have evolved."

"That would be an excellent edge on a battlefield," Trent said. "Focus on the one you're engaging, while seeing everything else around you."

"We've never fought like that, but you're correct—it could be useful in those circumstances."

"It may prove useful in the future," Trent said. "Learn your lessons, Miz—we don't know what we'll face before this is over."

"I understand that well," I said, reaching for the handle of the practice blade nearest me. "I will study the texts and be ready for my first lessons. *Soon.* My sister is waiting."

~

BlackWing XIII
Randl

We'd just entered Ca'Lex's orbit when the message came from Kooper. At least a family hadn't turned on itself this time.

Instead, a packaged food distribution facility had gone crazy during a night shift, and every employee on duty was now dead. Kooper's description of the scene made it sound worse than that of the Gant family.

The entire operation had been shut down, while other employees and the owners were having a meltdown. For now, the facility was off-limits to anyone except those sent by the CSD—the planet belonged to the Campiaan Alliance, this time.

"I'll be there shortly," I said. "We just arrived in Ca'Lex's airspace."

"Keep everyone staying behind onboard, then, until you get back," Kooper warned. "Bring Travis or Trent with you, if you want."

"I'll bring one of them," I agreed. "We'll have shields up and full security measures in force while we're gone—we don't need to be attacked while we're distracted."

"Just what I was thinking," Kooper sighed. "Let me know when you're on your way. We've set up in a nearby building while the forensics teams search the crime scene."

"Will do." I tapped the comp-vid to end the conversation before sending mindspeech to Travis.

~

BlackWing X
　Travis
"I'll go this time, bro," Trent offered.

"If you're sure," I began.

"I'm sure. See if Sabrina has any ideas on how to pinpoint irregularities while we're gone," he added.

"We'll work on that," I said. "Don't let it get to you. That first scene was brutal, and what Randl transmitted, mind-to-mind, was worse."

"I'll keep you posted," Trent said. "I'll even fold space if I need to barf."

We always laugh at Mom's use of that term—it makes no sense in any language except that of Old Earth.

"You'll be fine," I punched his shoulder. "Randl may want to see the bodies, though, so be prepared."

"I will."

~

Huyer Food Distribution Warehouse, Woord'l
   Randl

Mak and Jak wanted to come. I ended up settling for Mak and Vik, instead. The Blevakian brothers were satisfied with that arrangement. I figured both had seen their share of bloody crime scenes, so I didn't feel obligated to warn them ahead of time.

Trent, dressed in black leathers with both blades in sheaths at his back, was silent and determined as Kooper led us into a side door of the warehouse, near the loading dock where most of the carnage took place.

Kooper frowned at Trent's preparedness, but I didn't. From the moment we walked in, I knew there were survivors hidden somewhere, waiting. The stink of the Prophet's interference was everywhere.

～

Vik

If Randl hadn't shielded us as well as he did, we'd have died or been severely injured in the initial attack. I'm sure the investigators had no idea that there was enough space below the extendable deck to hide a dozen or more attackers.

You have individual shields around you, Randl sent rapid mindspeech. *Go to work.* Even Kooper held a laser pistol, shooting at attackers who were also shielded heavily. Most of his shots ricocheted away from those shields, pinging against metal columns or tearing chunks out of less substantial walls instead of hitting intended targets.

Several CSD agents who'd been standing guard were also engaged, but as they weren't shielded at first, we lost three quickly.

Somehow, in the midst of blasting the enemy, Randl formed shields around the other agents, who were now protected as they fired their weapons.

Randl couldn't bring the facility down—that would destroy the crime scene. For a moment, as I fired my pistol at an attacker, I wondered whether these men were the Prophet's minions or former warehouse workers.

～

Randl

I recognized this as the trap it was meant to be, right as we were attacked. The Prophet's reach had become long, it appeared, as I read in a few faces that they were from Campiaa, and part of those who'd been snatched away from there recently.

Miz's sister wasn't among them.

She was valuable to the Prophet, if he'd bothered to learn about the skills of those he'd taken.

So far, we'd only managed to kill one attacker, and that was because three agents fired at the same one, bringing an entire wall down on him.

The rest were well-shielded by the Prophet, although to a fault—unless those shields were breached by us, only air was allowed in.

Those he'd sent to attack us would die within their shields in a matter of days, as they could only fire their weapons past the shields.

Target the weapons, Kooper sent to the rest of us.

That was harder than it sounded, as the attackers had been instructed to keep moving.

That's when I stopped, closed my eyes and focused solely on their laser rifles.

～

"Now what?" Kooper asked as the attackers bumped into one another behind the containment shield I'd built around them—after destroying their weapons.

"I suppose we'll have to figure out how to destroy their shields, or take them somewhere so they can starve to death," I replied.

"Fuck," Kooper cursed as he watched obsessed attackers attempt to keep moving within the containment shield.

The bodies of three dead agents had already been removed when Jett Riffler arrived on the scene. He'd traveled by mundane means to get to us, and managed the distance in record time.

His dark skin glistened with sweat in the afternoon light as he walked onto the loading dock, flanked by two guards—he and they had run the remaining distance after a transport dropped them off half a mile away.

"They can't see outside the containment shield—I constructed it that way," I told Jett before he could voice his concern. "If the Prophet is seeing through their eyes, he's not seeing anything except a blank wall right now."

"So they laid a trap," Jett shook his head. "This makes things worse."

"I think he drew us in with the Gant family, and then set us up for this," Kooper said.

"If Randl hadn't been here, we'd be dead—most of us, anyway," Vik remarked.

"When did you know the Prophet was involved in this—and had troops hiding?" Jett asked.

"The moment we stepped onto the loading dock," I answered.

"I'll be sure to write up the fools who didn't examine everything, including the platform," Jett rumbled while looking around the loading dock. Instead of only seeing a bloody floor and walls, as it had been, one wall was now collapsed, the others pock-marked with laser blasts.

The concrete floor would be stained with blood, but I imagined it could be painted over. With the Prophet's small army nearby, although contained, the stink of his interference hung heavy in the air.

"We've removed the one crushed by the wall," Kooper said. "His shield collapsed when the wall did. No idea how that happened, but he's flatter than a ribbon lizard, now."

I turned to blink at Kooper. "It fell on him from overhead, didn't it?" I asked.

"If you mean the wall, yes."

"Maybe we can destroy the other shields the same way. We've been attacking them from the sides. Maybe we need to do that from the top —or the bottom."

"We can try both," Kooper said. He sounded as if he were willing to try anything at this point.

"I recognize some of them as those missing from Campiaa," Jett said. "Can you get anything useful from any of them?" He turned back to me.

"It's the same as usual—they bear the obsession of the Prophet. They don't even recall their names at this point, they just want to kill me and anyone else who gets in their way."

"There's no saving them, or any reason to question any of them?"

"Not at this point," I replied.

"Damn." Jett sounded weary.

"They'll try to fight anyone who makes an attempt to question them, and you may not get answers of any kind," I went on. "These are just killing machines, now."

"Are they clean, or is there forensic evidence we can collect to see where they've been?" Trent asked.

"Is there a way we can place them in suspension?" Vik suggested. "In case a cure or something is found?"

"That's an excellent idea," I blinked at Vik. "I think I can do that."

"What are we waiting for?" Kooper rumbled. "Get on with it, and once they're rendered harmless, we'll see if they have evidence on them."

～

BlackWing X

Travis

Things got complicated, Trent informed me in mindspeech. *There are now fourteen of the Prophet's minions in stasis, after they tried to kill us. We only managed to kill one.*

I'd sent out tentative mindspeech initially, after he'd been gone eight hours. It should have taken less than half that.

What about the warehouse? I asked.

Kooper says it'll have to be shut down until further notice. Looks like the owners will have to set up their operations in an empty facility nearby until this is cleared up. Randl says the stink of the Prophet is all over it.

Doesn't sound good, I said. *Was Randl the main target?*

We think so. Maybe next time, he ought to show up in heavy disguise.

Not a bad idea.

Yeah. Nothing happened until he walked through the door, and then all hell broke loose.

I guess the Prophet knows the coin trick won't work on Randl, I said.

Randl knew something was up the minute he walked through the door. The Prophet can't hide his signature from Randl, like he can from anybody else. I didn't feel anything the whole time we were there.

Does it feel like things are getting worse—like the Prophet's getting more devious? I asked.

I think he thought it was going to be easy, until Randl showed up. Now, the Prophet has to kick things into overdrive to thwart Randl.

Do you sometimes feel as if this is good and evil battling each other, with no way for either to win? I asked. *Like being evenly matched, or something?*

I hope that's not the case, or this could go on forever, with piles of bodies left in its wake.

Yeah.

When do you think you'll be back?

Maybe in an hour. We haven't had anything to eat, so Kooper may want a dinner meeting. If that happens, I'll let you know. Has Sabrina come up with anything there?

She's using a scanner she modified earlier. So far, nothing out of the ordinary, but it takes time to scan every inch of a planet, down to the core.

Nice. Kooper will probably be interested in that technology—right now, the only thing in production that'll scan to the core is huge and carried on a science ship.

She modified a regular scanner that'll fit in your locker, I said. *Appears to work just fine but it's slower than she likes. Now, she and Miz are working together to improve that.*

Sounds great. Let us know if you find anything, I said. *Kooper's back and he wants a meal and a meeting.*

~

Randl

For a while, we'd felt too nauseous to eat, so we'd used that time to write an official and an unofficial report for Kooper. The unofficial one would include my take on the Prophet's influence in the events—something that couldn't be proven for the official version that others would read.

Kooper, Jett, Ildevar Wyyld and Teeg San Gerxon would be the ones to receive the unofficial versions, for their eyes only.

The only other people who knew about those reports were the ones writing them. Mak had a good memory, so he wrote a report for the official files, with full understanding of what needed to go in and what needed to stay out. He and his brother had a good educational background, which I'd come to appreciate very much.

Their former employer, Jewl Yarro, had only cared about their bodyguarding capability.

"Ready for food?" I asked, slapping Mak on the back.

"Since about two hours ago," he said, scooting his chair back from the borrowed desk and standing to stretch cramped muscles. All four arms went behind his head as he bent from side to side, eliminating kinks and cracking joints.

"Good," I told him. "Kooper wants to have a meeting while we eat," I continued. "I'll buy you a beer or two, if you want."

"I'd take about six," he agreed with a wry smile.

"I hear that," I said. "Want to walk or fold space?"

"If it's all the same to you, let's walk. My legs are cramped after sitting so long."

We walked through the maze of hallways in the local CSD Headquarters, until we found Kooper, Trent and Vik standing near the front door. Jett was with them. He'd be coming to dinner with us; I could see it in his face.

~

"A round of drinks," Jett said when a waiter sidled up to our table in a private, upscale restaurant not far away.

Our drink orders were taken, with half of us ordering the largest beer they offered. "Room for two more?" Zaria arrived, and with her was another Blevakian. While I couldn't read her, I could read Bleek, who was one of her mates.

Mak blinked without speaking; I determined quickly that Bleek was a hero—a legend on Blevakia.

"How—is your son?" Mak found the courage to speak.

"Barc is fine. He's getting high marks in an advanced school on Wyyld." Bleek was happy to talk about his only child. "How is your family?"

"Thriving," Mak replied. "Very well, thank you." He knew they had things in common—both had worked for a criminal at one time, and had been rescued from that life by the ones they now stood beside.

"If your eldest wishes to attend college off-world, her tuition will be covered on Le-Ath Veronis," Zaria leaned around Bleek to inform Mak.

"Thank you—I'll remember that," Mak said.

"Just tell her to write a letter to the Queen, asking to be admitted. I'll tell Lissa it's coming," Zaria added.

"She loves studying history," Mak blurted.

"There is no finer college to learn that subject—from instructors who actually lived through much of it," Zaria replied.

Take her up on it, I told Mak in mindspeech. *Zaria is right about this.*

Kooper cleared his throat, taking us back to the reason we were here to begin with. "I'm not sure Randl should come to future sites, unless a way can be found to get him in without the Prophet knowing," Kooper said.

"That's why I'm here," Zaria said.

"Why are you here?" Kooper lifted an eyebrow when he turned in her direction.

"To change his outward appearance and a few other things. Don't worry—to those who matter, he'll still be the same. To the Prophet and anyone else who doesn't need to know, they'll see someone different. Every time."

"I'm not going to ask how that's possible," Kooper shook his head. "Whatever you need to do, I suppose."

I could tell Kooper saw this as usurping some of his power. I saw it as a potential life saver, and not just of my life.

"I'm not trying to take anything from you, Director." Zaria sounded frosty. "I'm attempting to preserve what you still have."

"I get that." He pinched the bridge of his nose. "We've had a trying day."

"I know." Zaria sounded more amenable.

"What do you need to do?" Kooper asked.

"It's already done," she shrugged. "Remain cautious, Director. Things will proceed as they will."

With that, she and Bleek rose from the table and disappeared. Mak was disappointed—he wanted to talk more with Bleek. Kooper's initial reaction to Zaria's assistance had precipitated her early exit.

I understood Kooper's frustrations up to a point. Being what he was, he was limited in what power he could employ to combat the threat the Prophet represented. Zaria, on the other hand, could do more, and didn't appear to have the same restraints.

Kooper found that frustrating, as would I.

I realized then that I held a unique position in this war with the Prophet—I was under no obligation to follow a set of rules delivered alongside the power I held.

Zaria was the same as I—we were rogue participants in the Hierarchy's eyes, I suppose. We'd come to our power through other means—I'd been born to mine. I had no idea how Zaria's developed.

Perhaps those were questions for Quin—when we had time to talk. *Director*, I sent to Kooper, *stop worrying about it. I know you're frustrated. I think we all are after today.*

Let's order now—we have plenty to discuss, he replied.

BlackWing XIII

Randl

I didn't know at first, until the restaurant manager thanked Kooper when we walked out of our private dining room later. The only person he remembered seeing was Kooper. All the rest of us looked different to him. I didn't delve too deeply into what he saw, only that he wasn't didn't recognize the rest of us.

Zaria had changed all of us, and not just me. The Prophet would be hard-pressed to put a name or identity to X's and XIII's crew from now on.

Thank you, I sent to Zaria as I approached the bridge. Dori would be there, and I'd tell her what we found at the warehouse. We'd also discuss any information she'd received from Sabrina regarding the deep scan of Ca'Lex.

Be careful, Zaria's reply entered my mind.

We'll do our best.

~

BlackWing X

Travis

Trent was exhausted, but he wanted to know if we found anything. I couldn't put him off until the next day; I knew Dori would deliver the news to an equally exhausted Randl when he arrived on XIII.

Beneath so much jungle growth and piled debris, we'd found two deep, square holes, where undoubtedly there'd been liquid concrete poured at one time.

Both holes were now empty, and mostly filled in with vines and detritus. We'd have to visit the planet to learn what we could on how long the holes may have been empty, and what, if anything, we could determine about the contents before they were removed.

We'll go to the planet's surface in the morning, Randl's mindspeech told me how tired he was.

Yeah, I responded.

CHAPTER 5

a'Lex
    Randl

"There's a trog-fly nest near the top of the hole," Miz pointed out as we stood at the edge of the first emptied crater. "It couldn't have tunneled in from the side like that if the concrete were still there. I estimate by the age of the larvae that the hole has been empty for around twelve days."

Miz was a walking science comp-vid, we discovered. Who knew what other sorts of information he had stored away?

"It takes eleven days for the eggs of the trog-fly to hatch, and these are newly hatched, according to the size—only a day or so old."

Do you think this could be another trap? Dori sent. *Is the Prophet hoping you'll come to check on this?*

No idea, I replied. *Zaria's disguises are in effect, though, and I don't feel anything overly strange, Prophet-wise, about the area, other than what's coming from this hole. I hesitate to touch the area around it, though, in case he's set a trap for me that way.*

I don't want you to touch it, she confirmed. *It scares me.*

"I'll take a soil sample," Travis said. We wore protective suits, and I had no desire to pull mine off to get a feel for what happened, here.

With a soil sample, I could place a shield around myself aboard ship and see what I could determine that way. I didn't want to frighten Dori or the others, either, but I felt a watchfulness about the area—as if eyes were on us. The feeling was vague—more of a slight discomfort, rather than a full-blown concern.

"Take enough for two testings," I said aloud.

Travis turned toward me; I could see his frown through the clear mask of his suit. *I need some for me, too, and not just the science team*, I sent. *I don't trust the Prophet in this.*

Understood. Travis took the trowel Miz handed to him and began shoveling dirt into a collector before sealing it shut. "The other location is two miles away," he said. "Prepare to be transported, everyone."

The second hole bore similar signs of age, according to Miz. More dirt was shoveled into a second collector. In both locations, jungle conditions were present. This entire section of the planet was choked with trees, vines and rampant plant growth.

Trees were closer to the second hole, however, and I became wary, as the feeling of being watched increased somewhat. I didn't detect malice in the watchfulness—not specifically, anyway, just a wary regard, as if whomever it was held deep concern—and curiosity—over our presence.

It wasn't animals or shapeshifters—those had a different feel. This —I had no explanation for it, as I hadn't felt it before.

"Ready for transport to the ship," Travis announced. Seconds later, we were taken away from the planet's surface. I'd folded my crew away while Travis did the same with his.

Half an hour later, my share of the soil samples landed in my office, courtesy of Miz, Trent and Markus.

"Properly sealed," Miz set both bio-containers on my desk. "If you'd like assistance in doing the analysis," he offered.

"Miz, I'm going to touch them," I admitted. "With my bare hands. I'll be shielded when I do it."

"What will that do?" Miz turned to Markus.

"He can feel the past through objects that were present during certain events," Markus shrugged. "I can't explain it better than that."

"I didn't do it while we were there in case the Prophet was watching, somehow," I hedged. "I didn't exactly feel his presence, but."

"Travis says he felt like he was being watched by something," Trent offered.

"Good. Then I'm not the only one," Markus said. "What I felt— David calls it the willies."

"Markus, Miz, interview everyone who went to the surface," I said. "Ask them who felt as if they were being watched. Send a report to me afterward."

"On it," Markus said. He and Miz strode out of my office, leaving me alone with Trent and the samples on my desk.

"You don't think it was the Prophet, do you?" Trent asked.

"No. This was something I hadn't felt before. Perhaps the Prophet has new allies," I said.

"That's not good."

"It may be something else," I said. "I may know more when I touch these." I tapped the containers in front of me.

"Need someone to watch?"

"I'll ask Vik. He should be able to intervene or call in the troops if needed."

"Good enough. Hard to come to terms with him being an older brother, you know."

"I think he feels the empty years between you and Travis," I said. "Things should have been different, but they weren't."

"Things should have been different with Reah, but they weren't," Trent sighed.

"Every family has its share of darker times, I think," I said.

"What about yours?" Trent asked.

"Except for my mother dying early," I began. I recalled my vision of her after touching the Prophet's coin. Someone had harmed her in the past. I still hadn't gotten to the bottom of that, yet.

"You may be luckier than most," Trent said. "I have to go. Trav's watching the bridge until I get back."

I watched him disappear in front of me. *Luckier than most,* he'd said. That remained to be seen.

~

Prophet's Compound

Mae'Sandar Keel

Le'Vestar tried to wake me from the stupor I suffered for days, before my brain came out of the fog placed by our captor. Until then, I'd been under the Prophet's influence, reacting to his instructions and those of his other trusted minions, while my brain struggled with its subjugation.

Lev, how are we going to escape? I asked in mindspeech as we worked together to rehabilitate a retired transport ship. Our engineering skills had kept us alive and out of less savory assignments.

Lev and I had already overheard that one such assignment had gone badly for nearly twenty of the Prophet's newest conscripts. The Prophet wasn't happy, we knew, as he'd missed an update on the progress Lev and I were making.

Somewhere, too, I imagined that Miz'Sandar was going crazy looking for me. He wouldn't care whether Lev was rescued or not—his concern would be only for me.

I cared that Lev survived. That's why I wanted more than anything to escape this trap, if only to stay together instead of being pulled apart. Miz and the Or'myr Council would see to it, if we survived.

Escape would take time, however. Whatever the Prophet had done to both of us still held sway on parts of our brains—the parts that allowed us to transform and protect ourselves. For now, Lev and I were working to compartmentalize that dangerous lock on our shapeshifting abilities.

Lev wanted the Prophet's death for what he'd done to us—and especially to me. I read his expression when he thought I wasn't looking; a determination to get us away, but not before making our captor pay for our kidnapping and suppression.

Lev and I—we loved one another. Had for nearly a year. Miz and the Council wouldn't understand, either; they'd force me to marry another to continue the race. Someone they considered more acceptable.

I cared not that Lev's grandfather had broken Or'myr law, shaming his family. Lev shouldn't be forced to pay for another's crime. At the moment it was moot, since Lev and I were captives and, if my guess were correct, nobody knew where we were. If they did, we'd have been rescued by now.

The other trouble, too, was that there was some sort of shield in place at the Prophet's massive compound, which kept mindspeech from traveling outside it. My first, tentative sending to Miz had echoed inside my mind.

Lev and I would only stay alive as long as the Prophet found us useful.

Therefore, we would remain useful—until we found a way to escape.

"Report?" Our supervisor, Yurik, arrived to ask us about our progress.

"Here is the list of replacement parts, as requested." Lev spoke in a monotone, handing the comp-vid to Yurik.

The comp-vid was useless as anything other than a recording device.

"Are there accompanying images or specifications?" Yurik demanded.

"Yes, Supervisor Yurik." He could have seen that for himself, if he'd bothered to look at the first screen. I had the idea that Yurik was out of his depth as far as engineering went.

"Are these parts readily available?" Yurik went on.

"Some may be more difficult to find—this freighter is nearly fifty turns old," Lev replied.

"Suggestions?"

"Look for scrapyards or ship recycling businesses," Lev answered. "Parts may be found there, perhaps, if new ones aren't available."

"All right. I'll expect another report tomorrow morning." Lev and I watched as Yurik stalked toward the door. He had no idea how to obtain parts that he had no knowledge of until a few moments ago.

The Prophet would be displeased if he failed. If Yurik failed and survived the Prophet's wrath, then Yurik would visit his displeasure upon us—we'd seen that sort of thing already, with other captives who'd been put to work.

Failure wasn't looked kindly upon in the Prophet's world.

Keep working, Lev turned my focus back to our task. *Tonight, we'll concentrate on forming teeth and claws.*

Teeth and claws. With those, we could defend ourselves. The rest would come afterward, and we'd win our freedom with wings and scales.

~

BlackWing XIII

Randl

I hadn't touched the soil samples, yet. Instead, I'd retrieved the small box containing the coin spelled by the Prophet, setting it beside the soil containers.

I worried that my mother's images would appear again, and I'd receive more disturbing information.

As for my father—I considered bringing him with me, but decided it was a bad idea. As much as I'd like his nearness and advice, I didn't want to place his life in danger again.

I left him on Campiaa—he'd gone to work as Wyatt's assistant, to organize his personal and business schedules. Organizing things was one of Pap's many talents, and it was an upgrade in pay from his previous job.

The Prophet thought him dead, and I preferred to keep it that way. Pap went by another name, now, courtesy of Teeg San Gerxon and Jett Riffler.

"You rang?" Vik walked into my study.

"That's an old one," I pointed a finger at him. Old Earth

communicating devices rang with a bell at first, before more sophisticated alerts became commonplace.

"Have you ever seen a rotary-dial telephone?" He grinned.

"Have you?"

"I saw images."

"But not in person?"

"No."

"Then neither of us has actually seen one?"

"I suppose that's true."

"I'll bet Dave has seen one."

"It isn't a contest," Vik rumbled.

"Everything with you two is a contest."

"You didn't call me to discuss rotary phones, did you?"

"No. You brought it up."

"We're literal today, aren't we?" He took a seat before my desk.

"I'm just putting off the inevitable," I admitted. "I need somebody with me when I touch any of these things—in case something goes wrong." I swept a hand over the three containers on my desk.

"You're saying something could go wrong? That only one of my kind might fix?" He understood faster than I'd expected.

"Harmful power is nullified by your kind," I agreed. "I'm hoping that remains true if something's here that isn't right."

"I can handle that part."

"There's something else."

"What's that?"

"If I become—dangerous, I expect you to take care of things."

"What?"

"What I said. If I no longer have control over myself and become a danger to anyone else, except for the Prophet or another criminally-minded individual, then I expect you to eliminate the problem."

"Damn, no pressure, man," Vik swore.

"I don't think it'll come to that; I only wanted you to be aware."

"Then consider me aware—and repulsed at the same time."

"All right. Want to come to the lab with me, so I can stick my hands in this dirt?" I tapped the container of soil. "If I survive that, then I'll think about handling the coin, too."

"Whatever you say, boss."

"I have an ulterior motive in this, you know," I told him while rising from my seat. "If there are any hidden spells in this stuff, then you'll neutralize them while I'm getting my hands dirty."

"Sounds like a plan," he grinned. "I'm right behind you."

≈

Vik never said anything during my hesitation to touch the soil, once the cover was removed. He and I stood in a sealed compartment, not far from the one that held the inert bodies of Akrinn and Lorvis.

Jamming my left hand into the soil, I waited for it to tell me something.

It wasn't long in coming.

≈

Vik

I didn't know what to expect. First, his body stiffened, as if he were having a seizure. Then, an indrawn breath, that wasn't released for far too long. Once I determined that he hadn't taken a breath after minutes passed, I reached out to touch, only to watch him disappear.

By the time I understood that he wasn't coming back, I realized the gold coin was missing, too.

≈

"Dori, you're in charge for now," Kooper said. We'd informed him, Travis and Trent of Randl's disappearance, and Kooper had demanded a meeting aboard XIII. "Travis and Trent will follow protocol while we continue our search for the Prophet," Kooper continued. "Leads will be pursued whenever they are substantiated at headquarters."

"This leaves us vulnerable, doesn't it?" Travis asked quietly.

Dori, who sat next to me, appeared stunned. She and the rest of us had attempted mindspeech, to no avail. Wherever Randl was, and if he were still alive, he wasn't answering.

I wished I'd seen what he'd seen; for now, the soil sample still lay on a table in the sealed section of the cargo hold.

Kooper ordered it left there, in case it was required to get Randl back. I'd have been more concerned if Kooper hadn't reported that the other soil sample was being analyzed, with no other disappearances to its credit.

That gave us some hope—that Randl had transported himself, rather than being pulled away by an unknown force.

I was back to what he'd seen to precipitate his disappearance—without telling me or anyone else before he left.

"If he's gone into *split-time*, that could account for the lack of communication," Trent pointed out during a short period of silence.

"True, I suppose," Kooper agreed reluctantly. "I hope if that's the case, he isn't exhausting himself too much to return on his own."

Randl

The Prophet's minions crawled like ants over the enormous block of concrete. I saw the vision of it, without accompanying sound. He'd pulled it out of the ground, and now they were checking it over.

When the transport lowered itself to the planet's surface, I watched as it loaded the concrete into its yawning mouth, using bots to do so.

Who would go to this much trouble to collect the concrete, and why? No doubt it was filled with the bones of those they'd shoved into it to die a ghastly death. Even if they chose to recycle the concrete, which made no sense at all to me, they'd have to clear the bones out of it, and any other impurities, to meet Alliance specifications for its reuse—in both Alliances.

Or did they?

I imagine I cursed embarrassingly as I throttled back to the ship's lab, landing on hands and knees and sliding across the floor while scrabbling for something to grab onto. I found Kooper and half my crew waiting there, their mouths open in surprise.

~

"Yes, I want the concrete analyzed. Grind it all down if you have to, to get a decent sample," Kooper growled at the face on his comp-vid. "Jett and I both want a report on your findings."

The communication was ended before he turned back to me. I sat in my office, behind the behemoth desk, sipping water and attempting to push back growing fear. "We should have a full analysis in an hour," Kooper set the comp-vid on my desk with a sigh.

He'd come to the same conclusion I had. If the Prophet's disease was in the victims' bones, and those bones were ground into recyclable concrete—or anything else, for that matter, then it could show up anywhere across both Alliances.

"This goes back to Phorde Gaster," I said. "And WildTree Industries."

"The imposter of Phorde, anyway," Kooper agreed. "We really need to look into their records, but it's possible we won't find everything we need on who they've sold recycled concrete to."

"Especially if there are obsessions in play—or maybe just a healthy fear of being arrested," I said.

"What about the Gant family, though? I don't recall concrete in any part of their kitchen." Kooper quirked his mouth into a half-frown.

"What about the rest of the house? Failing that, they may have come in contact with it elsewhere."

"I suppose that's possible, but we'd have to go through the entire house, and then retrace their steps as a family, prior to their attacking each other."

"We should probably do that, then."

"I know. I'll get people on it."

~

CSD Headquarters, Campiaa City

Jett Riffler

She'd told me long ago that she'd known me in another life. I had no idea what life that was, or how we'd met. I didn't doubt her words, though. She'd asked for a meeting, and said she was bringing two that I should hire.

I didn't know about the hiring, but I said I'd consider it once I met them.

That's why I was more than surprised to see Zaria walking into my private office, with Nari and Tiri behind her.

They'd made the news vids a few times, by retrieving relics others had spent centuries searching for.

"Director Riffler, I'd like you to meet Nari and Tiri," Zaria introduced both. The twins were identical in every way except their choice of skirt colors. I gaped at them. Dark eyes, clear, dark skin, hair beautifully swept back and intricately braided; I drew in a breath and held it for several seconds.

How was I to know they'd have this kind of impact on me?

"We think we can help in your search for—the one on your most-wanted list," Nari spoke first, while a lovely smile lit her face.

"I would welcome any help," I admitted, forcing myself to stop staring and behave in a more business-like manner.

"We sometimes get a feeling for missing things," Tiri said, while her sister nodded in agreement. "If we can focus on something the Prophet has, or someone, even, then perhaps we'll be able to track him in that way."

"It can't hurt to try," Zaria shrugged. "They're willing to give you a year, unless you find what you're looking for before then."

"I'm ah, sure I can get the Founder to agree," I said. "Are you willing to travel with some of our, ah, agents?"

"Of course," both dipped their chins in unison.

I'd never been reduced to such a blubbering fool in all my life, I think.

"I'll send you to a crew shortly, then. When will you be ready to go?"

"They're prepared to go now, and I can deliver them," Zaria offered. I wasn't sure I was ready for them to leave just yet, but didn't say it.

"May I have a word with you in private, Director?" Zaria asked.

"Oh, of course."

"Nari, Tiri, will you wait outside for me?" Zaria turned to the sisters.

They left my office quietly, the fabric of colorful skirts swishing about their ankles. I hated to ask them to wear uniforms aboard ship, but they could be safer moving about, if it came to that.

Once the door was closed behind them, I turned to Zaria.

"I have a few gifts for you," she said.

"What gifts?"

"I assume you'd like mindspeech, and the ability to fold space, unless I'm badly mistaken." Her words were dry.

Had I gaped before? I may have made a bigger fool of myself, this time. "I'll take that as a yes," Zaria smiled. The room filled with light. When it dissipated, I felt as if I were young again.

"You *are* young again, although you won't look much different to most people; I've left that disguise in place. Those around you who are immortal will know what you look like, and that you've been granted the gift of immortality, too. Also, I have this." She floated a small box in my direction.

A medallion, like the ones worn by Randl and his crew, nestled on silk inside the carved receptacle. "Don't take it off," she warned. "I've given medallions to Nari and Tiri, too. Just in case."

"Thank you." I placed the medallion around my neck and slipped it beneath my shirt.

You're welcome, she sent. *And it's long overdue. Don't misuse the power, or it will be recalled.*

I understand, I returned.

"There's nothing to prevent you from checking on BlackWings X and XIII, just let the Captains know you're coming aboard," Zaria said. "You know, for dinner and such."

A world of possibilities opened before me, then, and I blinked in astonishment. I'd already made up my mind to see Nari and Tiri as often as I could while they were employed by the CSD. Folding space would make that so much easier.

"I cannot repay this gift," I hung my head.

"Do you know what a true gift is, Director?" Zaria said softly.

She'd place emphasis on the word *true*.

"I don't understand," I said, lifting my eyes to hers.

"A true gift is one that is given, with no thought of repayment. That is what this gift is. Use it wisely and to your advantage, Jett."

I mulled her answer for a few moments. "What—was my name before?" I asked.

"I won't give you the proper name," she smiled at me again. "I'll give you the nickname I called you, even though you hated it at first. When I last saw you in that life, you'd gotten used to it, even if you didn't appreciate it. I called you Auggie. That's all I feel comfortable giving you."

"Auggie." I savored it on my tongue. "I don't dislike it," I said. "You may call me this anytime you want. I'll know it was a name given in affection, and that will matter more than anything else."

"We were friends," she said. "Good friends. Auggie thought of me as the daughter he never had, and that meant a lot."

"I find myself wishing to have a talk with this former self," I admitted. "Very much."

"I wish I could talk to him again, too. I should take Nari and Tiri to BlackWing XIII—they have the most room for extra guests."

"I'll prepare their hiring papers and catch up with them for signatures." I grinned at the realization that I could do that in person, rather than on a comp-vid.

"I'd say you can do whatever you want, Auggie," Zaria laughed. As I watched while she walked out of my office, I realized I felt happier than I had in days.

～

BlackWing XIII

Randl

I'm coming, and I'm bringing Quin and two new recruits for you, Zaria sent.

"Zaria's coming," I told Dori, who was still fussing because I'd barely touched the food I'd been served at dinner.

Kooper had left an hour earlier, after learning that humanoid bone detritus was scattered throughout the concrete used to form the loading dock at Huyer. Now, a carefully selected team had to research all recycled concrete used throughout the Alliances.

I realized what a hopeless job that could turn out to be—it was law in both Alliances that concrete and other building materials had to be recycled instead of dumped somewhere. That meant that every new construction had some portion of their building comprised of recycled substances.

"You really ought to eat your dinner—you don't look good," Quin said the moment she and Zaria arrived. With them were two other women. I blinked at them—their names were Nari and Tiri, and they were identical twins who had a talent for finding relics and such.

"Quin, can you help him?" Dori pleaded before I could stop her.

"I can." She smiled and sat beside me, before taking my head into her hands. I didn't argue—my head was still foggy from the unexpected trip into *split-time* that I'd taken. The fogginess left me feeling queasy, too, but I wasn't telling Dori that. She was worried enough as it was.

Slowly, Quin pulled the fog from my mind, and with it, the nausea affecting my gut. I felt so much better when she took her hands away, I wanted to laugh.

"If that ever happens again, I know to call you first," I grinned at her instead.

"I'd like to introduce Nari and Tiri," Zaria said, once I was healed. "They'll be joining you onboard, and helping you search for the Prophet."

"Any help is certainly appreciated," I said. Maybe they could get a lock on Mae, just by coming in contact with Miz.

"My idea, as well," Zaria confirmed my thoughts.

"Maybe I can help some, too," Quin offered. "Although Justis doesn't like me being gone for days at a time."

"We can communicate through comp-vid," Tiri grinned at Quin. They knew one another, that was plain, without my reading them.

"Then keep me posted," Quin smiled back. "I'll help as much as I can."

"We may need your help when Kooper gets information on recycled concrete," I said. "I'm sure he'll ask you to study images."

"He's already sent images of those who worked at the packaged food facility," Quin told me. "I just got them a few hours ago, and haven't had time to look, yet."

"Will you keep me in that loop, too?"

"I'll send you anything I get."

"Good. I need to revisit the Gant family, I think. Something about them raises my hackles. They feel different from Huyer Food Distribution to me."

"Then I'll pay close attention to these new images, to see if I get the same feel."

"I really appreciate your help with this, Quinnie," I said.

"It's no trouble. You know I want to see this resolved. We both would like for people to stop disappearing and being murdered."

"Yeah. That's exactly what we all want," Dori huffed.

You think the bones of victims have been crushed into a lot of recycled concrete, don't you? Quin sent.

Yes. And that, somehow, is spreading the Prophet's disease. We don't have any proof of it, and frankly, we may never be able to scientifically prove that an obsession can be spread like that. How do you separate an obsession from somebody's brain, so you can point it out to somebody else?

I know. It sounds impossible, doesn't it?

I just want to know how long the concrete blocks removed from those planets have been used as building materials in both Alliances. I think we can extrapolate the intent and point to the evidence from there.

"It's not going to be an easy job," she said aloud.

"We may have to do some snooping around all of WildTree's recycling facilities—off the books," I said.

"I want updated images on all their employees," Quin agreed.

"I think I can ask Travis and Trent to do some of the legwork," Dori said.

"We'd like to speak with Miz'Sandar Keel," Nari and Tiri chorused.

"He's at the shooting range with Chief Markus," I said. "They usually go after dinner, to get some practice in."

"I can take them," Zaria smiled. "Quin and I will leave after that."

"I'll find berths for you—unless you'd like to share a larger one," Dori offered.

"We'll share—it's easier to bounce ideas off one another," Nari grinned.

"Good enough. I'll find you after I get it set up, and we'll get uniforms for you, too," Dori said. "Welcome aboard BlackWing XIII."

iz'Sandar

"Most of us have an official, ASD-issued ranos pistol—with the new safety technology. That means the pistol assigned to an individual can only be used by that individual. If the enemy takes the weapon and attempts to use it, it'll probably kill them." Markus handed me one of Sabrina Kend's disposable ranos pistols to study. "That one won't fire a lethal blast—it's built for practice."

I'd passed Markus' tests on laser pistols and rifles. Ranos technology was the next step in my training.

"When we go on classified missions, we usually have one of these with us," he nodded toward the pistol in my hand. "They can be destroyed easily if we're taken into custody, and they only fire a limited number of times before destroying themselves anyway. This technology is so secret, only the BlackWing ships carry them."

"This is fascinating," I turned the pistol in my hand, checking the charge.

"Chief Markus?" Zaria appeared, with Quin and two other women I didn't recognize.

"Zaria?" He dipped his head respectfully to her and Queen Quin.

"I've brought Nari and Tiri to you—they want to speak with Miz," Zaria smiled at both of us.

"Nari and Tiri—the noted archaeologists?" I'd read about some of their discoveries—they'd found things others had searched for—sometimes for centuries.

"They want to help find the Prophet—and your sister," Zaria said, while both women nodded and smiled at me.

"Any help would be much appreciated," I blurted. At that point, I had no idea what archaeologists might do to help, but I was willing to try anything if it got me closer to Mae.

"Good. Quin and I will leave you to talk, then. Be sure to take your ideas to Randl," Zaria turned to Nari and Tiri. "He'll see the possibilities in them, I guarantee it."

Quin waved before she and Zaria disappeared; folding space was a talent I very much wanted for myself, and would never have. At least I knew people who possessed it, as it was an elegant way to travel.

"Now you've seen a Larentii—twice," Markus grinned at me.

I went still for a moment. "Zaria is Larentii?"

"I've never seen her that way, but some of the others have," Markus shrugged. "They say it's amazing, and that she has wings, too, if she wants to show you those."

"I didn't know Larentii had wings," I frowned while running through the catalog of information in my mind on the race of blue giants.

"Only Zaria has wings," Nari smiled. "We'll sit over here while you continue your lesson, and when you're done, we'll ask questions," she said.

"No pressure with an audience," Markus slapped my shoulder. "Come on, you can do this."

What I wanted to do was wrestle Markus to the floor for taunting me, but I didn't say that. Instead, I lifted the pistol as he'd taught me, took aim and fired.

∼

Randl

"Nari and Tiri need something belonging to Mae'Sandar," Zanfield informed me as he slid onto the chair opposite my desk. One of his eyebrows lifted high, as if he expected me to stare at the colors moving about in it, like wind moving wheat in a field.

"You know this how?" I set down my comp-vid, which held images to peruse, so I could turn my full attention to Zanfield and his bi-colored brows.

"Markus and Miz told me," Zanfield waved an arm. "Miz doesn't have a hair or a fingernail of hers with him. That means we need to go to her quarters on Campiaa, and find something the twins can use."

It was my turn to lift an eyebrow, although mine wasn't nearly as spectacular as Zanfield's. "I think we can ask Wyatt to get something," I said after considering the problem. "I think I'll ask him to collect some things that she may have used for a while, too. For me."

Zanfield's face morphed into a studied, thoughtful expression. "So you can touch them?"

"Yes."

"You won't disappear again, will you?"

"Thank you for your concern, Zanfield, but I was in control last time. I just didn't take time to tell anybody I was leaving to go into *split-time*, because somebody would argue, and I hate that."

"You should have taken somebody with you," Zanfield sniffed.

"You know those white streaks in Travis and Trent's hair? They're lucky that those streaks are the only thing affecting them after going into *split-time* with me. I wasn't shielding them at the time, so we got lucky. Splitting time for anyone else appears to be—detrimental."

"Are you saying that our lives could shrivel and turn white?"

"I think that's what I'm saying—except for the white part, unless it's your hair."

"Good to know," Zanfield now appeared troubled.

"I think Travis and Trent survived because they're immortal," I added. "I believe that a mortal, unshielded in *split-time*, wouldn't last long."

"What about you, then?"

"I can't answer that with full confidence," I said. "What I suspect is that I create *split-time*, therefore it has less of an effect on me, unless I empty myself of power while I'm there. That's not to say it doesn't affect me; this last time, it clouded my brain. That's why Quin had to help me."

"You don't suppose the Prophet is doing that somehow?"

"I don't know. I don't even know whether that's possible or not," I admitted. "It's something to think about, though."

"What about giving Nari and Tiri something from the Prophet?" He turned to a safer subject—in his mind, anyway.

"Zanfield, that just sent shivers down my back. I worry that the Prophet will know if they delve too far into something he's touched. They don't have the ability to shield themselves like I do. I feel it's dangerous to even suggest it."

"Then we're back to Mae's things," Zanfield said.

"Yes, we are. I'll communicate with Wyatt and ask him to find something for us."

"Thank you. I can mark that task as done," he pulled his comp-vid from a pocket and tapped on it for a moment.

"You're anybody's idea of a dream employee, you know that?" I teased.

"I'm just trying to get it right the first time," he grinned. "I'll let Markus and Miz know."

I watched as he rose and walked out of my office. Once the door was closed behind him, I lifted the comp-vid again to study images of the Gant family—those the ASD had gathered from recordings of the family outside their home. The images came from cameras at schools, shops and restaurants, days before the massacre.

I'd sent copies to Quin, so she was seeing them at the same time. So far, she'd sent me nothing in return—and she'd have seen whether they were affected before I did. Something was missing here—a piece of information, perhaps, that nobody had provided.

Kooper had interviews with neighbors, too, but those held nothing out of the ordinary.

I was back to the biggest question in my mind; *why did the Prophet choose the Gant family?*

What about the packaged food facility, too? Was it to lure me in? Did he know I'd show up to look? How could he? I was enemy number two in both Alliances, and had he known I'd show up at Huyer Distribution, he'd have come himself to destroy me.

Instead, he'd sent minions to do the job.

Travis, I sent, *I think there was another reason the Prophet attacked Huyer Food Distribution.*

Be there in a sec, he replied, showing up almost simultaneously with his mindspeech.

"What's up, bro?" He slid onto the chair Zanfield had vacated only minutes earlier.

"I think we need to check those crates and pallets at Huyer," I said.

Travis drew in a breath. "You think they were collecting food, don't you? They waited until the employees did away with themselves, before taking what they wanted."

"Only I think they got interrupted, and hid when someone else showed up."

"This means," Travis hesitated while he sorted his suspicions before saying them aloud. "This means the Prophet has control over what's in that recycled concrete. Doesn't it? Like turning it on and off."

"Just as he has control over the people he's infected. He can control the bones of dead people," I breathed.

"This goes back to his ability to reanimate the dead."

"And that terrifies me in ways I can't begin to describe."

"Kooper," Travis had a comp-vid in his hand quickly. For this, he wanted a face-to-face, rather than mindspeech.

"What do you have, Captain?" Kooper's voice was clear, his words curt.

"Have someone check the crates and boxes at Huyer. In other words, do an inventory. Randl and I think the Prophet's people were stealing food and got caught. They hid, but when Randl arrived, the opportunity to kill him was too good, so they acted on it."

"I'll have an inventory done before the day's out." Kooper cut off the communication.

"Fuck me," Travis sighed. "Fuck me running."

"I'll put the rest of our speculation in a comp-vid message to Kooper and Jett," I nodded at Travis. "They need to know everything."

"How far away can the Prophet be to reanimate bone dust? There has to be a limit to the distance, don't you think?" Travis asked the question now turning in my brain.

"I don't know," I said. "Or even if there is a limit."

"Don't scare me more than I already am," he held up a hand. "I don't know what Trent will think when I tell him this."

"Want to hold a joint ship meeting so we can tell the rest of them, after you tell Trent?"

"Yes. I'd prefer that you be there to answer questions, because I have no answers."

"You think I have answers?" I tapped my chest. "I'm trying to figure all this out on the fly."

"Let's have the meeting after Kooper lets us know about the inventory at Huyer," Travis suggested.

"Good enough," I agreed. "I'll clue Dori in while you tell your brother; that way neither will be mad because we didn't tell them first."

"Right on the money, as usual," Travis said. "I'll see you later."

After he folded away, I went back to studying images. Nothing. Not a damn thing stuck out. Borell Gant had never worked for anybody or anything that was tainted by the Prophet, as near as I could tell. His wives had never worked outside the home, either, and their past histories never listed a lover who'd be suspect.

Why? I was back to my original question, and the answer, just as it had before, eluded me.

~

CSD Headquarters, Campiaa City
Jett Riffler

"A quarter of the warehouse emptied," I handed the report to Kooper across my desk. "They were being selective, too. All the sealed meats were taken, sealed fruit was taken, certain vegetables, all in sealed containers, were taken, and a pallet of condiments, salt and such, was also stolen. The cameras, as you know, were compromised before the massacre began, so we don't know exactly how it started, or how the stolen food was transported."

"Outside security cameras recorded no images," Kooper crossed long legs and shook his head at me. "The Prophet may have been taking it by employing power. I don't know whether he has anyone on his staff capable of it."

"We can't discount that possibility," I toyed with my comp-vid. "Do you think he may have warlocks or wizards in his employ?"

"Or obsessed, you mean?" Kooper said what I was afraid to contemplate.

"Yes."

"I need to have a conversation with the King of Karathia and his father, I think," Kooper said. "They'll be more approachable than the Grey House Wizards."

"I may ask if Zaria can help."

"Good luck on getting her attention," Kooper huffed.

"I can try. You interview the King of Karathia. I'll let you know if I get an answer from Zaria."

~

BlackWing XIII
Randl

"You're saying he can command the bone fragments in recycled concrete?" Miz asked after Travis and I made our announcements at the joint meeting. Before his sister disappeared in front of him, he'd never suspected anything like this was possible.

"I can't say that with full certainty, but it looks that way," I told him. "We've checked the records for that warehouse—some of the concrete flooring was replaced more than eight months ago. There wasn't an incident until recently, when the Prophet decided to replenish food supplies. We've handed him a few setbacks after he attacked transport ships, so he's looking at other ways to feed his flock."

"For the longest time, we couldn't determine why he was driving people into wet concrete," Travis said. "Until now, we thought he was feeding his dark fantasies, by forcing them to die in such a hideous way. Then, the first concrete block we found disappeared—and the hole was filled with dirt. After that, half the dirt disappeared, to get Randl's attention."

"We have no idea how many of those mass graves exist," I said. "The ones we've found have been flukes, mostly, when someone notices an anomaly on one of the Prophet's chosen planets."

"He's booby-trapped some of them, too," Trent grumbled.

"I think it's only a matter of time before he wriggles his way into an important facility—through its building materials," I said. "Imagine if everyone at ASD Headquarters turned on each other. Not only would it wipe out everyone in charge, but it would send the rest running, because they'd finally understand that nobody is safe."

"Uh, Randl?" Vik sounded worried.

"What is it?" I asked him.

"What was used to rebuild those casinos in Campiaa City?"

"Holy, fucking, hairy weirdballs," I cursed.

"I'll let Wyatt know," Trent offered.

"Do it now," Travis said. "They need to start checking everything, as of yesterday."

Trent's eyes unfocused as he put our fears into mindspeech to Wyatt. "He's telling his dad now," Trent was back to the present. "They're going to dig through the records, and trace every bit of the materials used to rebuild. They're in contact with Jett, too."

"Good."

"I have a question," Nari raised her hand.

I didn't tell her she didn't have to raise a hand to ask. "What do you have, Nari?" I asked her.

"Will you give us a chip of that concrete—from the warehouse?"

"I don't think it's safe," I said. "Unless you can build an impenetrable shield around yourself, the Prophet may become aware of you and spend his energy to take you over—or kill you. I don't want either of those things to happen."

"That's scary," Tiri said. She'd sat beside her sister at the long table in XIII's meeting room, listening quietly until now.

"Stick with something of Mae's for the moment," I told them. "I doubt the Prophet will expect us to come at him from that direction."

~

Avii Castle

   Quin

I found Charla and Barkins sitting on the terrace outside Gurnil's Library. She'd climbed up all the way from her suite near the lowest level of the castle to look out over the ocean.

"That's a long walk to make," I said, announcing my presence.

"I never thought I'd wish to have wings before," she admitted, turning to look at me. "My mother had a huge, nasty parrot when I was little. She let it attack me if I did something wrong."

"That would certainly give anyone pause where birds are concerned," I agreed, sitting on the chair beside her bench. "I also know what it's like to climb stairs instead of flying from terrace to terrace."

"I needed the exercise," Charla sighed.

I read in her expression that someone had offered to fly her to the Library terrace, and she'd declined. An off-duty male guard offered, actually. Charla was too terrified of his wings to accept.

"Oskar is a good man," I told her. "He just happens to have wings."

"He introduced himself," she turned her head away. "He seems nice. I just—can't. Not right now."

"I know. Don't let your fears keep you from making friends, Charla. You're free for the first time in your life to do that—on your own terms."

"Barkins liked him. He tried to lick his face."

"Animals are usually the best judges of character," I agreed. "And I have it on good authority that his shift goes to dinner at eight bells—in the guard's mess. They accept visitors, and since Barkins is so well-behaved, I think he'd be a star at dinner."

"I don't have wings," she reiterated.

"Neither do most of the women and men in Casino City and Sun City. That doesn't keep the guards or anyone else in Avii Castle from getting to know any of them."

"I'll think about it," she said, sounding glum.

"It's better than having dinner alone in your suite, sometimes."

"Oh, no, somebody fell off the ship," she rose and pointed at the tourist boat far below.

"Jumped, more than likely," I said. "Wait, here comes a guard, now." She and I watched as a guard, with two strokes of long, multi-colored wings, dropped like a well-aimed rocket toward the cold water surrounding the tourist boat.

Charla held her breath as the tourist was plucked deftly from the waves. The guard then flew the jumper to the boat, where he was deposited, soaked but intact, on the deck. A waiting security officer took charge of the miscreant and saluted the departing guard.

"The tourists try that all the time, thinking we'll haul them to the castle rather than putting them back on the boat," I explained as Charla bounced with glee. "We only allow those we've invited to come here. Those people on the boat would pay a lot to have what you do—you're a special guest of the King and Queen of the Avii."

"That—I've never seen anything like it," Charla giggled. "It was so—efficient. And fun."

"We see at least two jumpers a week," I said. "The guards train for water rescues."

"Has Oskar rescued anyone?"

"More than he can count, I'm sure," I said. "He's one of the regulars on boat duty. It takes what Justis calls *finesse* to snatch them out of the water like that on the first try. Not all the guards are as good at it."

"Do you think he'd talk to me about that?"

"Are you kidding? What man doesn't like to brag about his exploits?"

Charla laughed again. To me, it was a sign that she understood her new-found freedom to be a normal person—for the first time in her life. I couldn't wait to tell Randl about it—he'd seen what I had in her —that deep within, she'd hated what her mother made of her.

I'd been made for a purpose, too, and had it not been for the intervention of three powerful ones, Zaria included, I'd have traveled a far different path. Like Charla, I wouldn't have liked it, either.

"Not every wrong will be righted in the universes," I said, startling Charla with my swift, inexplicable change of subject. "Therefore, we must right as many wrongs as we can, if it lies within our ability."

"That sounds—deep." Charla blinked at me. She didn't say what else she thought—that she was confused by my statement.

"Tell me," I turned toward her. "If you saw someone trip and fall, would you hold out a hand to lift them up, or sniff at their clumsiness and walk past?"

"I'd help them up if I could."

"And that is why you are a special guest of the King and Queen of the Avii. Want tea? I think Gurnil may have some in the Library."

"I'd love tea."

~

Randl

"This was a futile search," Kooper said, sounding more than a bit accusatory. "We found nothing that could have affected the Gant family that wouldn't have affected others, too. We've even interviewed friends and relatives who'd seen them up to a month before their deaths, and they recall nothing out of the ordinary with any of them."

He hadn't delivered the lecture by comp-vid, either. He paced before my desk while snake scales appeared and disappeared on his neck and arms. He was more than frustrated, and felt helpless in the face of this mystery.

"How's the baby doing?" I asked as quietly as I could.

"The baby is fine—nothing out of the ordinary with it," Kooper grumbled. "For now, it's in government custody, but there's nothing to prevent the release to the closest relatives, who are waiting to take it in."

"At least that's one bright spot in this awful mess," I sighed.

"We've gone through the local waste recycler, but that's just a mash of everything they've discarded, plus what came from their neighborhood."

"Do you still have it?" I asked.

"We moved it to a holding tank. You're welcome to go take a whiff —but I warn you, it's completely foul."

"I'll come take a whiff, then," I offered.

"I'll transport us," Kooper offered.

Dori, I'm taking a short trip with Kooper. Be back in a few, I sent mindspeech.

All right. Keep us posted.

Will do.

With a nod, Kooper folded us to the ASD facility, where the holding tank was located.

"Something's off, here, and it's not just the stench," I said after studying the tank for a few minutes.

Kooper, standing not far away, hadn't taken his eyes away from me the entire time. "Can you be more specific?" he asked.

"It's minute, but there's a bit of a feel from the Prophet."

"You think they threw something away that he'd contaminated?"

"That's what it feels like for now. Since this has already been ground up for recycling, and it's as much liquid as solid, I don't know how you're going to pinpoint any particular source," I said. "Especially since none of that ever shows up on any scientific measuring device."

"Fuck." Kooper swiped the back of his neck with a hand. At this point, we were both frustrated.

He didn't say it, but he was concerned about the same thing I was —that however this had happened to the Gant family, it could happen again to another unsuspecting household.

"I'll ask somebody to do an analysis, to see if any concrete components are in this tank," Kooper shook his head. "This is infuriating."

"Don't let this overwhelm you," I advised. "We have to take a longer road than we want on this, and as you said, it's infuriating."

"I've chased Vardil Cayetes from one end of the Alliances to the other, and I never felt this frustrated," Kooper said.

"Vardil used methods we could eventually name and define," I said. "This—defies anything anyone has ever seen or dealt with."

Kooper didn't add that Vardil's death had come at the hands of Zaria—that kill wasn't his. He'd wanted it, though. Again, it revealed the differences in his position and the one Zaria held.

She wasn't constricted by a set of rules mapped by the Hierarchy. I didn't point out to Kooper that even if he weren't held to those rules, he'd still be no farther along that we currently were, and hadn't held the necessary resources to track Vardil Cayetes at the end, either.

He'd be no farther along with the Prophet than he'd been with Vardil's locations and dealings, had Zaria not become involved.

Pulling out his comp-vid, Kooper tapped commands to a science team. It could take days to go through the contents of the entire tank.

"So, I found the stink of the Prophet in their house, but not on them. Then, we find more evidence here, in the waste from their neighborhood. This is mind-boggling," I said. "Will you forward the autopsy reports to me? I think I'd like Markus and Miz to take a look, after I go through them."

"I'll do it now," Kooper tapped his comp-vid again. "You should have it by the time you get back to the ship."

"Thanks. I'll let you know if anything sticks out."

"You do that. I assume you can get yourself back?"

"Yes."

I disappeared before I could read more frustration in his features.

～

"Are you sure it won't bother you?" I did a comp-vid conversation with Quin, rather than sending mindspeech. I asked if she'd review the autopsy reports, too.

"I'll get through it," she said. "If you're concerned, then I am, too. At least we know they weren't poisoned—Kooper's people went through the food and drinks at the home and found nothing."

"They found nothing they can detect with normal devices," I said. "We're not looking for those things."

"True. How long before we know whether there were any components of recycled concrete or human bone in the collected waste?"

"Kooper says it could take days to go through the entire tank."

"Horrible, isn't it?"

"Yes."

"At least they got to it before it went through the treatment facility, to break it down further."

"I know." The thought of it made me want to shiver, and certainly turned my stomach. If Kooper hadn't held up the process, the whole thing could be on its way to being used as compost, somewhere.

"Randl?" Trent tapped on my open office door.

"Quin, I'll talk to you later. I think Trent has information."

She signed off quickly, so I turned off my comp-vid and nodded for Trent to take a chair.

"We know Nari and Tiri are working with some of Mae'Sandar's things," he began.

"They have hair from her brush, some favorite jewelry and such," I agreed.

"What if we had something a bit more—personal?"

"Like what?" I refused to read Trent, so he could reveal his story at his own pace.

"Well, Sabrina looked at what you did to search for evidence of the kidnap victims—in case they showed up on Alliance cameras or scanners. She thinks that if we had something of Mae's from when she turns, that it could be used like a beacon to identify her—even from a distance. She says that she can take the scanner tech she just developed for Ca'Lex, and with your spellwork or whatever it is you do, you may be able to hone it to recognize Mae out of thousands of other individuals scanned."

"Now there's a thought," I said. "Like if we were flying by empty or abandoned planets, we could scan them, to see what's there?"

"That's what she's aiming for."

"Damn. We need that like yesterday," I stood and rubbed my forehead. "I'll talk to Miz. Maybe he knows of something we can use. Tell Sabrina to get to work on her end, and I'll see what we can do on the power side of the equation."

"I think you can do whatever you did for the scanners in the Alliances," Trent added softly. "I know Sabrina wants to find Mae, but I'd like to find any of them. It could lead us to the Prophet's hideout. Once we have that information, we can deal with him and his remaining minions."

"Is she already working on this?"

"Yes. She was refining the design we used for Ca'Lex, when this idea came to her."

"See if she wants help from Miz—I know he wants to be involved any way he can."

"I'll ask. He's like a walking comp-vid anyway."

"Keep me updated on the progress," I said. "I'll consider the best way to hone in on Mae while Sabrina is working with the design."

"I'll do that." Trent rose from his chair, nodded and folded away, leaving me standing beside my desk, considering all the possibilities.

It might have been helpful to us if we'd preserved even a shred of the Prophet's dead army on Campiaa to analyze. We may have been able to pinpoint their worlds of origin from DNA samples.

Instead, I'd transported all the active, reanimated dead to Tiralia, and they'd been consumed by the planet's poisonous atmosphere. When the attack on Campiaa was over, every scrap and ash of those bodies blasted well enough to disable them disappeared, leaving us with only wrecked buildings and the dead and injured of Campiaa to deal with.

V'dar had carefully thought out his attack, start to finish.

What he hadn't done, though, was consider himself the loser in the fight. Because I'd hurt him afterward, I was now his main focus for revenge.

I worried that everything else that was happening had been planned for a very long time. Tapping my comp-vid, I gave it a voice command. "Bring up the records of the Prophet's attack on Campiaa, and any information prior to the attack," I said.

"Retrieving requested information," a pleasant voice replied.

Perhaps there was something we'd missed in the landslide of other occurrences on Campiaa. The only way to determine that was to go through everything, line by line.

Again.

CHAPTER 7

*B*lackWing XIII
  Randl

I toyed with the gold coin from Vogeffa II while I read information on my comp-vid. That's where Dori found me when it was time for our evening meal together.

"Stop spinning that coin and come eat," she pretended gruffness.

"All right." I gave her a lop-sided grin before standing and pocketing the coin. I'd considered delving into its history again, but couldn't bring myself to do it. Searching its past could prove too painful, now that I knew it had once been in my mother's possession.

I wasn't ready to see more mistreatment aimed at her. Besides, I could still hear Pap's words in my mind—*you find this bastard, and you teach him a lesson he'll never forget.*

"Let's go," I gestured toward the door of my office. "Lead the way, my lady."

~

"Hey." Dori and I were nothing more than a tangle of naked limbs when we woke. Our food was still sitting on the table inside our suite

91

—I'd placed a warming spell on it before we'd turned to other things, and now I was quite hungry.

Reaching in, I smoothed blonde hair away from her forehead as she growled her satisfaction at being next to me in bed. "Hmmph," I chuckled at her and dropped a kiss on her nose.

"Hungry," she yawned and opened her eyes.

"Me, too. Wanna eat?"

"Yeah. Can you have the server-bot bring it?"

"I can transport it to the bed. If you spill your soup, though, that's on you."

"You're so funny." She pulled away and scooted into a sitting position.

As promised, I floated the food to the bed, setting the plates gently on our laps, while keeping the soup bowls suspended several inches above the covers.

"Nice." Dori lifted a spoon and dipped into the floating soup bowl. "Tomato. I love tomato soup."

"Me, too. And nowadays, I don't have to wait until my mental vision adjusts before I can eat it."

"Cori and Marco's baby is teething," Dori said as she dunked her spoon into the soup bowl again. "Cori says it's driving them crazy, but they didn't want to ask for help, because it's a natural part of a baby's growth."

"They still mad because we're together?"

"Not after what you did on Campiaa. Marco gave you props for that, and Sal may have had a few words with him, too. The family is good with us being together. Mom and Dad keep asking when we can visit."

"That's a good question. I don't have an answer," I admitted.

"I sort of told them that. They'll have to accept that we can't drop everything and turn up every eight-day or two. Besides, their only grandchild is keeping them busy—they help with the teething fussiness half the time."

"Isn't that what grandparents are for?" I grinned at Dori.

"I think so. Cori wouldn't get any sleep at all if it wasn't for Mom and Dad. And," she hesitated for a moment.

"What?" I stopped cutting into my pork roast for a moment to look at her.

"They're hoping you can see what sort of shifter the baby will be."

"Penny's tiny, still. She should be allowed to grow into her shifter, whatever that turns out to be," I frowned.

"Well, you and I may know that, but when it comes to parents," she shrugged.

"Yeah. I get that. Maybe I'll have a look. In a few years."

"Jerk." She elbowed me half-heartedly. "This is my niece we're talking about."

"You know," I said, "My father never placed expectations on me. Maybe it was because I was born blind, and on Vogeffa II, being blind was often a death sentence. My father loved me anyway. Had I not been born with the talent I have, he'd still have done his best to see me raised to adulthood and able to function as well as I could on my own."

"Randl," Dori set her fork on the plate in her lap and dipped her chin, making blonde curls fall forward to cover half her face, "You were never just a blind man. Or a blind child. Do you know how grateful I am for that?"

She lifted her head and turned to blink at me. Love for me shone in her eyes. "I never thought somebody would love me like this," I confessed and leaned in to kiss her. "That is what I am more than grateful for."

"We're just a mutual admiration society of two, aren't we?" she murmured and kissed me again.

"That works out great for me," I said. "How about you?"

"Wouldn't have it any other way."

Randl, mindspeech came from Travis, interrupting the moment between Dori and me. *There's another family dead—this time on Pyrik.*

❧

The differences between the Gant family and the Lindom family were that Pyrik was a CSD world and there were two of the Lindom family who weren't at home when the carnage started.

The father and eldest son had gone out of town for a school trip, and they'd found the other three members dead on their return—the mother, the middle son and younger daughter.

Like the Gant family, the dining room was a scene of carnage. The stink of the Prophet was all over it. Kooper and Jett were already at the home, waiting for us when Travis and I arrived.

I showed Jett how to shield himself, since he was new to his power. Kooper glowered at the brief interruption; he was angrier now than he'd been when he saw the Gant family's home.

"The initial search of all records reveals nothing," Jett told me as we surveyed the well-appointed kitchen and dining combination room.

Blood was everywhere; the ASD forensics department was allowed to take point on this rather than the CSD, since they had previous experience with the Gant family murders. Investigators from both teams were in the process of recording images before removing the bodies.

Father and son had been taken away from the scene, lest they become contaminated—at Kooper's command. It was the wisest thing to do. I'd check them later for contamination—when we were done, here.

"I sent images to Quin," Kooper growled as he stalked across the adjoining living space, where the rest of us stood. We hadn't walked into the affected area, to keep from disturbing evidence.

"Now that you've seen these bodies, what do you think?" Jett asked.

"That they have the Prophet's stink on them," I said. "I wish I'd seen the Gant family earlier. By the time I saw them, it was gone. I can't believe that one family would have it, when the other wouldn't. I just can't determine how it disappeared in the Gant family within a day's time."

"I agree." Jett's jaw worked, making the tattoo on the left side of his face jerk. It was the only indication that he was angered by what he saw.

"I want you to check the bodies again—tomorrow," Kooper growled as he stopped in mid-pace.

"I can do that."

"Good. Jett and I will get things moving on this and keep you advised."

"Thank you."

Travis lifted an eyebrow at me. He hadn't spoken during our stay; he didn't want to set Kooper off any more than I did.

Kooper was so frustrated he was ready to explode, I think.

Zaria, I sent, *somebody needs to help Kooper calm down.*

I'll see what I can do.

Thank you. I hadn't expected such a prompt reply, but it came immediately. I was grateful. We didn't need our lion-snake-shifting Director of the ASD to out himself in front of underlings, that's for sure.

I was ready to go, and opened my mouth to ask Travis if he wanted to fold us back to our ships when the feeling hit.

I'm sure it was aimed at Kooper, but the rest of us felt the backlash. Kooper dropped to his knees, it was so intense.

Love.

Love had been sent to him—and to the rest of us.

Zaria, somehow, had contacted the Mighty Heart, and she'd done what she could.

She is mated to Kooper, came Zaria's soothing response. *She just needed to know that he needed her.*

"Koop," Jett said softly, holding out a hand to lift him up.

"Yes. Thank you." Kooper let Jett pull him to his feet.

"I must say, you're a lucky man, Kooper Griff," Jett said.

"I am. Randl, I'll talk to you and Travis later," Kooper nodded at me. "Jett and I will handle things from this end," he reiterated.

"Thank you, Director," I dipped my chin to him.

"Ready?" Travis asked.

"Yeah. Let's go back."

~

BlackWing X

Miz'Sandar Keel

"I have it programmed to look for certain elements in a planet, but I haven't figured out how to set it to search for DNA from such a distance," Sabrina said as I studied the prototype scanner she showed me.

"That will be more difficult, as the scanner will have to search an entire planet for a single source of the DNA—like finding a marble the size of my thumb in the vastness of space," I agreed. "With elements, those are generally located in swaths—like gold or other metals."

"I know." Sabrina sounded stumped. "I have to keep working on this, to refine it. Wyatt found hair from Mae's hairbrush, which I had to share with Nari and Tiri, but I'm going through all that faster than I thought I would."

"My DNA should show a familial similarity," I said. "You can always take something from me if you need it."

"That may be a possibility," she considered my suggestion. "Especially when we test it. That could help a great deal."

"Do you think it would help to send out micro-satellites—to boost the signal when you search for a particular set of DNA?" I asked.

"You mean position those things around the planet?"

"Yes."

"My concern is if we find the Prophet's planet, he'll detect anything like that. It could give him time to get away—and take everybody else who's with him, too."

"That's a no, then," I sighed.

"It's a good idea, and under normal circumstances, would help tremendously," she said. "In this case, he's too powerful. We don't want to let him know we've arrived if we can avoid it."

"He really can animate the dead?"

"I've seen it. You've seen some of the vids—before the comp-vid cameras died, anyway. All those scenes of the army marching down the street in Campiaa City—those at the front were already dead.

They'd been handed a weapon and the Prophet instructed those corpses to fire at anything that moved."

"I need to sit for a moment and digest this," I told her. My hope was dimming that we'd find Mae soon with Sabrina's new technology.

"Want something to drink? Tea in the galley?"

"Can they put something stronger in it?" I begged.

"I sure hope so. Let's go find out."

Markus, carrying a bottle of bourbon, found us at a table in the galley half an hour later. Without a word, he nodded to Sabrina and took a seat adjacent to mine. Lifting the bottle up, he silently asked if I wanted liquor added to my tea.

"Yes. Please," I pushed my cup toward him. He poured a generous portion in my cup, which was only half full.

"None of this is your fault, Miz," he told me, while adding bourbon to Sabrina's tea next. "We're working as fast as we can. I know time appears to be dragging as far as results go, but we're still the best option for finding your sister."

"I understand that—the logical part of my brain does," I agreed. "But the emotional part is drowning in fear."

"I read a study once that says shifters require larger portions of alcohol to get drunk," Sabrina said, lifting her cup of tea to sip.

"Here." Markus pulled the top off the bourbon and poured until my cup was full of the amber liquid. "There's more, too, if you need it."

~

Travis

"Markus had to carry Miz over his shoulder when Vik came to take them back to XIII," Sabrina told me over dinner. "He was too drunk to stand."

"He's terrified for Mae—and you know what Randl and Dragon said—that Mae is a Queen Or'myr and the hope of their race. Miz has the weight of his love for family and the survival of his race resting on his shoulders."

"No pressure," she set her fork down with a heavy sigh. "I'm working on the scanner, but trying to program the thing to search for DNA? Nobody's tried that before—not from such a distance."

"I know the med scanners have to be close to the patient—if not connected to them," I said. "Even Randl's spelled cameras have to be close enough to get a reading. Baby, are you sure this is even possible?"

"I'll make it possible." She sounded determined.

"That's what I love about you—you never give up," Trent slid onto a chair on Sabrina's other side and leaned in to give her a peck on the cheek.

"Anything new on the Lindom family?" Trent asked. Gerrett arrived to set a plate of food in front of him—Trent was Captain until tomorrow, when I'd take over.

"I haven't heard from Kooper. Randl hasn't reported anything. Same type of scene as before, except two family members were away when it happened. They're terrified and confused about the whole thing, and I'm sure Kooper's people are asking questions that don't make any sense to them."

"The Prophet does that to people."

"Kooper was about to unravel," I said. "Randl sent mindspeech to Zaria. I'm glad she answered—she convinced Breanne to send *Love* to Kooper to calm him down."

"Zaria can communicate with the Mighty Heart?"

"Hmmph," Trent snorted. "Zaria can probably communicate with anyone she pleases."

"Can she communicate with the Prophet?"

"I could, but that could make things worse for everybody else—after all, people tend to retaliate against an easy target," Zaria appeared and took a seat across from the three of us.

"I didn't consider that," Sabrina blinked at Zaria. "If I could, I'd probably taunt him as much as I could in mindspeech, and then everybody would pay for it afterward."

"Yes. Exactly," Zaria nodded. "There's no reasoning with a madman, either. Anything can set them off."

"You think the Prophet is crazy?" I asked.

"I think he's programmed for it."

I didn't ask how that was possible—Zaria knew things I'd never know.

"How did you know we needed that information?" Sabrina asked.

"Nexus echo," Zaria smiled. "It's an old Larentii trick. Ask Lissa about it—she can do it, too."

"I can tell you—Mom told me," I offered.

"Okay—go ahead. I'm curious," Sabrina bumped my shoulder with hers.

"Mom says it's like setting an invisible spider web across the universes, and tuning it to a single thing—like a spoken name or a subject being discussed. Whenever that name or subject is spoken, it causes the web to vibrate, telling the Larentii where, when and who. It's their decision whether they wish to interact past that point."

"That must take a great deal of power," Sabrina breathed.

"It does. As things tend to go, only the most powerful, immortal races have the ability," Zaria explained. "Sadly, too, if a Sirenali is involved, they can mask those terms from anyone. We'll never hear the Prophet's minions addressing him, because of their unique talent for concealing themselves and those about them from the powerful."

"It's never easy, is it?" Trent asked.

"Hardly ever," Zaria replied. "While Gerrett keeps you hidden here, I am connected to him, and to your medallions. That enables nexus echo to work between us."

"It's like a vid game," Sabrina offered. "Every time you master one level, the next one is harder. Unless you design the game, and then you cheat," her laugh was humorless.

"Baby, did you do that?" I nudged her.

"Maybe."

Zaria smiled at Sabrina. "Keep working on this level, all right?" She reached across the table to pat Sabrina's hand. "The rest of us will do what we can, too. I have to go, now. Someone else is calling my name."

Zaria disappeared. Sabrina appeared stunned by the brief contact with Zaria—as if she'd been given an amazing gift. I slipped an arm around Sabrina's shoulders and drew her close. "Love, you, baby," I whispered against her hair.

I love you too, she breathed into my mind.

Trent, I sent, *our girl just got mindspeech*.

~

BlackWing XIII

Miz'Sandar Keel

After passing out from drinking too much, I woke in my own bed aboard XIII with a pounding headache.

I blamed Markus—and myself—for the headache.

I didn't regret the sleep I'd gotten between, however. Sleep had become elusive the longer Mae was missing.

I had vague memories of being carried by Markus, before we were transported away from BlackWing X. The next thing I recalled was Markus pulling off my boots after placing me on the bed.

Had I told him I loved him when he did that?

I couldn't remember, and considered it was a mistake if I had. Time to stop thinking—it only made my headache worse. Rolling off the bed, I staggered to the bathroom to find painkill. It would take half a bottle to dull this pain.

Once I had the headache under control, I'd compartmentalize things again, emotions included. Alcohol always muddled my good sense and let too many things wander out of sealed, mental boxes.

"Miz?" A knock sounded on my door, followed by David's voice.

"Come in—I'm looking for the painkill," I said, each word stabbing painfully into my brain.

"No worries," David said, opening the outer door as I poked my head out of the small bathroom. My vision was blurred; I struggled to make his image clear as he stood inside my cabin, hands on hips.

"Damn, dude, you look like hell," he said flatly. "Markus asked me to stop by to see if you wanted something to eat. He'll bring a tray if you do."

"I suppose I should eat something," I rumbled while attempting to get the cap off the painkill bottle.

"Let me," David held out a hand.

I gave the bottle to him without hesitation. "I'll let Markus know," he said, passing the opened container back to me. "I figure you have time to shower and wake up a little more before he gets here."

"Yes. Thank you," I said as David walked out the door and closed it behind him. Maybe I hadn't embarrassed myself in front of Markus after all.

One could only hope.

~

Pyrik

Randl

"Barely a tingle," I told Kooper as we studied the bodies found the day before.

"How can he do that?" Kooper asked the rhetorical question. "How can they be soaked in his stench one day, and barely anything the next? You'd think that if the Prophet wanted to pull the evidence away, he'd do it right after his targets died, instead of a day after."

"Has forensics or the examiners found anything?" I asked.

"No poisons, just as before," Kooper shook his head. "No other obvious diseases or injuries—except those inflicted right before their deaths."

"Like the Gant family."

"At least we stopped their waste from joining that of their neighbors, this time. We had everything inside the house shut down the moment we got the call."

"Maybe this will be easier to go through," I said.

"It'll certainly be less."

"There's that."

"Any connections between this family and the Gant family?" I asked.

"We're researching that, now. Quin has studied the images I sent to her—she said she saw nothing out of the ordinary—just a family preparing to have a meal together, then the violence came."

"Then this family, like the Gants, had no idea they'd been targeted. If they had, Quin would certainly find it."

"As would you," Kooper huffed.

"Quin may be better at it than I am—she's been doing it longer."

"So. No poison in the food, no evidence through the victims that they were a target, and we're following their recent footsteps, like we did with the Gant family. I worry we'll find nothing. Again."

"Director, there has to be something here; we merely don't know what we're looking for," I said. "We'll find it. We have to."

"I wish we'd hurry, then. This frustration is making the snake angry."

"How do you calm a snake down?" I asked.

"Not easily," he sighed. "If the Prophet were here, I imagine biting him a few dozen times would help a lot."

"He'd be dead by the fourth bite," I pointed out.

"But it would give me satisfaction to bite him more."

"Then everyone else would stand aside and allow it," I shrugged. "If the Director's not happy, nobody's happy."

"Damn straight." Kooper grinned for the first time in days. "Come on, there's a drink calling our names, I think."

～

"I haven't been here in a while," I said as we chose a table for four in New Fangled, Le-Ath Veronis' favorite vampire bar. I'd already seen in Kooper that Kell and Opal were joining us. I waited to see what Kooper wanted to discuss.

Those two—Kell, a modified vampire, and Opal, a powerful shapeshifter and member of the Hierarchy, often carried out undercover operations and research for Kooper.

"I assigned them to this case—to look into everything concerning the Gant and Lindom families. If there's something we missed, it's their job to find it," Kooper said as Opal and Kell took their seats.

"We'll be coordinating with you, if we do find anything out of the ordinary," Kell told me. "We'd like you to stay in contact with us, too, if you come up with any ideas."

"I can do that," I agreed. "Want to be included in shipboard meetings, if we're covering the subject?"

"If we're available, yes," Opal said.

"Right now, Sabrina is working on a portable scanner," I told Kooper. "She's attempting to adjust it to search for DNA long distance, instead of elements or other substances."

"I don't know how that could be possible," Kooper said before motioning a waiting comesula over to take our orders.

I don't argue with Sabrina where technology is concerned, I said in mindspeech while Opal and Kell ordered their food.

I won't either, but it sounds far-fetched to me, Kooper replied before opening his mouth to order a steak sandwich and fries, plus a bourbon and soda.

"I'll take the Earth-burger, please, with mustard, lettuce, onion, tomato, pickles and cheese," I said when my turn came. "Also with fries and a Refizani Blue."

"I'll have your orders out soon," the comesula dipped his head to us and strode toward the kitchen.

"I'm starved," Kell smiled at Opal. Both were older than dirt, looked young and had waited centuries for the right person to come along.

A smile from Kell, as an ancient vampire, was a rare occurrence. I reckoned he saved most of those for Opal.

"I hear you have Nari and Tiri working on the kidnapping," Opal said.

"We do. They're occupied with locating the missing through more personal items," I explained as the comesula set our drinks on the table. Kooper had a sound shield around us, but it never hurt to take every precaution.

Personal items? Kell sent mindspeech.

Hair and such, I replied. *I'm not exactly sure how their talent works, but I can't argue with the results they've gotten in the past.*

Understood, Kell said, lifting his glass of bourbon. I held up my beer in a silent salute and we both drank.

❧

BlackWing XIII
Nari

"This isn't like historical artifacts," I dropped onto a chair in our lab with a weary sigh. "We don't have a ready supply of paper or metal or anything else from a particular era to help us do the search," I added.

"I know," Tiri agreed, taking a chair nearby. "We have a few hairs to work with, and even though we're using only a microscopic bit at a time, we have an entire universe to search, rather than a single planet, like we usually do."

Our talent was inherited from our grandmother, who'd been dead for years. At least we'd improved on what we'd learned from her, employing something that vibrated at a similar frequency to search for like items in the same era.

Not-so-important scroll fragments from the same time period could be used to search for a much more important set of writings. Bits of clay pots would assist us in finding caches of ancient pottery, which in turn could pinpoint ancient cities or burial grounds.

We'd discovered so many ancient things this way, including buried coins and other treasure, by using a single coin minted by the same dynasty.

If we knew the planet where Mae'Sandar Keel had been taken, we'd likely have found her already.

"We have to keep looking," Tiri said. "Just not right now. I need a long bath or a swim or something."

"I want a swim," I said. XIII was large enough to have a lap pool near the back. Swimming was our exercise of choice, to get a series of failures out of our minds through physical effort.

"I really wanted to see Director Riffler again," Tiri stretched and yawned. "He certainly appeared interested."

"You know we intimidate men," I pointed out. "We're not helpless or stupid, and you know how that goes, sometimes. He's had plenty of time to rethink his attraction."

"Then let's go swim and get everything out of our heads for a while."

"Right behind you." We walked out of our lab together.

~

CSD Headquarters, Campiaa City

Jett Riffler

I'd called myself a fool and sent required records for signatures by comp-vid to Randl, instead of showing up on BlackWing XIII, hoping to have dinner with two beautiful women.

What if they didn't want to be paired or courted together?

A Fi'Gu, or leader of his race, required at least two wives when he married. It was tradition.

They probably knew that by now; the tattoo on my face announced what I was to those who knew, and those two were more than knowledgeable of ancient races and customs.

Perhaps they weren't attracted to tattoos—some weren't. Half my body was covered in tattoos—a Fi'Gu's markings.

You're overthinking this, I scolded myself. Truth was, I hadn't been attracted to anyone for nearly a century. I'd been too busy handling things for my race and for the CSD—sometimes at the same time.

It would be comforting to have wives who not only cared for one another, but who understood customs and traditions.

"Damn." I rubbed my forehead. "Get back to work," I ordered myself. Things would either work out or they wouldn't, and I had no time to make myself crazy over what lust and attraction could do to the best among us.

~

Prophet's Compound

Le'Vestar Limn

Mae and I were halfway to our goal of sequestering the hold the Prophet held over us when he walked into our laboratory, followed by a terrified Yurik. I saw the struggle in Mae's eyes, first—getting that close to the one who held our reins made the obsession more virulent.

"Yurik has been unsuccessful in obtaining certain replacement parts for my ship," the Prophet said, his words and voice sounding as well-oiled and poisoned as a venomous snake's. His left hand moved continuously as he clacked two round objects together. From the sound of it—they were made of solid glass.

"It is an older ship, my Lord," I ignored the questions in my mind and dipped my head to him before he could accost Mae about parts we didn't have.

"What shall I do? I want my ship functional," the Prophet snapped.

"If we had proper equipment, we could fabricate the parts ourselves."

"You're sure of this?"

"Yes. I am an engineer, as you know, as is my colleague." I nodded toward Mae, whose eyes held unblinking terror.

"Very good. Yurik, find what they need to manufacture parts. I wish to send my pilots out in search of other ships."

"It will be done, my Lord," Yurik bowed low.

"Of course it will be done." Tossing out his right hand, the Prophet casually forced power through his fingers. Yurik was knocked off his feet and into a nearby table, jarring everything we'd laid upon it and causing a few important things to fall.

As ringing metal fittings clanged and rolled across the concrete floor, the Prophet disappeared from our presence in an angry burst of light.

CHAPTER 8

*Q*ueen's Palace, Le-Ath Veronis
Kooper

"Searching through the waste from an entire neighborhood has turned into a foolish quest," I told Queen Lissa. "As for stomach contents and such, there's nothing out of the ordinary there, either."

"Have you had Randl check what's been removed from stomachs?" Lissa asked.

"No, we only checked for poisons. I'll have Randl on it by the end of the day, though."

"Sounds good. Doesn't hurt to check everything, does it?"

"Of course not." I silently berated myself for not thinking of it already. "I'll have Opal and Kell look into it, too."

"Kell would know poisons better than anyone." Lissa's words were dry.

He would—as the creator and head vampire of the Order of the Night Flower, Kell was the expert on such in both Alliances. Subtle poisonings were his specialty.

Had the Prophet taken up the craft, too, with less than honorable intentions? Had he created something that would get past our most sensitive equipment?

What poison would turn a family against each other? Had he found a way to infuse it with obsession?

"I believe we just had the same thought," Lissa said. "And it's terrifying."

~

BlackWing XIII

Randl

"We're treating this as a biohazard," Kell said as he directed the sealed carry-bot to my desk using his comp-vid. "We haven't touched any part of it, and don't intend to."

Stomach contents of the latest victims sloshed inside the clear globes of the carry-bot. I shoved the idea of where the brown mushiness had originated and concentrated on finding any connection with the Prophet.

"There's absolutely nothing there," I shook my head at Kell.

"Well, it was a thought," Kell sighed.

"No, I didn't make myself clear," I said. "This—stuff, whatever it is —didn't come from the Lindom family. I don't know where it came from, but it isn't from anyone's stomach."

"Fucking hells," Opal hissed. She'd stood behind Kell, a silent witness to our exchange. Her anger had come quickly, however.

Someone, somewhere, had switched the contents removed from the Lindoms' stomachs for something else.

"I just sent mindspeech to Kooper," Kell growled. "He's not pleased."

"Find out what happened to the same contents from the Gant family," I said.

"Already on it," Kell replied. "Keep that contained and sequestered," he pointed to the carry-bot. "We'll be back."

~

Avii Castle

   Quin

"He's obsessed," I handed the photograph of Kooper's Chief Forensics Officer back. Kooper looked angry enough to blast his comp-vid to pieces once I told him what I'd seen. I'd gone through images of everyone in the forensics lab, getting to the Chief at the last.

The Prophet was extending his reign of terror to include innocent families, and we still hadn't determined how he'd done it. Both families had ingested something infected with the Prophet's disease, that much was clear, and he'd reached out to command one of Kooper's employees to remove the evidence of it.

I didn't want to tell Kooper what I thought—that this was the Prophet's way of retaliating against him and Jett for standing against him on Campiaa. The Prophet had lost an entire fleet of stolen ships in that battle, along with his dead army and many of his minions on the ground.

Randl was obviously first on the Prophet's list to destroy, but Kooper and Jett were close behind.

"He wants me, too—doesn't he?" Kooper guessed what I was thinking.

"And Director Riffler. He has all along, remember? Randl has inserted himself deliberately onto the Prophet's kill list, but the Prophet was targeting Jett and you on Pyrik, and then again on Campiaa. Getting you and the Alliance leaders out of the way would allow him to take over. You've managed to fight him back every time, plus, the ASD and CSD, working together, destroyed his new fleet of ships. He's furious, now."

"Do you think he may have counted on jealousy between Directors?"

"That's possible. If he did, he's more than disappointed that you continue to work together, rather than pursue him separately."

"Something to think about," Kooper said absently. I knew he was thinking about Randl, now, and how Randl often was a step or two ahead of both Directors. Kooper couldn't feel jealousy, but he could feel envy and frustration. Randl could and did do things that Kooper couldn't.

Saying something to Kooper about that could only make things worse, too, so I didn't. "It's going to take all of us, working together, to bring the Prophet down, Director Griff," I told him instead.

"You're right. Thank you, Quin. I have a Chief of Forensics to corner, now."

"I hope you find him," I said.

Kooper closed his eyes for a moment as his shoulders slumped. He didn't have to ask what else I'd seen in the image—that the man Kooper now hunted had disappeared, even from my finding skills.

~

BlackWing XIII

Randl

Kell and Opal returned for the carry-bot, and to let me know the information Quin had given Kooper. The Chief Forensics Officer for the ASD had been compromised and obsessed by the Prophet.

He'd replaced stomach contents with mush and then disappeared. The Prophet was telling us that he could get to anyone he wanted, just because he wanted, and for now, we were powerless to stop him.

If it were the Prophet's intention to stretch Kooper and Jett's resources to the limit, he was doing a fine job of it. I had no idea how many people they'd already assigned to track down sources and uses of recycled concrete; every ship in the BlackWing fleet was either searching for the bone-filled concrete stashes the Prophet had already made or looking for his kidnapped victims, and then there were the usual criminal activities that they were already investigating.

"This is impossible," Opal shook her head as Kell directed the carry-bot to follow him.

"Yeah. That's it in a nutshell," I agreed. "We may never know what those two families ate that the Prophet contaminated. It could be a single ingredient—or the entire meal."

"One family had salad and a noodle casserole; the other pork and apples," Kell agreed. "Not much in the crossover department. Have you considered that some of the stolen items from the food warehouse may have been used?"

"I've considered it, and concede it's possible," I said. "But how did he get it into two households? Security vids show nothing, as you know."

"I'll look into the food shopping habits of both households, then," Opal offered. "I'll let you know if I find anything."

"Thank you."

"He could be dead, for all we know," I told Travis and Trent at a private dinner meeting. I'd filled them in on the Chief of Forensics disappearance, after he'd sabotaged the investigation into the deaths of two families.

"I worry about the food supply being compromised," Trent rumbled. "This could affect anybody anywhere."

"I've spoken with Gerrett about what those families used to cook their meals—ingredients and such, and there's not much to go on. No similarities in components that we can tell."

"Then the Prophet isn't limiting his influence on a single thing," Travis grimaced. "Fucker."

"And, like the recycled concrete, he can choose whenever he wants to activate his influence," I pointed out.

"Fucker is too nice a term for the Prophet, bro," Trent told Travis. "It gives ordinary, everyday fuckers a bad name."

"Agreed. I'll certainly revise my description. Thank you for the input."

"Anytime. It's the least I can do."

"You've always been helpful that way."

"You know it, bro. Want to settle this in the dojo?"

"What just happened?" I asked, after looking from one brother to the other.

"Come on, dude. You need to work off some anger and anxiety, too. Grab your blades and we'll get on it." Travis stood and stomped out of my office.

~

Miz'Sandar

"A laser rifle has more kick than the newest version of a ranos rifle," Markus told me as I took aim at the target. "These replicas will give you the weight and feel of the real thing."

I held a replica of a ranos rifle in my hands, wondering how much less a kick it had. I'd always braced myself when I was learning how to fire the laser rifles. I was about to fire when Captains Travis and Trent, followed by Randl, walked into the exercise facility.

All three carried swords. Not practice swords—these appeared real in every way.

"Those aren't their Grey House blades, or Randl's personal swords that nobody else can use," Markus found me gazing at the new arrivals. "Those are just everyday blades that a warrior on Falchan might have."

"A Falchani warrior's blades are serious enough," I said, blinking as blades were set aside while all three went through a stretching session.

Vik showed up then, armed just like the other three. I was going to see all of them fight with two blades and found myself looking forward to it.

"We can take a break," Markus grinned. "It's fun to watch them," he added.

By the time stretching was over, a larger audience had arrived, including Sabrina, Dori, David and several others.

"They blow off steam this way," David said as he settled on the bench beside me. "I figure they got some not-so-good news and they're working their way through it."

"Don't worry, we'll hear what it is before long," Markus, on my other side, patted my shoulder.

112

"But what if it's about Mae?" I asked, struggling to keep my voice steady.

"They'd have come to you already," David replied. "I think it's something to do with those two families who turned on themselves. We already know the Prophet is involved—they may have some disturbing updates for us."

"Stop worrying about it and watch," Markus said softly, rubbing my back for a brief few seconds. "Here we go." Markus dropped his hand; I jerked in my seat as Travis and Trent attacked one another so swiftly I almost missed it.

~

Randl

"I doubt the Forensics Chief was kidnapped. He's obsessed, so all they had to do was crook their finger and he'd go willingly," I answered Miz's question at the ship's meeting later.

The sparring session had helped a great deal—things were falling into place and there was less panic as they did so. "The powerful can't find him anywhere, so he's hidden by a Sirenali, just like the Prophet and his minions," I went on.

"He's probably with the Prophet, then, advising him on new ways to contaminate food and interfere with the investigation," David complained.

Those were my concerns, too, so I didn't respond. Having a Chief of Forensics expert on your staff could lead to all sorts of criminally-induced ideas.

"Are there any other obsessed employees at the ASD or CSD?" Dori asked.

"Quin is going through all the rosters again," I said. "It's a long and tedious process, and could require repeating almost daily."

"That's not good," Vik growled.

"It's easier than having them followed—they'd be following themselves," Trent said. "The Prophet is deliberately spreading our resources thin. With these random murders, he's forcing us to scramble to make sense of any of it, when there likely isn't any to be found."

Trent was probably right—if I wanted to create chaos, it's exactly what I would do. I just couldn't figure out, yet, how the Prophet arranged for those killings to happen so randomly.

"Do you suppose it's like putting one piece of poisoned fruit in the barrel, waiting for an unsuspecting innocent to come along and take it?" Miz asked. His brow was creased as his mind sorted through possibilities.

"Miz, I think you may be right," I said, forcing myself not to shudder. Wherever the poisoned items had been placed, it had been completely random, in my opinion—a bomb waiting for someone to pick it up and take it home with them.

Kell, I sent mindspeech. *I want names of markets and grocery outlets where both those families shopped, and then we need vid images covering the days they last shopped there.*

On it, Kell replied. *I'll have it for you by tomorrow. Want me to report this to Kooper?*

I can do it, I said. *I need to speak with him anyway.*

Good. Thank you.

I'd already decided to have a meeting with Kooper—and Jett, Teeg San Gerxon and Queen Lissa. She'd relay important information to Ildevar Wyyld, the Founder of the Reth Alliance.

It was only a matter of time, now, before the Prophet played his hand—offering to stop murdering innocent families in exchange for information.

On me.

∾

Founder's Palace, Campiaa
Wyatt San Gerxon
When Randl asked to have a meeting with Dad, Kooper, Jett, Gran and me, we had it put together in record time. We now sat in Dad's meeting room to discuss new information regarding the family

murders on Pyrik and Lordinus. Opal and Kell accompanied Kooper when he arrived, as they had information to share, too.

Jayna sat beside me; Dad wanted her and Tybus in the meeting with us.

"We've gone through security images from the grocery shops both families frequented," Kell began. "There's nothing out of the ordinary in either. We do have a list of items purchased, however, so we're backtracking to packing facilities, growers, everything. Somewhere along that chain of food handling, the Prophet placed something he contaminated, waiting for someone, somewhere, to consume it."

"I get angry, every time I think that going into the kitchen to cook could result in somebody's death," Gran huffed. She loved to cook. As she was powerful, the infection might not affect her, but it could destroy the comesuli who worked in the palace, along with any unsuspecting humanoids.

Dad was furious about it, too; he merely hadn't voiced his opinion as yet. I watched his jaw work as he ground his teeth. *How do you fight this?* I had no ready solutions. The Prophet was playing Russian roulette with people's lives, as Gran would say.

"Do you think it's as simple as dropping a single apple into a barrel?" Tybus asked Kell.

"I worry that it is exactly like that," Kell replied. "There's no reason to target either of those families. They have no ties to any government, have only the standard military service if that, and never served in the field while there."

Kell and Opal had done thorough research on both families—up to a point. "Were any of them having affairs outside the home?" I asked.

"We're working on sorting that out, too," Opal said. "We've found nothing so far, but we still have a few friends and neighbors to interview."

They'd considered the transmission by sex angle, just as I had, but to our knowledge, the Prophet wasn't aware of that possibility, yet. I worried that he'd discover it if he hadn't already, and then we'd be in more trouble than we already were.

"We're still working on how and when the Chief Forensics

Specialist got away," Kooper said. "I'm having all his recent movements tracked, hoping to uncover more information."

"We're having a real manpower problem," Jett said. "Too many things to investigate, and not enough people to do the work," he directed his remarks at Dad.

"I'm asking Ildevar for investigative resources from the RAA," Kooper said. It was a good idea—the Regular Alliance Army had their own arm of intelligence operatives, some of whom were on par with Kooper's people.

"Can we do that, too?" I asked Dad. "Conscript Regular Campiaan Army operatives for a temporary assignment?"

"I'll speak with Generals and Admirals this afternoon," Dad said. "Jett, I'll let you know how many they can reassign temporarily afterward."

"Thank you," Jett said. "That will relieve some of the pressure."

"Randl, what do you have?" Kooper turned to him, now. He'd remained silent up to now, listening intently to everything said.

"I'm telling you what's likely to happen in the future," he said.

"What's that?" Kooper didn't sound happy.

"He won't identify himself, but the Prophet will be asking for information on me. He knows you have a price on my head, now, and is likely following every scrap of information published in any way about me. He may go so far as to offer an exchange—making the slaughter of innocent families cease—for any reliable word on me, so he can more easily track me down."

"What does this mean?" I asked.

"It means I have to step up my game on crimes committed—without actually committing any. Kooper, whenever you catch any real pirates in the act of committing a crime, then those crimes, whenever possible, need to be attributed to me and the BlackWing fleet. Feel free to tell everyone that I've taken over the BlackWing Pirates, because that much is true."

"You mean, take what the real pirates do and twist those crimes slightly to lay the blame on you?"

"Yes. If any pirate ships get destroyed while attacking transports, then lie and say more got away. It'll be better if the criminals are killed in the commission of the crime, but use your own judgment. The more false information we can feed the Prophet, the better off we may be."

"He'll be gunning for the entire fleet," Jayna said, sounding alarmed.

"That's why we need to leave at least half the BlackWing ships out of this. Let them keep their alter egos in place during this operation. Only ask those who are willing to have the Prophet target them to fly under the BlackWing flag."

"I can do that," Kooper appeared thoughtful.

"Queen Lissa, will you coordinate with Quin, and make the final decisions on whether a serious crime is suitable to attribute to me?" Randl turned to Gran.

"I can do that," Gran nodded. "Easily."

He was asking her to employ a certain amount of power to make reasonable determinations. I didn't blame him in this. With Quin and Gran both considering the crimes in question, I felt we'd be relatively safe in twisting the facts a bit.

"Does he have any ships left to chase you down?" Tybus spoke for the first time, to ask Randl a question.

"I don't know. If he doesn't, I figure he's working to get some. He's able to fold space, but I doubt many of his minions can do it. Having ships enables his troops to be in several places at once."

"He wasn't counting on the RAA and RCA to fight his newly-acquired fleet in Campiaan space," Dad said. "We destroyed his fleet—or most of it, I'm sure."

"I feel confident he threw everything he could at us," Randl agreed. "He'll be looking for more ships, if he hasn't found some already."

"I'll make sure the word gets out to increase security in shipyards and such," Jett said.

"As will I," Kooper blew out a frustrated breath. "Fuck. Knock one head down and a dozen more pop up."

"Well, it's either a hydra or a game of whack-the-mole," Gran drawled. "The hydra is more evil. I'll go with that one."

"Are there any criminal factions left with a fleet of ships?" Jayna asked.

"There may be a few. I'd say most of those are outside both Alliances," Jett replied.

"I agree. After the Prophet took over two of the Big Three, and Randl took the third one, the rest have only a few ships here and there inside Alliance air space." Kooper made a face as he considered the possibilities.

"The Big Three had a sizeable fleet available for the Prophet to take, and he managed to take two-thirds of it easily. What remains is more scattered and would require more time and effort—unless he decides to go after military fleets. Perhaps it is time to consider unusual uprisings that would require their presence," Jett offered.

"Do you think he has something planned?" Dad asked.

"It's possible," Randl responded. "Are there any missions scheduled that require more than one or two Alliance ships?"

"There's nothing now," Kooper said.

"That doesn't mean the Prophet won't manufacture something," Jett pointed out. "He could easily start a rebellion on an Alliance world."

"True," Gran said. "We'll be keeping a careful watch on anything like that from now on."

"I want his head," Kooper growled. "The Prophet. I really need suggestions on how to find him—faster."

"We're working on that, but we need time," Randl said. "He won't make it easy, you can bet on that."

"Nothing has been easy where he's concerned," Dad noted. He was still angry that the Prophet had not only destroyed much of Campiaa City, but had killed or kidnapped so many of its citizens. Like Kooper, he felt helpless against an enemy of this magnitude.

Unlike Kooper, Dad didn't blame Randl for not capturing or killing the Prophet already. He knew, as did I, how long it had taken to track and destroy Vardil Cayetes and his bunch.

It had taken decades, and Zaria was the one to destroy him at the end.

The Prophet wasn't going about his takeover in the usual fashion, though, and Kooper didn't like scrambling to combat new threats he couldn't fight with his regular troops.

This time, Randl was working against the Prophet, with Zaria's help. Somehow, that irked Kooper, too.

Gran, I sent. *Why is Kooper upset that Randl is the one going against the Prophet?*

Because he can't, even with the power he has. The Prophet is a special case, and Kooper is frustrated that he has little in his personal arsenal to take him down.

This stems from frustration?

Kooper isn't used to this kind of threat, and a feeling of impotence is never a good thing. Your Aunt Bree is aware of the situation.

Aunt Bree. The Mighty Heart. I hoped she could redirect Kooper's frustration, then, to keep Randl unfettered in his search for the Prophet. He didn't need another worry to weigh him down.

Is there anything we can do?

I'm not sure. I'll think on that, Gran replied.

~

Kend Industries Warehouse, Jaledis

Le'Vestar Limn

Yurik wanted to growl at the Prophet's recently-acquired servant, Jiles. Jiles was young, a criminal, and a warlock. Folding space and petty theft appeared to be his complete repertoire. I imagined he was a low priority as criminals went on the King of Karathia's wanted lists.

With an obsession placed by the Prophet, that low priority status could change quickly. Jiles was the Prophet's new toy, and he'd employed his limited talents already to steal food and other necessities. Now, Jiles had gotten us into a warehouse, so I could search for a suitable machine to manufacture missing parts for an old starship. I hoped to find raw materials, too, or we'd be forced on another trip to get them.

If Mae and I had been sent together, we'd have attempted escape. She'd been commanded to stay behind, so I was accompanied by Yurik and Jiles, who were particularly unhelpful in looking for the proper machine and materials. While I searched the massive warehouse for a suitable parts replicator, however, an idea was forming in my brain.

An idea that involved repairing an ancient starship, and then convincing the Prophet to allow Mae and me to stay on board, in case more repairs were needed.

Once aboard and away from the Prophet, we'd make our escape—provided we could successfully throw off the Prophet's hold and become what we truly were.

Neither Yurik nor Jiles understood what was needed; they merely wandered through a cluttered warehouse like lost souls, staring at things they didn't comprehend.

"Here," I called out softly. I'd found what was needed—granted it was an older model and quite large, but it would certainly get the job done.

"This," I pointed to the machine, sealed in clear plastic. On the outside, it bore an inspection sticker, telling me that it still worked. Not far away lay crates of manufacturing materials—metal, plastics and such.

"Those, too," I pointed to the crates.

If Jiles weren't obsessed, he'd have balked at moving such a large amount. As it was, he'd been instructed to do whatever Yurik said. Squaring his shoulders and shoving back a swath of too-long brown hair, Jiles prepared to move the required materials, the machine and three people.

∼

Founder's Palace, Campiaa
Kooper

The alarm went off on my comp-vid the same moment Jett's

sounded. We were wrapping up the meeting when the emergency messages arrived.

Jerking my comp-vid out of a pocket, I scanned the message. "Kend Industries' main warehouse was just burgled," I snapped. "A replicating machine and raw materials were taken."

"By whom?" Randl stood immediately.

"They don't know—all the security vids were killed while the thieves were in the warehouse. The alarm sounded the moment several items were removed from their pressure sensors."

"Perhaps we should take a look," Jett said.

"Randl, Jett, you're with me," I said and folded space.

Kend Industries Warehouse, Jaledis

Randl

"Power was used to temporarily disable the security vids," Kooper said, staring at the static images recorded by security cameras.

We stood behind the Chief Security Officer, who worked the console to show us what they had—or in this case, didn't have.

"This warehouse holds most of our older, working models of replication machines and such," the chief told us. "One of the larger ones is missing," he tapped the console to bring up the image of an empty space in the warehouse. "And raw materials, too." He switched the camera to other empty spaces.

"Do you know how it was done?" the chief asked Kooper. "These are state of the art security cameras, and it's impossible to use a device to take them out of service."

"I'd say it was either a wizard or warlock," Kooper said. "Randl, do you think you can tell anything if we go down to the floor?"

"I may be able to see something."

"With your permission, Chief?" Kooper turned to him.

"Come with me," the chief said. Jett, Kooper and I followed him to the trans-vator down the hall.

~

Instead of going to the empty spaces, I chose objects that stood next to the empty spaces. Without the advantage of a wall, it was the best I had. Placing my hand on a large machine that lay adjacent to the missing replicator, I took a deep breath and closed my eyes.

The images came immediately. "Three were here," I breathed. I didn't report it then, but one of those three I recognized immediately.

Le'Vestar Limn, one of our missing Or'myr.

The other thing I knew from seeing his image, was that he was working his way out of the obsession placed by the Prophet.

The other two were so consumed by their obsession, I couldn't get anything other than their images.

Kooper had a database, however, and I could employ power to recreate images to feed into that database. If there were any records anywhere, we'd learn who Le'Vestar's companions were.

"Kooper," I said, opening my eyes and removing my hands from the machine I'd touched. "We may have big problems coming our way."

CHAPTER 9

SD Headquarters, Le-Ath Veronis
Randl

"You think he's found a wrecked ship, or one that needs repairs, and he's commanding Le'Vestar and Mae'Sandar to get it ready to fly?" Kooper shook his head. His worries, like mine, had just increased ten-fold.

"I think so," I said. "If they can repair one, then they can do the same for others. I never considered protecting impounds and scrapyards, but it looks like we need to."

"Fuck. I have lists longer than the Kletic River of stolen goods from scrapyards," Kooper cursed. "Those are considered the lowest of low priorities. Nobody investigates those cases if they can help it."

"No doubt that's why the Prophet has targeted them." Jett was already convinced that the Prophet was scavenging scrapyards for parts or junked ships. "In fact, he could have obsessed who knows how many scrapyard employees, to let him know when anything arrives that he'd want."

"It makes sense when you put it like that," Kooper tossed out a hand. "Fuck. Planet-fucking hells," he growled.

"Can you get images and information on scrapyard owners and

employees to Quin?" I asked. "We really need to know if they're obsessed, and if they are, what's been taken from their businesses."

"We should be discreet—we don't want to alert the Prophet that we know of this new enterprise," Jett cautioned.

"I know," Kooper kneaded his forehead. "I'll get Quin on this right away. Randl, did you see anything else in Le'Vestar?"

"Only that he's working on throwing off the obsession. It still lingers and prevents him from changing to his dragon or protecting himself. I imagine Mae is in the same state, and he won't leave her behind—that's why he didn't attempt to escape while on Jaledis."

"We have information on one of the two thieves," Kell and Opal arrived. Kell handed a comp-vid to Kooper.

"Jiles Tamber, Second-level warlock and petty thief," he handed the comp-vid to me after scanning information quickly.

"That's him, all right. The Prophet now has a warlock, and may be looking for more."

"I'll let King Rylend know where this one is," Jett said when I handed the comp-vid to him. "This will certainly move Jiles up the wanted lists."

"Any suggestions before I send you back to work?" Kooper asked.

"I do have a suggestion, and a gift for you," I said.

"What's that?"

"Here," I handed a memory chip to him. "Travis offered. I didn't have anything to do with it."

"What is it?" Kooper fingered the tiny chip.

"An invitation from his father and grandfather," I said.

"Drake and Dragon?" Kooper was puzzled and curious at the same time.

They want to teach you meditation. Dragon was Warlord on Falchan during the worst wars that planet ever saw. I think he knows a thing or two about stress, and how to relieve it. I hope you will take this in the good spirit it was offered, I added.

At that moment, I could read Kooper easily. If he admired anyone, it was the Dragon Warlord. *I'll give this serious thought,* he replied.

Thank you. Tension drained from my body—I worried that Kooper would find it an insult and refuse the help.

"I'm gone," I said. "Contact me if you need anything." I folded space back to the ship.

~

Avii Castle

Quin

"He used to work for my mother," Charla said when I showed her the image of a scrapyard mogul. "I saw him many times—I had to allow him to stay at my house on Campiaa whenever he wanted to gamble. My mother insisted."

I'd seen Jewl's image in Ex'ero Plumb's. Thankfully, he wasn't obsessed. Some of the others were, and I'd already sent that information to Kooper.

"He's Crillie," Charla admitted, turning pink. "I always assumed he and my mother," her face turned a deeper pink.

Crillie. I wanted to turn pink, too. Crillie men were equipped with two penises instead of one, each operating independently of the other. There were plenty of jokes about Crillie men, too. I cleared my throat and pretended I hadn't heard any of them.

I need images of all of Ex'ero Plumb's employees, I sent to Kooper.

Is he obsessed, too?

No. Not yet, but he has more than seventy scrapyards, and there's nothing to keep his managers and employees from being obsessed.

That's true, Kooper agreed. *He's Crillie, you know. There's a joke about him fucking his patrons twice on the costs of his parts and scrap,* Kooper added.

I think that joke may be told about any Crillie business owner, I responded, feeling my face turn hot.

That could be, Kooper said.

Charla says she saw him plenty of times—that he worked for Jewl, I changed the subject quickly. *She says that her mother and Ex'ero may have been lovers.*

I'll let Randl know. This may work to our advantage in some way, Kooper sounded thoughtful. *Find out everything you can from Charla, and keep me informed.*

Of course, Director.

~

BlackWing XIII

Randl

"He's Crillie?" Dori's eyes were wide as she stared at Ex'ero Plumb's image. She, Travis, Trent and I sat at a table in the galley, discussing the latest information.

"Yeah, and he owns seventy-six scrapyards—they're huge, like scrap warehouses. Several of them occupy small moons, they're so large," Travis said, consulting his comp-vid. I appreciated the fact that he'd skirted the double-dick phase of this conversation.

"Do we know whether he keeps good records of his sales and purchases?" Trent asked, pulling Travis' comp-vid closer to get a better look.

"Doubt it," I said. "Charla said he used to work for Jewl. I think that has criminal intent written all over it. Look at it this way—if Jewl misappropriated something, how easy would it be to hide said misappropriation in a warehouse so vast, you'd have to use a shuttle to go from one end to the other?"

"What about scrapped or disabled ships?" Travis asked the question I wanted answered.

"We don't know. All Kooper has at his disposal are the legal records Ex'ero keeps. There's nothing to prevent him from keeping other objects, let's say, in case they're called for, or if the right buyer comes along."

"What if he worked for the other two of the Big Three?" Dori asked. "We know they got killed in the Battle of Campiaa, but what about their assets and hidden employees?"

"Perhaps we need to pay a visit to Ex'ero sometime," Travis

suggested. "Did you tell Miz that Le'Vestar was on Jaledis and part of the robbery at Kend Enterprises?"

"Not yet. I'll tell him that Mae is safe for now—if nothing else, at least that information should give him some hope."

"You didn't see where they are?" Trent asked.

"That's buried in the part of Lev's obsession that's still in place," I shook my head. "That would be the most difficult nut to crack in the Prophet's repertoire, you understand."

"Damn, that would have made our lives so much easier," Trent rubbed the back of his neck.

"Yeah. Now, we know where all seventy-six of Ex'ero's scrapyards are. I say we approach the nearest one without delay, and find out if they've had any unusual requests for starship parts or fittings."

"I'm all for it," Travis agreed. "Now that Opal and Kell are working on the family murders, I feel better about looking into this. Who knows, if we find anything, it could either lead us to the Prophet, or allow us to set a trap for him."

"Exactly what I was thinking," I said. "And I believe we may be getting some company."

"Who?" Dori asked.

"King Rylend wants to send someone who can help us track Jiles Tamber. He says he has someone who is a power-scent tracker. They can recognize Jiles' power residue if he's used it anywhere, without casting a more elaborate spell. After a while, most power signatures deteriorate. The power-scent outlasts that, and this is where the tracker's talents come in."

"That could turn out to be more than handy," Travis said. "Those trackers are sort of rare, too. I've only heard of four or five who are currently working, and those were born in the last hundred years."

"If the Prophet gets addicted to having warlocks at his beck and call, then we'll need all the help we can get," I sighed. "Jiles is a Second-level warlock. We don't need the Prophet getting greedy and setting his sights on the more powerful ones. Bel Erland said he'd bring the power-scent tracker to us in time for dinner."

"I hope he's able to settle in with the crew," Dori said. "Do you think he's been made aware of the particular talents onboard?"

"I'm sure Bel will fill him in," Trent grinned. He should know; Bel Erland was his nephew.

"Good. We don't need somebody wanting to pet the Ocelot, now do we?"

Travis snickered. Every now and then, Dori let the Ocelot loose and patrolled the corridors of XIII. The crew knew to greet the Captain and then get out of her furry way.

Even I knew not to pet the Ocelot when someone else was watching. "Come back for dinner tonight," I told Travis and Trent. "Bring Sabrina and a few others if you want, to meet the new arrival and share a meal with Bel."

"We'll be back," Travis rose from his chair in my office and stretched. "Come on, bro, we have time for a sparring session if you're interested," he slapped Trent on the shoulder.

"Right behind you," Trent agreed. Both folded space at the same time. Only a few seconds passed before there was a knock on the galley's outside door.

"Come in, Zan," I called out and opened the door with power.

"Here are the flight plans for Captain Dori," Zanfield handed a comp-vid to her. "Mapping out all of Ex'ero's scrapyards, from nearest to farthest, as requested."

"Thank you, Zanfield," Dori grinned. "Tell Phillip he did a great job."

"I'll tell him." Zanfield turned to go.

"Zan, will you inform the crew that we'll have another temporary agent joining us tonight? Ask them to come to dinner in the main dining area, so I can make introductions."

"I'll see to it," Zanfield said.

"Zan, did you, ah," I studied the side of his head. He'd added green and red streaks to the yellow and purple, making his head look like a dyed, ripe jori-wheat field.

"Like it?"

"It's stunning."

"Good. Exactly what I hoped for." He grinned, waved as he turned on his heel and sailed out of my office.

"Do you think he's begging for attention?" Dori asked softly.

Yes, I answered in mindspeech. *Zanfield doesn't know how much we care for him, so he's keeping with his old ways.*

Money isn't everything, I guess, Dori responded.

Not even close, I acknowledged.

~

King's Palace, Karathia

Bel Erland

Every time Perri reported to us, she'd change her hair with power. Not just lengths and styles, but colors, too.

Today, her hair was shaved on the sides, while the top remained a medium length. She'd tied those lavender and pink strands into a neat bun at the top. Dad always said she looked as if she should be working in a clothing-and-jewelry boutique, rather than ferreting out power-scents for the Crown of Karathia.

At twenty-six, she was the youngest and best power-scent tracker we had. And, as she could detect the power-scent through a touch of her palms, she generally wore fingerless gloves unless she was working.

"I don't want to wear an ASD uniform," she announced, as if she were conversing with a friend instead of the King of Karathia.

"I doubt a uniform will matter to Randl Gage," Dad's words were as dry as petrified wood. "What matters to him will be your talent and your ability to get along with the crew."

"I can get along—if they leave me alone."

This, of course, stemmed from her childhood. Even among other Karathian children, she'd been different. Her family was quite poor, too, which further ostracized her. It wasn't until she was re-evaluated at age eighteen that the power-scent ability was recorded as a specific talent.

The Crown offered to pay her way into a prestigious Alliance school. She now held a degree from Le-Ath Veronis University, and had a Vamp U shirt to show for it. All through those four years, however, she'd retained her loner status.

She'd worked for the Crown for the past three years, and her tracking success rate was the best we'd seen.

She was eccentric and somewhat disrespectful, but managed to get her work done in spite of it.

If anybody could handle her, I figured Randl could. He'd take one look at her and know exactly what her troubles were. Dad agreed with me on that.

"Bel will take you to the ship in three hours. You're to meet the crew at dinner. I hope you can handle that much," Dad said.

"As long as they don't try to discuss the weather or their cats," Perri sniffed.

Dad and I turned toward each other, then. Dad grinned. I stifled a laugh. "Be ready to go when Bel comes for you," Dad turned back to Perri.

This will be interesting, I sent to Dad.

Big time, Dad replied.

❧

BlackWing XIII

Randl

I found the boxed medallion on my desk after a workout session with Vik.

For the new member of your crew, was written on the box in Zaria's hand. I recognized her writing, having seen it several times. *Send mindspeech if there are problems getting the new recruit to wear this* appeared on the box as I read the initial inscription.

Dinner was in an hour; Bel would likely send mindspeech before his arrival with the new agent. I wondered if uniforms would be needed.

"You asked to see us?" Markus tapped on my open door. Right behind him stood Miz, the one I really needed to see.

130

"Come in," I invited. "Have a seat. Want a drink before dinner?"

Miz was immediately suspicious. He stiffened, expecting bad news. "It isn't bad news, Miz," I told him, pulling a bottle of bourbon from my desk drawer and floating three glasses toward my desk. "I'm sure you've heard about the theft from Kend Enterprises?" I asked as Markus and Miz took their seats.

"We heard it from Vik," Markus nodded.

"Good. The news I have is this," I began pouring bourbon. "Le'Vestar was a part of that crew, sent by the Prophet. While that may not sound like good news, it actually is. I could see in the images I got that he was in the process of peeling away the Prophet's obsession. It's not halfway gone or even close, but I could see enough in him to know that Mae'Sandar is safe."

"Thank the gods," Miz blew out a breath. Markus handed him a glass of bourbon, which he emptied in one swallow.

~

P'loxett

V'dar

The two spheres in my left hand clacked together softly as I turned them over repeatedly while thinking. More and more, I was finding the new captive, Lev, quite useful. He and the female—both engineers, had done more to get my ship up and running than all my remaining pilots and workers combined.

Too, he'd been the one who'd pointed me in the proper direction, without realizing it. Scrapyards and recycling plants were everywhere, and many of them held parts, pieces, hulls and disabled ships in their inventory.

With the machine recently stolen from Kend Industries, we could manufacture what couldn't be found, and we'd have a fleet of ships again—enough to pull the Alliance fleets into another battle.

Only this time, they wouldn't find it so easy to defeat me.

Yes, I had plans. My recent experiments with food items were quite successful. Many of my workers were engaged in furthering that endeavor, while I watched over it carefully.

Time to pull back on the deaths of innocents, perhaps, letting Alliance Directors think I'd turned my thoughts elsewhere.

Soon enough, I'd initiate my plans against both, and they'd never know what hit them.

As far as my main enemy, Randl Gage, went, I still searched diligently for him. He'd turn up sooner or later, or I'd convince the Alliances to hand me information in exchange for—wait.

Ah—that was it. I could let them know that I'd curtail my efforts to murder innocents, in exchange for information on Randl Gage. *Yes*. If I killed one more family, then made my offer, they'd be more than willing to give me whatever I wanted.

"My Lord," Varok approached me with a comp-vid in his hand.

"Yes, Varok?" I stopped rolling my spheres and gave him a smile—I was feeling magnanimous suddenly. You'd have thought I'd given Varok his fondest desire, he was so pleased by that small gesture.

"Randl Gage, my Lord." He handed the comp-vid to me. I blinked at the news distributed by a reputable news conglomerate.

One of Alliance's most-wanted, Randl Gage, is now in charge of the BlackWing fleet, reliable sources report, the headline read. *The BlackWing Pirates, scourge of the shipping lanes, are now more dangerous than ever*, the following text began.

"Hmmph. We shall see who is more dangerous," I sniffed and handed the comp-vid to Varok. "I have plans to make," I told him. "Randl Gage has ships I wish to take—along with his head. See that I am not disturbed."

"Of course, my Lord."

I resumed the clacking of my spheres.

∾

BlackWing XIII
Perri Wilker
A fucking BlackWing Pirate ship? What the hells was going on? The

Crown Prince smiled at my confusion and didn't say anything in explanation.

He'd given me a list of crew members to study, but I hadn't bothered to look at my comp-vid, yet. More than anything I wanted to know why the Crown of Karathia had anything to do with the BlackWing Pirates.

"Welcome," the man said as Prince Bel steered me into a spacious office. He stood behind a solid wood desk that would bring thousands—if not hundreds of thousands, if it were as old as I suspected it to be.

"The desk belonged to Jewl Yarro before I stole it," the man said, the corners of his eyes crinkling as he grinned.

I took a closer look at his eyes—and blinked.

He was blind.

"You know, that's the first thing everybody notices when they meet me," he said, pointing to chairs before his desk. "Please, sit."

"Perri, this is Randl Gage, who works undercover for the ASD and CSD," Prince Bel said as he sat comfortably on one of the offered chairs. "The entire BlackWing fleet is an undercover operation for the ASD, and occasionally operates in conjunction with Jett Riffler's department. The one they're hunting now is a threat to both Alliances. I'm sure I don't need to tell you that you can't repeat this information to anyone else outside the BlackWing fleet. That includes other ASD or CSD operatives."

"Are you saying you don't trust them?" I frowned at the Prince.

"They may have been unwillingly compromised," Randl said.

"Unwillingly?"

"By a Sirenali's talent. Are you familiar with that race?"

"Not really."

"Dad told you that we were hunting Jiles Tamber," Bel explained. "He has been obsessed by a Sirenali's talent, to serve the Prophet."

I drew in a breath, then let it out slowly. I'd read about the Prophet and his dealings on Campiaa. A criminal like that terrified me.

"He can order almost anyone obsessed," Randl said. "Only the most powerful can hope to deflect that power. Don't worry, hunting him is my problem. We're only asking you to sniff out warlocks or witches that he's taken."

"Doesn't he have power, too? That's what I assumed when I read the reports on Campiaa City."

"He does. Terrible power, actually," Randl said. "That's why I'm going after him, rather than anyone else."

I frowned again and a derisive statement almost left my mouth.

Almost.

"Randl is the only one who's ever faced off against the Prophet and survived," Bel said. He'd read my reaction quickly.

"He thought he killed me. You see I survived," Randl held out his hands. "He knows it, too. I'm at the top of his hit list, now, because we beat him back on Campiaa."

"Why isn't that in any of the reports?"

"Because we're undercover, remember?"

"Hmmph."

"I have something for you," Randl slid a small box across his desk. "Wear this at all times, including in the shower. Never take it off."

"What is it?" I couldn't keep the suspicion out of my voice.

"A gift from a Larentii," Zaria appeared at Randl's side, all eight feet of her, blue skinned and blonde-haired. "If you wish to survive on this mission, then wear it. Ultimately, the choice is yours. It will only work for you and nobody else," Zaria added.

I stared at the female Larentii in shock, afraid to blink while thinking that the vision would disappear.

"I'm really here," Zaria said gently. "That medallion is of my own making. Wear it. For me, if nobody else."

With a nod to Randl and Bel Erland, Zaria folded away.

"You know a Larentii?" I stumbled over the words.

"Zaria is the one who brought my Quin back to me," Bel Erland sighed. "The Crown of Karathia owes her much."

"Zaria has helped me greatly in my search for the Prophet," Randl declared. "Wear the medallion as she asked. I have a feeling it will prove a necessity before this is over."

~

Randl

With shaking fingers, Perri draped the fine gold chain over her neck, tucking the medallion beneath the white shirt she wore. Leather pants and boots rounded out her outfit; clear evidence that she admired the Falchani, much like another I knew.

I didn't want to tell her that not only was Ilya Ironsmith known to me, he was one of Zaria's mates. Ilya was Karathian, like Perri, and, like Perri, he admired the Falchani. Unlike Perri, however, Ilya had actually fought beside the Falchani.

I would enjoy introducing her to Travis and Trent. If she wanted to learn bladework, they'd probably volunteer to teach her.

Perhaps they could convince her to come out of the shell she'd built around herself, too. When time permitted, I'd have a private conversation with the King of Karathia about her background and upbringing. For now, that would have to wait.

"I believe dinner is waiting for us," I said, rising from my chair. "Shall we?"

~

Perri

I knew who he was the moment he sat at a nearby table.

Zanfield Staggs. The man who was so rich, he could buy planets. What the hells was he doing here? I thought this was a dangerous undercover operation, which, in the natural order of things, would exclude anybody rich enough to keep their hands clean of it.

Zanfield is a valuable member of this crew. I received mindspeech from Randl Gage. *I expect everyone in the BlackWing fleet to treat their coworkers with civility and respect.*

How did he know what I was thinking—from the beginning?

"Randl knows everything," a smiling Falchani—a real Falchani—sat across from me. Then, another, identical to the first, sat beside him.

The woman who sat next to the second one? I knew immediately that both were hers.

Damn. Always the way.

"Captain Travis Tetsuya," the first identified himself. "Captain Trent Tetsuya," he introduced his brother. "Sabrina Kend," he indicated the woman.

"Related to Ruther Kend?" I asked, sounding ruder than I intended.

"His daughter. She's working with us, designing new weapons and such."

"Why are Falchani working with the ASD?" I suppose I still hadn't worked through my spiteful thoughts.

"A better question would be why are Queen Lissa's twin sons working for the ASD," Sabrina said.

This one could bite back if bitten first. Good to know.

Civility and respect, or this will be the shortest assignment you ever had, Randl informed me.

Yes, sir, I replied unwillingly.

Good. The food is excellent; Gerrett and Susan worked hard on it. Try it —who knows, you may even like some of it.

It is good, I grudgingly admitted.

We'll have a meeting with the Captains after dinner. Please behave in a professional manner.

I was a fourth-level witch. What did he think he might do to me if I ignored his commands?

I waited to find out.

"I like your hair," Zanfield spoke to me.

"Well, Master Staggs, I've never received a compliment from someone who could wipe his eyes and his ass with money and toss it out with the other garbage," I sniped.

"I've never been accosted by one who only knows how to be rude," Zanfield shot back. "My money I can wash. You, on the other hand, no amount of washing will clear up that bad attitude."

"That's enough." Randl was now standing next to Travis across the table. "After I told you in the last fifteen seconds to behave professionally, this comes out of your mouth in response to a compliment?"

I only meant to set his uniform on fire.

Nothing happened.

Nothing.

I reached for the full force of my fourth-level talents, only to find them—gone.

"What did you do to me?" I attempted to shove my chair back and stand. I couldn't move. My chair was stuck to the floor, and I was glued to the chair.

"You're lucky I'm still letting you speak," Randl snapped at me. "I don't give a damn what your childhood did to you. I can show you fifty other people who had a rotten childhood, too. All of them are courteous when spoken to, and most of them are more powerful than you. Now, if you can't be civil to everyone aboard this ship, I can send you back to the King of Karathia and let him deal with your insubordination."

"I'll take her back," Bel Erland materialized behind me.

"No." I hung my head. "Please, I don't know why I said it."

You've done it so long, it's become habit, Randl spoke into my mind. *Nobody here is going to hurt you unless you hurt them first. Understand?*

I nodded while tears threatened.

Nobody had ever looked past the shields I'd built around myself. Randl Gage, the blind man, saw straight through them.

"I'll take her back to my father," the Crown Prince reiterated.

"Do you want to stay?" Randl asked me. I lifted my head to stare into sightless eyes.

"Yes," I admitted, dropping my eyes and clasping my hands together to stop their shaking.

Randl sighed. "We'd like you to join us, Perri, but we want you to be a part of us and not just someone who makes herself an unwelcome outsider."

Is that what I'd done? I shivered.

"Finish your dinner," Randl said. "I've released your power. I'll know if you misuse it, though." He turned and strode back to his own table.

"I'm sorry," I apologized to the table as a whole. "I get uncomfortable in strange surroundings, and it brings out the worst in me."

"No worries," Zanfield waved a hand. "I still like your hair."

"Thank you," I sighed.

"Then I'm no longer needed," the Crown Prince smiled and folded space.

CHAPTER 10

Randl

"Zan?" I knocked on his door.

"Come in," he called out. I walked inside his cabin. In all likelihood, Zanfield had never lived in such a small space in his life. He never complained about this one.

"I came to talk about Perri," I said.

"I know. She's got claws, and not in a good way," he said, waving me toward the single chair next to his bed.

"She doesn't know a damn thing about you, Zan," I said. "She needs to learn to be better than this."

"I saw plenty of the same attitude from rich people, who didn't have a reason for it," Zanfield sighed. "People who'd step on anybody they thought they could, because they could."

"You and I know there's no excuse for that—no matter whether they're rich, poor, pretty, or not so pretty. Mean or evil, on the other hand—once you figure that out about them," I snorted a laugh. The Prophet came to mind in that category.

"I totally agree. Want tea or something stronger?" Zanfield opened a drawer. I found it contained all sorts of bottles, some of it exotic liquor not easily obtained.

"I'll have what you're having," I said.

"Good." He fished two glasses from a shelf over his bed and set about pouring drinks for us.

Once a glass was in my hand, Zanfield held his up. "To wiping my ass with money if I want to," he quipped. I laughed so hard I almost spilled my drink.

~

Travis

Bel asked for a private meeting with Trent and me before he went back to Karathia. We sat in the Captain's cubby, having a drink and talking.

"I know it may not be easy," Bel said, sipping bourbon, "but if you could arrange to train her in bladework, I think it could help her develop discipline in her life."

"She'd have to, or we'd refuse to continue training her," Trent thumped his empty glass on the desk.

"She admires the Falchani, and her hero is Ilya Ironsmith, because he's a Karathian who fought beside the Falchani," Bel explained. "I hope her hero-worship will lead her to accept the discipline needed to achieve proficiency in the art."

"Too bad we can't get Ilya here to walk her through it," Trent shrugged. "Is there a chance she might admire High Demons, too? Vik can fight with blades better than most. He could work with her when we're busy." He pointed between himself and me.

"I don't know, and Vik may not be ah, willing to let that information out right away," Bel guessed. All of us were related to Vik, and that was something none of us were willing to tell.

"Does he stay in contact with Ry?" I asked, meaning his father, the King of Karathia.

"Fairly often. They talk late at night, sometimes. Dad's the oldest, but only by a few days. They grew up together. Went to lessons together." Bel sighed and emptied his glass. "Dad never said anything, but he was pretty upset when he thought Vik was dead."

"A lot happened at the time," I admitted. "Wasn't easy on Mom, either, as you can imagine."

"Quin says she went with Zaria to ah, pull him back from death, but that's all she'll tell me." Bel was mated to Quin, and would know of Quin's involvement in this before we would.

"What about Perri's family?" I asked. "Anything there we should know about?"

"She has a younger brother who was born void," Bel said.

I went still. Trent lifted an eyebrow. A void on Karathia was one born without power of any kind. It was a rare occurrence, and they were often outcast or adopted off-world because of what many parents saw as a disability.

Those who were raised by their families often faced adversity in their daily lives through no fault of their own. "Where is he now?" I asked.

"With her uncle, last we heard. She visits him whenever she can, and always comes away irritable and angry—likely at the way many Karathians treat him—as if he doesn't belong. For now, he's still in school, but he has obvious learning disabilities."

"Perhaps she should try to send him off-world; there are plenty of places that can help him in this," I said.

"The uncle has custody, after the parents disappeared. The uncle is adamant that Pauley stays where he is. And, as Pauley's considered incompetent, I'm sure the uncle will petition the Crown for permanent custody when he comes of age next year."

"What about giving Perri custody?" Trent asked.

"Dad will consider all requests when the petitions cross his desk. Look, I need to go—there's an early audience in the morning."

"No rest for the wicked—or for the crowned head," Trent teased.

"Have you ever tried to sleep in one of those things? It's impossible," Bel chuckled.

~

Zanfield

I'd gone to the dojo to work out, and found Vik there already. He grinned, tossed me a wooden blade and waited while I stretched.

I could fight with a blade, but only one. Slowly, Vik was teaching me how to handle a second one. First though, I had to go through all the forms with the blade in my off-hand, to get used to it.

I had bruises on my arms and ribs from being clumsy at it, too.

Shortly after we finished, while I was checking my wooden practice blade for nicks along the edge, Zaria arrived.

"You need something?" Vik asked. If Zaria asked, he'd be ready to go anywhere or do anything—because she asked. He told me once that Zaria and Quin, the Avii Queen, were the only reasons he was alive.

"I need to speak with Zanfield," Zaria smile at Vik. "You can stay if you want."

"Stay," I told him. I couldn't imagine she'd tell me anything he couldn't hear.

"Zanfield, this is about Perri," Zaria sighed. "I need your help."

"What kind of help?" I wasn't sure what I could do to help her—something had happened to her in the past, and it affected every part of her life. She'd attacked me first because she'd grown up poor, I had no doubt about that. People generally had two kinds of reactions to me—to kiss ass, as David said, or they became angry, because I had things they never would.

Except for the BlackWing crew. I was treated as one of them—no better and no worse. I liked it.

"I need a bribe placed with her uncle," Zaria said, and then proceeded to tell me things—about Perri, her brother, and the uncle—that nobody else had heard.

Until now.

"I can do that," I said. "I'll reach out and make contact when I get back to my cabin."

"Be discreet," Zaria warned.

"Oh, you can count on that," I grinned. This was subterfuge at the highest level. I liked it. And it was for a good cause, which made it even better. "I'll have it done by the end of the week."

"Thank you. If there are any problems, send mindspeech," she turned to go.

"I don't have," I began.

"Now you do," she turned back to give me a brilliant smile. "Have fun. Don't misuse it."

"I—I," I stammered.

In response, Zaria tapped her temple.

Thank you, I sent.

You're welcome, she replied and disappeared.

"Holy shit-show, dude," Vik slapped me hard on the back. I was so stunned, I didn't even yelp.

~

Randl

We pulled into orbit around Horlak the following afternoon. Ex'ero Plumb lived on Horlak, and leased its smallest moon from the Horlakian government to house his scrapyard and recycling business.

Records indicated he was home at the moment, rather than visiting his vast empire of scrapyards spread across the Alliances. We wished to have a few words with him, while we sent spies to the business to scope out his inventory and employees.

With Kooper's help, the meeting was set up as an interview—with a local news personality asking questions while I acted as an assistant.

I'd know everything I needed just by looking at him. I had to disguise Mak and Jak, who refused to let me out of their sight.

To outsiders, they'd appear to have two arms and no weapons. The three of us were scheduled to meet at the news vid station, and ride with the journalist to Plumb's residence.

Dori wanted to go with Travis, Trent, Vik, Perri and Gerrett to Horlak's moon, to search it. I planned to join them the moment I learned what I could from Ex'ero.

Nari and Tiri were set to monitor the scrapyard from the ship; if anything tripped their senses, they'd let me know. David would receive comp-vid images of anything our spies couldn't identify; he was good at sorting components for ships from other items.

Zanfield and Markus were in charge of XIII while Dori and I were off the ship; Zan was more than happy with his temporary promotion.

"You're the emissary from the Governor?" I was led toward Journalist Wilm Bedard's office by a receptionist. To her, I looked perfectly normal—Zaria's disguising efforts were in place.

"Yes," I said. "We only wish to accompany Wilm during his interview."

"So many others have tried and failed to get an interview with Plumb," the receptionist said. "Wilm's status and popularity, and our news station's credibility convinced him."

Mak snorted softly at her remarks but didn't say anything. I pretended I didn't notice the puffed-up importance of it all.

Sal would say somebody had drunk the cool-ade, whatever that meant. "Thank you for your cooperation," I told her. "The Governor and his entire staff appreciate your efforts in this."

"We're happy to help," she cooed.

She's trying to come on to you, Jak sent.

This disguise is damn good, then, I replied. I could tell he was trying not to laugh.

~

Ex'ero's Shipyard and Recycling, Horlak
Travis

"We're looking for spare parts for older ships," I told the employee. He stood behind a desk built of scrap metal melted together, some of it still resembling the metal parts it was made of.

It could have been a work of art, if someone had bothered to put a little thought into it. They hadn't, and it showed.

"Don't have much," the employee rasped, raking a finger down a list on a comp-vid. He either had a cold or spent most of his days yelling at employees. My bet was on the latter.

Are those supposed to be coveralls? Dori sent. She'd noticed what he was wearing, just as I did. On a small patch over his left breast was the name Jincus. The remaining fabric had been covered in grease and lubricants too many times to reveal its original color, and now appeared as a mix of blacks, blues and grays.

Studded boots clomped across a concrete floor as he walked toward a rear shelf to lift another comp-vid.

Two sets of records? Trent asked.

Possible, I returned. *We need Miz or somebody to get into their records, I think.*

"I can show you what I have," Jincus said, returning to the misshapen desk with the second comp-vid in his hand. "This way."

We followed him through a wide door to the left, then down a long corridor toward a trans-vator. *Ex'ero needs to update,* Dori said, glancing at the poor condition of the trans-vator's interior as we loaded into it with Jincus.

Did they repair ancient hover-cars in here? Vik asked. I wondered the same—it smelled of oil and other vehicle fluids, made worse when the door closed on us, trapping scents inside. Jincus tapped a button that was so darkened by use and dirty fingers that I couldn't read the designation on it.

When we left the trans-vator after our arrival on a lower level, Dori sniffed the air. *Rats here,* she informed us. *Maybe a few other things, too.*

I'm not surprised, Vik said. *Is anybody surprised?*

Either the junk business isn't as lucrative as Ex'ero makes it out to be, or he's funneling money elsewhere, Trent observed.

He was probably laundering funds for Jewl, and that source of income has dried up, I pointed out.

That's recent, Vik said. *This has taken a while.* He meant the condition of the warehouse we walked through. *I'm amazed the air containment systems and circulators are still in operation.*

"We have to get out of here," Perri shouted aloud, as my skin began to itch furiously. Vik reacted faster than I could; he skipped us away as half the moon exploded, destroying everything on that half, including Ex'ero's massive warehouse.

~

"Well, Jincus, I don't suppose you know anything about that explosion, do you?" Kooper wove a path around Jincus' chair aboard BlackWing X, while the man sat there, sweating. He wasn't supposed to survive the explosion; I'd bet Zanfield's entire bank account on it.

He understood that, too.

It's my fault. Perri, who stood in a corner as far away from Kooper as she could get, sent mindspeech to me. *A warlock put up a perimeter alarm. I think it was set to trigger the explosion if another warlock, wizard or witch crossed it. I felt it when I walked through it, but it was already too late to stop it.*

"Director," I said aloud. Kooper stopped mid-pace and looked in my direction. "It was a perimeter alarm set up by a warlock," I said. "Perri accidentally set it off by walking through it. It was created to go off if another power-wielder passed through."

"A perimeter alarm? Why were they worried about a power-wielder coming in?"

"Th-theft," Jincus stuttered. "All of our warehouses have b-been ransacked in the last few eight-days. The boss had some warlock in to scry two days ago. Paid a lot of money, too. I g-guess some of that money went toward the spell."

"What was stolen?" Kooper demanded. Jincus shifted uncomfortably on his chair. "Same as what he was asking for," he nodded in my direction. "Old ship parts. In the past eight-day, several hulls and old clunker ships were taken. The warlock said it was the same thief stealing from us, and that he was a warlock, too."

"Do you know this warlock's name? The one who set the perimeter spell?"

"No." Jincus dropped his head. "The boss does."

"What did we miss?" Randl folded in with Mak and Jak. I could see he was already aware of the explosion—half of the moon had blown up along with the warehouse and everybody on Horlak knew it by now.

"We need the name of the warlock Ex'ero hired to set a perimeter spell," Kooper growled.

"I have that already," Randl said. "The minute he found out the warehouse blew up, Ex'ero cursed his name. Apparently, the spell he paid for was to trap the thief, not destroy the entire place."

Jincus sagged in his chair at Randl's news.

$$\sim$$

Randl

"Stone Wicke?" Bel Erland reacted to the name in shock. "We thought he was dead."

"Apparently not," Kooper said dryly. "Perri already said it wasn't anyone she'd ever scented before."

"He's been out of sight for nearly five centuries," Bel grumped. "Dad is having a cow, as Gran would say."

"We'll be having a talk with Ex'ero—an official one, this time, to find out how he came across warlock Wicke," Kooper said. "He may have to scramble to get rid of the spells Wicke placed on his other warehouses. I imagine it cost him in the millions to get the work done, only to have it blow up in his face."

"Literally," Trent nodded. "What do you want us to do with Jincus? I still want to ask him if Ex'ero keeps two sets of records."

"Then keep him on board—in a holding cell if you want," Kooper said. "Maybe he'll give you more information on what was stolen, since Ex'ero didn't report it. Perhaps he'll give evidence against Ex'ero, too. If not, send him to the lockup on Le-Ath Veronis for a few days. If there's nothing to charge him with, he'll be sent home. For now, I consider him a suspect, until we know otherwise."

"We'll keep him here," I said. "Other than doing what Ex'ero told him to do, I doubt he's a criminal."

"Then have Gerrett help him forget where he is and who he's with, if he's dropped off on Horlak," Kooper ordered. "We're taking Ex'ero into custody, to question him about his involvement with Jewl Yarro.

Let me know the final decision on Jincus, in case we have to pull him in again."

"We'll do that," Trent agreed.

~

"You're letting me walk around the ship?" Jincus sounded surprised.

"If that's what you want. I warn you not to be rude to the crew—they're going to be feeding you and protecting you while you're onboard."

"Hmmph," Jincus shook his head. "I was scared to death Director Kooper would haul me off to an ASD lockup and forget about me."

"I doubt you've done anything to warrant that," I said.

"Where is Ex'ero?"

"He's been detained for questioning about the warlock he hired—and a few other things. Seems the Karathian Crown has been looking for the warlock for a while, and they want information."

"Trust Ex'ero to find somebody like that," Jincus snorted.

"Is there something we should know?" I asked.

"Ex'ero may be the worst judge of character I've ever seen," Jincus shrugged. "I tell him not to hire this one or that, he hires them anyway, and they end up taking things and disappearing. It hasn't been just thieves breaking in, you know. In the past year, parts and pieces of older ships have become a much-desired commodity."

"Do you know why?"

"No idea, unless it has something to do with that battle in Campiaan space. I hear a lot of criminals lost their ships that day. You know both Alliances keep a close watch on anybody who orders ships, now."

Closing my eyes, I drew a deep breath. Now it was beginning to make sense. The Big Three had their fingers in a lot of pies as Sal would say, and a multitude of other criminals under their thumbs. They couldn't place orders for a whole new fleet—Kooper and Jett would be notified.

The ships destroyed in the Campiaan battle had been taken away from who knew how many criminal operations, to give the Prophet what he wanted.

"Jincus, you just became a temporary member of my crew," I said. "How do you feel about being a pirate? Also, will you mind wearing something other than what you've got on?"

"I've never worked on a ship," he said, although he sounded intrigued. "I don't know what I'd do for you."

"I'm putting you with my ship's engineer," I said. "I'm assuming you know the parts and pieces taken from the scrapyard."

"I do. I've gotten used to listing them as missing," he admitted.

"Good. David may be able to show you a thing or two about how the ship works, if you like to get your hands dirty."

"You can't tell?" He held up both hands and grinned. His hands were stained from years of handling old parts and pieces of vehicles and appliances.

"Good enough. David will be along to take you to his department," I said.

"You rang?" David walked into my office.

"I'm assigning Jincus to your department temporarily," I said. "He knows the parts and pieces of older ships that have come up missing lately. It's now your job to tell me whether full ships could have been assembled from all that, and how many of them we need to be concerned with."

"Can you still get into the records of Ex'ero's businesses?" David asked Jincus.

"Sure," Jincus shrugged. He didn't even blink at David's stature, which made my opinion of him rise considerably.

"Good," David said. "Come with me; we have a lot of work to do."

"Get him decent clothes," I said as they walked out of my office.

"On it," David called back. At the last, Jincus turned toward me and flashed a grin. I think he liked his new job already.

⌇

"Somebody already had this idea, before the Prophet got on board with it, too?" Travis asked. I'd gone to X to have this conversation with him and his twin.

"It looks that way. This means we may be chasing after common criminals rather than the Prophet, when we start looking for this stuff."

"Just when you think things can't get any worse. It's a cinch Stone Wicke works for one of the criminal concerns, and is doing his best to keep others away from what he deems their property."

"Maybe he knows they also have warlocks or wizards in their employ, and his boss or bosses don't want the competition. Ex'ero may have been caught in the middle of a feud," Trent offered.

"Somebody wants to take over where the Big Three left off," Travis said. "This means a power struggle, just as we're attempting to chase down the Prophet."

"This isn't fucked up or anything," I said.

"Want a beer or something stronger?" Travis offered.

"Let's have a beer. Damn. We don't need more complicated. We need less complicated."

~

Dori

"You're different." Perri twisted her mouth as she considered me from across the table. I'd sat down to have a cup of tea in the galley; Perri walked in shortly afterward and plopped onto the chair opposite mine.

"Shapeshifter," I said. May as well get it out in the open and see how she reacted.

"What kind?"

"Ocelot."

"A big cat?"

"Essentially."

"Nice. Any other shapeshifters on board?"

"Yes. Phillip, my pilot. David, too. X has several on board."

"Have I met them?"

"Susan. Travis and Trent."

"What are they?"

"That's their secret—you should ask them." I didn't say it, but telling her to ask politely when she knew them better was certainly on my mind.

"Sorry—I've never really met shapeshifters before—I have no idea what the protocol is."

"Then say that. I'm sure they'll accommodate you as well as they can. There's something else you should know about us, too."

"What's that?"

"Never touch a shapeshifter in their other form without their permission. It's impolite."

"Why would I—isn't that the same as touching them otherwise? That would be rude."

"You may fit in here after all," I said. "Welcome to BlackWing XIII."

~

Zanfield

"We're about to go in, sir."

"Make sure you impress upon him that I only wish to study the young man and nothing else. That I'm very curious how someone with power on both sides of his family can be born without it. Ensure that he understands that he's giving me all custody rights to his ward, who will come to live with me. Record every bit of the conversation, from multiple angles, if you can."

"Of course, sir."

"Are we about to see whether he can be bought?" Vik asked.

"You'd be amazed at how many there are who will jump at the smallest offer," I said.

"You sound disgusted," Vik observed.

"Because I am. Have a seat; you can watch this with me if you want." Vik took a chair in my cabin while I turned the standing comp-vid to a better angle.

"Looks like recent work on the house," Vik said as my agents walked to the front door of Alken Wilker's home.

"I'll make note of that," I said as Alken answered the door himself.

"You the ones from Staggs?" Alken asked.

"We're his agents, yes."

"Good, come in," he invited. "The boy's in the kitchen."

Vik exchanged a quick glance with me. Were there going to be no questions? No requests for reassurances that the boy would be in safe hands? Drawing a breath, I turned back to the screen.

The house was cluttered as my agents walked through it, following Wilker's lead. The boy sat at a kitchen counter, slumped on his stool with a small, packed bag lying beside it.

"Fucking hell," Vik whispered as Alken spoke.

"These two are taking you to your new home," he said gruffly to the boy.

"Perri," the boy whined.

"She isn't here. She has work and nobody has time for you. Now go with these two. They have a new place for you to stay."

"I could be running a sex slave operation and he wouldn't care," I growled.

"The ah," Alken held out a hand while the boy dejectedly slid off the stool. Teren, my lead agent in this, handed the credit chip carrier to Alken.

"We need the signed agreement," Teren said as Alken took the carrier and stuffed it in his pocket.

"It's right here," he lifted a comp-vid. The document we'd sent him was pulled up on it—Teren came close enough to see. Alken signed with a stylus and sent the document while we watched.

"Good," Teren said. "The boy will be well-cared for."

"Doesn't matter to me," Alken patted his pocket. "Tell your boss it's a pleasure doing business with him."

"Pauley, come with me," Teren held out a hand to the boy. "We're taking you home."

"Perri," Pauley mumbled a second time.

"I'm sure we can help you with that," Teren said, leading him toward the front door. Franc, my second agent, lifted the boy's bag and carried it with him.

Vik and I watched until everything was loaded into the hovercar and it drove away. "Damnation," Vik rumbled. "If we hadn't promised Zaria to wait to report this to Ry, he'd have the information already."

"I'm sure she wants the boy off Karathia first," I said. "She sent Ilya Ironsmith to transport them away from the planet. They're going to Campiaa from there, where Zaria and Quin are waiting."

"They're going to help the boy?"

"I think they're waiting to see if there's anything they can do. Then, we wait a little longer, to hear how Alken breaks the news to Perri. I'll be interested to learn what sort of lie he tells her."

"How much is that credit chip worth?"

"A million. I was prepared to go higher. He jumped at the first offer."

"Fucking hell."

≈

Founder's Palace, Campiaa

Quin

Justis and Dena insisted on coming with us to Campiaa. Zaria transported us, and Wyatt and Jayna waited to greet us.

Ilya Ironsmith folded Zanfield's agents and the young man to us shortly after our arrival.

"Pauley," Zaria approached him—he looked terrified to be where he was. "There's no need to fear, you're safe, now," she soothed.

He may have shrunk away from anyone else. Zaria's hands, when she touched him, let him know (as only the Larentii can) that he really was safe.

Quin, he has a mind-dampening spell, Zaria sent. *Let me remove it, then you can help him deal with the injustices of his life.*

I'll be happy to.

Bel Erland would get an earful, too, once I was done. Neither he nor his father, King Rylend, had thought to check on the boy, believing the uncle when a status report was required.

Now, only the blackmail between the uncle and Perri remained to be dealt with.

Wyatt, standing nearby, helped catch the boy when he almost fell after Zaria removed the spell.

"Perri?" The boy was now weeping. For years, his thoughts, speech, everything, had been stunted by a conniving uncle.

"We'll bring her to you soon; she's safe," Zaria smiled at Pauley. "This is Quin, my daughter," she introduced me. "She's going to help you, too."

"Feathers," Pauley blinked as if he'd just noticed me and my wings.

"I'm Avii," I told him gently. "We all have wings. I'm going to touch your face, now. Is that all right?"

He dipped his head in a trembling nod. Placing my hands on either side of his face, I closed my eyes and searched for the hurts to heal.

CHAPTER 11

*B*lack Wing XIII
    Randl

"I originally intended to handle this one way, but I think it will be better if we do this, instead."

Zaria sat on one of my guest chairs, explaining what she, Zanfield and Quin had done for Perri's brother, Pauley.

"He's safe at Avii Castle, with Quin watching over him. Gurnil is secretly pleased he has a student to teach, so Pauley now has a suite adjoining the Library."

"How bad was the mind-dampening spell?" I asked.

"He has no real education past the first year," Zaria shook her head. "He was sent to special classes, but essentially learned nothing. He's safe now, and relieved of that infernal spell. I wish it were this simple to deal with Perri's trauma," she added.

"I know. I also know of other people who've dealt with similar circumstances."

"I wish she'd told the King what was going on, but she had no idea about the mind-dampening. She imagined that Pauley wasn't a power-void only—that he had other problems, too."

"What will be done with her uncle?"

155

"I just came from Rylend's palace. He has all the records Zanfield supplied, including the vid recordings and the record that Alken has already emptied the account created for him and transferred the money. I figure it won't be long before Ry's troops knock on Alken's door."

"How did he hide that spell from a power-scent tracker like Perri?" I asked.

"We're still working on that. It could be that he'd laid so many spells throughout the house that she couldn't differentiate one from another. There's a chance, too, that a counter-talent may also run in the family, so to speak. I promised Ry I'd come have a look at Alken when he's taken into custody."

"Is Pauley normal, other than having no power?"

"We think so, but his growth and maturity level have been drastically compromised. I hope Gurnil and Quin can bring him along carefully, until he's where he should be."

Bel Erland appeared in my office at that moment, interrupting my conversation with Zaria.

"Alken has disappeared," he said, sounding winded. "As if he knew we were coming after him. The money has disappeared, too, and we can't find him anywhere; we've already attempted scrying."

Zaria sat, silent in her chair, her eyes unfocused.

"I believe he's either joined a criminal faction with a Sirenali, or has gone to the Prophet," she said, blinking after a moment. "I can't find him, either."

"What does this mean?" Bel Erland demanded.

"I can't say for sure," Zaria shrugged. "I do believe that Perri will know his power-scent anywhere," she went on. "It may make our job easier, if we come anywhere close to Alken Wilker from now on."

Vik, will you and Zanfield bring Perri to my office, please? I sent. *I have news concerning her uncle and brother.*

On our way.

~

We never discussed where the money came from to pay Alken, and Perri didn't ask. Zanfield visibly relaxed when the topic was glossed over. Instead, we talked about Pauley, how he was now safe on Le-Ath Veronis and in the care of the Avii Queen. Perri had permission to visit whenever she wanted, while her brother worked through years of no learning and stunted emotional growth.

"Don't beat yourself up that you didn't know—you were too young to understand it when it first happened," Zaria said.

"But how did you know to help him?"

"Just a suspicion, which turned into a reality," Zaria replied. "The Karathian Crown now has Alken Wilker on a list, as do your colleagues, here. We worry that he may have joined a criminal faction, and, as he is a fourth-level warlock, his talents will be viewed as most desirable to any new boss."

"They'll have his crimes to hold over his head, too, if he gets any ideas," I said. "He may have hemmed himself in with his choices."

Perri dropped her eyes and nodded. She never said anything about what her uncle had done to her over the years. A part of her was grateful he was gone. Another part was overjoyed that Pauley was being cared for.

Overall, Perri was still overwhelmed by years of molestation by her uncle, and, after she was employed by the Crown, the theft of a good portion of her wages, too. This was more than a delicate situation, as she had to be the one to ask for help. She'd rebel if anyone forced it on her, or suggested it, even.

Perri hid behind a hard shell. Inside that shell was a frightened girl who'd been harmed too many times by her own flesh and blood.

"Can I see Pauley soon?" Perri raised her head.

"You can see him now. I'll take you." Zaria stood and smiled at her.

"Sir?" She turned to me, asking permission.

"Go. Stay and have dinner with him if you want," I waved a hand.

"I'll go with them, if that's all right," Vik said.

"Good enough. You can bring her back when she's ready." I watched as they disappeared. Zanfield sagged against the wall.

"Don't worry, Zan," I said. "Your secret's safe with me."

"But what will she say when she learns I'm Pauley's legal guardian, now? Her uncle signed those rights over to me."

"If she doesn't ask, who's going to tell her?" I grinned.

"I sent a message to the Avii Queen, with access to an account I set up for Pauley," he said. "I told her to buy clothing, supplies, whatever he needs and a few things he wants."

"Zan, you're one of the best people I know," I said.

"Having money doesn't hurt, either," he finally grinned at me.

"Well—who cares about that?" I teased. Zanfield laughed.

Avii Castle

Quin

The moment Perri arrived with Zaria and Vik, Pauley was up from his seat at a library table and running toward his sister.

I may have brushed a few tears away as they wept and laughed in each other's arms. At least Pauley's mind was clear, now. Before, his mind was held in check so strongly that the only thing he knew for sure was that his sister cared for him.

Here he was, now, a seventeen-year-old with the learning level of a seven-year-old. Gurnil and I intended to rectify that. He had the capacity—now that Zaria had removed the spell that held him back, and I'd healed the damage it had done to his brain.

"I have a room," Pauley was more than proud of that fact. "Come see." He grabbed her hand and pulled her toward it.

Once, that same room had been mine in Gurnil's Library.

"Zanfield set up an account for him," I whispered to Zaria as brother and sister disappeared behind a door. "He'll be taken care of for a very long while. Eventually, I think he'll be the same as anyone else his age."

"He'll be his own person," Zaria agreed. "His uncle, on the other hand," she snorted.

"I feel the same way. You know Perri was molested by him, and then he stole her earnings."

"I know. We can help, but she has to want our help."

"I understand that, too." I moved closer so I could put my arm around Zaria's waist to give her a hug. Like me, she couldn't stand to know that an innocent suffered. I knew, too, that if Perri came to either of us, help would be more than willingly given.

Sometimes we have to wait for the hurt ones to come to us, Zaria sent.

And that makes it harder for us—to practice that kind of patience, I replied.

I love you, my daughter, Zaria put an arm around me to hug tighter.

Thank you. I love you, too.

Karathia

Bel Erland

"This would be easier if Zaria were here," Dad sighed as we surveyed the clutter of Alken Wilker's home. We'd come the following day with several guards, to see whether there was any evidence that would indicate where Alken had gone.

We already knew that Randl suspected he'd fallen in with criminals. It was a good supposition—where better to hide a criminal that among others who were as bad or worse?

If they hid behind Sirenali, his hiding would be even more effective. Like Dad, I worried that the Prophet would lure him in. If that were the case, how had they contacted one another?

Nobody heard from the Prophet. Generally, he took whatever or whomever he wanted.

"I figure Stone Wicke has been working with someone else for a long while—if he were with the Prophet, I believe we'd have gotten wind of his presence before now," Dad surmised.

He was thinking the same as I—which ones on the wanted list could be taken by the Prophet, and which ones had gone elsewhere. Karathia's most-wanted list was no secret to anybody—the Prophet could find it easily enough as it was public information.

Wilker, though—he hadn't been placed on that list until after he disappeared. That raised a question, the answer to which could be more than frightening.

"Do you think he'll attempt to contact Perri, now?" Dad asked.

"Not if he's with the Prophet."

"Good point."

"I'll take the latest images we have to Quin. Maybe she can tell me something about him we don't know—after she's finished telling me off for not guessing Alken was guilty of crimes against his niece and nephew."

"We still don't know where their parents are," Dad said. "We've never been able to track them."

My head jerked up, then. "Do you suppose?" I stared at Dad.

"My alarm bells just went off, too. Take the comp-vid recordings we have from Zanfield's crew and get them to Quin right away."

❧

Avii Castle
Quin

"That's what I see in him—that he was going to join his brother—at an arranged meeting place. He already had it planned when Zanfield's people arrived to take Pauley."

"Where was the meeting to be?" Bel Erland asked. "Can you see that?"

"A bar on Brakkus," Zaria arrived and spoke. "I just came from there," she added. "It was a meeting place only—wherever Alken's brother took him, the location was kept from Alken. I believe that they're with a criminal faction somewhere that has nothing to do with the Prophet, though. At least for now. I doubt the Prophet has much in the way of warlocks or witches at the moment, but I think he's beginning to see their usefulness."

"Gillen Wilker is a stronger Fourth-level than Alken," Bel Erland mused. "His wife, Qatti, is Third-level. They probably abandoned their children to Alken, so they could make serious money somewhere. The deal may have been to bring Alken in later, after the children were grown and living on their own."

"But it's likely that Gillen never counted on Alken molesting the children—and then blackmailing Perri with Pauley's continued well-being unless she paid him and kept her mouth shut," I said, feeling angry again. Every time I saw Pauley struggling to read even the simplest words, it made me furious.

"It boils down to their being among the worst parents I've met," Bel Erland grumbled. "With Alken being among the worst uncles I've ever met."

"Their status as relatives no longer concerns me," Zaria said. "Their status as criminals, on the other hand, does."

"Do you want me to visit Randl, to let him know our latest suppositions?" Bel Erland asked Zaria.

"Yes. Tell him to send mindspeech if he wants—this needs to be sorted out before the Prophet decides to add to his stable of warlocks and witches."

"I want to know who hired Stone Wicke," Bel said. "Dad and I both do. Whoever it is, they really want to destroy the competition for parts and hulls of older ships. Dad and Uncle Teeg are working with Kooper and Jett to determine whether there are spells laid at other scrapyards."

"Ilya and I have already removed the spells at Ex'ero's other businesses," Zaria told him. "Those would have been nasty if they'd detonated. Warlock Wicke has some explaining to do when we catch up with him."

"Is that what you came to tell me?" I asked.

"And tell Bel Erland and his father," Zaria smiled. "Whoever laid those spells won't even realize they're gone."

"What about Ex'ero?"

"A few crimes uncovered so far," Zaria said. "Kooper and Jett are still trying to get information on his involvement with Jewl. Both may be laying charges, since Ex'ero operates in both Alliances. They may be convinced to look the other way on some of those infractions, if he allows the ASD and CSD to put in their own surveillance in his businesses, which will be most discreet."

"To catch the ones coming in to look for parts and such," Bel Erland nodded his approval.

"Yes. And they may find it more difficult than usual for a power-wielder to cause those cameras to go offline temporarily, as they usually do."

"Nice. Can you teach me that trick?"

"Sorry—it's Larentii need-to-know only."

"Damn."

"Ask your grandfather Erland—he may be able to come up with something similar," Zaria laughed.

"Oh, good. I'll ask Grampa, then."

"I think that whatever faction the Wilkers work for, they knew of and understood Quin's ability to see things about them," Zaria said. "That's why information was held back from Alken, and we don't have good images of Gillen and Qatti to work with."

"Pauley barely recalls his parents," I said. "Perri hates them for abandoning her and her brother. Her memories are faded, too."

"Bel, when you see Randl, will you do something for me?" Zaria turned to him.

"Of course."

"Ask him to take Nari, Tiri and Perri to Pyrik, where the Prophet's stronghold was. They may be able to read things from the site that will be helpful in tracking him and his minions."

"I'll let him know."

"Are you leaving?" I asked him.

"Yes. May I have a kiss?"

"Yes."

～

BlackWing XIII
Randl

"That's actually a good idea." Bel Erland relayed Zaria's message to me, in addition to what the consensus was on Alken Wilker. "We've heard from Kooper—Ex'ero has given permission for the ASD and CSD to place cameras in his businesses, and they're working on some of the other scrapyards, too. A few BlackWing ships have been dispatched in those directions to investigate thefts and items unaccounted for."

"I think I'd like to come with you when you take those three to Pyrik," Bel said.

"I'll probably have other volunteers, too. Mak and Jak won't let me go without them."

"Take Vik with you."

Like me, he wanted a High Demon presence, to nullify any malicious power left behind to trip someone up. "I was planning to," I said.

Bel Erland, like his father, King Rylend, didn't like the shaky ground we all stood upon where the Prophet was concerned. After Campiaa, every ruler in both Alliances walked carefully. One misstep and too many to count could die or be taken by an unseen hand.

"What do you suppose he wants?" Bel asked. "Besides taking over both Alliances?"

"There's something to want other than that?" I was puzzled by the question.

"It's just—what's left after that? You control everything —then what?"

"No idea. What if there isn't anything after that?"

"Just a thought," Bel waved a hand, dismissing the idea. A worry began in my mind at that moment, however.

What if we were wrong?

What if the Prophet ultimately wanted total control—*and something else?* I really needed more information on him to make a determination.

I knew where he was from. That he'd spelled a coin that once belonged to my mother. How did those pieces fit together?

"I'll arrange to take those who want to go to Pyrik tomorrow at nine bells. Are you available then?" I asked Bel.

"I'll be here," he agreed.

When he folded away, I rose from my desk and walked out of my office. I wanted to ask Perri questions, and worked on how to tactfully do that while I strode to the trans-vator.

~

Vik and Zanfield ended up coming to the galley with Perri. Dori arrived a few seconds later.

"Tomorrow," I said, "We're going to Pyrik to visit the Prophet's former stronghold—what's left of it, anyway. We'll see if there's anything you can scent about the place. Nari and Tiri will use their talents, too, for the same reason."

"I've never been to Pyrik," Perri said.

"Not much to see, really," Dori said. "They have a few nice vacation spots."

"The place we're going has radiation poisoning readily available," Vik said. "Keep shields up when we go."

"I've developed a shielding technique that won't affect my scenting ability," Perri confirmed.

"Mostly what I want to know from you is whether the Prophet had any warlocks, witches or other power wielders with him while he was there," I said. "Nari and Tiri will be looking for artifacts to help with their work."

"Does this place have a name?"

"Lee'Qee," I shrugged. "I have another question for you. If it makes you uncomfortable, tell me."

"What is it?" Perri stiffened slightly—she was afraid I'd ask her about her uncle.

"What do you recall of your parents? Did anyone ever say where they went?"

"I don't think anybody knew," she said, grateful that it wasn't as personal a question as she'd feared. "All I knew about it was our—uncle, coming to get us one morning because our parents left during the night. As far as I know, they left no note or anything else for us, including money to take care of us."

She didn't add that her uncle berated her often, saying that she and Pauley were a burden to him and she should shut up and put up —*with him.*

Filth, Vik spat in mindspeech.

You mean her uncle?

And her parents. Who knows which are worse? Surely they knew about his proclivities.

Without seeing them, I can't say for certain.

I'm not giving them the benefit of the doubt. They abandoned their kids and didn't care enough to check on them.

You know—I think you're right.

Damn straight. I know what I'm talking about. Those people had a choice. I didn't.

I know.

Vik was referring to his own past, when he'd been helpless and controlled by others. He'd done things as a result, and turned his own family against him because of that. Zaria and Quin had given him a new life, with a new name, but there were ghosts in his past that still haunted his memories.

Quin, Zaria and I—we could see that history in him, and he was aware that we knew. He understood that we didn't hold those things against him, either. If he hadn't been worth saving, Zaria would have left him dead in the past. Vik was still coming to grips with that—that he was found to be worthy.

He would never have abandoned his children if he'd been himself all those years ago. Gillen and Qatti Wilker had chosen to abandon their own, and another family member had abused them afterward. A curl of smoke escaped Vik's nostrils. His demon was angry.

Perri failed to notice; she hunched in her chair, making herself smaller as memories of her family washed through her mind. None of those memories were good. No wonder she lashed out at times—the pain had to be overwhelming upon occasion.

"I don't remember much about them," Perri considered my first question, now. "I remember my father yelling at Pauley, because he couldn't do some things for himself. He was so little. My mother hated farming. That's what they did—they grew vegetables to sell to the markets on Karathia. It wasn't a high-paying occupation, and they leased the land from someone else. I remember them saying the rent was too high."

"This may be difficult for you to hear, but they may have found employment with a criminal faction," I said. "We believe that your uncle has now joined them—we have some evidence that Alken met with your father at a bar on Brakkus. Nobody knows where they went from there, and that's troubling."

"They don't care about us—Pauley or me. You can't use us as bait," Perri sounded resentful.

"Perri, that would never occur to any of us. I feel bad enough, asking you to dredge up memories so we can try to track them in a normal fashion. We don't hold children hostage. It's illegal and repugnant in the extreme."

"Quin would consider murdering anyone who threatened Pauley," Vik said gently. "As would Queen Lissa of Le-Ath Veronis."

Perri lifted her eyes to Vik, who sounded sure of himself. He should; Queen Lissa was his mother and nobody mistreated children around her.

"Can you say for sure that he's safe where he is? That they can't just show up and take him away if they want?"

Here was something that troubled her. Alken had sold Pauley once. What would keep him from trying the same thing again?

"I would hate to be anyone who thought to take Pauley away," Zanfield spoke for the first time. "Zaria is formidable. I wouldn't dream of making her angry, and someone taking Pauley would definitely do that."

"How do you know that?" Perri demanded. Tears threatened; the roughness of them were in her voice.

"Because she gave him one of these," he pulled his medallion from beneath his uniform. "I doubt anyone will touch Pauley from now on without permission." We watched as Zanfield placed the medallion under his shirt and patted it into position.

"I thought these were secret identification tags," Perri grumbled, pulling her own out and staring at it.

"The one Sabrina wears protected her from a kidnapper," I said. "Blew him against a wall and knocked him unconscious when he tried to touch her."

"You're joking."

"No. Ask her yourself."

"You mean these are like Grey House protection jewels?" Perri's eyes widened as she studied the gold medallion.

"I think it's much more than that, but Zaria won't say exactly what, other than don't take it off," Zanfield said. "So, don't take it off —all right?"

"I won't." She placed the medallion under her shirt, much like Zanfield did. I could see her relax somewhat as she did so. She'd been terrified for Pauley, that much was certain.

Somehow, too, Zanfield had been having conversations with Zaria. That intrigued me. It was obvious that she held a high opinion of him, just as I did. There was something else, too, about him.

Zan, are your agents protected well enough? I asked in mindspeech. *The two you sent to Karathia? I'm worried Alken may try to destroy the witnesses to his indiscretions.*

Zaria said they would be protected. She gave them a medallion, too. I think we can send them out again, if we need to. They're trained bodyguards, you know.

Zaria gave you mindspeech. That's outstanding, I sent.

I'm grateful. With all the money I have, this is something that I couldn't buy. It came as a gift, instead.

I'm grateful, too. We'll keep your agents in mind if we need boots on the ground.

They liked rescuing Pauley. Frankly, they're bored most of the time, so this was a nice adventure for them. They liked Pauley, too. They don't get to spend time with young ones very often.

You think they'd consent to live at Avii Castle between assignments?

I think they'd be impressed—and happy.

Good. I'll ask Quin and let you know. If she says yes, be prepared to help me transport them to their new home.

Ready anytime, Commander.

Go ahead and tell them to pack their gear, I sent after several seconds passed. *Quin says yes.*

∼

A'pelur

Gillen Wilker

"You sold Pauley?" Qatti hissed at Alken.

We wondered where his money came from. Now we knew.

"That fool, Zanfield Staggs, paid me a million for him. You know Perri works for the Karathian Crown. She'll find him soon enough, I think. Could become an incident, but she'll get him back."

"He paid a million? For Pauley?" Qatti's interest had turned to the money and not the child.

"Without blinking. I didn't see him personally; his agents brought the money to me and took the boy with them. They said Staggs wanted to study the boy—why he was born without power."

"The names of those agents?" I asked casually. Anybody who had access to Staggs' money interested me a great deal.

"In this comp-vid," Alken handed it to me. "Only first names and a bank account set up for a single purpose, in case you have your sights set on his other money. I already checked."

"We get our hands on even a fraction of that money, and we can stop working for anybody else," I snapped. "Why didn't you tell us this when I picked you up on Brakkus?"

"Because the Karathian Crown was about to pull him in for questioning, right?" Qatti always arrived at the answer before anybody asked it.

"I don't know that—they didn't contact me," Alken replied stiffly.

"I'll bet your house has been turned upside down and too many spells to count have been set on it, looking for you," Qatti said.

"That's beside the point," I growled. "They won't find him here—

we're hidden well enough behind the boss's spells. I don't know where he got them or who he paid; we know Stone didn't lay them, but they work. Nobody can find us, guaranteed." Stone, the boss' favorite warlock, was talented, but not *that* talented.

"Spells? Laid on what?" Alken asked. A spell had to be laid on something.

"They're in the walls," Qatti whispered. "Every wall in the place, according to the boss. It's like we're invisible, here."

"You still haven't told me where we are," Alken whined.

"We won't tell you—not now," I interjected smoothly. "Eventually, you'll know—that, and the boss's name, too. For now, keep your head down and do as you're told. In between, you can eat, drink and do whatever you want here at the compound. Just stay out of arguments or fights—the boss will get rid of all of us if you do that."

"We can't afford to be sent away," Qatti added. "We're protected here, and we're paid. I don't want to give up either of those things, unless the price is right."

"Let's see who Staggs' agents are," I tapped Alken's comp-vid. "We'll work on making the price right."

~

Avii Castle
   Randl

"I hope you don't mind sharing the suite—it has separate bedroom and living quarters on either side of the balcony," Quin led us through the door. Teren and Franc, Zanfield's agents, walked with the rest of us, amazed by thick, glass walls of multiple hues.

"The whole thing is made of glass?" Teren asked.

"The base structure, yes," Quin turned to smile at him. "There are other materials laid over it in places—wood and such, like for the doors and furniture. The glass is said to be impenetrable. You're on the third level, so not a lot of stairs to climb to and from the dining hall. Feel free to eat with the guard, if you want," Quin went on. "If you'd like, you can work out with them. They have hand fighting and blade practice four days out of every eight-day."

"What do they do on the other days?" Teren asked.

"Flying drills—formation, midair battle training, practicing pulling not-so-smart tourists from the water—that sort of thing. They all have two days off per eight-day, too."

"I wouldn't mind working out with the troops—when they're on the ground," Franc said.

"I'll let Ardis know—he's in charge of the troops," Quin replied. "He may visit you in the next day or so. Between now and then, make yourselves at home. If you'd like a tour of the castle, I'll send someone to guide you through it."

"What about Pauley? I wouldn't mind seeing the boy again," Teren said.

"He's near the top, in the main Library. Gurnil, our Chief Librarian, is teaching him, now that Alken's foul spell is gone."

"That's what Randl told us," Teren nodded at me. "That Pauley's uncle did that to him."

"Is it possible to go ashore and visit the cities?" Franc asked.

"I'll make someone available to take you; you only have to ask," Quin said. "Go to Niff's, first thing. The ice cream and sweets are heavenly."

CHAPTER 12

BlackWing XIII
Randl

"Jincus, what can I do for you?" I asked. He'd come to the table where I was having breakfast with Dori, as if he were warily approaching a superior who could fire him at any moment.

"I'd like to ah, train with the others," he began. His hands were much cleaner, now, and his black and silver uniform was also clean and neat. He liked it, I could tell, and held himself straight and proud while dressed in it.

"You mean hand fighting and such?"

"Yes. And with your permission, with firing pistols and handling blades. I watched those Falchani go after each other. I've never been so impressed in my life."

"Ask Markus to take you on—he's training Miz, too, on most of those things. Master what he has to teach you and I'll let you approach Vik about training you with blades."

"Jincus. Want coffee?" Gerrett walked up to place a pot of tea on our table.

"Join us," I slid a chair out with power. Blinking, Jincus took the offered seat and nodded at Gerrett.

171

"Gerrett likes you. He doesn't speak often to anyone," I told Jincus.

"I'm still trying to get used to this. I figured I'd be sitting in jail, somewhere, after I didn't get blown up like some of the others did. And not for the reasons you might think," he added.

"We know you didn't have anything to do with that explosion," I held up a hand. Without a layer of ancient dirt and grease on his skin, Jincus looked much younger. Probably seventy-five or so, and in his prime. His hair, a sandy red, was thick, clean, and combed neatly. When I first saw him, it had been just as dirty as his hands, from raking fingers through it often.

Gray eyes studied me—to him, I was an anomaly and he still didn't understand why he was now working as a pirate sponsored by the ASD. Regardless, the whole idea appealed to him greatly.

After all, who didn't dream of being a pirate at least once in his life?

"Where are you from?" Dori asked as Gerrett set a mug of coffee in front of Jincus.

Jincus rolled his shoulders uncomfortably for a moment. "Most of my family was on Vic'Law when it was destroyed," he confessed. "I'm not a legitimate citizen of either Alliance. That's why I thought I'd be hauled off to jail. My brother and I stowed away on a ship leaving the planet about two years before the planet was destroyed. Back then, it was either work for a criminal or ruin your health and wreck your life, trying to make a living in hiding or off the soil. Our father died at the hands of the criminal boss he worked for; we decided we wanted something better. We hid ourselves aboard a freighter and eventually made our way into the Alliances."

"Where's your brother, now?" I asked.

"Dead. He was on Campiaa when they got hit not long ago. His body was barely recognizable when it was recovered from the casino where he worked."

"Damn," Dori swore softly.

"Well, Jincus, the one who's ultimately responsible for your brother's death is also our number one target. Glad to have you aboard. Stick with us; we intend to take that bastard down," I said.

"Thank you," Jincus whispered, wiping moisture from his cheeks.

"I think we may be able to do something about your citizenship, too," I shrugged. "Le-Ath Veronis offered for most of those who were rescued from Vic'Law before it blew apart. I think we can grandfather you into that arrangement."

"I heard about those," Jincus ducked his head. "I didn't think I'd be eligible, since I wasn't with them. You'd have to know the Queen, I think, before anything of the sort could happen."

"Hmmph," Dori snorted a laugh.

"Jincus, I think we can get you in—if you want to keep working with us, that is."

"Please—I think this is exactly what I want to do."

~

Queen's Palace, Le-Ath Veronis
Travis

"Randl approves of him?" Mom studied the images we had of Jincus—both before and after the grease spill.

"Randl offered him a job immediately."

"Good. I can get him grandfathered in with the others. Tell Randl I'll have the paperwork done in a few days. Officially, he just became a citizen today, but the files have to be placed in the archives."

"I hope Kooper doesn't have a fit about this," I said.

"Kooper doesn't have anything to say about each planet's naturalized citizenship, provided the candidate isn't a known criminal. If Randl gives him a clean record, I think we're safe."

"David likes him a lot, too. Says he's really good with engine repairs and such."

"If he wants to apply for housing on Le-Ath Veronis, tell him to submit a request to Renée. She'll get it to me for approval."

"Thanks, Mom." I leaned in to peck her on the cheek. "I think he'll be so happy it'll overwhelm him."

"Anything new on the Prophet front?"

"Nothing, but we've got feelers out everywhere, and we're going to Pyrik to see if we can pick anything up in Lee'Qee."

"That cesspit? Make sure everybody is triple-shielded."

"We're on it," I grinned at her.

~

Lee'Qee, Pyrik

Randl

"I'm not so sure this was a good idea." Vik shook his head at the devastation of Lee'Qee before us. We stood on the edge of the deepest pit, where the worst of the blast damage lay. There, only the occasional concrete wall or metal fixture emerged from the dirt and debris. While Vik, as a High Demon, wasn't susceptible to radiation sickness, I shielded him so he wouldn't carry anything back to the ship.

The others with us, if they couldn't form their own shields, wore protective gear and a shield I'd provided on top of that. Bel Erland, standing not far away, frowned at the pit of rubble before us. Perri stood close to him, as if she felt obligated to provide protection for the Crown Prince of Karathia.

Nari and Tiri stood near me, waiting for my signal so they could start digging.

"Do you feel something?" I asked them.

"There's a vibration here, certainly," Tiri replied.

"What about you, Perri?" I turned to her.

"There are several signature scents here, but most are ancient."

"Likely when the spells were first laid to hide Lee'Qee," Travis observed.

"That feels right—it goes back centuries, I think," Perri agreed. "There may be something newer, but I'd have to get closer to the location of the spell to know for sure."

"Let's go, then," I nodded to my crew. "Watch your step—we don't know what's out there or whether there are still traps waiting."

"You trying to scare us or something?" Vik lifted an eyebrow at my statement.

"I'm scared," I said. "I didn't even have to try very hard. I could have died here, remember? The Prophet did his best to end me."

"I read the report in Kooper's files," Vik sighed. "Come on, let's go have a look." We began our trek downward into the pit, Mak and Jak so close behind me I could hear them breathing.

Nari

The vibration was like a beacon to us—somewhere in this wretched, demolished ruin, ancient gold lay. When Randl gave the word, Tiri and I strode toward it as fast as we could, while watching where we placed our steps. Somewhere behind us, Randl, Vik and the others followed. My sister and I'd become like hounds to a scent, however, and strode ahead of them quickly.

For Tiri and I, gold had become a vibrational standby—we'd found so much of it in the past we could feel it from a distance if it were there.

A strong signal emanated to the northeast of where we began our trek into the pit. Somewhere to the sides and behind us, the others fanned out, looking for any likely object that might give us a clue to the Prophet's whereabouts.

A half-buried metal rod caught a leg of my uniform, so I stopped to pull the fabric away from it. Tiri, who'd gone several steps past me, screamed as the ground suddenly caved beneath her feet. Shouting came from the others as I hopelessly reached out to her.

In ghastly slow motion, I watched the dirt and filth swallow her scrabbling body, while clods, pebbles and detritus rained down after her. A sickening, metallic clang sounded as Tiri hit the bottom of a black pit.

Terrified, I screamed Tiri's name. When I received no reply, I shouted for Randl and the others. The gaping hole spread before my eyes, and before I could back away, the cavern's maw opened wider and pulled me into throat-clogging darkness with my sister.

~

Randl

At least my shield around Vik expanded to cover his Full Thifilathi; before anyone else could react, the winged, black-scaled High Demon was digging into the cave-in, huge, clawed hands pulling out limp bodies in only seconds.

It felt like forever.

"They're not breathing," Travis shouted at me as he raced past, Bel Erland right behind him.

Quin, I need your healing ability, I sent.

I have to find someone to transport, her mindspeech came immediately.

No, lend it to me. Shove it into your communication, please.

I don't know how. Can you pull it to you?

I think so. Prepare yourself.

~

Travis

By the time Randl reached the bodies, he was glowing brightly—as I'd seen Quin glow in the past when she'd healed someone.

Vik, still in Full Thifilathi, held a body in each massive hand, a frown of concern on his face as he waited for Randl to do something.

Randl motioned for Vik to bring his hands closer together. Once that happened, Randl placed a hand on each woman's chest. The power expended was so bright it was blinding.

Tiri coughed first, followed by Nari. I folded space to stand beside Randl, to give him a hand if needed.

"Welcome back," Randl smiled at the twins.

"There's gold down there," Tiri's croaked. Her hand shook as she touched her forehead. "A lot of it."

"Vik, can you get them back to the ship?" Randl asked.

"I'll transport them," Bel Erland offered.

"What the," Nari blinked as Vik's clawed hand moved slightly beneath her body.

"Nothing to worry about," Randl held up a hand. "Vik's High Demon pulled you out of that hole pretty fast. He and Bel will get you back to the ship, where you'll be checked over by the med-bot in the infirmary. You can rest and eat after that."

"What about the gold?" Tiri demanded.

"We'll get it, don't worry," Randl said. "Good work, by the way. You led us straight to it."

Vik nodded to Bel, who folded space with him and both women.

"I feel something coming from that hole," Perri sounded timid.

"A warlock or witch's power?" Randl turned to her.

"No. Something—different. I don't know what it is, but there's a power-scent to it. A strong one. It didn't reach me until this hole opened." She held up a handful of dirt she'd collected from the edge. I was grateful she had a shield placed between that dirt and her hand.

"That's not scary," I told her. "Are you still planning to go down there?" I asked Randl.

"No. I think I'll remove the entire thing and dump it out on Ca'Lex," Randl said. "If there's another trap, we can stand back from it," he added.

"Good plan," Perri agreed. I could tell she didn't want to be swallowed and strangled like Nari and Tiri had been. She dropped the dirt she held and cleared her hand of debris with a quick spell.

That caused me to wonder—had there been a spell around the gold —to trap and choke anyone who happened on the cache? I'd ask Randl that question later.

"Ready?" Randl turned toward me. I nodded. Holding out his hands, Randl employed his power to separate a rather large section of the ruins from what surrounded it. In moments, he, his bodyguards, Perri and I stood on Ca'Lex, while Randl let the enormous glob of ruins fall.

It dropped with a resounding, metal-rending crash, and if we hadn't been heavily shielded from even a quarter-mile away, the shockwave from the released spell would have killed us.

~

BlackWing XIII

Randl

"It takes time to spell individual coins," Bel Erland set the gold disk on my desk. It was one of thousands—perhaps hundreds of thousands, that I'd pulled away from the dirt and debris I'd dropped onto Ca'Lex.

"You're saying none of the coins was spelled?"

"Perri says there's nothing, and I haven't found anything in that sample pile you have, there," he pointed to the mound of gold on my desk. "It was a hoard, guarded by a spell, yes, but Nari and Tiri set off the preliminary spell, and you destroyed the secondary one."

"Why didn't the Prophet take this with him?" I mused, not expecting an answer.

"He probably thought it safe enough there—the place is quarantined, remember, and without shields, or the knowledge that it was there to start with, I figure it would be hidden well enough—with the spells around it, of course."

"Except we managed to get past all that," I said. "Nari and Tiri say there's nothing they've seen so far in that hoard that's less than a thousand years old."

"Then each of those coins is a museum piece, worth much more than its equivalent weight or face value," Bel Erland said.

"They also say that some of the coins aren't anything they've seen before."

"From dead civilizations that have no written history?"

"Either that—or they never existed in these universes."

"What?"

"I'm just giving you a theory, that's all."

"It's a terrifying theory."

"No joke," I grumped. "I think I need to speak with the Larentii Archivist. If anyone knows—he will."

"Zaria is his daughter-in-law; ask her. Does Perri have any idea on who or what may have laid the spell on the cache?"

"It's nothing she's ever felt before. Not a warlock, witch or any wizard, she thinks."

"What does that leave, then?"

"The really powerful? A sorcerer, maybe?"

"You think the Prophet did it."

"I think it's possible."

"If he did, then he knows the cache was compromised."

"I worry about that, too. Here are my thoughts on that, though. If he had gold, why is he stealing everything, including food? He could buy whatever he wanted on the black market with that kind of currency. Gold, platinum, jewels and such are happily accepted by criminals everywhere."

"I don't have an answer," Bel Erland said. "It's something to think about, though."

"There's the possibility that even the Prophet didn't know about the gold. We have no idea how long he used Lee'Qee as a base of operation, or whether he even stayed there much at all. I get the idea that he didn't—that he only visited now and then."

"Then someone else may have hidden their treasure there, long before the Prophet came along?"

"Maybe."

"Someone whose power signature Perri doesn't recognize."

"That, too," I agreed. "I can put my hands on some of these coins to look for information, but I hesitate to do so."

"I'd be wary of it, too. Who knows where you could end up?"

"And that's what worries me most."

"Yeah."

"Commander?" Zanfield rapped on my door.

"Come in, Zan. We're just finishing up," I invited.

"Director Riffler arrived a few minutes ago. He's in the infirmary, talking with Nari and Tiri," Zanfield announced.

"No surprise," I smiled at Zanfield. "Let me know if he needs to see me afterward."

~

179

Avii Castle

    Quin

"I'm fine," I waved Dena's concern away. "Randl borrowed some of my healing ability. I just feel hungry and thirsty, now."

"Is it back? Your ability?" She sounded worried, despite my reassurances.

"It is; I felt it go and return," I said. "It was to save two lives, and they're fine, now. I supervised everything he did."

"Here's food," Dena said, rising as a servant brought in a tray.

"Oh, good, noodles," I said, lifting a fork and dipping into the bowl.

BlackWing XIII

    Randl

"You're sure they're all right?" Jett stood between the beds holding Nari and Tiri, as if he dared anyone to remove him from the ship's infirmary.

"Quin supervised their healing; they're fine," I assured him. "The med-bot's information confirms that."

"Oh, good," Jett visibly relaxed.

"You should have seen us—we were covered in dirt," Nari smiled at Jett. Tiri beamed at him from her bed, too.

"You released a preliminary spell, which could have been enough to do anyone else in," I told both women. "The dirt was meant to cover you up afterward. Thankfully, Vik was close enough that he nullified the brute force of it, and his High Demon lifted you out of that mess. He was the best person to be there for both of you at that moment; anyone else coming in would have tripped the primary spell, too, and that could have taken anyone else down."

Jett's frown was very deep by this time; I didn't want to downplay how much danger Nari and Tiri had been in. At least he wasn't terrified for them until after the fact.

Don't worry about Vik; Nari and Tiri are young enough to be his children, I told Jett in mindspeech. *He'd have done the same for anyone.*

Besides, if you haven't noticed, you have two adoring women staring at you whenever you're not looking. You should come for meals now and then, I added.

"Might I join you for dinner tonight?" Jett turned to the twins.

"Please," Nari struggled to hide a huge smile.

Jett, delighted with her answer, lifted her hand and kissed it.

~

Queen's Palace, Le-Ath Veronis

Lissa

"I didn't want to keep hauling it around on XIII," Randl said. He and Trent had transported the bulk of the gold from Lee'Qee to my treasury. It took up an entire, unused room there. Kooper, Randl and I were the only ones to have access to it afterward; it was heavily warded by all three of us.

"Did you keep a sample?" Kooper's forehead creased as he asked the question.

"I did—Nari and Tiri helped select a good cross-section to examine. Some of it is stamped in designs and languages they've never seen or heard of, before."

"We need a higher power on this," I said. "I'll see whether Charles is willing to take a look."

"I was hoping for Nefrigar," Randl countered. "Who is Charles?"

"The Mighty Mind," Kooper snorted. "He shows up when he's interested, not until and certainly not before."

"Zaria is his daughter," I half-whispered. "She doesn't like to talk about that."

Randl blinked. If I were honest, I'd say he hadn't considered that Zaria had parents who weren't Larentii.

"It's a long story, and not one for me to tell," I waved a hand at Randl's confusion.

"Now I'm more confused than I was," Randl sighed.

"Most of us stay confused," I patted Randl's shoulder. "You'll find answers eventually—if you're meant to have them."

"The Prophet is my main goal as far as answers are concerned," he said. "After that, well, maybe my curiosity will be satisfied in other ways."

"What's your first move?" Kooper asked. "Now that you have a basket full of gold to examine?"

"I suppose I ought to get on that," Randl admitted, although he didn't sound enthusiastic about the task. Kooper lifted an eyebrow—that's exactly what he wanted Randl to do.

"You don't sound comfortable about it," I said.

"Because I'm not. I'm worried I'll be pulled into *split-time* to investigate, and I'll come back exhausted."

"Hmmmm," Kooper cleared his throat.

"Fine. I'll get on it," Randl waved a hand and folded space.

~

BlackWing XIII

Randl

"Some of it we recognize—those are the coins that drew us toward the cache," Nari said. She and Tiri sat in my office, discussing the gold we'd kept aboard ship. Two piles of it now lay on my desk.

"What about the others?"

"They vibrate differently," Tiri explained. "Not by much, but enough to be noticeable."

"We've seen plenty of gold in our lives," Nari picked up the narrative. "Nothing vibrated like this stack." She pointed to the pile in question.

They'd separated the pieces with the vibrational differences from the others. Those separated coins were also the ones with unrecognizable markings.

"Then you take the pile you recognize," I said. "I'll take the others."

"Dori says that could be dangerous," Nari and Tiri said together.

"Orders from Kooper, so there's nothing I can do about it," I replied.

"Oh." Both, again.

"Take your pile and start working with it," I pointed to the proper pile of coins. "Send Vik to me—we have work to do."

"We'll find him," Nari said.

I could have sent mindspeech, but I wanted to put off this task as long as I could. Nari and Tiri scooped up their gold and headed for my door. I hoped they'd take their time passing my message to Vik.

~

Miz'Sandar

"Always make sure your weapon is fully charged and ready," Markus instructed Jincus, while I watched. I'd already had this lesson, so Jincus had to catch up.

"Don't want to run out of juice, I take it," Jincus grinned.

"Exactly. Every time the weapon is used, it must be inspected before it is charged again. If you've been in a firefight, a weapon can sustain damage in a number of ways. It's best to repair that damage before it's needed again. Most times, a weapon will only be fired a few times. It's built to fire continuously for more than an hour, before the charge runs out. If you're in that situation, you'll need another pistol or rifle to replace the empty."

Jincus handled the laser pistol as if it were a raw egg with a slight crack in it. "First time holding one?" I asked him.

"Yes. Never thought I would, you know."

"I thought the same thing, until Markus started teaching me. Civilians generally don't need weapons in the Alliances," I added.

"They were everywhere on Vic'Law, but they belonged to the bosses, who handed them to trusted employees," Jincus said. "My father said to never pick one up unless you intended to use it, and to prepare yourself to die that way, too. Vic'Law wasn't a friendly place, if you know what I mean."

"Did your father carry a weapon?" Markus asked.

"He did. He didn't like it, but he worked for one of the bosses. That's the way things were, and he was right—that's how he died. The boss killed him, because he thought he'd betrayed him. Found out later that wasn't the case, but he was already dead. Good luck on getting an apology or a sentence leveled against one of the bosses who ran the planet."

"Then handle that weapon like you mean it, Jincus," Markus advised. "I'll teach you how to defend yourself against criminals."

"Good. Thank you."

Randl

"You rang?"

"I did."

Vik slid onto a guest chair, frowning at me. He'd seen the pile of gold on my desk; he understood what was about to happen.

"Kooper's orders," I explained with a shrug.

"Fine."

"Pick one," I told him.

"Me?"

"Yeah. I don't want to."

"All right." Vik reached out to scramble the pile of coins, before lifting one up and offering it to me. Taking a deep breath, I leaned forward to take it. Perhaps it was because we were touching it together for a small moment, that we were both flung into *split-time*.

BlackWing X

Travis

"Dori is frantic. Says they both disappeared—she checked the camera recording from Randl's office," Trent reported.

"How long?" I asked.

"For nearly an hour."

"Fuck. I hate this," I growled, rising from the captain's chair on the bridge. "There's no way to tell which coin he touched?"

"Nari and Tiri are going through their inventory to find out," Trent said as we walked toward the captain's cubby. "Even if they find out, those markings aren't readable to us—we need somebody who might know what they are."

"Send a message to Reah. We need to speak with Nefrigar," I said. Nefrigar was Reah's Larentii mate. He was also Chief Archivist for the Larentii, and the best resource on unusual languages and artifacts that I knew.

"I am here," Nefrigar arrived himself, only moments after Trent contacted Reah. He'd shortened his height, to fit more comfortably in the captain's cubby aboard ship.

"Trent, do you have the information from Nari and Tiri, yet?" I asked.

"Here are the images," he handed the comp-vid to Nefrigar.

Nefrigar's brows drew into a frown as he studied both sides of the coin depicted, before blinking. I'd never seen a perplexed Larentii, before. Nefrigar was certainly perplexed.

"I do not recognize this as anything from any of the known universes," he handed the comp-vid back to Trent. "I have transferred these images to the Archives, so they can be further studied."

"I think you should take a look at the rest of the coins, then," I said.

"There are more?"

"All different from that one, and nothing we can find records on, anywhere."

"Lead me to them," Nefrigar sounded worried.

If the Chief Archivist of the Larentii sounded worried, then I figured everybody ought to be worried.

I know I was.

∼

Randl

Where the hell are we? Vik asked. He and I stood on a rustic street corner of a rustic town on an unknown world. People, dressed in rough-spun shirts and trousers, walked past us, their hand-made leather boots and shoes making creaking sounds on the walkway made of wide, wooden boards.

The walkway was to protect shoes and clothing from the mud and filth of the adjacent, unpaved roadway, where horse and ox-drawn carts and carriages rolled past.

It looks like the old west on Earth, sort of, as Mom describes it, Vik added.

I—this isn't Old Earth, I said. I looked into faces—faces worn and drawn by fear. The language spoken had nothing to do with any language ever spoken on Old Earth. Two women passed by us, not even bothering to look up from their whispered conversation, bonneted heads held close together, as if that would ward away the curious listener.

They're terrified, I told Vik.

Maybe we should follow them. I don't think they see us, he added.

He was right. People walked around us as if we weren't there. *Let's go,* I nodded at Vik's suggestion.

The layout of the town was simple—a single main street, with a few roads crossing the main one, all dirt, of course. The whole place might have a population of three hundred.

Maybe.

When we turned a corner to follow the women, what lay before us didn't belong in this town, and probably not on this world, wherever it was.

A temple, made of marble, stood at the end of this side street, and roughly a quarter-mile in front of it, the street went from dirt to paved.

Which of these things doesn't match the rest? Vik quoted an old Alliance nursery rhyme.

Come on, I said. *We need to find out what's going on, here.*

It took a few minutes to get to the edge of the paving. *Look at this,* Vik pointed out the edge of it. *It doesn't touch the ground.*

It didn't—it hovered nearly four inches above the dirt and muck of the street beneath.

I don't think this was built here, I began, as we stepped upon the paving to follow the two women.

I don't think it stays here, either, Vik said.

You know, I think you're right, I agreed. Once we were close enough to the temple, I could see that it had set down atop a tree, the limbs of which were broken and splayed beneath the western edge of the temple grounds.

The whole thing, built on a platform and complete with a paved entrance, was ready to travel elsewhere at a moment's notice.

What do you think this means? Vik asked before he drew in a sharp breath. We'd almost come to the gates of the temple, where two men walked out to open the tall, iron frames for the women.

Ra'Ak, Vik growled mentally, while a plume of smoke blew from his nostrils.

Stay calm, I cautioned, worried that he'd go Full Thifilathi and destroy the two Ra'Ak standing at the gates. *Come on*, I grabbed his arm to pull him forward. *They're going to close the gates again.*

We barely made it through before the Ra'Ak, in humanoid form, closed the gates, just as I feared.

Another man appeared, then, from nothing. He'd folded in, there was no doubt. Both women dropped to their knees, weeping and terrified.

They had a right to be.

This one wasn't Ra'Ak. This one—*rogue god* whispered into my mind. I could see plainly what would happen to the women.

They were dinner for the rogue god's pet Ra'Ak.

We're moving, Vik's mental shout woke me up from a near-trance. *We have to get out of here.*

I think you're right, I agreed. *But first.*

Pulling the women away with power wasn't difficult. And, as it was a surprise to the rogue god and the Ra'Ak, who hadn't expected anything of the kind, we lurched back to BlackWing XIII. We fell in a heap at the feet of a surprised Larentii; Vik cursing, the women weeping.

CHAPTER 13

BlackWing X
Travis

"Thank goodness Nefrigar was here. We'd never have made sense of what those women were saying," Trent slouched onto a seat in the captain's cubby.

"He had to give them Alliance Common, or he wouldn't have understood them, either," I pointed out.

"They're with Mom, now—she may have to lay compulsion to keep them from hyperventilating," Trent sighed.

It was true—Randl, Vik and Nefrigar had transported the women to Mom's palace, so they could be questioned. I had no idea what would be done with them afterward, but it wasn't as if they'd have survived where they came from—that much was verified by both women— they'd been chosen by a town lottery, which only took women's names.

Because Ra'Ak preferred female meat over that of a male.

Randl said a rogue god held the Ra'Ak's leash, in a temple that could be moved from place to place.

Likely, there were lotteries taking place in many towns similar to the one he and Vik had been flung to.

188

We'd looked more closely at the coin, too, which Randl set on his desk with a thump once he was on his feet again.

Made of soft gold and roughly minted, the coin now bore the imprint of Randl's thumb, he'd held it so tightly.

"At least Vik came back without a white streak in his hair," Trent observed.

"True. But he's High Demon, bro. They're immune to a lot of things. Maybe *split-time* is one of those."

"Did you see him? He was still breathing smoke. He wanted to tear into those Ra'Ak."

"It's probably a good thing he didn't. Randl may have made a mistake, taking those women away."

"You mean the timeline and all that?"

"And all that."

∼

Queen's Palace, Le-Ath Veronis

Lissa

It's possible, Nefrigar informed me in mindspeech, *that somehow, the coins were taken from worlds that never existed in our timeline.*

Randl and Vik stood nearby in my palace library, waiting, while Nefrigar and I finished our silent conversation.

They'd given us their story; the two women were currently in the palace kitchen, guarded by two vampires and eating as if they hadn't seen a decent meal in a decade.

You mean in one of those eras, I said, for lack of a better term, *before the God Wars in their timeline destroyed everything?*

It's possible, I suppose, but how did those coins survive that total destruction, and make their way to this one, unharmed and locked away?

Nefrigar had trouble with that theory, just as I did. Total destruction was total destruction, no matter how you looked at it.

Someone would have to deliberately do it. Someone who survived from one period to the next, I suggested.

I agree. Which leaves us with a conundrum. I doubt any of the Three would do this. There is no purpose in it.

Yeah. But there has to be a purpose—doesn't there?

One would tend to believe that, yes.

Do you think Randl would be willing to examine those other coins? This worries me in ways I can't define. Not yet, anyway.

Has anyone else attempted to do what Randl has done, to go where the coin originated?

Nef, whenever I hold one of those coins, nothing happens. Nothing. Randl is the only one who has any sort of reaction to them. I get the idea that if Alliance coins hadn't been included in the cache, Nari and Tiri wouldn't have been drawn to it, either.

Disturbing, Nefrigar sighed aloud.

Oh, it's that, all right. I've sent a message to Charles, but he hasn't responded.

The Mighty Mind is the only source of information that may unravel this conundrum, Nefrigar agreed. *Will you keep me updated, if you learn anything new?*

I will. What should we tell Randl?

Perhaps he should examine other coins. He and your son say they passed through that world invisibly—nobody saw them. I hope he'll find something to lead him to the Prophet, or whomever hid those coins on Pyrik.

I suppose it couldn't hurt, but I'll warn them to be careful and try not to bring anyone else back.

Good idea. There's something else, too, Nefrigar went on.

What's that?

This cache, in its bunker, was buried far beneath Lee'Qee. It was only uncovered well enough after Randl and the Prophet created the explosion and the resulting pit.

You've looked into this, haven't you?

While we were discussing it, yes. The explosion muddled many things, but I found no evidence of a passageway or steps leading downward to the cache.

It was buried and covered over?

I believe that to be so. It may be that the Prophet was the only one with that knowledge, else why would his minions be instructed to steal food and supplies, with so much gold at their disposal?

This is a mess. I rubbed my forehead. A headache was coming; I could feel it already.

I suggest you place sensory devices, or a spell, perhaps, in case the Prophet sends someone to investigate recent events in Lee'Qee.

That's—a great idea, I confirmed. *I'll have Erland lay a warlock's web. If anyone breaks the invisible strands, we'll know.*

Be prepared to go quickly if that happens, Nefrigar warned.

Right. "Randl?" I spoke aloud. He turned quickly, with Vik close behind.

"We think you should continue to examine the coins, as Director Griff instructed. We hope you will find clues as to the Prophet's involvement in this, and perhaps find information on how to locate him, too," Nefrigar said.

"All right. At least we didn't come back exhausted, like in the past."

"Something else that's different," I looked up at Nefrigar.

"Very true. I will consider this, among all the other facts uncovered so far."

"Lissa?" Winkler and Gavin folded into to the library, although Winkler was the one to speak.

"What's wrong?" I knew immediately that something was.

"Another family has turned on itself. Six are dead."

"Who and where?" My heartbeat was rapid and irregular at this information.

"It's not good news," Gavin growled. "Six members of the royal family on Ru'beq are dead, including the Crown Princess."

T'beq, Capital City of Ru'beq
Randl

Vik had brought Perri, at my request. The Prophet's stink was all over the royal dining room, but that's not all we found.

"Jiles Tamber's spell scent is here," Perri confirmed. "I feel it most strongly here." She pointed to a dish of spiced apples.

"So the Prophet really is contaminating food and getting it onto tables," Kooper said. "Only this time, he chose his target, instead of letting the contaminated food go to a random family."

"How do you know he chose this one?" Lissa asked. At least the bodies had been removed shortly after our arrival, but the blood and carnage remained.

"Because we have a message," Kooper turned his comp-vid toward Lissa.

I froze. Here it was—the one I was expecting—and dreading. The Prophet had reached out to Kooper, just as I thought he would. I waited to hear how he'd done it, and whether there was an intermediary involved.

"*Greetings,*" Lissa read aloud. "*In exchange for information currently held by your agency on one of your most-wanted, Randl Gage, we are willing to exchange information on those responsible for recent, royal deaths.* There's no name, only an electronic contact," Lissa added.

"Which will be shut down automatically if we attempt to trace it," Kooper hissed.

He was right—criminals had become quite adept at covering their communicative tracks. By the same token, undercover agents could conceal communications with official departments, too, so the criminal factions where they were embedded couldn't get information on the agent involved, or who they worked with, if they were discovered.

"I suppose we have to consider what information to give him," I said. "I'll let someone else handle that."

"I'll talk it over with Jett, Ildevar and Teeg," Kooper said. "I'll keep you informed. Go back to your ship, Commander. You have work to do."

～

"Not today, you won't." Dori, hands on hips, blonde curls crackling and blue eyes blazing, glared at me when I told her what Kooper said. He wanted coins examined quickly; there were more than thirty left in the pile I was responsible for.

"I agree," I held up a hand to circumvent the argument she'd prepared. "Not today. Vik and I've had enough for one day."

"Good. When did you eat last?"

"I don't remember."

"Come with me. Gerrett will find something for you."

Gerrett already had food waiting; Vik was eating when we arrived in the galley. David and Zanfield kept him company; both were having a beer and discussing the day's events.

"Want to join us?" Vik invited, nodding toward empty chairs.

"Sure."

Gerrett arrived with a plate of food, giving me a slight frown as he put it in front of me. "I'll bring more beer," he said to the others. "Want one?" he asked Dori.

"Yes, please. This has been a trying day."

"Agreed." Gerrett strode away to pull beer from the cold keeper. He returned with a tray full of opened bottles, set it on one end of the table, took one for himself and sat down in the last empty chair to drink it.

"Where do you think you went?" David asked.

"I don't really know," I said. "The language wasn't anything we recognized, and a rogue god was there. There shouldn't be any rogue gods left anywhere during this timeline, so I think we may have gone to a now-defunct one."

"Defunct?" Zanfield grimaced at the term I'd used.

"As in destroyed. That's the idea I got from Mom and Nefrigar," Vik lifted his beer and emptied half the bottle in two swallows. "No longer existing," he went on, setting his empty bottle down and silently asking for another.

Gerrett passed a bottle down the table without a word.

"That almost happened with us," Dori said softly. "Ashe doesn't like to talk about it, but the God Wars came and went, here. I think it's happened before, and every time, the entire set of universes is destroyed and has to be constructed from scratch again. This may be the only one that survived."

Ashe. The Mighty Hand. One of the original Three. He'd know about that, I suppose.

"But not this time, you say?" David asked.

"No. This time, they either destroyed the rogue gods or locked them away elsewhere, where they can't escape. Anyway, that's how I understand things. As I said, Ashe doesn't like to talk about it."

"Does anyone else ever feel like you're still a child and the grownups are talking about things they don't want you to know about?" Zanfield asked.

"Every fucking day," David lifted his beer. Vik clinked his bottle against David's and laughed.

~

P'loxett

V'dar

"This is the warlock responsible for laying those spells in the scrapyards?" I studied the image of Stone Wicke on the comp-vid handed to me by my chief subordinate, Varok.

"He works for Mebbers," Varok said. "We've learned that Mebbers is attempting to take his previous boss' place."

"Well, as I commanded his previous boss at the end, don't you think Mebbers works for me?"

"It may be difficult to get past the spells and shields he's placed around himself," Varok informed me. "We managed to get this information from an ah, dying associate."

"Did we have anything to do with his death?"

"Most certainly, my Lord."

"All the better. No trail of information to lead back to us, then. Study this further, Varok. I wish to have a meeting with Mebbers and his ah, warlock. Soon."

"I'll see to it, my Lord."

"Good. It's my hope that when we receive information from the

Reth Alliance concerning our enemy, Randl Gage, that we'll have a more powerful warlock at our disposal to assist us in destroying him —and taking his entire fleet of BlackWing ships."

"Anything else, my Lord?"

"Yes. It has come to my attention that the ground inside Lee'Qee's quarantine perimeter may have been disturbed, recently. Will you send someone to investigate and report to me?"

"I'll go myself—with your permission. May I borrow Jiles to transport?"

"Of course," I waved a hand magnanimously. "Soon enough, that's all he'll be good for—once we have more warlocks at our disposal."

"In all things, you are wisest," Varok dipped his head respectfully and backed away.

"It goes without saying," I sniffed. "Leave now. I want reports by tomorrow. Send Yurik to me before you go. I wish to speak with him."

~

Founder's Palace, Campiaa

Kooper

"The royal family on Ru'beq is asking more questions than I can comfortably answer," I explained to Jett, Teeg and Wyatt. "The Prophet chose his target carefully, this time. I told them what I could concerning this menace, but like everybody else, they want to know why they were singled out. They have no dealings with him or any other criminal. How do you explain that they were chosen because the Prophet wants Randl Gage, who, in all the official records, is also a wanted criminal?"

"They'd demand that you hand over everything you have," Teeg leaned back in his chair, making it creak softly with the movement. He sat behind his desk; Jett and I sat on guest chairs, and Wyatt stood by the closed door.

"If they ever found out that Randl works for us, they'd want your head and his, too," Wyatt said.

"And mine," Jett snorted.

195

He was right. Perhaps this was a side game the Prophet played—if he couldn't destroy Jett and me in one way, there were other ways to eliminate our threat. If certain information reached the media in both Alliances, Ildevar and Teeg would have no choice but to release us from our positions, because the populations of both Alliances would demand it.

We played a dangerous game, holding sensitive information back from the people, but that was far better than facing mass panic everywhere.

It's the way things have always been done, Jett sent to me. He understood my expression; he felt the same pressure. Most of the time, he handled it better, too.

"We can't give them this information," Teeg said. "I've spoken with Ildevar, and he agrees. I understand that your positions are on the line if the people feel they've been in danger all along and have purposely been kept in the dark. This happens now and then; you both know that."

"My problem is with being held accountable if that happens, when I've done nothing wrong," I snapped.

"I know. Kooper, your predecessors knew the risks, too, when they accepted the job. Some handled it well; others didn't. Please don't make yourself one of the latter."

I knew he spoke of Norian Keef, my immediate predecessor. Norian had let power go to his head, over-compensating, perhaps, for the constant pressure he felt in his work.

"It's bad enough," Teeg went on, "that every royal family, planetary leader and so on, has now beefed up their already tight security. If the Prophet strikes any of them, how will we explain that no matter what they do, neither we nor their security forces can protect them from this menace?"

"The only way we could do that would be to have Randl in every household, waiting for the Prophet's stench to enter it," Jett grumbled. "Which is impossible."

～

BlackWing XIII

    Randl

"I'm not sure my pay grade covers this," Vik said as he stared at the pile of coins on my desk.

"I hear that," I agreed. "Just pick one and hold onto it while I touch it, too."

"What if we can't get back?"

"I've considered that," I said with a sigh. "I hope Zaria is keeping tabs," I tapped my chest where my medallion lay. "Dori has already threatened me twice, today."

"That's never a good sign," Vik quipped. "I'm glad we're taking our blades with us, this time."

"I thought about ranos pistols, but last time, the technology wasn't even close to their environment."

"Blades work everywhere," Vik grinned.

"Then pick a coin and let's get this over with."

～

Avii Castle

    Quin

"I think they might fit into New Fyris easier than most places," Lissa said. The two women Randl rescued from a long-dead world stood nearby, gaping at the view from the King's balcony. Where they'd come from, an ocean was a myth at best. They'd never seen one and had barely heard of it, too.

Lissa had brought them to me, so I could read as much about them as possible before making a final decision on where to place them.

"New Fyris is a mix of old and new—I agree with you," I told Lissa. "They'll do all right there, I think. Do we have anyone lined up to act as a liaison?"

"Winkler has petitioned Amlis, so I think they'll be fostered in some way. I've asked for regular reports, too, while they're educated on Alliance laws and customs. How is Pauley doing?"

"Eager to make up for lost time. He doesn't talk about his uncle much, though, and when he does, it upsets him."

"No surprise. How about Charla?"

"I think she may be on the road to conquering her fear of birds," I smiled. "She has lunch or dinner with the guards now and then."

"That's a lot of wings to deal with," Lissa laughed.

"It is, and they're all laughing and talking. I think she needed that—to be a part of a happier group."

"Her mother is a piece of work," Lissa rolled her eyes. "We've placed compulsion twice for her to stop complaining about inconsequential shit."

I wanted to laugh at her terminology. I stifled it, settling for a grin, instead. "I have to go," Lissa rose from her seat. "Drake and Drew are coming with me to deliver the women to New Fyris."

"Good luck," I said, rising with her. "I feel sorry for them—that they have to make a new life for themselves in a strange land."

"I'd feel sorrier for them if they'd been a Ra'Ak's dinner," Lissa snorted. "I can't say this was the best solution, but Randl did what he thought was right at the time."

"He always does that," I agreed. "Even when I first met him on Vogeffa II, as a nine-year-old blind clairvoyant. He knew Lafe, Terrett and I were coming, somehow, and prepared his village for our arrival."

"Why didn't we know how important he was, back then?" Lissa asked the question I'd already considered—why hadn't we seen that in him early on?

"No matter, he's working with us, now," she smiled suddenly. "I'll let you know how things go in New Fyris."

"Thank you." I nodded as she folded away with both women.

~

Le'Vestar Limn

"The ship is almost ready," I replied to Yurik's question. "Only two parts more to complete the engines."

"How long?" Yurik demanded. "The Prophet wishes to—visit someone."

"Perhaps another eight-day," I said. "The parts have to be calibrated after we manufacture them."

"Then make it soon. Mebbers awaits a visit from his overlord."

Mebbers.

I recognized that name. Mebbers was a known criminal who'd disappeared in the last century. Many speculated that he'd been killed by one of the Big Three. How had he stayed hidden? Better yet, how had the Prophet found him now?

"We will make it soon, supervisor Yurik," I dipped my head to him.

Mae exchanged a glance with me as we watched Yurik stalk out of our workroom. We had more of our minds to work with, now, but were still no closer to making the change, which could lead to our freedom. Still, it was vital that we be allowed aboard the ship when it launched.

Vital—for both of us.

~

Alken Wilker

Mebbers. It didn't take long for me to put it together. Since I'd come here, I'd caught whispered conversations, here and there. Conversations on how the boss liked things done.

Less than a century ago, there were plenty of tales about him—how he liked to share a meal with those who'd crossed him, and if the tales were true, proved quite entertaining as a host before he killed them after dessert was served.

One such dinner occurred not long after my arrival. Word of it eventually reached me, as I have sharp ears. I hadn't informed Gillen that I knew; he was still embroiled in searching for Zanfield Staggs' agents.

Qatti was becoming impatient; Teren and Franc, Staggs' agents, had dropped out of sight and no amount of scrying would reveal them.

So far, I'd only been asked to provide low-level spells. Gillen said it was customary, until I could prove myself trustworthy. Only once, too, had I seen Mebbers' most trusted warlock, Stone Wicke, from a distance.

Stone did the heavy lifting, as far as spells were concerned, with help from Gillen and Qatti. They never spoke about what they'd done or where they'd gone when they went with Stone. *Boss' orders*, Gillen always said.

Even my family didn't trust me. Here, too, none of the few women who worked for Mebbers were interested in me. Most walked away the moment I came close to them. Gillen warned me, too, that Mebbers was prone to hosting a special dinner with anyone he employed who attacked another employee—for any reason.

The last thing anyone here wanted was to have dinner with Mebbers, and that included me. Yes, I was a warlock, but Stone was a stronger warlock. My own brother would look the other way, I'm sure, if I were targeted by the boss.

∼

Queen's Palace, Le-Ath Veronis
Lissa
I'd just returned to the palace when Erland appeared.

"You must come," he said, urgency in his voice.

"What is it?" I asked.

"The warlock's web I laid over Lee'Qee has been disturbed. Someone is there, now."

"Lead the way," I said, ignoring the fact that I was still dressed for a royal visit with the Prince of New Fyris.

Erland folded us to Pyrik, and to the area in question. He wasn't wrong; there were three who'd come, and one of those three was Jiles Tamber.

Kooper, I snapped, sending him images of what I was seeing.

He didn't bother to reply; he, Kell and Opal arrived together. Erland tossed a shield around Jiles, or the Second-level warlock would have let loose with every spell he knew to keep himself from being captured.

The other two attempted to fight Kell. That was a mistake—you don't take on an ancient vampire and expect to come out the winner. Both were unconscious in seconds—a single blow delivered to each accomplished that.

Kell knew exactly how to throw a punch to keep his quarry alive and render them unconscious at the same time.

"May we borrow your dungeon?" Kooper walked up to Erland and me.

"Of course. Erland will place a power-light cage around our young warlock; wouldn't want him getting away, now would we?"

Randl

Do you suppose civilization is here, somewhere? Vik asked.

We'd been walking at the edge of a forest for what felt like forever.

I think I hear something, I said, coming to a stop and holding out a hand to keep him from walking past me.

Above the sound of our breathing, we heard it—the low drone of chanting, coming from somewhere ahead. Again, it wasn't a language we understood, but chanting is the same, no matter where or when you are.

Let's check it out, Vik strode ahead.

The moment the circle of chanters came into view, I understood they were a mix of rogue gods and Ra'Ak; Vik was blowing so much smoke it clouded around both of us.

Hold, I grasped Vik's upper arm. The tight muscles clenched under my grip; he wanted to tear into these just as he wanted to tear into the others.

This time, their prey wasn't two women.

It was sixteen children—to feed the eight Ra'Ak present.

Before you take the children away, a man appeared before us. I blinked—he felt familiar, somehow. Was familiar, perhaps, in more ways than one. Vik, I understood quickly, hadn't seen him at all.

Couldn't see him.

What? I demanded quickly in mindspeech. If we didn't take the children soon, they'd die.

This. He flipped a gold coin toward me. Without thinking, I reached out to pluck it from the air.

The world you visited last time is no more—just as this one will be when you leave, he said. *Take those children and go quickly.*

Who—are you? What is this coin for? I asked, fingering the coin before gripping it tightly in my fingers.

You'll figure it out, he said, and disappeared.

What are you waiting for? Vik demanded. He hadn't seen or heard anything that passed between the strange man and me.

Nothing, I snapped and raised my hands.

Like before, I employed power to pull the children away, causing Ra'Ak to turn to their serpent form and bellow to the skies as we left their world behind.

~

Queen's Palace, Le-Ath Veronis

Randl

"I think it was meant to be. I can't explain it better than that," I told Queen Lissa. How could I tell her about the strange man's appearance, that only I had seen?

Or the coin, which I now carried in my pocket?

"We have sixteen children to find homes for," Lissa turned to Winkler, Drake and Drew, who stood with her inside her private study.

Like the previous women, the children were in the palace kitchen, being fussed over and fed by an army of comesuli.

"You say they were chanting before they ah, ate?" Lissa turned her next question to Vik.

"That's exactly what it was. No idea who they were chanting to, but it was somebody who held sway over rogue gods and Ra'Ak, too."

"A more powerful rogue god—or their version of the General?" Winkler asked. It was a valid question.

"Has to be one or the other, doesn't it?" Lissa frowned.

"That makes sense," Drake agreed. "I wish we had more information, but Randl had to do what he did quickly, or the children would have been eaten by Ra'Ak."

"I might not have held back, either, if he hadn't pulled us away when he did," Vik confessed. "I was really pissed."

"Oh, honey," Lissa went straight to Vik and hugged him hard. His arms were around her, too, and he released a relieved breath. His mother loved him—quite a lot, as it turned out.

"I ah, think we should prepare for more rescues every time I examine a coin," I said. "I don't know how or why, but I think this was meant to be."

"Then I hope you'll be safe when you go," Lissa leaned away from Vik and reached up to pat his cheek.

"Thanks, Mom," he grinned.

CHAPTER 14

BlackWing XIII
Randl

"I'm grateful Queen Lissa is helping place those children," I said. "Quin is also volunteering—she'll meet with them to determine their specific needs."

As usual, our meeting was held in the dining hall, and X's crew had come to hear the news, too.

While I spoke, I fingered the coin in my pocket. So far, I'd been too busy making reports, settling children and having a meeting with the crew to examine it.

"You've seen Ra'Ak and rogue gods in both places?" Travis asked.

"Yes. I think there is some significance to that, but I don't know what, yet," I replied. "So far, too, there has been no evidence of gods, High Demons or any other powerful race in residence." I wanted to shiver at that thought—that those things might have been eliminated already. Or, in the case of the High Demons, they may not have existed there at all, leaving Ra'Ak free to do as they willed, once they went rogue.

We'd found no black Ra'Ak so far; Vik confirmed that the ones we'd seen were all copper Ra'Ak. As a High Demon created to stand against them, I suppose he'd know as well as anyone.

"They were chanting before the meal?" Dori asked.

"It looks that way," Vik said. "I can tell when a Ra'Ak is close to the change—these were close. If we hadn't pulled those kids away when we did, it would have been too late for them."

"Why would they bother to chant? Why didn't they just eat?" This question came from David.

"We don't know. Since we couldn't understand the language, we may never know."

"Do those kids know?" Perri asked.

I went still. "Maybe they do. I'll ask Lissa and Quin to look into it," I said. "Good point, Agent Wilker."

"I'd prefer Perri, if that's all right."

"I'll make a note of it." She didn't want to be associated with her family any longer. I figured we could fix that, if she wanted. *I can petition the Crown of Karathia for a name change if you want, and it will be granted without hesitation*, I sent to her.

I want it, she replied. *Thank you*, she added.

I'll send it right away. Bel Erland, I sent, *Perri wants to change her last name.*

I'll do the paperwork and have Dad sign it by tomorrow.

Thank you. Perri, the Crown Prince says it will be done by tomorrow.

What will they change it to? She asked.

I think something suitable can be found. Don't worry, all right.

It will be changed to Ironsmith, Zaria's voice informed both of us. *It's an old family name, and Ilya already said yes. Your brother's name will be changed to that as well. Ilya says welcome to the family.*

I watched as Perri stood up from her chair, sobbed once, and ran to embrace me.

"Sorry, everyone," I hugged Perri as well as I could. "She just got her last name changed, and it's amazing."

～

Perri

I had no idea. Really. I'd never felt I'd belonged anywhere, until I found my way onto a BlackWing Pirate ship.

I barely slept after going to bed following the meeting. My name would be Ironsmith when I woke, and I was too wound up to fall asleep. Pauley's name, too, would change. I doubted he'd have any regrets, after years of mistreatment at the hands of our own kin.

Ilya Ironsmith, himself, had given Pauley and me permission to use his name. How amazing was that? Randl told me after the meeting that Ilya had been there when Pauley was removed from our uncle's home, and had transported my brother to Campiaa, where he was met by Zaria and Quin.

Too bad Uncle Alken hadn't tried something then—Ilya would have fried him where he stood.

My eyes must have closed sometime after I had that thought; I didn't remember anything until my alarm went off.

~

Randl

"Shhhh—here she comes," Dori whispered. The rest of us had gathered early in the dining room, waiting for Perri to arrive.

We were having a birthday party—for her—and her new name. I suspected there hadn't been a proper celebration for her real birthday in a very long time—if ever.

Perri jumped when the crowd shouted surprise. Her eyes grew round as she stared at decorations looped about the dining room.

"Happy new name day," Dori said, placing a bouquet of flowers in Perri's arms. "Randl has the new records for you, and everything is official. Signed personally by the King," she added with a grin.

"Come, sit," David waved Perri to a table. "We'll have breakfast in a minute. For now, we have other stuff to do."

"What other stuff?" Perri became wary.

"Just gifts," Nari and Tiri exclaimed together. "Here. You'll be one of the few to have one of these." A small, velvet box was presented to Perri after she took a seat.

"What is this?" Perri carefully lifted the lid.

"A coin, from the lost city of Haribauld," Tiri explained. "Only a few of them exist, and most of them are in museums. We were allowed to keep a few since we found them, and one of them is now yours."

"You're joking." Perri stared at the small, silver coin nestled on a bed of silk.

"Not joking. You can keep it or sell it, but remember, it's extremely rare."

"I'm keeping it," Perri breathed, shutting the lid and hugging the small box to her chest.

"Good choice," Nari laughed.

"Next," Vik stepped forward, an envelope in his hand.

"What's this?" Perri took the envelope as if it were made of crystal and could shatter at any moment.

"Look inside," Vik said.

Perri lifted the flap and pulled the single slip of paper out. I knew what it said already.

"Read it," Dori coaxed.

"This entitles Perri Ironsmith to blade lessons with Vik, Travis and Trent while she is aboard any of the BlackWing fleet. Is this for real?" She looked through the crowd until she located Travis and Trent.

"It's real," Travis confirmed.

"And now," David stepped forward with another envelope. "This is something everyone contributed to," he said, handing the envelope to Perri.

A hush dropped through the crowd; we waited for this final gift to come. Yes, we'd all contributed in some small way, but the idea—and the bulk of the funds—had come from Zanfield.

"This entitles the bearer to two Falchani-made swords, custom made by the best bladesmith on Falchan," Perri read aloud. "But only when her Sursees say she is ready to receive them."

"And you can't begin blade training without this," I carried a box to the table and set it in front of her. "This is from the King and Crown Prince of Karathia."

She lifted the lid carefully. Inside was the traditional, white training garb given to a new trainee on Falchan. Beneath that lay another envelope. "The Crown of Karathia is most pleased to see another Ironsmith training in the Falchani way," Perri read aloud. "The Crown will also buy your first set of black leathers when you attain master's status. Signed, King Rylend Morphis and Crown Prince Bel Erland Morphis."

"Training begins tomorrow. You'll rise two hours before breakfast and meet us in the dojo, ready to begin your training," Travis said. "Wear those," he nodded toward the trainee's whites.

"Thank you. Is my name really Ironsmith?" she turned to me, then.

"I have the images of signed documents on my comp-vid, and I'll transfer those to you, along with copies of Pauley's documents. Everything is now legal and official. Welcome to the BlackWing fleet, Agent Ironsmith."

~

Avii Castle

Quin

"Pauley, you and your sister have a new last name," I sat beside him to deliver the news. Gurnil, sitting on the opposite side of the library table, beamed at both of us.

Pauley's face formed a deep frown as he considered this. "Uncle Alken can't hurt us anymore, can he?" he finally said.

"That's right. Your new last name is Ironsmith. From now on, you'll be Pauley Ironsmith. How does that sound?"

"Ironsmith," he practiced the name. "Perri likes it a lot, doesn't she?"

"She does."

"I like it too."

Gurnil smothered a laugh; I hugged Pauley and laughed with him.

~

BlackWing XIII

Randl

The coin lay on my desk. One side bore the image of an eagle-like bird, with four wings. The opposite side bore the face of a man. I suppose coins were tributes, no matter when or where you were.

He said the first world Vik and I visited was gone. What was that supposed to mean? I'd already determined that it was a defunct world —if not a defunct universe. Why would someone go to the trouble of telling me what I already knew?

Blowing out a breath, I pulled the coin I'd used the day before from a desk drawer, to compare it to the one I'd gotten from the ghost. I don't know why I called him that, but he'd appeared only to me.

Vik had no clue that anyone else was there, or that he'd given me anything.

"They don't match," I turned the coin used the day before, comparing it to the one I'd been given. Not only did they look different, they *felt* different, too.

As for its purpose, he said I'd figure it out.

How?

"Problems?" Zanfield walked into my office. The door was open, so that was expected.

"Hey, Zan. Have a seat," I invited. "Want tea?"

"I'd take tea."

After sending mindspeech to Gerrett, he told me when two cups were ready to be *Pulled* into my office. I transported them in, and set one in front of Zanfield while I gripped the other with one hand.

"Thank you for signing off on the papers for Pauley's name change," I said as Zanfield drank from his mug of tea.

"No trouble," he waved his free hand. "What did you need?" Yes, I'd sent mindspeech, asking him to come by my office when he had a moment.

"I'd like for you and Perri to train with blades together, when she reaches that point in her training. I know Vik is teaching you to fight with your off-hand, so you'll be able to handle two blades eventually. Perhaps it'll help Perri, to have someone to spar with."

Zanfield's mouth quirked as he considered my request. "Well, I suppose it wouldn't hurt for her to see that even the wealthy can fall flat on their faces," he said. "As they say, money isn't everything."

"But it helps," he and I said in unison. He laughed.

"Tell Vik," I saluted Zan with my mug. "He'll know what to do."

"I sure hope so. I see plenty of bruises in my future."

"As long as it isn't broken bones. I forbid you to get broken bones, and that's an order, Agent Staggs."

Zanfield stood and saluted smartly. "Aye, Commander," he said, then turned briskly and marched out of my office as only Zanfield Staggs could.

~

Vik

I found David and Jincus in the bowels of the ship, going through an engine check together. I figured Jincus had never seen an engine this new or complicated before.

"These are the energy crystals, where the ship's power comes from," David said. "They were designed by Kend Industries, and are the best available anywhere." He pointed through the window, past which the huge crystals were lined up along that side of the ship.

"I figure you're used to seeing the older, natural crystals, that weren't as energy efficient as the manufactured ones," David went on. "They ran out of juice faster. As for these, we usually open the door guards to charge the crystals when we're in a regular orbit around a planet, to soak in as much sunlight as possible. We can go two weeks on a single charge, as long as we're not engaged in a firefight with someone. The backup engines require fuel, and we have enough to get us to a destination if we deplete the crystals."

"What kind of weapons do we have onboard?" Jincus asked.

"The usual—laser cannons and such."

"I think the best weapons we have are the crew," I said.

"I never thought about that, but you could be right," Zanfield walked in to join us. "I wouldn't want to mess with Randl or Vik, even with a fleet of ships behind me. And that's just from XIII. X has its own set of formidables."

"Formidables?" I blinked at Zanfield's description. "Sounds like a name for an athletic club."

"Maybe we should call ourselves that," David laughed. "Formidable David. That sounds good to me."

"Formidable David, can you stop what you're doing?" Dori joined us. "We just got a call from Kooper. An old shipyard was hit just outside the Campiaan Alliance. Not much left there, but Kooper wants us to investigate—there are a few survivors who should be questioned, and this requires us to go in undercover. Stone Wicke may have been involved in this—or the Prophet. We need to know which one."

"Not an Alliance world, I take it?" Zanfield asked.

"Right. We need everything online in five minutes, Dave. If you can."

"Hmmph." David waved a hand and went to the nearest console to pause the engine check. "You're online now, Captain."

"Good. Phillip," Dori spoke into her communicator, "the engines are back online. Let's get going."

"Yes, Captain," came his muted reply.

"Randl wants both of you in his office," she nodded to Zanfield and me. "To discuss what we know so far."

"Want me to skip you back to the bridge?" I asked Dori. "I can skip Zan and me to Randl's office from there."

"Sure. Makes things go faster," Dori agreed.

Gripping Dori's and Zanfield's arms, I skipped to the bridge.

Randl

"We didn't know about the facility, until it blew up," Kooper informed us in a vid feed. "Spy-bots recorded the explosion, so we sent more in to investigate. Doesn't look good, and we have no idea what was stolen before the shipyard was destroyed."

"What if the survivors won't cooperate?" Zanfield asked.

"That's where Gerrett can help, Zan," I said. "If I can't tell things for myself, that is."

"I doubt many of those ships fit Alliance specs, unless they were stolen to begin with," Vik pointed out.

"We think that, too. I'm concerned that the Prophet may be depending on his new engineers to get around that obstacle—especially since they have a stolen fabricator to use, now."

"What if it's Stone Wicke, instead—and whoever he works for?" I asked. "His Second-level warlock is missing, and I figure the Prophet may be pissed and looking for a replacement."

"What if the Prophet has his eye on Stone Wicke—and his boss? What if he knows who that boss is? It won't be a stretch, I think, for him to go in and take over, like he did with two of the Big Three." Zanfield offered his thoughts on the matter.

"I think you could be right, Zan. It makes sense that the Prophet would be looking for others to absorb into his plot, just as he did last time. He's gotten a taste for warlocks, perhaps, and is searching for more to add to his team."

"How long will it take to arrive at the destination? From your current location—by mundane means?" Kooper asked.

"Dori says three days."

"Do you think you can get in at least two more coins before then?"

"If that's what you want."

"I do. Something bothers me about all this."

"Something bothers me about it, too." I didn't add that it wasn't the same kind of being bothered. Kooper wasn't the one going to places unknown, to witness horrific things about to happen. He didn't mind sending me, though.

Fuck.

"I'll keep you posted on our progress—in both," I said.

"See that you do." Kooper terminated the conversation.

"Well, we have our orders," I studied Zanfield and Vik. "How did Perri's training go this morning?"

"It went well," Vik said. "Travis came to help, and we went through the care and cleaning of blades, followed by beginning stretching. I'm glad Travis was there to tell her that this is how training has been done on Falchan for thousands of years. She wanted to pick up a practice sword first thing."

"Good. Let me know when it gets to the point where Zan and Perri can practice together."

"I will."

"Can you make yourself available after the midday meal? Looks like we have another coin to examine."

"Yeah. I'll be there."

~

Queen's Palace, Le-Ath Veronis

Kooper

"Our instructor would hit us on the head if we let our minds wander or talked during meditation," Crane, Dragon's brother, informed me.

"How old were you?" I forced myself not to be angered by his words.

"Four. You have a lot of catching up to do. Your comp-vid is being watched by a reliable assistant, who will rush in if the universes implode. Now, clear your mind and begin again."

Here we were, in the Queen's arboretum, while I attempted to contain my thoughts and my temper. Crane chose the area because we were surrounded by plants and trees, and nearby, a fountain made soothing water noises.

Soothing to him, perhaps. I just felt aggravated.

"Honey, just close your eyes." I jumped when Breanne appeared at my side, already folded into the proper pose for meditation.

My first thought was to pull her into my arms. The look in her eye and lift of an eyebrow told me to stay where I was. "I'll give you enough to get you relaxed," she told me. "After that, you really need to try for yourself. This will do a lot of good, if you'll stop telling yourself that you don't have time for it."

Stop behaving like a shedding snake, she told me in mindspeech.

They're half blind when they do that, and it makes them grumpy, I defended snakes everywhere.

You're not blind so you're over-compensating on the grumpy part. Now close your eyes and I'll send you what you need.

All right.

My breath caught as the first wave of love hit me—not as strong as she could send—not even close, mind you, but it was just enough. It helped me relax immediately.

We begin, Crane's mindspeech sounded pleased.

~

BlackWing XIII
Randl

"Dragon and Crane insisted on teaching Kooper how to meditate, after he kept putting it off," Vik grinned. "Mom sent mindspeech. He tried to wriggle and talk his way out of it today, too, but Bree showed up and things are going better, now."

"At least it's good news," I said, eyeing the pile of coins which had lain, undisturbed, on my desk since the last time Vik chose one.

Would someone need our help again? Would I meet another that Vik wouldn't see? I carried the coin I'd received the last time in my pocket, which was tightly buttoned. It felt right that I should carry it, somehow—*as if it were safe with me.*

Why it needed protection I had no idea, but I wasn't going to have an argument with myself over it; I had no facts to support either side.

"Ready?" Vik asked, his hand hovering over the pile of coins.

"I suppose," I said and watched as Vik lifted a disc of gold away from the others.

~

Founder's Palace, Campiaa
Wyatt

Opal and Kell stood in Dad's study, waiting with me. Dad hadn't come back from a meeting with the Fruit and Vegetable Growers of the Campiaan Alliance, or FVGCA. I didn't know which was harder to say when pressed to say it quickly.

Jett was on his way, too, but he'd been in a meeting with security from the member planets across the Campiaan Alliance. None of them wanted what happened to the Reth Alliance world of Ru'beq to happen on their worlds. Jett was forced to give advice on how to increase security, at a time when the Prophet was almost unstoppable if he targeted someone.

If we had that sort of information, we'd have employed it to keep him from nearly destroying Campiaa.

Opal and Kell had done some reconnaissance on the shipyard destroyed on the small planet of Gis. They'd gone in undercover, of course, while Kooper and Jett got Randl and BlackWings X and XIII there as fast as mundanely possible.

I had no idea what their information was, but I asked them to wait until Dad and Jett arrived, so they wouldn't have to tell it twice.

"What do you have?" Dad walked into the office faster than most people ran.

"Kooper asked us to represent him in this meeting," Kell said. "We have some disturbing news."

"What's that? Ah, Jett, good," Dad said when Jett folded in.

"We found that Stone Wicke caused the original destruction of that shipyard," Kell reported. "We tailed a few employees after our arrival, and we're almost certain that they all have new obsessions. Our supposition is that the Prophet came looking into the matter, shortly after it happened."

"Not good news," Dad shook his head.

"Oh, there's more," Opal said. "We found out who Stone Wicke works for."

"Who?" Jett demanded.

"Mebbers." Kell's voice held anger.

"We thought him long dead," Dad frowned.

"Evidently not," Opal sniffed. "It appears that the owner of the shipyard was invited to one of Mebbers' famous dinners, when he refused to hand over his inventory without payment. We found a servant who ran when the blood and guts started flying, so he escaped the obsession placed on the others who stayed behind."

"Is this information reliable?" Jett asked.

"I placed compulsion. It's reliable," Kell growled as his eyes narrowed.

"Not to worry, I believe you," Jett held up a hand. Kell was possibly the oldest living vampire, next to Tybus. Compulsion placed by either was as fool-proof as you could get, unless the subject had an obsession in place or a King Vampire at their elbow. Had an obsession been in place, Kell would have gotten no information at all.

"Then we need to get Randl there as quickly as possible," Dad said. "We should fold the ships in, rather than waiting for regular space travel to get them there."

"I agree," Opal said. "But there's a problem."

"What's that?"

"I tried to reach Randl in mindspeech. When he didn't answer, I contacted Travis. Travis says Randl went into *split-time* with Vik earlier, at Kooper's command. He hasn't returned, yet."

"Fucking hells," Dad rubbed his forehead.

"With your permission, I'll ask Travis and Trent to get the ships there and wait for Randl and Vik to arrive."

"Will they know where to go?" Jett asked.

"I think Randl focuses on the ship, so I hope that's the case."

"I don't know whether we should risk it," Dad said. "We don't need to fuck this up by moving too quickly."

"Then I'll tell them to stand by until Randl returns," Opal agreed.

"Thank you," Dad told her.

❧

BlackWing X
   Travis
   "How long have they been gone—in our time?" I asked Dori.

"More than two hours," she said. She'd come to X to have a private conversation with us.

"Sending the ships ahead and letting him catch up was discussed," I began.

"I will claw whoever made that suggestion myself if we're ordered to leave this space without him," Dori growled.

"I get that," I held up a hand. "It was just a suggestion, and it was shot down."

"Good." Her arms were now crossed tightly, as she glared at Trent and me. I understood without asking that she didn't like Kooper's orders in this matter—that Randl examine the coins, which would send him into *split-time*. She had no idea where Randl would end up, or whether he was in danger, even with Vik at his side.

"Randl ought to be able to make his own mind up about these things," Trent sighed.

"Exactly," Dori said quickly, unwinding her arms to point a finger in Trent's direction. "Kooper doesn't have a clue what's waiting, and he just sends him anyway." She tossed out the same hand in a gesture of frustration. The other hand now rested on her hip; a dangerous position for any man to be near.

"We understand what you're saying," I attempted to calm things down. "It almost made us crazy when the Prophet took Sabrina."

"That was only once," Trent took up the narrative. "I have no idea whether we'd be sane if she kept disappearing."

"Are you saying I'm not sane?"

Now you're in trouble, Vik grinned as he and Randl landed inside the captain's cubby.

"Dori, it's okay," Randl held up a hand. "We had to deliver merpeople to a compatible ocean, and that took time."

Randl

"Kooper said to transport the ships two hours out, and make our way in under normal means," Travis informed the crew in our meeting. "We're underway, now, so be prepared for anything once we arrive in Gis' orbit."

"Merpeople? For real?" David asked. We were back to the *split-time* trip Vik and I had taken.

"For real, dude," Vik answered the question. "Randl had to take them and their tank of water so they wouldn't suffer shock, and it gave us time to analyze the water and look for the closest thing we could come to it. Turns out, it was the Eastern Ocean on Avendor."

"Were they in danger? Like the others?" Perri asked.

"Man," Vik shook his head and lowered his eyes. "First time we've had to fight our way in; the guards were packed so tight around that aquarium tank there was no other way. The tank was what they used to hold them, until Ra'Ak and rogue gods could have seafood for dinner."

"Holy shit," Dori hissed beside me.

What we hadn't told them yet was that we'd fought while invisible. The enemy couldn't see us to fight back properly. I wasn't worried about killing innocents—all of them were tainted and served their masters willingly.

I also didn't mention to anyone—even Vik—the one who'd appeared to me before I lifted the merpeople and their tank away.

Another man coalesced the moment we reached the tank; I felt a connection to him like the one before, only this one tossed a small bag containing several coins to me.

His message was much like that of the first man's—a variation of *you'll figure it out*. I wasn't sure about that. All I had was a growing list of questions, while answers were as rare as a speeding inky-sloth.

Speeding or not, inky-sloths were extinct—just as the answers I sought could be.

～

P'loxett

V'dar

The spheres clicked at a rapid pace in my left hand as I considered my next move. I could transport myself to Mebbers' homeworld, but I preferred to take my workers and engineers with me, to dismantle Mebbers' compound and bring it back. That included Mebbers' ships and whatever information they could gather, which could take time.

Besides, I had to determine who had taken Varok and Jiles. They'd disappeared from Lee'Qee, and my connection to Varok had been broken, somehow. I could no longer determine his location.

That angered me.

I needed Mebbers' warlock—that was more than evident. He and Mebbers had recently raided and destroyed shipyard on Gis. I'd gone with a few of my people to get information shortly after. We'd gotten everything the remaining employees could give us, so I left them with obsessions to keep that knowledge from anyone else.

The best information was this, however. Mebbers had more than one warlock, although the one I wanted most was the strongest of the three who'd attacked the shipyard. Mebbers had walked in after the theft and destruction, like a Lord surveying his conquest.

I wanted that, too. Powerful warlocks or wizards under my command would convey how powerful *I* was. Why hadn't I done this before?

Besides, I could pull names of others from Stone Wicke—I felt confident of it. Ensnaring more of his kind held much appeal.

With power wielders working on where my missing slave could be, I would surely find Varok.

And I would kill his captors.

CHAPTER 15

Queen's Palace, Le-Ath Veronis

Lissa

"I only see the fog of obsession," Quin sighed. We could easily see the warlock and the other two captured in Lee'Qee. We on the other hand, were shielded from their sight and hearing.

"I imagine they're important to the Prophet," Erland said. He held the sight-and-sound dampening shield around us, while Quin examined the captives in my dungeon.

"You know he sent them to find out what the recent disturbance was in Lee'Qee," Kooper said.

"How long had they been there before we arrived?" I turned to Erland.

"Seconds," my handsome warlock mate shrugged.

"Do you suppose the Prophet saw anything?"

"No idea. I hope it was unexpected; Jiles certainly wasn't strong enough to detect the net I placed."

"Then I hope he doesn't know where to come looking for them," I said. "I don't need obsessed vampires."

"This gives me the shivers," Quin said, turning toward me.

"We can't put them in a normal facility—the Prophet will have them back in a blink, and destroy anybody in his way while he's at it," I said. "We have plenty of shields around this place, but we don't have shields around the people outside the palace or in any of my cities."

"We can't even feed them to a Ra'Ak without assuming that their obsession will be transferred to the Ra'Ak," Kooper sounded grim.

"That's—terrifying," I said after a moment's hesitation.

"It's like a virus, isn't it?" Quin asked.

"Yeah. It is." My shoulders sagged at the thought. "The universes are getting infected with all of this, and we don't have a cure. We don't even have the idea of a cure, or where to start on one."

"Do you think that's the ultimate goal—to infect everyone with the Prophet's disease? It can be transmitted through sex, blood, body fluids, the concrete we stand on and now ingested by eating something tainted with it."

"We've never put it together like that," I said. "Your statement is true, of course, but we've been fooling ourselves about it all along. What it could come down to, is that everyone except the very powerful could be affected, and pass it to their newborn children, too. All the Prophet would have to do is crook a finger, and anyone would do whatever he wanted."

"Fucking hells," Kooper hissed through clenched teeth. "What good is the Hierarchy, when even we can't control this?" He folded space before I could attempt to calm him down.

I'll find him, Bree sent.

She'd have to; I had plenty to consider, and little to help me do it. Kooper might need a babysitter, but I had babies of my own, the Prophet's minions in my dungeon, Le-Ath Veronis to protect and a way out of this to consider. I couldn't spare him any more of my time.

"I worry the Prophet will turn his sights on Karathia," Erland shook his head.

"We may all be in the Prophet's sights, we just don't know it yet," I countered.

"We'll find a way," Quin whispered, as she stared at the space previously occupied by Kooper. "We have to."

~

Gis

> *Randl*

The man shivered in my presence. Kell laid compulsion on him to answer questions truthfully; this was the only employee of the shipyard to escape the Prophet's influence.

The others obsessed by the Prophet's command had been rounded up already, although the CSD and the Governor of Gis were negotiating their fate. I didn't want to be Jett in that scenario; he had to convince the Governor that those men were a danger to anyone else, should the Prophet decide to command them further.

"You have nothing to fear," I told the man standing before me. He was terrified of Kell, Travis, me and anyone else in the room. That included Mak and Jak, who stood behind me as usual.

"Aren't you going to ask me anything?" He stumbled over some of his words out of fear.

"I don't have to," I held up a hand. The initial murder scene at Mebbers' table—the one that sent him running—still haunted him. Perhaps someday he'd be grateful that his mind was still his own, but it probably wouldn't be this day, or any in his near future.

"You were right to run," I added. "It saved your life and your mental health. Someday, I think you'll appreciate it, but not now. I understand that."

"I didn't do anything wrong," he dropped his eyes.

"I know that, too. I think we should keep you safe, however, since you're the only real survivor in all this mess."

"But there are others," he argued.

"They are not themselves, and may never be themselves again," I explained. "Do you have family here?"

"A son. My wife died two years ago."

I'd seen that in him already—living on a non-Alliance world meant he couldn't afford the medical procedures that would have saved her life.

"Where should we take them?" Kell asked.

"He's a good father," I said, causing the man to jerk his head up to stare at me. "Queen Lissa is placing orphans. Perhaps Cheel, here, would be willing to help. He could apply for Alliance membership and change his name, too, if he wants."

"How did you know to call me that?" Cheel asked. Cheel was his nickname and not his given name. At least he hadn't said the obvious —that I was blind, like everybody else I'd met.

"It's a gift," I shrugged. "Kell will take you and your son away from here, in case Mebbers or any of his crew come looking for you. He doesn't want anyone who doesn't work for him to recall seeing him, you understand."

"I know." His shoulders sagged in a helpless gesture.

"The Alliances aren't so bad," Kell said. "Come, we will find your son, gather your things and transport you to Le-Ath Veronis. A home will be found for you, once it's determined where those orphans will go."

"Where are they from? The orphans?" Cheel asked.

"We don't know," I said. "And that's the truth. They don't even know Alliance Common, so we're having to teach them."

"My son will be educated with them?" Cheel's hopes had risen. On Gis, only the more fortunate were educated. Cheel's mother had taught him, because she'd once been of that class. After she died, Cheel worked long hours and had barely taught his son to read.

"I think your son will receive a fine education," I assured him.

"Then I'm willing."

"Good. Come now, we will collect your son," Opal coaxed. She, Kell and Cheel disappeared. I blew out a long breath.

"What do you think will happen to the obsessed ones?" Travis asked.

"I don't know, yet. I have no idea how much Jett will have to tell the Governor to convince him to let him take them off the planet—for its own safety. Cheel consented—and that was the only obstacle we had to overcome. At least they have permission by law to leave Gis if they wish to. With an obsession, we can't rely on their permission being their own."

"And if they're ordered to kill their neighbors, no choice there, either," Mak snorted.

"Ready to go to the shipyard, or what's left of it?" Travis asked.

"Yeah. Let's go. Perri?" I turned to her. "We'll set down at the perimeter. You tell us if you sense warlock interference, or a spell left behind to harm anyone who comes looking. I'm not sure there's a spell still in place, since that would be a waste of a warlock's talents after they already destroyed it, but it never hurts to check. Vik, if you'll transport her," I nodded to him.

If a spell had been left behind to destroy a witch or warlock, then he'd keep her safe while she did her scenting routine.

"On it," Vik said.

"Ready?" I asked the others. After Travis' nod, I folded space while Vik skipped to the crime scene.

~

"Nothing so far," Perri reported as we took careful steps toward the ruin that once was an enormous scrapyard. Once I knew more about hidden spells, I'd place my hands on a broken wall to see whether I could tell what was taken by Mebbers.

My mind was on that when Perri drew an audible breath and froze.

"What?" I asked quickly. Everyone else had stopped in their tracks the moment Perri did. Vik, standing beside her, cast a questioning look in my direction, silently asking me if I knew what the trouble was.

I could see why he wanted that information; Perri was now visibly shaking.

"Perri," I said. "Tell us." My mindsight was already seeing her fears, however. She'd come across the remnants of a spell.

Placed by her father.

We know who her parents work for—and her uncle, I sent to Vik and Travis. *She sensed a spent spell of her father's,* I added.

Fucking hells, Vik swore.

Take her back to the ship, I said. *I think I can handle this from here.*

Vik disappeared with Perri, while Mak, Jak and Travis drew closer to me.

~

BlackWing XIII
  Perri

"What happened?" Dori asked when we arrived in the galley. Vik had contacted people on the ship and several were waiting for us. I didn't appreciate that. I didn't want Dori to see me so weak. Or David or Miz or—*Zanfield*.

"We found out that her father is one of Mebbers' warlocks," Vik's voice sounded rough and angry as he set me down. I was shaking so hard, I could no longer control myself. Deep down, embarrassment warred with my shock and fear.

"We need to get her to the infirmary," Dori snapped.

"No," Zanfield said. "I don't think she wants that."

"I don't," I stuttered through chattering teeth.

"Then what do you suggest?" Dori almost shouted at Zanfield.

"I need a blanket," Zanfield sounded calm as he approached me. "Now, while they're searching for that, it's time for you to sit," he said firmly, pulling me toward a chair. Sitting down sounded like a good idea, until he sat down first, pulled me onto his lap and wrapped his arms tightly about me.

"They're not worth it," he whispered against my hair. "Never have been, never will be. Gerrett is bringing something warm to drink, and Dori's gone for a blanket," he soothed. "You just got rattled by the surprise," he went on. "This happens, sometimes. Nothing to worry about."

He understood as well as I did that wherever my father was, my mother and uncle were, too. I think that troubled me more than anything—that Uncle Alken was with my parents, and they'd done nothing about him harming me—or Pauley.

"Shhhh, don't think about it," Zanfield murmured. "They can't hurt you here."

Had I already embarrassed myself? I made it worse by wrapping my arms around Zanfield's neck and sobbing.

∾

Randl

"I'll touch this wall," I said, reaching out to the broken concrete.

"Randl," Travis warned. Yes, I was aware that the Prophet could have his disease in any concrete anywhere.

We were about to find out if that were true here. "I don't feel his taint," I said. "But we can't discount any possibility. Trav, put a shield around my bodyguards."

I felt it when Travis' shield replaced mine around Mak and Jak; I was now on my own if anything went wrong. There was a possibility of an unexpected trip into *split-time*, too, but I didn't want to add that to the equation.

Stretching out a hand, I let it rest on the smoothest part of the broken wall. The visions came immediately.

∾

Kooper paced inside my office, while Travis stood nearby. I'd sent Mak and Jak to the galley for a meal—they were starving after my prolonged bout of visions at the ruined shipyard.

"Six hulls?" Kooper stopped to stare at me for the third time.

"And at least four engines which could be repaired to drive them," I said. "Plenty of other things were taken, too, including used solar drive crystals, although they're the old ones and prone to draining faster than the newer kind."

"They're in Mebbers' hands for the time being," Travis offered. "The Prophet doesn't have them yet, I don't think."

"Then we need to find Mebbers," Kooper growled. "Before the Prophet does."

"Too bad Mebbers didn't leave anything behind for us to examine, or anyone that we could question," I said.

"What?" Kooper had taken three steps into another bout of pacing, only to stop short at my words.

I saw it, then.

We had the shipyard's owner—his body, anyway. I had no idea whether that would give us the information we wanted, but it was a start. "What about the dinner—was it held at the shipyard?"

"No—at the owner's home," Kooper said. "Come on, we have things to do," he snapped. Before Travis and I could argue, he'd folded us back to Gis.

"At least there's no taint from the Prophet," I said as we studied the owner's body on a metal table. The head had been removed, courtesy of Stone Wicke, and lay at one end, near the neck. Blood had been washed away from the severed parts; seeing that on an empty stomach could have precipitated dry heaves. Stone wasn't neat about his work, and he'd made this death as painful as he could.

"It's a good way to get the employees to hand over whatever Mebbers wanted, I suppose." Travis shook his head at the grisly remains.

"Nothing on where Mebbers is located?" Kooper frowned at me.

"Nothing, Director."

"Then we'll go to the scene of the crime." Once again, he folded us away.

"Nice place," Travis looked about him. "Looks like junk pays well."

It did—the home was large and lavish—three stories of it, with a grand entrance and wide, curved steps leading upward.

"He wasn't held to the Alliance standards of pricing," Kooper grunted. "Let's go to the dining hall. I want information," he said, his eyes narrowing at me.

"If there's anything to find," I held up a hand. "I'll let you tap into what I see," I added. That way, he couldn't accuse me of holding anything back.

I turned to follow Kooper as he strode to the left, toward a wide doorway that led into another room, and then another after that, before we reached the formal dining hall. Chaos had happened here—that was evident. Several chairs were overturned as some guests attempted to flee.

"At least most of it's intact," I said, surveying the dining table. Blood stained the floor at one end of it—no guesswork involved as to whom it belonged to. Plates of smelly, congealing food lined both sides, still, and markers set out by the local police remained in place.

I studied the scene for a few moments, deciding what I wanted to put my hand on and where. Eventually, I chose the end where the blood left a dark stain on the Serendaan carpet, and laid a hand on the edge of the table.

I heard Kooper's intake of breath as he saw what I did—the last dinner held at this table.

~

Travis

I was included in Randl's visions. There we were, silent, invisible witnesses to Mebbers' latest murder at a dinner party.

I watched as the shipyard owner lifted a glass of wine to Mebbers, who sat at the opposite end of the table. Nearby, Stone Wicke sat, watching both men surreptitiously. He waited for a signal from Mebbers—I understood that much. We were about to watch the owner be relieved of his head in a torturous way.

"Give me the ships you have. I'll ensure you are rewarded later," Mebbers nodded to the owner. I knew—as did the owner, that Mebbers' words were insincere.

"Nothing leaves my business without payment first," the owner countered. "I'll give you a very good deal, sir, I assure you."

"But that's not what I want," Mebbers said. "Try harder to see my way in this."

"I cannot. I have employees and taxes to pay," the owner snapped.

"Well, then, I suppose I'll have to consider things while I taste the wine."

That was Stone's signal, apparently, because what followed had people running and screaming as the owner's head was sawed off by a warlock's power, and the victim screamed as long as he could before his throat was severed and gurgling was the only sound made past that.

It was ugly, unnecessary, and bloody. Another warlock, followed by a witch, went after fleeing guests. Those guests died or were coerced elsewhere; their blood wasn't on the floor like their employer's was.

Cheel ran the moment the carnage began; he'd been standing by the servant's entrance, waiting to refill wine glasses. He'd been lucky, too—he'd escaped, running in the opposite direction from the others. That had saved his life and kept him from being obsessed.

Randl, though, wasn't watching or listening to the owner after a while. Instead, he watched Stone Wicke carefully.

Abruptly, the vision stopped, and we found ourselves back in the dining room as it was, now, where the stench of rotting food was suddenly more apparent.

Without hesitation, Randl walked straight to the plate that Stone Wicke had eaten from, and slapped his hand on the remaining food. Kooper almost jumped as the delicate plate rang in protest at the assault.

Randl, when he turned toward Kooper and me, had stars in his eyes. "Mebbers is on A'pelur," he stated, his voice low and deep, like that of a bourdon bell.

"Where on A'pelur?" Kooper demanded.

"I don't know," Randl was back to himself. "I'm not sure it has a name."

~

Queen's Palace, Le-Ath Veronis

Lissa

"I saw it, Mom. I don't know whether Kooper registered it or not, but it was there." Travis had gotten away for a short visit, telling me he had news.

"This is interesting," I agreed. For now, the only ones I'd seen whose eyes had filled with stars were the Mighty and a few others in the Hierarchy—it was an indication of power.

"Should I put it in a report?" he asked.

"No. Honey, I think this is important, that we keep this to ourselves for now. You can tell your brother, but nobody else, understand? That means not discussing it with Randl, too."

"I can do that."

"Good. Are you hungry?" I knew he was, he just hadn't said anything.

"I could eat."

I wanted to laugh. Instead, I folded him to the kitchen to get him a plate of food.

~

BlackWing XIII

Randl

"Jett barely managed to convince the Governor to release those obsessed employees to him," I told Dori as I wolfed down food in the galley.

"We've set a course for A'pelur," she told me. "It'll take four days. I hope we get there before the Prophet does."

"I may go hunting before the ships arrive," I said, before biting into a roll dripping with butter. Gerrett had a magic touch when it came to baking bread, in my opinion.

"You better take somebody with you," she warned.

"I'll take Vik," I said.

"What about the coins?"

"I'll do one more tomorrow, and then turn my sights on A'pelur."

"Has Kooper agreed to this?"

"Haven't asked him. How's Perri doing?"

"I think she's fine. Of all the people to be able to calm her down, I'd have said Zanfield was last in that category."

"Hmmph."

"You know, you should keep me better informed," she pointed a finger at me. I ignored it and went after the squash casserole on my plate. I didn't explain that Zanfield had scars of his own where parents were concerned, so who better to understand the hurt and fear? No, they hadn't molested him, but he'd been neglected or punished, depending upon their mood or whim.

When faced with those events during childhood, one either became his tormentors, or transformed himself into their opposite. Zanfield was in the latter category. He was determined never to make another suffer as he'd suffered.

He felt strongly about Perri's treatment—by both her parents and her uncle. Thankfully, Perri had responded well to Zanfield's efforts, rather than rejecting them. I hoped it boded well for her future, convincing her to accept help when it was offered.

"Where is she now?" I thought to ask.

"Asleep, I think. She's in her cabin."

"Good. Going after her parents and uncle on A'pelur won't be easy on her. I may have to talk with Kooper about keeping her out of this."

"That—may be a good idea," Dori said after a moment's consideration. "It could end badly for any of them, and that could be a problem."

"I believe the ASD regulations support it," I said. "If you're related to a target or a victim, you're kept out of the investigation."

"Or in this case, the fight," Dori huffed, turning her head away.

"You're right. Whether it's just Mebbers and his power wielders, or Mebbers and the Prophet, it'll be a fight for sure."

"You're not making me feel better about it."

I'm sorry, baby, I sent to her. *Somebody has to do this, and that somebody is us.*

"I know." Her admission came with a weary sigh. "It would be nice to have a break from it, though."

"I understand that." She wanted some time alone together, when neither of us had to worry about the job or someone else's health or happiness. "I'll try to make it happen, I promise."

"Try to make it soon."

"I'll see what I can do."

"Want dessert?" she asked, as I scraped up the last of my food and stuffed it in my mouth.

I nodded while chewing, so she rose from the table and headed for the cold keeper. Shortly after, I had a dish of ice cream sitting in front of me. "Want some of this?" I offered.

"I had two bowls earlier," she waved away my offer. "Eat it—it's gishi fruit ice cream from Niff's."

"Even better," I grinned at her and dipped my spoon into cold heaven.

~

Vik

"We don't know where Mebbers' compound is on A'pelur," Miz said. "Sabrina, Nari and Tiri will do what they can when we get close enough to orbit the planet, but there's nearly two billion in population, and it's roughly the size of Avendor, with two moons."

Once we'd learned which planet housed Mebbers' hideout, we'd set our course for it at best possible speed. Miz, I knew, was hoping to find his sister at the end of this journey, or the Prophet, in order to locate his sister.

He, David, Markus and I had settled inside Zanfield's cabin to discuss strategy while Randl had a private dinner with Dori. Zan's quarters were crowded with that many people, but a case of beer made everything better.

"That's a lot of ground to cover," David said. "Any idea where to start?"

"I'd say start with the less populated areas," Zanfield said. "If I were a criminal, I wouldn't want the common crowd knowing anything about me. Reports get filed that way."

"Unless he's paid off the A'pelur government," Markus suggested. "That's happened in the past. A'pelur is a Campiaan Alliance world, and they weren't always on the straight and narrow."

"Excellent descriptive phrase," David lifted his bottle of Refizani Blue.

"Stole it from you," Markus grinned and clinked his bottle against David's.

"He has to be hiding behind Sirenali—or Sirenali bones," I said. "Ry and Bel Erland have already done a scrying spell, and found nothing."

"How did they know to do that?" Miz asked.

"I asked them to," I shrugged. "While we were waiting for Randl to get back."

"Must be nice to just contact the Karathian King and Crown Prince and say, 'how about a scrying spell?'" Zanfield said.

Ry is my brother, I sent to Zanfield. *That's not common knowledge. I also trust that you can keep that secret?*

Does this mean Queen Lissa is also your mother?

It does.

That means you're also a brother to Travis and Trent. Damn, you have more connections than I do.

I'll try not to get all puffed up about it.

Zanfield stifled a snicker at my choice of words.

"Do you think Sabrina can get us close to Mebbers with her new contraption?" David asked Miz.

"It could," I broke in. "It isn't held back by Sirenali cloaking; that only works against the powerful. In this case, mundane could become quite handy."

I didn't say what else I was thinking. After Randl slapped his hand on congealed, rotting food to divine information about Stone Wicke, perhaps he could forge a connection with Sabrina's newest technology and force it to give him answers.

Travis had taken information to Mom about the change in Randl as he'd divined information on the warlock; she said to keep it quiet. I agreed with her. Something was happening, but I trusted Randl with my life—and the lives of everyone else aboard the BlackWing ships.

"I worry that the Prophet may know exactly where Mebbers is, while we're still fumbling around trying to find him," Markus said. "Are we only taking X and XIII?"

"I don't know. Maybe Randl does," I lifted my beer and drank.

"Might be nice to get some help," Markus observed. "We have no idea what kind of forces Mebbers has, and if the Prophet is waiting, too, he can command the dead."

"That opened up a few unexpected graves," David shuddered.

Randl, I sent. *I think Jett needs to pay attention to any cemeteries and mausoleums on A'pelur.*

Dude, you just gave me the willies. I'll pass that along, for sure.

A'pelur was acustomed to burying their dead, and a quick search on my comp-vid revealed that graveyards were everywhere.

Fucking hells.

~

P'loxett

V'dar

"We have no new information to report," Perill informed me. Perill was more than motivated to find Varok; they were brothers.

"Any guesses, then?" I toyed with my spheres. They and others like them had been gifts from my father before his death. More and more, they weighed on my mind, until I had at least two in my pocket at all times.

"It could be anywhere, my Lord, including Wyyld II, Le-Ath Veronis or Kifirin."

"Hmmm," I considered his choices. The High Demons of Kifirin would be formidable foes, but they'd never volunteered for such duties before. That left Le-Ath Veronis or Wyyld II. I doubted the Founder of the Reth Alliance would want my employees anywhere near him, because of the threat I represented.

That left Le-Ath Veronis. Its Queen was also formidable, but its people could become vulnerable if I turned my attention to them. Not the vampires, mind, but the comesuli and humanoids.

All would come to me if commanded.

Still, the difficulty with Mebbers was nagging at me, too. "If Le-Ath Veronis holds Varok and the others, then they will continue to do so. They have a convenient habit of keeping prisoners safe and well-fed while they have them, and neither Varok nor Jiles will give them information. Is my ship ready?"

"It went for a trial run this morning," Perill dipped his head.

"Very good. I should make a short trip to A'pelur to do some advanced recruiting; this way, things will go much easier when we arrive."

"It will be as you say, my Lord." Perill dipped his head again and turned to leave. The moment he closed the door behind him, I rose from my seat, straightened my clothing, and folded space to A'pelur.

CHAPTER 16

BlackWing XIII
Randl

"No disturbed graves so far," Trent slid onto a guest chair in my office.

"Are they watching the graveyards and such, now?" I asked.

"With as much manpower as they can spare, which isn't much," Trent grumbled. "I'm not sure they took the concerns seriously, either. Jett is having a standoff with the A'pelurian Prime Minister."

"Fuck. I have a coin trip with Vik today, or I'd go myself."

"I could go," Trent began.

"No. If there is even the slightest chance the Prophet could show up," I said. "That's from your Commander. And your friend."

"What about security forces on the ground, then?" he countered.

"I think they'd have the good sense to run if they saw a grave opening."

"Well, there's that," Trent agreed.

"As long as I'm in *split-time*, I don't want anybody going ahead with that idea."

"All right."

"Tell Jett to compromise with the Prime Minister. Tell the Prime

Minister to aim discreet cameras on those places. If any of them are disturbed or interfered with, he should inform Jett right away."

"Because that could be the Prophet's doing," Trent nodded.

"Exactly. That cuts down on necessary manpower—one person can watch several camera feeds at once."

"I'll relay the information to Jett now."

"Good. Send a message to Dori when you get his answer."

"You rang?" Vik rapped on my open door.

"I did. We'll talk later," I waved as Travis disappeared.

"Road trip time, huh?" Vik, with both blades strapped to his back and his black leathers on, slid onto a chair with a slight creaking sound.

"I call it a coin trip, but it's the same thing." I rose from my chair, stretched and *Pulled* both my sheathed blades into my hands. Strapping on the harness, I watched as Vik considered the pile of coins on my desk before selecting one.

"Ready?" He stood and held the coin out to me.

"Would it change anything if I wasn't?"

"Hmmph. Not likely," he grimaced. Reaching out, I touched the coin and slipped us into *split-time*.

Is anybody here? Vik sent as we walked through empty hallway after deserted corridor, inside a massive, dome-shaped building.

I don't sense anything, and I don't hear anything either, I said.

Why did it bring us here? He asked, meaning the coin. We were traveling toward the center of the building, because the curved halls were getting sharper in their turns.

Prepare for a trap, I cautioned. Would someone finally be able to see us, here? The air held the heavy scent of fear, and I had no explanation for it. Everything was spotless, too, without a mote of dust anywhere. If the place had been abandoned, as it appeared to Vik and me, it should have been otherwise.

Doorways on our journey were all open, revealing empty rooms beyond. No furnishings of any kind were left there for us to consider. The walls were a pale, hazy blue, with no signs of normal wear on them. The stone floor, of variegated browns, looked the same—as if ours were the first feet to walk upon it.

The last turn we made led us straight to the center of the building, opening onto an enormous, grand theater of sorts—also empty. Row upon row of circular, stone seats stretched downward toward a large, round dais. I blinked at my surroundings, while the fear in the air increased.

It is a sanctuary—for sacrifices made to the god, the woman sent while coalescing.

Vik, as usual, saw nothing.

Which god? I asked, tasting bile in my throat.

The god who always comes at the last, she replied. *We have to go; time is running short and we are in danger.*

But, I protested. Except for the feel of increasing fear, I saw no danger here. The building was empty and I'd seen none but her.

We are in what you call split-time, here. I cannot hold it long—there is a sacrifice taking place now.

My breath stopped at her words.

Vik, I turned toward him, *we have to go now.*

Take these with you, the woman said. My mouth opened in a silent shout when gold and silver coins poured from her open hands, flew in a curved flight and pounded into my back—so forcefully that I staggered as some of them hit me.

Go. Now. She shouted at me after the last coin struck. Swiftly, I turned toward Vik as she faded from my sight and the sanctuary came to life with the roar of a huge, bloodthirsty crowd. I grabbed Vik's arm, flying out of *split-time* and back to the ship.

Vik screamed in anger the entire way; it seems he'd also caught sight of what had been hidden from us all along—the sacrifices being made on the dais far below.

Sacrifices to the god who always comes at the last.

~

BlackWing X

    Travis

Vik couldn't stop breathing smoke. Clouds of it rose and dissipated about his head as he paced inside my quarters.

So far, he'd been too angry to speak; he'd growled instead as he made turns in the short space opposite my bed. I wasn't sure how long it would take for him to calm down enough to form coherent words.

"Can you tell me anything?" I asked after a while.

"Sacrifices. Fucking, bloody Ra'Ak, rogue gods, who the hell knows what else was there," he flung up a hand and went back to pacing.

"You didn't bring anyone back this time, did you?"

"Something happened, so we didn't see any of it until the last, and that's when Randl grabbed me and got us the hell out of there."

"He probably did the right thing. He'd stay and fight unless the odds were overwhelming."

"It was that, all right. To the tenth power, at least."

"Where is he? Randl?"

"Went straight to his office and shut the door. He's probably fuming, too. When I left, Dori was knocking on the door and yelling at him to let her in."

"That's not good. Look, want a drink? I think I need one."

"I'll take a bottle of the strongest thing you have."

"All right." Reaching into the bottom drawer in my bedside chest, I pulled out a full bottle of bourbon and handed it to him. "Pour one glass for me—the rest is yours," I said.

～

BlackWing XIII

    Randl

The sun and moon of my back tattoo now glittered gold and silver, because that's where the coins had embedded themselves.

How the fuck would I explain this to Dori, let alone anyone else? Vik hadn't seen the people I had in *split-time,* so my refusal to talk about it had now come to haunt me.

I'd finally sent mindspeech to Dori after she kept pounding on my office door; I told her we'd seen a sacrifice happening, and I needed to collect my thoughts. She'd left me alone after that.

I did need to collect my thoughts—after colliding with hundreds of coins, which were now attached to my body. I couldn't remove them, even with power. I'd tried that already and it was painful, so I let them be.

Dori my love, will you meet me in our cabin? I sent.

I'll be right there.

Thank you. I folded space to our shared cabin and removed my shirt. Time to come clean with my beloved, first.

~

"What is it?" she asked, the moment the door closed behind her.

"I want you to look at my tattoo and tell me if anything's different."

"Turn around," she made a circle with a finger. I turned my back to her, so she could see for herself.

"Did something happen?" she said. "Because I'm not finding anything."

"What?" I whirled to face her.

"It looks like it always does," she shrugged. "So, what happened?"

"I uh, got hit with some stuff. I thought it might have damaged the tattoo."

"Let me look closer." She gripped my arms and moved me around to look at the tattoo again. Her hands on my back sent shivers through me—it was something she often did in foreplay. I chewed my lower lip when my body responded in the usual way.

"Honey, I don't see it. You must be tougher that you think," she swatted my shoulder. "Now, do you want to talk about what you saw, or do you want to think about it some more?"

"I still need to digest it," I said, turning to kiss her. "Give me a few, all right? Vik's talking to Travis about it—as much as he can. It was really bad."

"I don't know how you can just walk into those situations and not come back scarred for life," she said.

"Just kiss me again, and get it out of my head," I coaxed.

"I'd be happy to," she replied.

Zanfield

"Two more days before we reach A'pelur," David said. "We'll recharge while in orbit."

"Vik's drunk," I said.

"Is that what you came to tell me?"

"It is."

"Where is he?"

"Asleep in his cabin. I had to ask Mak and Jak to carry him there; he passed out right after he skipped into the galley."

"You think he needs to be in the infirmary?"

"No. He just needs to sleep it off, I think."

"Did you report it to Randl?"

"No—he and ah, the Captain are both in their cabin."

"I—see," David nodded.

"It can happen—people often turn to sex for some reason after a death or deaths, as in this case."

"How did you find that out? That there were deaths?"

"From Travis. He said to let you know, since you're the senior officer in charge at the moment."

"I am, eh?"

"That's what he said."

"Nice. Well, carry on," David made a shooing motion. "I'll contact Markus and Miz. They shouldn't wake anyone unless it's an emergency."

Perri

"Do you know what happened?" I asked.

Zanfield set a cup of tea on the other side of my galley table and sat down with a sigh. "It ah, appears that Vik and Randl saw something horrible and came back to the ship in a rush to get away from it." He stared out the nearby window without really watching stars slip past. I watched his face as he sipped tea—it had become a mask to conceal what he knew.

"You don't want to tell me what it was, do you?" I couldn't decide whether that upset me or made me feel protected because he wanted to hold it back from harming me in some way.

"I don't—but not because I don't want you to know. I don't want it to upset you. Vik is drunk and passed out in his quarters because of it —so it's not an easy thing to hear."

"Tell me in the shortest, blandest terms, then," I said.

"Sacrifices. The humanoid kind. They couldn't save any of them."

"Oh." After a moment, when all sorts of scenarios passed through my imagination, I shivered.

"I wanted to keep that from happening." Zanfield noticed the shiver, since he was now watching me carefully.

"I appreciate that," I told him. "But what kind of agent will I be if bad news or horrible things wreck me every time?"

"Vik has been an agent for years," Zanfield pointed out. "You see how he's sleeping off a drinking binge after seeing horrible things."

I blinked at Zanfield. He was right. Plus, Vik was High Demon, and they were scary as hell to begin with. "That puts things into perspective," I nodded at his assessment. "How do you know all this?"

"I've had plenty of time to study anything I wanted," he shrugged. "I know enough about psychology, because well, because. I could get a practitioner's certificate if I wanted. I do have a med-tech's license, and can set a broken bone if I have to."

"You have a med-tech's license? Why?" I couldn't figure out why a very wealthy man would bother with that sort of thing.

"To see if I could do it. I could have gotten a physician's license if I'd kept at it and attended classes, but I didn't want to be stared at every day because I was the one with all the money."

"That sets you apart, doesn't it?" I was only beginning to understand that.

"Yes. Everybody in both Alliances knows about Zanfield Staggs. A lot of people outside the Alliances know about me, too. I'm envied, cursed and targeted no matter where I go. That's why it's nice to be here. Randl and the crew don't look at me that way, so I'm grateful. And, this is a wish fulfilled. I've wanted to do this since I was young. I had no idea it would ever be possible in the real world."

"What did you have to do to convince them?"

"I didn't. They initially came to me, because they needed help getting into a casino undercover. I provided their cover. Randl, though—when he acquired this ship, he asked me to be a part of the crew. That was the proudest moment of my life."

"So, what are all those vids of you in costume at casinos about?" I asked.

"People expect a show from eccentrics. I gave them that. Plus, I loved the uniforms."

"I'd never have known," I teased him. He always looked as if he were freshly laundered and pressed, with the creases perfect on his uniform. I'd never seen him out of uniform, and only now realized that.

"Do you wear something else for blade practice?" I asked. "Travis says we may be sparring soon—you with your off-hand, of course."

"I do. Vik says it's stupid to ruin a uniform with practice, so I dress like a Falchani," he grinned.

"Authentic to the smallest detail, I presume?"

"What other way is there?"

I giggled.

I don't giggle.

Ever.

A smile curved Zanfield's lips; it lit his entire face.

"We have a problem," Markus rushed into the galley, Miz right behind him.

"What's that?" Zanfield was standing in a heartbeat, his chair scraping across the floor with a sharp squeak.

"Those two dead bodies are flailing inside their sealed container," Miz said, then shivered.

At least I wasn't the only one to react that way to something horrific.

~

Randl

Akrinn and Lorvis stopped jerking shortly after they'd started. That's why Travis, Trent and I watched the recorded vid of it, over and over.

"There aren't any planets for light years, except for A'pelur," Trent shook his head as we ran the images back to watch again. "Here's the time and location data," he pointed out the information on his comp-vid.

"How close were we to A'pelur at the time?" I asked.

"A day and a half out," Travis replied. "The other planets in that system are uninhabitable. As in you'll melt, your ship will melt—that sort of thing."

"Do you think the Prophet visited A'pelur, then?" Trent asked.

"I don't know what or who else could animate those bodies," I said. "Any word from A'pelur on interrupted vid recordings in graveyards?"

"Nothing yet, but I'll contact Jett."

"Send him a copy of this recording," I said. "This concerns me. Even if there's no evidence from A'pelur, it concerns me."

"Are there maps of all graveyards on A'pelur?" I asked.

"Pulling those up now," Travis said. "I've sent the information to you."

"Send it to Quin, too."

"Done."

"Have Miz and Markus contact me immediately if those bodies so much as twitch again."

"Will do."

"Good. I'll be in my office, looking at graveyard maps."

"I think there may be a song in that, somewhere."

"Yeah. We'll write that one later," I waved a hand and folded into my office.

~

I have an uneasy feeling about this, Quin sent. She and I were doing the same thing—scanning the maps of graveyards on A'pelur. *How many are buried there—in your estimation?*

The records show nearly a billion marked burials, but you know he's always chosen the fresher graves. The trouble is, A'pelur has a very stringent embalming process, which preserves bodies sometimes for centuries, without much decomposition. Something to do with an old king who wanted to be preserved for eternity, so he laid down the law, as Travis would say. It survived through the transition to a Campiaan Alliance world.

Because of tradition or superstition or whatever, Quin sent a mental sigh. *That's not good.*

Not for us, anyway, if the Prophet has been there and managed to hide the evidence of it.

That's what I would do—make sure nobody knew I was there if I could.

Same here. We still don't know where Mebbers' stronghold is, so the Prophet likely is ahead of us, there.

All he has to do is grab an employee of Mebbers' and have compulsion laid. They'd tell him anything he wanted to know.

Or play the torture card. That works, too. Plus, if he can find several employees, he could walk right into the compound without lifting a finger.

I've always wondered how long it takes him to work his necromancy spell.

No idea. It's possible that we happened to cross paths, too—him just before leaving A'pelur, while we reached his range of effect. The bodies flopped and jerked for ten minutes.

Do you think the reaction of the bodies may have been stronger outside their sealed container? Quin asked.

It's possible. We won't know unless they're out of it and back in proximity to the Prophet, and I don't want them out of that container.

I understand. They're too dangerous. I have to go—Justis has put dinner on hold.

The bodies were dangerous—and capable of spreading the Prophet's disease. As a sealed barometer of his nearness and influence, they were useful. Outside that purpose, they were hazardous to an extreme.

Go have dinner with Justis—I'll let you know of any new developments.

Thank you.

Absently, I pulled the first coin I'd received in *split-time* from my pocket. The bag I'd received on my second trip lay in a desk drawer. I wanted to carry them, too, but there were too many to fit easily in all my pockets.

Unless you make them smaller—and carry them like the ones on your back, whispered into my mind.

Opening the drawer, I pulled out the bag of coins and dumped them on my desk, being careful not to mix them with the other pile for coin trips.

Like the last coins—these were gold and silver, mixed.

How hard would it be to stamp them into my skin—like the ink of a tattoo?

Not hard, as it turned out.

Afterward, I surveyed my work; the all-seeing eye of Horus on my back was now filled in with gold and darkened silver. I hoped that nobody could see it—as Dori hadn't seen the others.

"You're the last," I told the first coin, and feeling contrary on its placement, I stamped it into my right upper arm, where tattoos generally lay. Then, I gave it rays of gold, as if it were a shining sun.

Somehow, it felt right.

I didn't notice the added weight of the coins, either, and I was grateful. For better or worse, if I ever faced the Prophet again, I'd carry the remnants of dead worlds with me, perhaps as a reminder.

A reminder of what could happen to the worlds currently in existence, if I failed to destroy V'dar.

I'd asked her which god the sacrifices were made for—the woman I'd seen on the last coin trip. She'd said, *the one who always comes at the last.*

Sacrifices.

I'd seen sacrifices.

Men, women and children, driven into holes and drowned in liquid concrete. Those whose bones were apparently being ground into powder and used as building materials in who knew how many places, so the Prophet could control whomever came close or inhabited those places.

The Prophet could control anyone through the very food they consumed if he wanted. Even after their deaths, he could control them for his own purposes.

How could V'dar be considered a god?

Were gods always gods in the beginning, or had they drawn power to themselves to become stronger—to become the gods they were —over time?

Was V'dar becoming?

Was he the one to come at the last?

Could we stop him before he controlled everything?

The deep breath I drew trembled with these new revelations. How could we stop him? Already he was too strong and elusive. We'd been chasing after him for nearly two years and hadn't come close to finding him.

All we'd done was beaten back his army. I'd angered him. Wounded him, perhaps, which only fueled his fury against me.

I had no doubt in my mind, now, that he could raise another army of the dead on A'pelur, should he desire it.

Kooper, I sent.

Randl? He sounded surprised to hear from me.

It's time, I told him.

Time for what?

To offer me in exchange for leaving A'pelur alone.

No.

You need to listen to me in this. There's too much at stake.

Come to a meeting on Le-Ath Veronis in three hours. We'll discuss this with all pertinent parties.

I'll be there.

~

P'loxett

V'dar

I had more than thirty of the small spheres. I couldn't carry all of them with me, so the two largest ones had been my choice to hold in my pocket and toy with upon occasion.

I'd been drawn to the box containing the others after my return from A'pelur.

What would Father's advice be in this?

Failing that, what would my uncle have said? He'd perished not long after my father's death.

Uncle V'ili wore a frown whenever he visited me—as if I were an aberration to his race. Father always said to ignore it—that Uncle V'ili acted that way most of the time. It no longer mattered; he was dead.

Father was also dead. All I had left of him were my spheres. *You were born for a purpose,* Father always said.

What purpose is that? I'd asked him when I was younger.

You were born to rule everything, he'd told me. I'd learned much from him throughout my life. He was quite powerful. Still, someone had killed him. I'd never learned who or how. Should I discover their name, I'd target them with the full force of my anger and power. They were an enemy, just as Randl Gage was an enemy.

I will avenge you, Father, I vowed silently to the spheres.

"Greetings," a wispy figure rose from one of the spheres in my box. "We are gifts from your father. Gifts of power, to make your transition complete."

I stared at the cloudy, ghost-like vision before me.

"Transition?" I couldn't decide whether I appreciated the sound of it.

"Your father, Liron, decreed it; therefore, our power now belongs to you," the wisp informed me.

"But," I held up a hand.

I staggered and fell as the might and energy contained in thirty-four spheres ripped into my body.

CHAPTER 17

*Q*ueen's *Palace, Le-Ath Veronis*
Randl

Travis, Vik and Dori insisted on coming with me. Dori knew something was up, and I also knew how strongly she'd object to my idea of a trade—me for A'pelur.

It won't stop the Prophet from taking other worlds, and if you die this time, what will they do next time? My conscience continued to nag at me.

If we laid a trap instead, would he suspect and prepare for that possibility?

"Even if you do this, as you suggested," Kooper's deep voice contained suppressed anger, "the damage is already done if the Prophet has invaded those graveyards. He can call on them anytime. This is foolish and you know it. You'll be throwing your life away for nothing."

What have you done? Dori turned toward me with a frown.

"I haven't done anything, yet," I said, hoping to calm her and Kooper at the same time.

"We have troops on the way," Jett informed us.

"Ships, too?" My breath stopped for a moment.

"Yes. Why?"

249

"Oh, no. No, no, no," I shook my head forcefully. "He may be hoping for exactly that—that we'll send ships he can take from us."

"He lost that game last time," Kooper growled.

"And has had plenty of time to reconsider and plan his next moves to prevent it from happening again," I said. "He has an idea of what he's up against, now, and he's not stupid, Director. Far from it, actually."

"He also has a weapons expert at his command," Travis pointed out quietly. "Le'Vestar Limn could be building whatever the Prophet wants, with the materials and expertise at his disposal. Face it—if he and Miz's sister could have broken away from the Prophet's obsession, they'd have done it by now. A single ship, armed with ranos cannons, can do a lot of damage. If the Prophet is on board, well, we've seen what sort of damage he can do, all by himself."

"We still don't know where Mebbers is, and we could be dealing with him and the Prophet at the same time when we get there," I said.

"Then I suggest you go now," Kooper snapped. "I'll send the other BlackWing ships to join you, to support Jett and his people. Surely you can take out one ship, no matter how it's armed or protected. We will not offer a trade for you. Not now. That is my command."

This will kill Miz, if it kills his sister, Travis remarked in mindspeech.

I know. Come on, we have preparations to make. Will you contact the rest of the BlackWing fleet? Have them flying their pirate flags when they arrive in A'pelur's orbit. I'll inform Jett not to shoot at us.

On it.

"Director," Vik said, his voice thoughtful. "I understand it's your job to send your agents into danger now and then. Generally, they have a chance at survival when they go. I'd consider this carefully, if I were you."

"You're afraid of the Prophet?" Kooper demanded.

"Hell, yes. I'm not worried about me, though. I'm worried about the rest of the fleet. You're sending them into grave danger, and you know it."

"Then what's your suggestion, Agent Roth?"

"Keep the ships away who have nobody with power aboard. They're the most vulnerable to the Prophet's influence."

"I agree with Agent Roth," Jett spoke for the first time. "Leave them out of it. You know what could happen to them, otherwise."

"That only leaves BlackWings I, II and VII," Kooper complained.

"Then only send those," Queen Lissa said. "Vik is right in this. At least the ones with power have some kind of defense against this menace."

"Fine. What about Jett's ships?"

"I'd like to leave them out of this fight, too," I said.

"I can pull them back far enough that a ship's sensors won't detect them," Jett offered.

"Then do that." Kooper's anger was heating up again.

"I'll ride on XIII, with Randl's permission," Jett turned to me.

"That's fine," I agreed. "Are you ready to go now, or do you want some time before boarding?"

"I'll come now. Do you have a ranos rifle I can borrow?"

"Of course."

"Director." I jerked my head in a half-nod at Kooper. It wasn't anyone's fault that he wanted to tear into the enemy and destroy them. He was welcome to come, take up a rifle and use it if necessary.

I hadn't made the rules that bound the Hierarchy. Perhaps it was time someone reminded him of that; I sure as hell didn't want to.

"Let's go," I said, my voice sharper than intended. Travis folded us away from Le-Ath Veronis; my anger was showing, too.

P'Loxett

 V'dar

"You're sure of this?" I asked. I felt more powerful now than I ever had, and with my new power came new advisors. I found I trusted their opinions and advice.

Very sure. The same one spoke for all, I learned quickly.

"Then I should go now to lay the trap." I smiled at the thought.

They said he'd come—the one I wanted more than anything. I would be most pleased to kill him this time. With my new companions inhabiting my body, how could I fail?

∼

BlackWing XIII
Crew Meeting with X and XIII
Randl

"Zan, I want you to monitor Akrinn and Lorvis. If they so much as move a little finger while we're in orbit around A'pelur, I need to know it," I said.

"What can I do?" Perri asked. She and Zanfield sat next to one another. I didn't want to speculate yet; things would work out or they wouldn't.

"Perri, how far away can you sense a warlock or witch's talent? I know this is difficult for you, but we have to find Mebbers' hideout. If we don't and the Prophet gets there first, then he'll have an entire nest of criminals at his disposal to fight us."

"Usually I have to be close," she began, although she sounded better about performing the task than I thought she would.

"We may be able to help Perri with that," Nari and Tiri volunteered. "And, with the support of the technology that Sabrina is developing, we may be able to pull all of us together to find Mebbers —or those who work for him, at least."

Sabrina, who sat with Travis and Trent, turned toward the twins and blinked. "You think so?" she asked them.

"We have DNA from Perri, which will be close enough to that of three powerful Karathians on the surface of the planet. If we work our talent of vibration locating into your equipment, and bring Perri's ability to sniff out power signatures with us, I think we have a chance," Nari explained.

I stared at the twins—*could this work?* "Go, then," I said. "Keep me advised."

"On it," Sabrina stood, as did the twins and Perri.

"Good luck," Zanfield said softly to Perri, who turned briefly to give him a grateful nod.

If what they proposed actually worked, it could be a first—when multiple talents were combined with technology to achieve a specific result.

I liked the idea.

"Who's bringing the other three BlackWing ships?" Jett asked.

"They're bringing themselves—there's someone powerful enough aboard all three," Travis replied. "When they meet us here, we'll fold space to a designated orbit around A'pelur. If Sabrina and the others have their machine working, I hope we'll find Mebbers quickly."

"We don't know when the Prophet will come, do we?" Vik said.

"We don't. If we find Mebbers, though, then we may have enough time to clean out his nest and substitute BlackWing crew members," I responded. "Mebbers' people won't know how to fight the reanimated dead the Prophet will send against them. Opening fire and blasting them will only release the Prophet's disease and infect anyone close enough. We on the other hand, have handled this before."

"On Campiaa," Zanfield agreed.

"Prepare yourselves for battle," Travis stood. "When the other ships join us, we'll fold space to A'pelur. Good luck, everyone."

The only coin I now kept in my pocket was the coin from Vogeffa II. The one I'd seen my mother's image in. I sat at my desk, fingering the coin and contemplating a coming battle. I considered what we had to work with, what might be thrown at us, and how to counter V'dar's cunning with that of our own.

Was it Destiny? Did it happen on its own? I was thrown into *split-time* to see my mother again.

That was the last thing I wanted—at such a volatile time.

BlackWing X

    Travis

Bear Wright and Amos Thompson arrived first, in BlackWing I. BlackWing II wasn't far behind, and two of the eight reptanoid brothers, Farzi and Nenzi, joined us in the ship's galley. Jett had only met them a time or two, so they were catching up over cups of tea or coffee.

When VII arrived, I was surprised to see it captained by Lynx, the former Saa Thalarr. With him was Lion, a tall, well-muscled black man who was also retired from the Saa Thalarr. Lion grinned and almost crushed me in a hug; we hadn't seen one another in a while.

"Jett, this is Lion, and this is Lynx," I introduced them. Jett's eyebrows went up when he clasped hands with Lion and then Lynx. *They're powerful,* he sent to me in surprised mindspeech.

Very, I replied. *Although they have a strict set of rules to follow. That doesn't keep them from protecting themselves or those around them,* I was quick to add.

I didn't say that Farzi and Nenzi were more powerful than that, and also had a set of rules to follow.

Kooper could be here with them, I reminded myself. After the last time he'd faced the enemy on Campiaa, though, I felt as if it angered him that Randl had acted to keep him from breaking the Hierarchy's rules and tearing into everyone.

I had no idea how he'd have come out of that fight, if he'd done as he wanted to do. Was that why he was hanging back now? Because he was afraid of losing his temper—and his power—by breaking the rules?

He had a lot to lose—I realized that. The most important thing in that could be his mate, Breanne.

"Where Randl?" Nenzi asked in a reptanoid's standard, shortened version of Alliance Common.

"Thinking in his office," I said. "He's probably looking at this from every angle, and calculating what the Prophet will do in any situation."

"He do well with that," Farzi gave me a nod. I agreed with him.

Lately, Randl had been a half-step ahead of the Prophet in most things. There'd been a few surprises, but how could there not be?

~

Commander Randl Gage's Office, BlackWing XIII
  Zaria
For a moment, I studied the pile of gold coins remaining on Randl's wooden behemoth of a desk, considering how these particular coins had come to be there.

Randl still thought of them as coin trips.

They weren't.

They were designated for other assignments. "You know where you belong," I told them softly. "Go now. Time is short and you are needed."

The coins disappeared quickly while I watched. This—had been long in the design and the doing. Many fates rested on those ancient plans. Allowing my shoulders to sag with a sigh, I turned my thoughts to Randl, and how things were going with him.

There was no easy way in this for him, and the timing couldn't have been worse. *We live or die together, as it has always been,* I breathed the oath silently. It was a borrowed oath, from a long-ago time. It was true then, and true now. I had already waged war in this battle. Only time would tell if I needed to take a more active role.

Now, to wait. Perhaps I would keep myself busy in the meantime.

An idea formed.

Yes.

I folded space.

~

Avii Castle
  Quin
I leaned over the glass balcony outside Justis' and my suite, to get a closer glimpse of the tourist boats below. Somehow, six tourists had

planned a concerted jumping, all of them landing in the water simultaneously.

We had four guards on boat duty at all times, and none of these jumpers were close together.

"Justis," I shouted at him; he was puttering about inside our suite and heard me clearly.

"There are two more jumpers than the guards can handle," I told him.

"Let's go." His wings unfurled with a mighty snap; I was right behind him as he raced toward the edge and leapt off the balcony in a perfect dive.

Take the woman to the east, Justis sent mindspeech as we hurtled toward the water, chill air whistling past us at such great speed. The woman in question, and a man south of her, were struggling to stay afloat in rough, freezing waters.

Four guards were already collecting the others, but there was no time for them to drop off their first rescues and go after the others before they went under.

Make a hook of an elbow, I sent to the struggling woman as I neared the water's surface. It was so choppy, I could be swept into it if I had to dive in to save the woman. Not far away, Justis already had a grip on the man's arm and was pulling him out of the water.

I barely managed to hook my arm into the crook of the woman's elbow as the tips of my wings touched the sea's surface.

Lift, Quin, Justis shouted his mindspeech.

I did, flapping my wings furiously to gain height, pulling the woman from greedy waters sucking her under. Her arm suddenly went limp, forcing me to drop again to grab a hand.

That's when it happened.

My strength improved; with only her fingers clinging to mine, I jerked her from the water and flapped swiftly toward the nearest tourist boat. Releasing the hand I held while hovering over an empty section of the deck, I let her drop. She flopped and rolled ungracefully before coming to a stop against Justis' feet.

Justis held his rescued man in a tight grip; he'd determined exactly what I knew the moment I saw the woman's face; they'd planned this in an attempt to get to us—and Pauley.

In all the rush of tourists to watch the rescues of six who'd leapt overboard, three others had dropped into the water from a smaller, private craft not far away. They were clad in diving suits and carrying portable breathing gear.

They were swimming even now to the crevice at the base of Avii Castle.

"Hmmph," I glared at the woman. "See where this got you?" I turned, and lifting my arms, used newly-acquired power to *Pull* three men straight from the water and back to the boat.

They were quite surprised—and fearful—when their masks were forcibly removed by the Avii King.

I could see many things in their faces besides fear. *I know where Mebbers is,* I informed Justis. *We have to tell the others.*

"Oskar," Justis turned toward the guard who appeared at his elbow. "Take all nine of these into custody, and have them transferred to Queen Lissa's dungeon for questioning."

"It will be done, my King," Oskar dipped his head. The crowd gasped as four winged guards rounded up the jumpers and the swimmers, to take them to Queen Lissa.

Justis drew the medallion that Zaria had given him from beneath his shirt and stared at it before lifting his eyes to mine.

We both wore a medallion given by her.

Zaria had given us gifts beyond price.

Pauley is fine, Teren reported. *He's quite taken with the rescues, actually.*

Teren, Franc and Pauley all wore a medallion. Teren's had given him mindspeech. I wondered what else he might have.

We'll be right there—we have information for the BlackWing ships, Justis reported. Before he released his wings to fly back, he winked at me.

The oohs and aahs of the tourist crowd came the moment we lifted off the boat to fly back to our terrace.

∼

BlackWing X

Travis

Where is Randl? He's not answering my mindspeech. I was surprised to hear from Quin. I was even more surprised to learn that Randl hadn't replied to her.

He's in his office—or that's where he was, I told her. *Wait—I'm folding in there, now.*

The moment I materialized inside Randl's office, I knew something was wrong. Not only was he gone, but so was the pile of coins he'd gathered to take coin trips.

"What the bloody fuck?" I said aloud. *Quin, he's gone. I don't know where he is,* I informed her.

Oh, no. Travis, I know where Mebbers' compound is. We have to find Randl, and get him there as quickly as possible. Somehow, this is really, really important. I can't explain how, I just know that it is.

I'll alert the others and start looking—we have to have him in this fight, I said. I understood her urgency—I was beginning to feel it myself.

Here are the coordinates, Quin said, relaying them to me. Hastily, I jerked my comp-vid from a pocket and tapped the information into it, before sending it to Trent, Jett and Kooper.

Fucking hells, Kooper responded quickly, before landing in Randl's office. "Where is he?" he demanded, after finding Randl's desk chair empty.

"I don't know," I snapped back. "I came in here to see why he didn't answer Quin's mindspeech, and he was gone."

Jett, Vik and Dori arrived together; I assumed Jett had alerted the others already, although I hadn't told him about Randl's disappearance.

That fact was obvious to Dori, the moment she arrived.

"Do you know where he went?" she asked. I could see she was frightened; I would be terrified if anyone I cared deeply about vanished without a word. Nobody, myself included, had been able to reach him in mindspeech.

I was almost as worried about Randl's disappearance as Dori, but when Miz, Zanfield, Perri and Markus arrived, concern tightening their features, my worries ramped up exponentially.

"Where could he have gone?" Vik demanded, before discovering that the pile of coins on Randl's desk was missing. "What the bloody, head-banging hells is going on?" His words were punctuated by a cloud of smoke pouring from his nostrils.

"We know where Mebbers' compound is," Kooper growled, his voice and expression hard as stone. "Set your course accordingly. We'll be underway in five. If Randl isn't back by that time, then we'll do this without him."

Trent arrived with Farzi and Nenzi at that moment, and both reptanoids frowned fiercely at Kooper, as if they were having a heated discussion in mindspeech.

Kooper's skin turned from scales to flesh and back again as they silently argued. I'm sure Farzi and Nenzi were saying exactly what I was thinking—that we needed Randl in this fight, and to go without him was stupidity we could measure on a massive scale.

Mebbers we might be able to handle. An army of the dead and the Prophet at the same time?

Idiocy.

"We're going." Kooper snarled at the reptanoids. "Captains, set your courses now." He gave Dori a hard look. She gave him a harder frown back.

Do it, I sent to her. *We need you. If Randl gets back, I hope he can find us. It's not like it's a secret that we're going to A'pelur.*

"I'm not doing this for you," Dori hissed at Kooper. "I'm doing it for the people on these ships."

She turned abruptly to walk out of Randl's office. "We'll discuss insubordination after this is over," Kooper growled at her back.

"Take your best shot, Director," she whirled to snap at him, before striding through the door.

Walking to the bridge would give Randl a few more minutes to appear. I considered that Dori had the right idea in this.

"Well?" Kooper turned to me.

"On my way, Director." I folded space to X—and the farthest place inside it from the bridge. Like Dori, I began my trek toward the seat of command, casually inspecting the ship as I went.

I can hold things off for a bit longer, David sent. *XIII may be having issues with the solar cell connection to the ship's engines.*

Do it, I said. *With Dori's permission, of course.*

She already said yes. I just wanted to pass it by you to make it official.

Consider it official.

Aye, Cap'n, he sent in his native English.

He sounded like an Earth pirate—even in mindspeech.

~

Vogeffa II, Past
Randl

She had no idea who I was.

My mother.

She'd been so deep in labor when I found her struggling to stay in the shadows of Gungl, that she'd accepted the help of a stranger to get back to her small apartment over a crumbling marketplace.

Gungl wasn't a friendly place, and many would have taken advantage of the situation, robbing her of what little she had and leaving her to die in the streets. She wasn't pregnant with me—I'd been born in my father's village, which was more than two day's ride out of Gungl.

"Only a little farther," I coaxed as another contraction hit. She'd declined my offer to carry her—she didn't trust me that much.

She didn't trust anyone.

Except.

She'd met my father. She trusted Brandl Gage more than any other. I'd been connected to Quin's healing power once; I hoped I retained enough of that knowledge to help now.

The outside door, with stairs just beyond, was hanging off its hinges and clinging at a desperate angle as I helped her inside. Before long, someone would steal the door altogether, and there'd be nothing to keep the weather out of the stairwell.

"Step," I said softly as we came to the bottom tread. She groaned and leaned heavier against me.

"Let me carry you," I pleaded again. In her pain, it took a moment to register my words. Eventually, she dipped her head in acceptance. Lifting her easily, I took the steps two at a time, hoping the dilapidated wood could hold our combined weight.

Once inside the tiny apartment, I laid her on the narrow bed inside the small space. Next to the bed was a tiny table, and I saw it, then— the same coin I also carried in my pocket. Somehow, the Prophet had obtained it after this event.

"It's coming," she groaned, diverting my attention to more important things. Arching her back, she half-screamed when another contraction hit. I was forced to act quickly, removing her clothing as carefully as I could so as not to tear anything. She had precious little to replace anything she owned.

"Push," I told her. "And breathe," I added. The grunt she made as she pushed told me how much effort it took. Panting breaths followed, as her body attempted a short recovery.

"Aauuuugh," her groan came again as she arched, writhed and pushed, before collapsing onto the bed and panting again. Putting my hands on her, I attempted to give her strength to get through this.

"I see the head," I told her. "Push again."

The rest of the child came out in a relative rush, along with a gush of blood and fluid from the womb. Rising from the kneeling position I'd taken beside the bed, I made my way to the end, to lift the child and cut the cord.

When I reached out to touch the baby boy, who was now wriggling and making mewling noises, I saw it. Beneath smears of my mother's blood, flesh-colored scales covered his face and body. Gripped by a moment of fear and recognition, I was blown against the wall of my mother's tiny apartment when *they* appeared.

∾

BlackWing X

Travis

"You've delayed long enough," Kooper thundered. "Get underway or I'll move all these gods-forsaken ships to A'pelur myself."

He'd caught us doing exactly what we were accused of doing—stalling. Even Farzi, Bear Wright and Lynx had added their efforts to the mix. They understood what Kooper didn't—we could be hurtling toward our own death. Suicide by impatience, in my estimation.

I was issuing the command to get underway when Kooper made good on his threat, tossing us so violently toward A'pelur that many of us were thrown off our feet in the abrupt launch, and then again when we abruptly reached his chosen destination, coming to a ship-somersaulting end before settling into orbit.

We had injury reports immediately.

The Director had taken his anger to the extreme and harmed his own people.

∼

Vogeffa II, Past

Randl

When my addled senses returned, I understood who they were.

V'ili, perhaps the vilest Sirenali to ever live, and Liron, a rogue god, had arrived in my mother's room. Neither could see me where I lay, crumpled against the wall where I'd been tossed during the forceful blowback of Liron's arrival.

The other thing I knew?

Liron had taken V'ili's sperm, manipulated it, and then chose my mother as the vessel to bear the child—which bore his and V'ili's DNA. He had no care for my mother, or the fact that she'd initially refused him.

He'd ordered V'ili to lay compulsion to allow his violation, and then added to that terrible act by tossing a gold coin at her afterward. The same gold coin that lay on her bedside table now.

Do not interfere, a voice warned. The warning wasn't needed—I was in shock and felt powerless against what was happening before me.

"Bring the child," Liron snapped a command at V'ili.

"I don't want to touch that," V'ili drew back from the blood-and-fluid covered baby. "It's still attached," he whined back at Liron.

"Hmmph." Liron reached out and pinched the umbilical cord, severing it with a searing noise of fire.

"What about her?" V'ili asked as Liron *Pulled* a blanket of sorts into his hands and wrapped the child in it.

"She is of no further use to us," Liron snapped. "She'll die and we'll be done with her. The child is my objective."

With that, Liron disappeared.

V'ili hesitated for a moment, before his gaze fell on the coin atop the bedside table. He snatched it up and folded space while I stifled a gasp.

My mother moaned, then, and shifted in pain.

Liron was correct—she was dying.

That couldn't happen. Gathering my strength, I pushed myself to my feet and went to her. *Quin, help me now*, I begged silently, knowing she'd never hear me when and where I was.

Dredging up what little I'd learned during a brief healing session while Quin and I were connected, I went to help my mother as best I could.

~

Vogeffa II

Brandl Gage

I hadn't seen Mariana for several months. I'd been to market twice a month and looked for her every time, afraid to ask anyone for fear it would place her in danger. More and more, however, I imagined that the danger had already come to her, else she'd have visited my vegetable stall as she always did.

That's why, as I removed the planks from my now-empty makeshift tables and stowed them on my wagon, I was surprised to see a man approaching, carrying an unconscious woman in his arms.

As he came closer, I knew two things. First, I had no idea who he was; I'd never seen him before. Second, the woman he carried was Mariana.

"What happened?" I rushed toward the two.

"She's been ill," the man explained. "She asked me to bring her to you."

"What can I do?" I held out my arms to take her. Fear gripped my heart; it raced out of control as I searched her wan face for signs of life.

"She needs rest and care," he said, as I turned to carry her to my wagon. At least he'd wrapped her in bedclothes; I had nothing in the wagon to keep her warm against the chill of the trip home.

He helped me get her settled against the front of the wagon bed, directly behind the driver's seat. She'd be safer and warmer there, and I could keep an eye on her.

"She wants you to have this, too," the man drew a worn gold coin from a pocket and handed it to me.

"But," I protested.

"She wants you to have it." He pulled my hand toward him and slapped the coin into my palm.

"All right. Fine. Please say she'll make the trip—it's a long one," I said.

"Plenty of water, rest and food," the man told me.

"That I have," I nodded. Both were beneath the wagon seat and hidden against theft in Gungl.

"Good. Take care of her—and yourself, Master Gage."

"How do you know my name?" I frowned at the man.

"From her," he jerked his head toward the wagon.

"Oh. Of course. What's your name? So I can thank you properly?"

"Randl."

"That's it?"

"Just—Randl."

"Sounds like a good name for a son—if I ever have one."

"I'd say that's your choice to make," he lowered his head, but I saw the slightest smile curve his mouth.

"Consider it made, then. Thank you. I was beginning to think she was dead or taken by a sinister force."

"Not dead. The sinister force will be reckoned with. Go, now. Leave Gungl quickly."

"I will."

Leaping onto the wagon seat, I grabbed the reins and slapped them on the horses' backs. "Go, on," I told them, as I usually did. When I turned again to look at the stranger behind us, he was already gone.

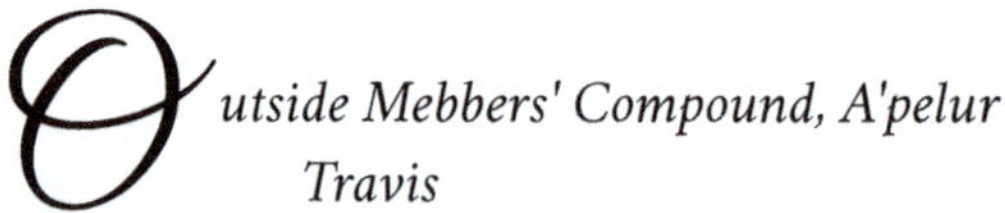

utside Mebbers' Compound, A'pelur
Travis

Bro, be ready to go to dragon, Trent sent to me. *I don't like this,* he added.

Kooper had forced us to put boots on the ground outside Mebbers' walls, where there was little to no cover. At our backs, the thick, dark, stone-and-concrete wall loomed above us, while Mebbers' people lined the top, weapons pointed outward.

A warlock's spell, no doubt, had alerted them the moment our feet touched the ground. I figured Zaria's medallion kept us hidden from their sight—for now.

Nearby, Miz, Zanfield, Perri and Markus knelt amid a pile of fallen leaves, Perri ready with a ranos pistol and a spell, the others armed with ranos rifles.

Farther along the line, Dori, Vik, David and the others were scattered, Susan, Jincus and Gerrett included. Kooper had even ordered our cooks to attack, leaving the ships in auto-orbit. Only Harlee, X's engineer, was left behind, because Jett refused to take him. He had absolutely nothing to protect himself; Zaria had never given him a medallion. The rest of us wore one, and that was some sort of defense.

Jett stood on one end of our line, looking formidable, while Nari and Tiri held rifles they'd barely trained to use at his side.

Kooper had the other end, worried, no doubt, that Jett would tell him what kind of fool he was for acting this rashly in a volatile situation. We could find ourselves caught in the middle of a horrific battle, being attacked from both sides. Kooper hadn't included us in his personal plans, and we were afraid to ask.

Just as we were almost afraid to breathe. Footsteps echoed above our heads as more of Mebbers' troops joined their fellows. As yet, we had no evidence of the Prophet's presence, but that could change in half a blink.

And it did.

~

Vogeffa II, Past

Randl

I'd *Pulled* the worn coin from a passing thief, who wouldn't learn of its absence for a while. I'd handed it to my own father, telling him my mother wanted him to have it. Had she ever realized it hadn't come from her—if she knew about it at all?

No wonder I hadn't seen anything when I'd held it before.

She'd never handled it to begin with.

I sat in what passed as a bar in Gungl, wondering how my life had gotten so fucked up.

V'dar was my half-brother.

How in the name of every god in existence, including the rogue ones, had that happened?

Fathered by a god, with the added curse of a Sirenali's DNA, V'dar had been created for a purpose. Liron had no care what happened to anyone else; he had his own plans and they included vengeance.

Even if it came years after his death.

The Prophet didn't have Sirenali at his beck and call; he *was* Sirenali —up to a point. And, with Liron's machinations at work, he had the full gifts of any Sirenali, plus those his father gave him, no doubt.

"Another drink?"

Another would be just as bad as the first four. "Absolutely," I tapped a finger on the bar and flipped out another silver coin I'd stolen from the same thief. He'd be a beggar by the time he reached his home.

I didn't care. He'd steal again anyway.

V'dar was my own flesh and blood. In all my imaginings about him and his beginnings, that was never a consideration. *Did he know he had a half-brother, or was I the only one burdened with that dreadful information?*

V'dar—my kin. Still, I intended to kill him. I wished I could kill him a hundred times for what he'd done during his life. But then I wished I could kill Liron and V'ili, too, for their part in this. They'd left my mother to die alone in Gungl. They had no idea I was there with her, invisible and angry.

Already dead, those two, a small voice informed me. *Sometime in the future.*

"Yeah," I sighed as the bartender thumped another drink in front of me. Lifting the small glass, I downed it in one swallow.

～

Mebbers' Compound, A'pelur
Zanfield

Kooper disappeared the moment the dead army appeared from nothing. Jett and the rest of us realized it quickly. Above us, Travis and Trent's dragons flew, burning swaths of the approaching army, but their efforts were a cup of water tossed onto a roaring blaze.

Form a tight circle, Jett shouted orders at the rest of us on the ground. It wasn't the easiest thing to do; until now, all we'd been able to do since the dead arrived was to keep a short path before us cleared so we wouldn't be run over by the Prophet's army.

The dead were marching—sometimes running—between us; we had no way to stop them from doing that unless we could form a circle, as Jett requested.

Take a step inward, toward your neighbor, Jett shouted. We were lined up haphazardly before Mebbers' compound, with Jett now at the center, but more of the dead than we could blast were getting through and attempting to scale the walls behind us.

With Mebbers' witch and warlocks firing spelled blasts, and the rest of his crew shooting ranos rifles, we were in as much danger from the back as from what we faced in front of us.

A circle would ease that problem somewhat, if we could get close enough together to make one.

Where was Kooper in all this? Where had he gone? I didn't want to consider insubordination, but, wait—yes. Yes, I did.

Asshole, I sent in his direction. He'd sent us here, when he should have known what kind of massacre it could turn into. My loyalty had never been to him, anyway.

Randl held my trust—in any situation. I just wished we'd waited for his return before instigating this madness, because I had no doubt that our arrival had done just that. The Prophet undoubtedly had been waiting for someone to make a move.

We'd become the target for two enemies, front and back. Not only that, but whenever we blasted another of the Prophet's deadwalkers, they exploded into gory bits of flesh and bone, spraying their infection everywhere.

If we escaped with our lives and without being affected by the Prophet's disease, I would kiss Zaria's feet myself.

I probably wasn't the only one who'd realized by now that we'd become invisible to both sides—that's why the zombies didn't bother stepping to the side; they kept walking toward us in an effort to reach Mebbers' walls, even though the ones in front of them were being blasted as quickly as our ranos rifles would fire.

Behind us, Mebbers' people were firing at the ocean of the dead— or so it appeared. If they'd seen us, they'd have targeted us better and more quickly. As far as we were concerned, they were firing blindly in our direction, and any blasts that should have hit us ricocheted in another direction. I hoped those altered blasts were hitting the dead, so the effort wouldn't be wasted.

If I were watching this battle on a vid rather than being in the middle of it, I'd probably enjoy the exploding, dead flesh flying high into the air every time a zombie was hit.

Being in the middle of it certainly changes points of view. *Draw closer together*, Jett commanded. I took two steps toward the center, after firing six quick blasts in succession to clear space.

I heard Vik's High Demon roar, first, just before my ranos rifle ran out of its charge.

Fuck.

Things had just turned deadly. Dropping the rifle at my feet, I drew the sword strapped to my back and swung at the first zombie close enough to bisect.

~

Mebbers' Compound

V'dar

They were here, just as my chief advisor promised. What did it matter that my newest conquests fired on the deadwalkers, in addition to the enemy? The deadwalkers were already dead—and it convinced our quarry to believe that Mebbers was still in control.

I chuckled as I watched the carnage outside the walls through the eyes of my newest minions—it was a new trick shown to me by my advisors. Yes, my enemy was hidden from sight—most of them, anyway.

The flying ones—we saw their flames and targeted those. As for the High Demon, he became visible to us the moment he turned.

What might I do with one of those—if I could command him?

No—better to kill this one and go looking for others. I could take them unaware. This one knew of me and would be wary.

"Your new ships are gathered around the *Prophet I*, my Lord," Mebbers bowed to me, as I'd commanded.

"Good. I feel there are other, enemy ships out there—when my enemy falls before us here, we will take those ships, too."

"As you command, my Lord."

Had Mebbers been in control of his faculties, still, he would have argued and fought before calling them my ships—those eleven vessels he'd carefully scrounged and stolen parts to rebuild before taking his place among the elite of all criminals.

Instead, I would hold that title; at least until they began to recognize me as what I was—their god.

The people would worship me as I commanded—my advisors said so. I looked forward to that day most eagerly.

~

Travis

If Trent and I, in dragon form, hadn't been able to shield ourselves while attempting to burn an encroaching ocean of the dead, Mebbers' warlocks would have fried us with the fireballs they tossed at us. Failing that, we'd have been killed by the rest of his crew, who were firing ranos rifles at us from the top of the compound's walls.

Once we'd made the change to dragon, we were visible because of the fire we breathed and the subsequent burning of the dead. *That* was more than visible to everybody, and they easily targeted the invisible sources of incinerated bodies.

Without our shielding ability, which was added to, no doubt, by Zaria's medallion, Mebbers' ground crew would have obliterated us in the first few rounds of shots at our dragons.

From my vantage point aloft, I couldn't see most of the others any longer—several were still shooting, but the dead swarmed so thick it looked like insects were marching over them like inconsequential sticks or leaves in their path.

I could have sent mindspeech, but was too terrified of not getting an answer. Too many rifles had gone silent, indicating they'd run out of their charge.

Where was Kooper in all this? He was the one who'd instigated this massacre; why wasn't he using his power to help?

Even if he turned to lion snake, no amount of poison would have an effect on what was already dead. The terrifying thing was this; Farzi sent mindspeech early on, telling me his power couldn't neutralize the Prophet's zombies. He and Nenzi had made that effort, yet the dead kept moving forward. It took more drastic measures—employing their power to blast reanimated bodies to bits instead.

That, of course, released the Prophet's disease into the air, which in turn would infect anyone it touched who wasn't sufficiently shielded.

The Prophet had grown much stronger, if he could take on the lowest levels of the Hierarchy like this.

Randl, we really need you, I sent, knowing my silent plea wouldn't be heard.

~

Vogeffa II, Past

Randl

The pain in my right arm, where the coin was grafted onto my skin, was debilitating for several moments, and that was soon followed by the relay of mindspeech—and a vision—from Travis.

Randl, we really need you, he'd said, while the images playing before his eyes had me standing immediately.

Mebbers' compound was under attack by a massive army of the dead, and Kooper had sent my people into the fray in one of the worst decisions he'd ever made.

Coming, I sent to Travis and the others, before disappearing in front of the bartender. His shout of alarm was cut off quickly, as I left his world and time behind; I'd somehow managed to zone in on Travis' location without even thinking about it.

We need help, I heard Dori's mindspeech quickly. *We're being overrun.*

She was right. Blasted body parts of the Prophet's zombies were piled high everywhere, along with gore, fluids and who knew what else—so much that the ground was slick with it. The army of the dead marched over their former allies, intent on reaching Mebbers' compound.

Or the ones standing before it.

Anyone who wasn't shielded properly could succumb to the Prophet's disease from coming in contact with any part of these zombies, and still there was a sea of the dead coming.

Baby, I just got here, I replied. *Give me a second to think, all right?* I was working my way through what I'd drank at a bar in Gungl, burning through the haze with power to clear my head.

As I stood inside my small island of shielded space, the dead bumped into my outer shield regularly, distracting me from the high wall before me and the encroaching dead.

To my right, Vik's twenty-foot Thifilathi suddenly roared to life as he changed and towered over his adversaries. He'd become visible—I understood why after a moment. He did it deliberately, to draw the dead away from the others.

Once he could be seen, scores of the dead crawled up his body, almost too quickly for him to burn them to ash. While bodies crawled and flamed over his legs and torso, Mebbers' people targeted and fired at him with ranos rifles.

All around Vik, I could see the short, quick bursts of light, telling me that a few of the BlackWing crews still fired their weapons at the dead. Those weapons were useful—if yours still held a charge and you had sufficient numbers firing into the massive army of attackers. We didn't have sufficient numbers.

Time for me to act, or someone could die.

If it hadn't happened already.

Miz

I'd lost sight of Markus, and was terrified he'd gone down beneath the onslaught of the dead.

If the Prophet had released this great a force against us, then what could we do in return? I'd never felt so helpless as I did then, firing my ranos rifle and watching the charge dwindle rapidly.

Still, I saw no end of the enemy coming against us. Until now, I'd never really considered that Mae might never be pulled away from the Prophet's clutches.

Miz?

Markus' mindspeech reached me. He was still alive and I was grateful.

Markus? I responded.

My rifle just ran out of its charge, he informed me. *If we—don't make it out of here,* he added, *I love you, too.*

~

David

Zombies bumped into the shield around me; my rifle had run out of juice and all it was good for now was bludgeoning zombies in the crotch.

That part of them no longer hurt; I realized it after the first few hits. I fell a time or two from the force of my blows—it didn't matter, they'd either walk over the shield covering me or slide over it when they blindly ran into it.

Randl's here, Vik informed me. I froze. I couldn't see over the zombies crowding around me, intent on marching to Mebbers' wall and crawling over it, no doubt.

In any other circumstances, I might have sent mindspeech to Randl, telling him I was on my way. With only the spent rifle in my hands, I was of no use to him and the less of a target I was, the better.

Time to help, a strange voice informed me.

What? Who the hell said that? I demanded.

I did. I am Ca'lex. I choose you.

Ca'lex is a forsaken planet, I argued as a zombie, leaking brain gunk and fluid from taking a hit to the head, slid across the top of my shield with an eerie squeak. The gore it left on the shield's surface made me want to heave.

I am Ca'lex—from before, from now, and from always. I choose you.

For what? I argued, whacking another zombie at the knees and causing him to fall. I was grateful that the shield allowed me to reach outside it with my weapon; otherwise, I'd feel more useless than I already did.

I am here. We will help.

The pain over my heart knocked me to the ground for brief seconds. Ripping open my collar, I saw it—one of the gold coins from Randl's desk had adhered to my skin, beneath Zaria's medallion.

Zaria's medallion hadn't stopped it from happening.

Why?

We know of her. We will help.

We?

There are many others like me. We are here. Come. We go to the one you call Randl.

What else would we call him? I snapped, attempting to cover my confusion and to buy time. The last thing I wanted to do was get between Randl and the Prophet, who was probably waiting somewhere to kill us.

We call Randl Reviendis.

What's that supposed to mean? In plain English?

Spirit of the universes. He is our defender, and we have come to help.

How? I was still attempting to buy time while I sorted through mind-bending information.

Like this.

The flood of power through me was terrifying at first—sort of like sap running through a tree. No, wait—it was *exactly* like sap running through a tree.

How did I know that? Who could understand how sap runs through a tree?

The nature spirit of an entire planet knows, he replied, easily reading my thoughts.

Ca'lex. An entire planet had filled me with power.

Fucking hells.

Let's do this. I tossed my useless ranos rifle on the ground and allowed Ca'lex to fold space.

~

Vik

Break the wall. We will do this together. No spell will harm you—you know that, he whispered to me.

Like a sun, the coin blazed on my Thifilathi's chest as I strode toward Mebbers' wall, intent on taking it down. Zaria's medallion, which had grown with me, swung with my effort, as I wiped out an entire section of the wall with a single blow of one arm.

Below me, a warlock cowered when he learned his power could do nothing to harm me. My companion, who called himself Meerius, had given me power I'd never thought to contain.

The dead still swarmed about my feet, but they no longer needed to come in contact with my scales. I could burn them with a thought, and I was thinking it most of the time. As for the ranos rifles aimed at me—no blasts hit. My Thifilathi, Zaria's medallion and Meerius' power and talents ensured it.

Raising a foot, I positioned myself to stomp the warlock below into oblivion. I recognized him, after all—Alken Wilker deserved to be stomped. I roared when something pulled him away, my foot landing on empty ground instead of that filth's body.

Nearby, Travis and Trent's dragons, each bearing a massive gold coin on their chests, burned into the solid rock of the wall with their fiery breath.

They'd been chosen, too. I was about to land another blow against the wall when Randl sent mindspeech.

Stand back, he ordered. *I'll take it down.*

~

Randl

Take down the wall and remove the dead, a voice told me. *Then stand against him.*

I recognized that voice. It belonged to the man only I had seen in the second coin trip. I'd felt a kinship with him when he'd appeared—because he was also blind, and yet he could see.

I am here with you, he said, as the gold coin on my right arm tingled. *Many others are here with me. Our power belongs to you, now. Use it. Take down the walls of this fortress. Turn the dead to ash. Then call out the god. He has grown stronger, as you will discover.*

Target the wall just there—in the concrete between stones, another voice said—the one belonging to the blind woman I'd seen in the last coin trip—before hundreds of coins had slammed into my back and adhered to my skin.

Focus, the male voice said as I studied the target she'd shown me. *Gather the power—it will come at your command.*

I focused as well as I could, while the heady sensation of power suffused my being. Somehow, I knew when it was enough, and released it against the walls that had kept Mebbers safe for decades.

～

Zanfield

We knew something was off the moment Mebbers' walls exploded in a blast that should have deafened anyone less than a mile away. The ground rocked beneath our feet, too, and only the shield around me kept me standing by tightening its perimeter briefly.

Mebbers is taken, Jincus' voice whispered in my mind.

When did he get mindspeech?

His companion gave it to him, a new voice informed me. *As I am your companion, now. You are more than you were, and Jincus is correct. See how the dead are veering away from the rubble of the walls? Their target has been you all along, as you have also been the god's target from within those walls.*

The god?

The one you and your friends search for, the voice replied. *Turn around. Reviendus is about to send these dead to their final rest.*

I turned, catching sight of Randl perhaps a hundred feet away. He faced the army of the dead after bringing the wall down, as if it were made of sticks instead of massive stones and concrete.

Travis' dragon, followed by Trent's, landed nearby with a considerable thump—they were prepared to protect us from Mebbers' people. Mebbers' guns had gone quiet, however, the moment Randl blasted the wall.

They're regrouping, Travis advised in mindspeech. *They'll start firing again once their new master commands it.*

Down the line, Randl lifted his arms. I had no idea what he was about to do. So far, only burning had been effective against eliminating the dead—enough that their parts and pieces were no longer a threat to anyone unshielded against them.

Yes, Trent's voice hissed in my mind when Randl, in an enormous burst of power, turned all the dead, including scraps and pieces, to winking sparks that flew away on the wind.

The hush that came after that feat told me two things. First, Randl was more than he was. Second, the Prophet was carefully considering how to destroy us all.

That's when we heard Randl's mindspeech; he'd included anyone who could hear him. *I'm here, V'dar*, he shouted. *Let's dance.*

∾

Kooper

The moment the dead appeared, I'd folded space to the back of that gruesome army, which stretched for miles. My first blasting against them threw dead bodies into the air and destroyed the ground beneath their feet.

I realized after several rounds of doing the same that the dead weren't affected at all. They'd drop to the ground, then stand again and either walk or run away from me.

That's when I was forced to focus on singles or a handful of the dead, and after discovering that I couldn't stop them with my power, I blasted them apart, instead. This, of course, released the Prophet's disease into the very air.

Small towns lay nearby, so I struggled to place shield domes around them, attempting to prevent their infection. The harder I worked at that, the more the winds blew, sending the disease everywhere. I couldn't contain the wind, either; it was useless to try.

That's when I began to curse myself, as more of the dead appeared from nothing to join the army already traveling at top speed toward Mebbers' compound. My people were there, shooting as fast as they could, no doubt, and there wasn't any way that the thousands they might destroy would make a dent in the hundreds of thousands heading toward them.

You could pull them out of there, I reminded myself.

That would be admitting my defeat—and my poor judgment in the matter. Too, it would open a clear path for the Prophet to take Mebbers and his entire crew—the ones who didn't die in the initial fight, anyway.

Who knew—the Prophet could already be inside the compound, taking over any or all of them. My power couldn't get past the protection Mebbers held inside his walls, and that left me blind to the goings-on there.

So, you'll sacrifice your people, to save your pride?

That voice wasn't mine.

It was Zaria's.

What she said. Breanne's voice was close behind.

Then what the hells do you want me to do? I shouted at Breanne.

How about going to protect them—some of their weapons charges have run out. You'd know that if you'd gone to help them already, or bothered to ask. Breanne wasn't happy.

Sometimes, I forget that she's one of the Mighty—one of the original Three. *Those are good people—the best people you have,* she added. *You're going to get them killed.*

What's this about, anyway? Zaria demanded. *You can't stand it if a woman outmaneuvers you? Is that it?*

You get to do whatever you want, I snarled in mindspeech. *While I'm held back.*

Oh, for fuck's sake. Everything I do, I do to protect people. Now, why is it you're doing this? So you won't look weak? That your man-pride won't take a hit?

Norian was always envious of what Lissa could do, Breanne said.

Kooper, you will not, and I repeat, not, end up like Norian. Get ahold of yourself, Zaria snapped at me.

Norian's dead, I flung at her.

Exactly my point, you stupid reptile. You're a hundred times the man Norian ever was. Now straighten up and act like it. Go help your people. If you don't, then I'll be forced to do it, and that won't go so well with your boss.

That's when the entire army of the dead went up in sparks, leaving only churned ground behind to mark their passage. I was ready to breathe a relieved sigh when the mindspeech came.

Somebody help, Farzi sent. *Randl—he call out Prophet. Prophet come. Things not look good.*

"Get everybody out except the crews of X and XIII," Zaria appeared at my side. "They can't help Randl in this fight. Get them out, now."

"What about Mebbers?" I argued.

"Mebbers is no longer Mebbers—or haven't you figured that out, yet?"

"Fucking hells," I cursed and folded space to the front wall of Mebbers' compound, which was no longer standing, I discovered. I may have mentally bellowed Farzi's and Bear Wright's names before gathering the crews of I, II and VII to get them the hell away.

~

Vik

V'dar, I heard Randl shout a second time.

My breath was stolen as even the air disappeared from Mebbers' compound, along with anything living—including Alken Wilker, no doubt. I wanted to roar, but there was no oxygen left to do so.

The Prophet had arrived, sucking the air from our very lungs.

~

Randl

He has grown, a companion voice informed me, as the Prophet appeared just inside Mebbers' compound, where the wall stood only minutes before. V'dar, as usual, wore his hooded cloak, half-covering his face.

The face covered in flesh-colored scales, I reminded myself. I understood that V'ili, his uncle, had made him ashamed of those scales, as they weren't the dark and menacing version that V'ili wore when he turned.

How much did V'dar hate V'ili, until V'ili laid obsession not to do so?

He holds others within him, too. We were afraid this would come, the companion's voice drew me away from my thoughts.

What others? I asked.

The legacy from his father, no doubt. A new voice spoke—a female voice.

Rogue gods, hidden within his infernal spheres, another said. *We cannot tell how many. They have enhanced his power.*

V'dar drew back his hood as he contemplated me—and my allies who'd gathered at my back. Without the hood to cover him, the Prophet's countenance vibrated with a hazy, violet light. His eyes stood out as black holes in his face, his flesh-colored scales emanating the same purple malevolence that enveloped the rest of him as he took a step toward me.

Sal would call this *High Noon* for some reason, although dusk was upon us.

I have released the air, my first companion said. *He cannot hold such for long anyway—he needs it, too. A small part of him remains human.*

Yes—the part of him that was from my mother.

Fuck.

The god that always comes at the end, the female voice spoke again. I thought she'd disappeared after the coins hit me.

She hadn't—she'd landed on my back with the others. She'd named the Prophet, too, during that coin trip, and I hadn't guessed her meaning at the time.

Look upon him, my first companion whispered. *He has never had an adversary before. Universes have fallen at his command—he is the ultimate destroyer.*

We have never gone to war, before, she told me. *Because the rogue gods were never destroyed in such numbers, before. We have waited long for this moment, to strike back for all the evil he has done to us in universes long dead.*

"Ah, Randl, how nice of you to come to me," the Prophet spoke. His smile revealed much—*they* lurked behind his falseness—the rogue gods he'd inherited from his father, Liron.

"V'dar." I only spoke his name. I refused to give my doubts credence here—if he killed me, then these universes would die like the others before them.

Behind me, the others gathered closer. Dori stepped to my side, the top half of her coin visible beneath the open collar of her uniform.

Jett took the opposite side. David had moved to stand beside Vik's Thifilathi.

I've gotten everyone else out who doesn't have a medallion, Kooper sent mindspeech. *We're aboard the ships. Call if you need me. I'm sorry, Randl. I had no idea this would happen.*

Water under the bridge, I replied, my words curt.

Vik stepped forward, his Thifilathi intimidating. David walked beside him, eyes blazing like the sun. Travis and Trent's dragons leapt forward with simultaneous roars. Then came Perri and Zanfield. Susan, Gerrett, Sabrina, Miz, Markus and all the others from X and XIII—except X's engineer.

Harlee had no combat training and no medallion. I couldn't decide whether he was the lucky one in all this.

"Give yourself to me and I'll consider letting your—*friends*—live," V'dar studied his fingernails, as if he were in charge of the universes already.

"Suck eggs, V'dar," David growled.

~

Starship Prophet I

Le'Vestar Limn

Something had distracted the Prophet; I had no doubt about that. The breath I drew felt like the first one I'd breathed in months.

"Lev?" Mae whispered beside me.

"My love?" I turned to her. Her eyes said it all—we were far enough away from the Prophet, and out of his thoughts for however brief a time, that I felt my wyrm-dragon stirring within me.

Mae and I stood in the engine room—we'd been stationed there to ensure the continued smooth operation of the ship the Prophet named after himself. He didn't have an enormous ego—he *was* enormous ego.

"Lev, we need to go before he," she didn't finish—I was already walking toward Yurik, who stood near the door.

"What do you want?" Yurik growled at me while leveling a ranos pistol in my direction.

"There may be an unusual murmur in the engines," I reported. "I need someone else to confirm before we alert the pilots and our master," I lied.

"Ah. Fine, then." Yurik holstered the weapon and approached me so I could lead him to the purported sound.

A human's neck is so easily broken, if one is strong enough.

Yurik's spine snapped with a sickly crunch, and I let him fall to the ground.

"Now?" Mae asked.

"Now," I agreed.

Together—we changed.

Together, our bulk was so great that it blew out the engine compartment and sent ship fragments flying into space.

We could protect ourselves long enough to reach the atmosphere —if we hurried. Our bodies were strong enough to survive the cold and lack of air for a short time.

Fly, I sent to Mae, who followed at my shoulder as we hurtled toward A'pelur.

~

BlackWing X

Kooper

You see that? I shouted in mindspeech to Farzi, Bear Wright and Lynx when the explosion lit the dark of space and sent shock waves outward. *That has to be one of Mebbers' ships—or the Prophet's. Fire on that location. He has others close by, I'm sure of it.*

I see ships, Farzi growled back. BlackWing II was far enough away that he'd caught sight of Mebbers' fleet coming around in their orbit.

Fire, I shouted at all of them. *Destroy those gods-damned things.*

In moments, more blasts streaked the dark around us. I targeted other ships lit by the explosions of the first few that were hit. I'd done little in this fight, but I could do this much at least.

The Prophet's ships would go down by my command, even if I couldn't stand against him myself.

~

Randl

Are we strong enough? Dori sent. The standoff was taking longer than I thought it might—I imagined that V'dar would level his worst at us, and we'd either be standing or dead afterward.

Not far down the line, Miz drew in a massive breath—and turned to his wyrm-dragon.

Mae, he bellowed in mindspeech.

Above our heads, in a darkening sky, explosions lit the atmosphere. Le'Vestar and Mae had done damage to the Prophet before making their escape, it appeared.

V'dar lifted his head to see the fireworks, before lowering his head to glare at me. One last bloom of light splashed the sky before V'dar released a blast so powerful it could—and did—take the planet apart.

284

CHAPTER 19

"We don't know anything. Haven't heard anything," Kooper settled onto a sofa in my library, a glass of Scotch in his hand. Something had changed in him—I could see and sense it. He felt responsible for deaths on A'pelur—and for the destruction of the entire planet.

The Prophet had destroyed it before disappearing. It was too much to hope that he was dead, too.

My worry now was the same as Kooper's—when and where would the Prophet reappear, and had his disease blown outward with A'pelur's destruction, to fall onto other, unwary worlds? We had no containment spheres to control this kind of threat. As long as the Prophet lived, his disease would remain a danger to every world it touched.

I'd sent mindspeech earlier to Quin. She sounded pragmatic about the entire debacle, which gave me the slimmest thread of hope.

Hope that not all was as it seemed. After all, I had three sons and a daughter-in-law on A'pelur when it died, and I didn't want to consider how heavy my grief would be if they'd died with it.

285

Only time would tell, I think. For now, the Prophet was likely plotting new revenge, for whatever imagined slights he could invent. He'd keep doing that, too—until he realized he no longer needed an excuse.

Bree already confirmed that much, in the brief mindspeech she'd shared with me. I'd asked other questions, too, and she'd refused to answer. Questions about the survival of family and friends, among other things.

"I wish I had better sense," Kooper sighed and emptied his glass of Scotch. I floated the bottle to him so he could pour a refill.

"Admitting your shortcomings is the first step in overcoming them," Master Morwin appeared, accompanied by Trajan, Ashe's right-hand man and high-ranking member of the Hierarchy.

"Morwin, what brings you here?" I asked, setting my glass of Scotch and soda on a nearby table. "Trajan, always good to see you," I nodded to the tall werewolf.

"I was informed that Pauley needs an advanced tutor," Morwin said, as if I should have known it already.

"But he's barely reading," I began.

"That is no longer true, according to the Mighty Hand," Morwin replied, his long, bushy red brows wiggling as he spoke.

"What happened? A miracle?" I stood, frowning at Morwin.

"I know not. I only know that my services are requested, therefore I am reporting to Le-Ath Veronis, to instruct a young one who is behind in his studies."

"I think I'd like to accompany you to Avii Castle," I said, speculation in my voice. Something was happening here; I just wasn't sure what it could be.

"Of course. You are always welcome, my Queen," Morwin bowed.

~

Avii Castle
  Quin

I'd sent mindspeech to Kay, and she'd relayed my request to Ashe, who'd approached Morwin for me.

Now, Trajan, Morwin and Lissa stood in Gurnil's Library, staring at Pauley.

Pauley was so happy, it shone through his pores, I think. Perhaps Trajan would know what the top of the gold coin peeking above the boy's shirt collar meant, but the others were clueless.

Just as they were meant to be—for now. As for Teren and Franc— they'd disappeared shortly after A'pelur was destroyed. I wasn't concerned for their whereabouts—I'd learn that soon enough.

Kooper still has a few lessons to learn, Zaria told me. But he did figure out how important Randl and the others were to him—when he believed them dead. He hadn't come with Lissa, likely because he didn't want to see more accusation leveled at him in the eyes of the Avii.

Word had it that Ildevar was waiting to have a meeting with Kooper. I wasn't sure what might be said, but Teeg San Gerxon was already searching for a replacement for Jett Riffler, after he'd disappeared.

Jett had stood with the others on A'pelur, while Kooper returned to an orbiting ship. I imagine that guilt ate at Kooper, too, even though he'd destroyed the Prophet's newly-acquired fleet of ships. I had no desire to assuage Kooper's guilt; it was part of his learning experience.

"You're Amterean," Pauley breathed when Morwin introduced himself. "I'm so happy—thank you for agreeing to teach me." He reached out and grasped Morwin's right hand in gratitude.

It is *a miracle, isn't it?* Lissa sent.

I like to think so, I agreed, pushing the edge of my blouse over the gold coin nestling on my breast, beneath Zaria's medallion. Her name was Tiralia, she'd told me, and already I appreciated her company.

~

Sirena

Phrinnis Tampirus

This is very nice, Revalus informed me. Together, we surveyed the palace around us. Revalus, his gold spread across my chest, saw everything through my eyes. *I was always blind*, he'd told me earlier, shortly after he'd adhered to my skin. *Most of us were, you know. We saw through others' eyes; humanoid and creature alike, and gathered everything we needed to know that way.*

Were you born? I asked. *Like other creatures?*

No. We became. From nothing, something. Until Reviendus came among us. He was born. We have no records in the Metal Library. We keep ourselves, he added. *As we are now, together, we are Ar'pex—meaning we hold one another. The Reviendus is Ar'pexi—he holds many, and they, in return, hold him. I am grateful for you—the rarest podl-morph among rare podl-morphs*, he declared. *We will be quite cunning together.*

Oh, perhaps even more cunning than that, I told him. He chuckled.

He and I—we'd helped other Ar'pexi remove the worthy from A'pelur before its destruction. They now inhabited Sirena, in cities built for them by Zaria. Most of those Ar'pexi were still among them, helping them settle and become accustomed to their new surroundings.

They were aware of A'pelur's destruction—Zaria ensured that there were news vids and other connections to the worlds outside Sirena, although no communication was allowed. And, if anyone wished to leave, they'd have to leave all their memories of Sirena behind, too.

So far, they were happy enough to be alive. I'd asked for employees for the palace, and currently it was fully-staffed, with a wait-list if more were needed. Zaria had seen to everything.

"Is everything ready?" Zaria appeared as if called, with Bleek and Ilya at her side. The Blevakian gave me a huge grin—he and Ilya were Ar'pex—they held coins, too.

"Everything is prepared, my love," I told her.

I bow to the Vhanaraszh, Revalus sent to her. He and I bowed, as indicated.

"Revalus, there is no need to bow," she smiled at me—and him. "We're in this together, you know."

At that moment, they came.

Twin Falchani brothers appeared, chests bare, medallions and Ar'pex coins proudly displayed. Miz'Sandar Keel and his new mate, Chief Markus, set their feet on the floor before us. Zanfield Staggs, one of his arms wrapped around Perri Ironsmith's shoulders, came next. Others arrived—the entire crews of BlackWings X and XIII, except one. The engineer had been collected from X by Kooper Griff, before the ships were sent to the hidden space station housing the rest of the BlackWing fleet.

Last of all, Randl Gage, Reviendus, Ar'pexi and Soul of the Universes, appeared with Dori, his beautiful mate, at his side.

"Welcome," I stepped forward to greet them, my arms held wide. "Here on Sirena, reclaimed from the dust of its destruction, are places for all of you. The planet is hidden from all except you, a few of the most powerful, and the Larentii. You will remain concealed by the bones of many Sirenali, buried beneath the planet's surface eons ago by their descendants. This is your safe place—to rest and enjoy. I imagine that you'll need it—the Prophet still lives."

"Will we still be the BlackWing Pirates?" Jincus asked. He'd enjoyed his new job; that was quite clear.

"We'll get the ships back," Randl told him. "Just not right away, for obvious reasons."

"Right now, the others think we're dead, so the Prophet will think we're dead, too," Vik explained.

"Then we may need a new name, to go with the old one," David pointed out. "Zanfield already named us, actually."

"What's that?" Randl frowned at him.

"We're the *Formidables*, a *very* special division of the BlackWing Pirates," David grinned, as if everybody should have known it already.

EPILOGUE

*R*andl

Soon enough, V'dar won't have to make excuses to kill—it will become too much of a pleasure for him, Bennall, my female Ar'pex, informed me.

He has too much of his father in him, Kev'Ril, my Chief Ar'pex, agreed. *That, combined with a gift of rogue gods to inhabit him, makes V'dar a terrible threat.*

"Who are you talking to?" Dori asked. She and I had just left our shared suite, to go to dinner in the dining hall. She knew I was having a mental conversation with someone.

"Bennall and Kev'Ril," I replied.

"Oh. Hariki says they're strong."

"While Hariki is made of stealth and cunning, Bennall tells me," I smiled at Dori. "Perfect for you, they both say."

"I think she's perfect, too," Dori sniffed.

"Come on, you, I'm starving." I pulled her against me and folded space to the dining hall.

~

Travis

We're fine, Mom. Really.

Tell me where you are. I want to see you.

We'll see you soon enough, stop worrying, I tried to console her. Half her sendings contained tears, that was easy to tell. *We can't tell you where we are—for obvious reasons. You have to keep this information quiet— share it with our dads and grampa only, all right? Zaria says she'll tell you where we are soon.*

Vik, too? Is he okay?

Mom, Vik is, well—I've never known him to be this strong and confident.

What about Trent—and you, too? Are you strong and confident after that fiasco on A'pelur?

Mom, stop worrying, I repeated. *Bro and I—we're formidable.*

∼

Le'Vestar Limn

It had taken some convincing—by Randl and Zaria, but Mae and I were together. Randl explained it to Miz in this way; Mae and I were infected with the Prophet's disease, so the very act of sex with any other would infect them, too.

I doubted anyone else would wish to carry that burden, as it was heavy and came with a terrible price. Mae and I had destroyed the Prophet's ship, which resulted in the ASD destroying the other ships. That, in turn, precipitated the Prophet's hasty engagement with Randl on A'pelur.

Randl considered our interference a blessing rather than a curse, because the Prophet may have been caught off guard. *Either way,* Randl said, *it prevented a drawn-out battle, with no certain victor.*

I still felt the total destruction of a planet was a terrible price to pay for that interference. Too, there was always the chance that the Prophet could command us again, if he were ever close enough to retake our minds. That meant we would be forced to stay far away from that possibility.

That's why we were now on Sirena, protected beneath layers of shields and hidden from the Prophet's meddling. The Or'myr High Council would have to understand—eventually—or choke on their own bile, as Randl pointed out.

For now—Mae and I shared separate-but-connecting suites, although our plans were to be together. The appearance of separate suites would placate Miz—somewhat. "I love you," I squeezed Mae tighter against me and whispered against her hair.

"Dinner," Miz rapped on my door, interrupting the subsequent kiss.

"I love you, too," Mae smiled up at me. "Now we just have to convince Miz to love you."

"He doesn't?" I teased.

"Stop it—I'm hungry," she patted my stomach. "Come on—before they eat it all."

"We'll be right there," I called out to Miz and kissed Mae again.

∾

Palace Library, Sirena

Zaria

He didn't look comfortable—probably because of the deep frown I wore. He looked just a bit guilty, too, which supported my theory.

I already knew that what was happening now had happened in the distant past—in other timelines.

Too many of them, actually.

"You and the other two closed the door and walked away, didn't you? Every time." I struggled to keep the accusation out of my voice.

"Those multiverses were all dying—or dead, and if we'd left the door open, as you say, then the perpetrators would have reappeared in every new multiverse we built. You wouldn't be fighting a single version of it now—you'd be fighting multiple versions, like a body infected with dozens of fatal viruses."

"Here's the problem with that statement," I pointed a finger at him. "It only takes *one* fatal virus. Any way you look at it, the body will still die."

"I see your point, but you're not seeing mine."

"Right." I shook my head at him.

"Things are different now—because I never had children before. Plus, you already know that the multiverse has never gone to war to protect itself. You had a hand in that, I believe."

"I imagined the multiverses were weary of dying—over and over."

"I never told you who your mother was," my father changed the subject.

My father. Also known as Charles, or Wisdom, or the Mighty Mind, thought to distract me from the topic at hand.

It was working.

"Are you going to tell me?" I demanded.

"I will—if you and Randl are successful in protecting this multiverse and keeping it alive."

With that carrot left dangling, he disappeared, leaving me silently cursing his strategy. Which, as it turned out, was successful in the extreme.

The End

List of Characters/Places Appearing in the BlackWing Pirates Series
(Characters from other series will be indicated by the series name for their first appearance. Those series will be listed in parenthesis after the names)

Adam Chessman: From Old Earth. Former chief of enforcers for the Vampire Council. Chosen to become a member of the Saa Thalarr. Mated to Kiarra. Also a member of the Al'Riyu. (Blood Destiny Series, Saa Thalarr Series)

Alken Wilker: Fourth-level Karathian warlock, and Uncle to Perri and Pauley Wilker-Ironsmith. Abused both children after they were abandoned by their parents (BlackWing Pirates Series)

Akrinn Lemm: Native of Jaledis, best friend of Fergue Bing. (BlackWing Pirates Series)

Amlis: Prince of New Fyris, a kingdom established on Harifa Edus after Siriaa's destruction. Father: King Tamblin of Fyris-deceased. Mother: Queen Omina of Fyris-deceased (First Ordinance Series)

A'pelur: Campiaan Alliance world and home to criminal kingpin Mebbers and his hidden fortress (BlackWing Pirates Series)

Ardis: Avii Captain of the Guard for King Justis. Mated to Dena, Queen Quin's personal bodyguard. Daughter: Dara. (First Ordinance Series)

Ar'pex: A nature spirit which has chosen to bond with another being, giving that being their power and cooperation (BlackWing Pirates Series)

Ashe Evans: The Mighty Hand, or Strength. Owns SouthStar Groves on Avendor, which houses many. SouthStar is a haven, and those who reside there will never age because of the power wielded by Ashe. Mated to Kay and Breanne. (Legend of the Ir'Indicti Series)

Astralan Starr: Fifth-level Karathian warlock, one of four brothers who protect Teeg San Gerxon. Mated to Queen Reah. Member of the Nameless Ones—see Hierarchy of the Gods. (High Demon Series, BlackWing Pirates Series)

Aurelius: Vampire from Old Earth. Turned Gavin Montegue. Mated to Queen Reah. Member of the Saa Thalarr and Mil'Karha—see Hierarchy of the Gods. (High Demon Series)

Ba'Moru: Small vacation resort on Pyrik and home to Caille Morr.

Bargel: President of Pyrik. (BlackWing Pirates Series)

Barkins: Charla Dare's fluffy, white canine best friend (BlackWing Pirates Series)

Barra Kend: Wife of Ruther Kend, mother of Sabrina Kend. (First Ordinance Series, BlackWing Pirates Series)

Bekzi: One of eight reptanoid brothers who are lion snake shapeshifters, although their births were manipulated by a criminal element to create assassins. Bekzi and his brothers had slightly slitted eyes, preventing them from passing as fully human, and therefore they were never forced into the role of assassins. Instead, they became well-versed in farming and the repair of mechanical things, providing maintenance and such to their criminal masters until they were freed by Reah and Teeg San Gerxon. Bekzi is mated to the Mighty Heart and to Zaria. Member of the Nameless Ones—see Hierarchy of the Gods. (High Demon Series)

Bel Erland Morphis: Crown Prince of Karathia. Fifth-level warlock and skilled at scrying and spells. Father: King Rylend of Karathia. Mother: Queen Reah of Kifirin. Mated to Queen Quin of the Avii. (High Demon Series, First Ordinance Series)

Bennall: A Campiaan Alliance world orbiting the same star as Kev'Ril.

Berel Charkisul: Son of Edden Charkisul. Mated to Queen Quin and serves as a liaison/ambassador for her after he was granted the blue wings of an Avii scholar by Zaria. (First Ordinance Series)

Bornelus: Non-Alliance world taken by the Prophet and guarded by mutant Ra'Ak.

Borell Gant: Patriarch of a family chosen randomly by the Prophet for his experiements in employing food to spread the Prophet's disease; deceased (BlackWing Pirates Series)

Brakkus: A Campiaan Alliance world, and chosen meeting place between Alken and Gillen Wilker (BlackWing Pirates Series)

Brandl Gage: Father of Randl Gage. Homeworld is Vogeffa II, until attack by Vardil Cayetes forced the population to relocate to New Fyris. Employed by Prince Amlis and later by Queen Lissa of Le-Ath Veronis and Queen Quin of the Avii (First Ordinance Series)

Breanne: The Mighty Heart, aka Love. (God Wars Series)

Bryan Riley: Vampire from Old Earth. Head of the News Conglomerate on Le-Ath Veronis. (Blood Destiny Series)

Caille Morr: Trail guide at a mountain resort on Pyrik—one of many hidden servants of the Prophet. (BlackWing Pirates Series)

Ca'Lex: Abandoned world; David's Ar'pex (BlackWing Pirates Series)

Calezia: Capital city of Fren'Ell, a Reth Alliance world, where Jewl Yarro had a home and a better reputation (BlackWing Pirates Series)

Campiaa: Small planet and home to the Founder of the Campiaan Alliance (Blood Destiny Series, High Demon Series)

Carek Prime: A non-Alliance world ruled by King Devarr, until it was destroyed by Vardil Cayetes. The population was subsequently moved to Cloudsong (First Ordinance Series)

Caylon Black: Falchani warrior and the best Falchani blademaster ever produced on that world. Caylon Black trained Dragon, Crane and Salidar DeLuca. Member of the Saa Thalarr and the Mil'Karha—see Hierarchy of the Gods. (Blood Destiny Series)

Celestan Starr: Fifth-level Karathian warlock, one of four brothers who protect Teeg San Gerxon. Member of the Nameless Ones—see Hierarchy of the Gods. (High Demon Series, BlackWing Pirates Series)

Charla Dare: Wealthy Campiaan resident who has been working as a smuggler and committing other crimes quietly while passing as one of the planet's elite. (BlackWing Pirates Series)

Cheel: Resident of Gis, a non-alliance world (BlackWing Pirates Series)

Chloe: Naturalized Amterean Dwarf, originally from Old Earth. Owl shapeshifter. Mated to Morwin Quiffilis. Sister to David Hiboux. (Latter Day Demons Series)

Cleaster Leech: Campiaan space station employee who has been infected with the Prophet's spreading obsession. (BlackWing Pirates Series)

Cloudsong: A world recently accepted into the Campiaan Alliance and ruled by King Devarr. Has a spotty, checkered past, and was once rendered barren and useless by a rogue warlock who tapped the core. Restored by Zaria and others, to become home to all the refugees from Carek Prime.

Connegar: Larentii. Mated to Queen Lissa. (Blood Destiny Series)

Cord'ilus: An empty world, devoured by Ra'Ak long ago.

Cori Anderson-DeLuca: Panther shapeshifter and Co-Captain of BlackWing VIII with her husband, Marco DeLuca. Mother: Lavonna

Anderson. Father: Nathan Anderson. Sister to Dori Anderson. (Legend of the Ir'Indicti Series, BlackWing Pirates Series)

Dara: Avii—daughter of Dena and Ardis. Named after Daragar of the Larentii. (First Ordinance Series)

Daragar: Larentii. Mated to Queen Quin of the Avii. (First Ordinance Series)

David Hiboux: Naturalized Amterean Dwarf, originally from Old Earth. Southern Boobook owl shapeshifter, who works as the ship's engineer for BlackWing X, before transferring to BlackWing XIII. (Latter Day Demons Series, BlackWing Pirates Series)

Dena: Avii bodyguard for Queen Quin. Formerly a yellow-winged castle servant. Now has multi-colored wings, like most Avii. (First Ordinance Series)

Devarr: King of Cloudsong. Husband to Hulce. (First Ordinance Series)

Derik: Prime Council of the Sirenali. (BlackWing Pirates Series)

Dori Anderson: Ocelot shapeshifter from Old Earth. Captain of BlackWing VII. Mother: Lavonna Anderson, a lioness shapeshifter. Father: Nathan Anderson, a vampire. One sister; Cori Anderson, a panther shapeshifter. (Legend of the Ir'Indicti Series, BlackWing Pirates Series)

Dormas: Ancient vampire who raised Gavril/Teeg after Kifirin removed him from Le-Ath Veronis. Taught Teeg woodworking, building and architecture. Now serves as Teeg's assistant in the Campiaan Alliance. (High Demon Series)

Drake Tatsuya: Falchani, serves as co-commander of Queen Lissa's army on Le-Ath Veronis. Father: Dragon Tatsuya. Mother: Devin of the Saa Thalarr. Mated to Queen Lissa. Twin brother to Drew Tatsuya. One son: Travis Tatsuya. (Blood Destiny Series)

Drew Tatsuya: Falchani, serves as co-commander of Queen Lissa's army on Le-Ath Veronis. Father: Dragon Tatsuya. Mother: Devin of the Saa Thalarr. Mated to Queen Lissa. Twin brother to Drake Tatsuya. One son: Trent Tatsuya. (Blood Destiny Series)

Edden Charkisul: Former High President of Kondar, a large continent on Siriaa. Now serves as an Ambassador for the Avii, after he was given the blue wings of a scholar by Zaria. (First Ordinance Series)

Edward Pendley: From Old Earth of Elemaiyan ancestry. Now owns EastStar Groves, producing gishi fruit on Avendor. Mated to Queen Reah. Member of the En'Nurifi—see Hierarchy of the Gods. (Legend of the Ir'Indicti Series, High Demon Series)

Erland Morphis: Father of King Rylend of Karathia. Mated to Lissa, Queen of Le-Ath Veronis. Fifth-level warlock with strong spell-casting skills. Member of the Ba'Mirha—see Hierarchy of the Gods. (Blood Destiny Series)

Ex'ero Plumb: Crillie resident of Horlak, and owner of seventy-six scrapyard warehouses. Formerly a business associate of Jewl Yarro. Crillie men have two functional penises, which is often the source of sexual jokes (BlackWing Pirates Series)

Farisa: Avii guild master who has persecuted Quin in the past. (First Ordinance Series)

Fergue Bing: Former boyfriend of Sabrina, native of Jaledis. (BlackWing Pirates Series)

Flavio: Vampire from Old Earth; took over as Head of the Vampire Council when Wlodek vacated the position to join the Saa Thalarr. Now a high-ranking Council member in Queen Lissa's court on Le-Ath Veronis. Mated to Kyler. Auxiliary member of the Saa Thalarr. (Blood Destiny Series)

Flyer: Falchani warrior, member of the Saa Thalarr and member of the Nameless Ones—see Hierarchy of the Gods. (High Demon Series)

Franc: One of two trusted bodyguards and emissaries who work for Zanfield Staggs (BlackWing Pirates Series)

Fyris: Small continent on Siriaa, a planet destroyed by Vardil Cayetes. (First Ordinance Series)

Galaxsan Starr: Fifth-level Karathian warlock, one of four brothers who protect Teeg San Gerxon. Member of the Nameless Ones—see Hierarchy of the Gods. (High Demon Series, BlackWing Pirates Series)

Gant Family: First family to turn against and kill one another in the Prophet's experiments with tainted food (BlackWing Pirates Series)

Gardevik Rath (deceased): Former High Demon Prime Minister to King Jaydevik Rath (deceased) of Kifirin. Mated to Queen Lissa. One son: Torevik Rath. (Blood Destiny Series)

Garwin Wyatt San Gerxon: Son of Teeg San Gerxon, Founder of the Campiaan Alliance. Goes by Wyatt most of the time, and acts as an ambassador for his father in Alliance dealings. Mother: Queen Reah of Kifirin. Grandmother: Queen Lissa of Le-Ath Veronis. (High Demon Series)

Gavin Montegue: Head of palace security for Queen Lissa. From Old Earth, he acted as the Vampire Council's chief assassin for centuries. Roman by birth, he served in the Roman army until his near-death in battle. Turned by Aurelius afterward. Mated to Queen Lissa. One son: Gavril Tybus Montegue, aka Teeg San Gerxon. Member of the Nameless Ones—see Hierarchy of the Gods. (Blood Destiny Series)

Gerrett: Sirenali, son of V'ili and Erithia Cordan, both Sirenali. Brother of Morrett and Terrett. V'ili had no idea that he fathered three sons with Erithia, and she held V'ili in such contempt that she only pretended to like him to get her way at times. Each time she bore V'ili's child, she sold that child into slavery at an early age, after removing his tongue so he could never place an obsession. (R-D Series)

Gillen Wilker: A strong, Fourth-level warlock, Perri and Pauley Wilker-Ironsmith's biological father, and brother to Alken Wilker. Employed by Mebbers, a criminal kingpin. Married to Qatti, a Third-level witch (BlackWing Pirates Series)

Gis: A non-Alliance world, raided by Mebbers in his search for hulls and scrap to build his fleet of starships (BlackWing Pirates Series)

Gord: Sabrina Kend's bodyguard, before she became an agent for the ASD. (BlackWing Pirates Series)

Grace: Member of the Saa Thalarr; she is the lace-feathered eagle, held in high esteem by all female Falchani warriors (Blood Destiny Series, Saa Thalarr Series)

Gungl: Largest city remaining on Vogeffa II (First Ordinance Series, BlackWing Pirates Series)

Gurnil: Blue-winged scholar and master librarian for the Avii. (First Ordinance Series)

Halimel: Vampire; former King of Hraede and member of the Order of the Night Flower on Hraede. Turned by Rigo. (Blood Destiny Series)

Haral Lebbon: Newly-elected president of Pyrik, after President Bargel's demise. (BlackWing Pirates Series)

Haribauld: An ancient city, long thought a myth, until Nari and Tiri uncovered its remains on an abandoned world (BlackWing Pirates Series)

Hariki: Nature spirit and Dori's Ar'pex (BlackWing Pirates Series)

Harlee: BlackWing X's new Engineer, after David transferred to BlackWing XIII (BlackWing Pirates Series)

Hierarchy of the Gods*:

The One

The Three (aka The Mighty)

Wisdom (Charles Hoffman) Strength (Ashe Evans) Love (Breanne Hayworth)

Ko'Ahmari

Ghi'Yisi

Al'Riyu

En'Nurifi

Ba'Mirha

Mil'Karha

Pan'Warha

Nameless Ones

Powers That Be

*members of the Hierarchy have strict rules of non-interference in the everyday happenings of mortals. Only the Three can completely override those rules, and they will only give permission for others to interfere when all the universes are in danger.

Horlak: Reth Alliance world and home to Ex'ero Plumb (BlackWing Pirates Series)

Hulce: Prince of Cloudsong, Chief of Sciences and husband to King Devarr of Cloudsong. (First Ordinance Series)

Ildevar Wyyld: Founder of the Reth Alliance. A Copper Ra'Ak, before the fall of the Copper Ra'Ak. Honest, trustworthy and of impeccable character. Member of the Ghi'Yisi—see Hierarchy of the Gods. (Blood Destiny Series)

Ilya Ironsmith: Powerful Fifth-level Karathian warlock, who has studied bladework and blade making extensively on Falchan. Before he was reborn as Ilya Ironsmith, he was Ilya Kuznetzov, a former Russian spy. (R-D Series and First Ordinance Series)

Jak: One of two Blevakian brothers who were hired by Jewl Yarro as bodyguards. (Blackwing Pirates Series) Now acts as bodyguard for Randl Gage, aboard BlackWing XIII (BlackWing Pirates Series)

Jaledis: Homeworld of Sabrina Kend and Kend Industries (BlackWing Pirates Series)

James Draper: From Old Earth. Now works as the pilot for BlackWing X. Mated to Nathan Cross, Navigator for BlackWing X. (R-D Series)

Jaydevik Rath (deceased): Former High Demon King of Kifirin. (Blood Destiny Series)

Jayna Dayle: ASD agent. Born on Vic'Law, a planet destroyed by Vardil Cayetes and his minions (First Ordinance Series)

Jerra: Avii daughter of King Justis and Queen Quin. (BlackWing Pirates Series)

Jett Riffler: Native Avendoran Fi'Gu, a dark-skinned race who tattoo the left sides of their bodies as a spiritual offering to their gods. Jett was named Director of the Campiaan Security Detail because of his bravery in the Campiaan Regular Army, where he rose to the highest position in its ranks. Jett is more than capable in his job, and is a good friend of Kooper's, as well as the Founders of both Alliances. (God Wars Series)

Jewl Yarro: One of the Big Three criminal kingpins since the demise of Vardil Cayetes. (BlackWing Pirates Series)

Jincus: Originally from Vic'Law, escaped before its destruction with his brother and made a home on Horlak. Worked at a scrapyard for Ex'ero Plumb on Horlak's moon, before the scrapyard warehouse was destroyed by a spell laid by Stone Wicke. Now works as Engineer's Assistant on BlackWing XIII (BlackWing Pirates Series)

Jurris (deceased): Former red-winged King of the Avii, and half-brother to the current King, Justis. Father of Liron, who was named after the god before it was determined that the original Liron was a rogue god. (First Ordinance Series)

Justis: Red-winged King of the Avii. Formerly had black wings and served as his brother's (King Jurris) Commander of the Avii army. (First Ordinance Series)

Karzac Halivar: Physician originally from Refizan. He is more than fifteen thousand years old, served as a healer for the Saa Thalarr and is mated to Lissa, Devin and Grace. One son with Grace—Kevis Halivar. Member of the Ko'Ahmari—see Hierarchy of the Gods. (Blood Destiny Series)

Kay Zahn: Known as R'Kita, or Changer in the Elemaiyan language. Mated to Ashe Evans. Member of the Ba'Mirha—see Hierarchy of the Gods. (God Wars Series)

Kell (Kellik of Abenott): Former noble in the Hraedan Court; became vampire before his natural death occurred. He was responsible for turning Rigovarnus I, who formed the Order of the Night Flower on Hraede. That order is comprised of former kings of Hraede, who have had their steady hand guiding the monarchy through millennia to ensure the safety and stability of that world. A master spy, Kell taught the order everything he knew, including a few things about the fine art of poison-making. Kell is mated to Opal. (First Ordinance Series)

Ke'Leru (skull) Pirates: A group overseen by the Prophet, to further his plans and desires. (BlackWing Pirates Series)

Kev'Ril: World destroyed long ago by nuclear warfare (BlackWing Pirates Series)

Kiarra: Strongest member of the Saa Thalarr. Father: Wisdom. Mated to Adam Chessman, Merrill Leopard and Pheligar of the Larentii. Also a member of the Ghi'Yisi—see Hierarchy of the Gods. (Blood Destiny Series, Saa Thalarr Series)

Kooper Griff: Director of the Alliance Security Detail (ASD). He is a lion snake shapeshifter, one of the few snakes that can blink. Their venom is deadly and so fast-acting that the use of an antidote must be immediate to save the victim's life. Member of the Ba'Mirha—see Hierarchy of the Gods. (God Wars Series)

Kordevik Weth: High Demon Crown Prince. Mated to Lexsi, Crown Princess of Kifirin. Father: Lord Nedevik Weth. Mother: Lady Verarok. (Latter Day Demons Series)

Lafe: aka Lafranza; Falchani Warrior and the ultimate tattoo artist. Mated to Quin. (First Ordinance Series)

Le-Ath Veronis: Reth Alliance world and home to most of its vampire population.

Lee'Qee: An abandoned city on Pyrik, quarantined because of a nuclear accident, centuries earlier. Home to the Ke'Leru Pirates, who became the Prophet's minions because they were hidden from the regular population and made themselves convenient for his takeover (BlackWing Pirates Series)

Len: Captain of the Furrow, a ship hauling food and supplies. (BlackWing Pirates Series)

Lenk: Captain of the Palace Guard on Cloudsong. (First Ordinance Series, BlackWing Pirates Series)

Le'Vestar Limn: Engineer and weapons expert; Or'myr wyrm-dragon from Campiaa, kidnapped by the Prophet alongside Mae'Sandar Keel (BlackWing Pirates Series)

Lexsi: High Demon Crown Princess of Kifirin. Mother: Reah, Queen of Kifirin. Father: Torevik Rath. Grandmother: Queen Lissa. Grandfather: Gardevik Rath (deceased). (Latter Day Demons Series)

Lindom Family: Second family turned against itself in the Prophet's experiments with tainted food (BlackWing Pirates Series)

Liron: A rogue god who manufactured Quin to carry out his plan to keep the Avii and Fyris safe, in the event of his demise. Quin was rescued from Liron's clutches by Zaria. (First Ordinance Series)

Liron: Avii; son of Jurris (deceased), former King of the Avii. (First Ordinance Series)

Lissa: Vampire Queen of Le-Ath Veronis, also junior member of the Mighty. Father: Brenten Arden, aka Griffin, a former member of the Saa Thalarr. Mother: Harriet-deceased. See "Hierarchy of the gods." (Blood Destiny Series)

Lordinus: Reth Alliance world and home to the Gant family (BlackWing Pirates Series)

Lorvis Verll (deceased): Native of Jaledis and former best friend of Sabrina Kend. (BlackWing Pirates Series)

Lukas: New Grand Master of the werewolves of Harifa Edus. (BlackWing Pirates Series)

Mae'Sandar Keel: Engineer and Or'myr Dragon Queen from Campiaa, kidnapped by the Prophet (BlackWing Pirates Series)

Mak: One of two Blevakian brothers who were hired by Jewl Yarro as bodyguards. (Blackwing Pirates Series) Now serves as bodyguard for Randl Gage aboard BlackWing XIII (BlackWing Pirates Series)

Marco DeLuca: Werewolf from Old Earth. Co-Captain of BlackWing VIII with his wife, Cori Anderson-DeLuca. (Legend of the Ir'Indicti Series, BlackWing Pirates Series)

Mariana: Married to Brandl Gage, mother of Randl Gage; from Vogeffa II (BlackWing Pirates Series)

Markus: Chief of local ASD Department in Turbak, on Jaledis. (BlackWing Pirates Series) Now serves as Chief of Security aboard BlackWing XIII (BlackWing Pirates Series)

Mebbers: Criminal Kingpin from A'pelur. He has successfully hidden from his criminal rivals for decades, behind walls filled with Sirenali bones (BlackWing Pirates Series)

Meerius: Nature spirit; Ar'pex to Vik Roth (BlackWing Pirates Series)

Melton Timble: Native of Pyrik; Shella Karp's fiancé, who killed her in a fit of jealousy. (BlackWing Pirates Series)

Merrill: From Old Earth. Roman by birth, was nearly killed in a battle. Turned by Wlodek, former Head of the Vampire Council on Earth. Merrill is a King Vampire, one who is not susceptible to any vampire's compulsion. Mated to Lissa and Kiarra. Member of the Saa Thalarr, and member of the Al'Riyu—see Hierarchy of the Gods. (Blood Destiny Series)

Miz'Sandar Keel: Comp-vid Engineer and Or'myr wyrm-dragon from Campiaa. Brother to Mae'Sandar Keel (BlackWing Pirates Series)

Morrett: Sirenali, son of V'ili and Erithia Cordan, both Sirenali. Brother of Terrett and Gerrett. V'ili had no idea that he fathered three sons with Erithia, and she held V'ili in such contempt that she only pretended to like him to get her way at times. Each time she bore V'ili's child, she sold that child into slavery at an early age, after removing his tongue so he could never place an obsession. (R-D Series)

Morwin: Often called Master Morwin, he works as a private tutor to the children of Kings, Queens and other important people. Amterean Dwarf by birth, who served twenty years in the Amterean military before become a scholar and teacher. (Blood Destiny Series)

Nari: Powerful relic hunter (Queen's Holiday short story, BlackWing Pirates Series)

Nathan Cross: From Old Earth. Now works as the navigator for BlackWing X. Mated to James Draper, pilot for BlackWing X. (R-D Series)

Nenzi: One of eight reptanoid brothers who are lion snake shapeshifters, although their births were manipulated by a criminal element to create assassins. Nenzi and his brothers had slightly slitted eyes, preventing them from passing as fully human, and therefore they were never forced into the role of assassins. Instead, they became well-versed in farming and the repair of mechanical things, providing maintenance and such to their criminal masters until freed by Reah and Teeg San Gerxon. Nenzi is mated to Queen Reah. Member of the Nameless Ones—see Hierarchy of the Gods. (High Demon Series)

Northon: Homeworld of WildTree Industries.

Opal Tadewi: Opal is from Old Earth—a Native American shapeshifting velociraptor. She was a member of the Old Ones—a line of long-lived shapeshifters on Earth who held a place of honor among all shapeshifters. Opal has served in many capacities, including law enforcement. Member of the Ba'Mirha—see Hierarchy of the Gods.

Ordin: Green-winged Avii master healer. (First Ordinance Series)

Oskar: Winged guard at Avii Castle (BlackWing Pirates Series)

O'Tunne: Presidential candidate on Pyrik, who lost the election to Lebbon. (BlackWing Pirates Series)

Pauley Wilker-Ironsmith: Born a void on Karathia—without even a trace of power. This condition is highly unusual among the citizens of Karathia, and is considered quite debilitating. Brother to Perri Wilker-Ironsmith (BlackWing Pirates Series)

Perill: A highly-placed officer in the Prophet's army. Born on Pyrik, in the poisoned, abandoned city of Lee'Qee. Father: Vrak. Brother: Varok. (BlackWing Pirates Series)

Perri Wilker-Ironsmith: Fourth-level witch with a power-scenting talent. Abandoned by her parents and abused by her uncle, she completed her degree at the University of Le-Ath Veronis before going to work for the Crown of Karathia, tracking down rogue warlocks and witches. Sister to Pauley (BlackWing Pirates Series)

Phillip: Originally a half-Elemaiyan child born on Old Earth, Phillip was a mountain lion shapeshifter. The tennis ball Ashe Evans once handed to Lissa belonged to him in his ghostly alter ego, as he was killed on Earth and brought back to life by the Mighty Heart (Legend of the Ir'Indicti Series, The God Wars Series, BlackWing Pirates Series)

Phorde Gaster: Imposter placed in WildTree Industries by the Prophet to carry out his plans. Now deceased. (BlackWing Pirates Series)

Phrinnis Tampirus: President of the Podl'Morphs, who can become anything animal, vegetable or mineral, according to their choice. Mated to Zaria. (First Ordinance Series)

P'loxett: A world destroyed by nuclear warfare; home base and hideout for the Prophet and his army.

Poll Endicutt: Small-time criminal from Campiaa, who is in love with his boss, Charla Dare. (BlackWing Pirates Series)

Qatti Wilker: Third-level Karathian witch; Perri and Pauley's mother, strongly motivated by money and employed (with her husband, Gillen) by Mebbers (BlackWing Pirates Series)

Quin: Queen of the Avii, a winged race from Siriaa, a planet destroyed by Vardil Cayetes. Began her life as a construct of the rogue god, Liron. Served as kitchen servant and page in Fyris, a small continent on Siriaa. (First Ordinance Series) Ar'pex: Tiralia

Rale Linn: One of the Big Three criminal kingpins to take over after Vardil Cayetes' death. (BlackWing Pirates Series)

Randl Gage: Blind clairvoyant born on Vogeffa II. Father: Brandl Gage. Mother is deceased. When Vogeffa II was attacked by Vardil Cayetes, most of the population was moved to New Fyris on Harifa Edus. Employed first by Prince Amlis, and later by the Alliance Security Detail (First Ordinance Series) Commander of BlackWing Fleet; chief Ar'pexi: Kev'Ril and Bennall

Reah: High Demon Queen of Kifirin. (High Demon Series)

Reemagar: Larentii. Mated to Queen Lissa. (Blood Destiny Series)

Refizan: Reth Alliance world; home planet of Karzac Halivar.

Renée Coffin: Queen Lissa's only female assistant, as female vampires are quite rare. Turned by Lissa herself, Renée has no knowledge of that and believes she was turned by Montrose, who acts as her sire and became her lover, once her five-year training period was over. (First Ordinance Series)

Revalus: Homeworld for the remnants of the Podl'Morphs and the Sirenali (First Ordinance Series, Latter Day Demons Series)

Reviendus: Randl Gage's title, given by the Ar'pexi, which means Soul of the Universes (BlackWing Pirates Series)

Rigo: aka Rigovarnus I of Hraede. An ancient vampire who was King of Hraede at one time. Founder of the Order of the Night

Flower on Hraede. That order is comprised of former kings of Hraede —all of them made vampires at the end of their reign. The order has had a steady hand guiding the monarchy through millennia to ensure the safety and stability of that world. Rigo was made vampire by Kellik of Abenott, who taught the order everything he knew, including a few things about the fine art of poison-making. Mated to Queen Lissa, and serves as the director of Lissa's hidden spy network. Member of the Mil'Karha—see Hierarchy of the Gods. (Blood Destiny Series)

Rodrik: Heir and Bodyguard to Prince Amlis. Father: Rath-deceased. Wife: Beatris, one child (First Ordinance Series)

Ru'beq: Reth Alliance world (BlackWing Pirates Series)

Ruther Kend: Owner of Kend industries. Married to Barra Kend, Father of Sabrina Kend. Kend Industries supplies the ASD and CSD with much of their weaponry and surveillance equipment. (First Ordinance Series)

Rylend Morphis: Fifth-level warlock and King of Karathia. Mother: Queen Lissa of Le-Ath Veronis. Father: Lord Erland Morphis. One son: Crown Prince Bel Erland Morphis. Siblings: Torevik Rath, Nissa Grey, Gavril Montegue (Teeg San Gerxon) Travis and Trent Tatsuya, Willow and Wayne Winkler. Mated to Queen Reah of Kifirin. (Blood Destiny Series)

Saa Thalarr: A term in the dead language of Neaboria, meaning Hope and Vengeance. It is a small race created and endowed with power specifically to destroy Ra'Ak and their spawn (Blood Destiny Series and Saa Thalarr Series)

Sabrina Kend: Genius daughter of Ruther Kend, owner of Kend Industries. Mother: Barra Kend. Kend Industries supplies the ASD and CSD with much of their weaponry and surveillance equipment. First mentioned in First Ordinance Series as an unnamed daughter of Ruther Kend. (BlackWing Pirates Series)

Salidar DeLuca: Werewolf shapeshifter. Taught the art of the blade by the Falchani blademaster Caylon Black. Mated to the Mighty Heart. (Legend of the Ir'Indicti Series)

Sandra L'Thorpe: Nurse and Nanny for Lissa's twins, Wayne and

Wynter (BlackWing Pirates Series)

Shella Karp: Native of Pyrik, works as one of President Lebbon's assistants. (BlackWing Pirates Series)

Soul of the Universes: A title the Ar'pexi have given to Randl (BlackWing Pirates Series)

Stellan Starr: Fifth-level Karathian warlock, one of four brothers who protect Teeg San Gerxon. Mated to Breanne. Member of the Nameless Ones—see Hierarchy of the Gods. (High Demon Series, BlackWing Pirates Series)

Stone Wicke: Low Fifth-level warlock, employed by Mebbers for decades. Prior employment was for one criminal after another for centuries, after which he faked his own death to remove himself from the Karathian Crown's most-wanted list (BlackWing Pirates Series)

Susan Plume: Hen shapeshifter (Buff Orpington). ASD agent who doubles as a cook for the crew of BlackWing X. (Latter Day Demons Series)

T'beq: Capital City of Ru'beq, a Reth Alliance world (BlackWing Pirates Series)

Teeg San Gerxon: Founder of the Campiaan Alliance. His given name at birth was Gavril Tybus Montegue. Mother: Queen Lissa of Le-Ath Veronis. Father: Gavin Montegue, one of Lissa's mates. His nickname, Teeg, was given to him by his foster-father, Dormas. He took that name when he was separated from his parents by Kifirin (the god, not the planet), who exacted payment for a request made by a young Gavril. His last name, San Gerxon, was acquired when he was named heir to Arvil San Gerxon, a criminal kingpin who built the small planet of Campiaa into a non-Alliance gambling mecca. Teeg's siblings include: Rylend Morphis, Torevik Rath, Nissa Grey, Travis and Trent Tatsuya, and Willow and Wayne Winkler. Mated to Reah, Queen of Kifirin. (High Demon Series)

Teren: One of two trusted bodyguards and emissaries who work for Zanfield Staggs (BlackWing Pirates Series)

Terrett: Sirenali, son of V'ili and Erithia Cordan, both Sirenali. Brother of Morrett and Gerrett. V'ili had no idea that he fathered three sons with Erithia, and she held V'ili in such contempt that she only pretended to like him to get her way at times. Each time she bore V'ili's child, she sold that child into slavery at an early age, after removing his tongue so he could never place an obsession. (First Ordinance Series)

Tim'Bek II: An abandoned world taken by the Prophet.

Tiri: Powerful relic hunter (Queen's Holiday short story, BlackWing Pirates Series)

Tiralia: World which destroyed itself with chemical warfare long ago. Still has a very poisonous atmosphere and none approach it. Only source of Tiralian crystal, a gem worth far more than any other. Also, Arpex for Quin (Saa Thalarr Series, BlackWing Pirates Series)

Torevik Rath (Tory): See Vik Roth.

Travis Tetsuya: (Tatsuya): Son of Queen Lissa and Drake Tatsuya. Takes after his father, who is Falchani (God Wars Series, BlackWing Pirates Series)

Trent Tetsuya: (Tatsuya) Son of Queen Lissa and Drew Tatsuya. Like their fathers, Drake and Drew, Travis and Trent are twins (God Wars Series, BlackWing Pirates Series)

Turtle: Falchani warrior, member of the Saa Thalarr, member of the Nameless Ones—see Hierarchy of the Gods. (Blood Destiny Series)

Tybus: A very ancient vampire, born long before the destruction of Le-Ath Veronis by the Copper Ra'Ak millennia ago. Le-Ath Veronis lay dormant for eons before Lissa arrived to rebuild it. (God Wars Series)

Ula Karn: Native of Jaledis and former friend of Sabrina Kend. Having an affair with Fergue Bing behind Sabrina's back. (BlackWing Pirates Series)

Vardil Cayetes: A criminal kingpin responsible for too many deaths to count in and out of the Alliances. Killed by Zaria (First Ordinance Series)

Varok: A highly-placed officer in the Prophet's army. Born on Pyrik, in the poisoned city of Lee'Qee. Father: Vrak. Brother: Perill. (BlackWing Pirates Series)

V'dar: aka the Prophet. Born on Vogeffa II. Parents deceased. Has skills of a sorcerer and necromancer. Not much is commonly known about him otherwise. (BlackWing Pirates Series)

Vik Roth: aka Torevik Rath. Brought back from death by Zaria, he now works under an assumed name for the ASD. High Demon son of Queen Lissa and Gardevik Rath. (Blood Destiny Series, High Demon Series, BlackWing Pirates Series)

V'ili: Sirenali Prince before the destruction of Sirena by the Larentii. Was rescued from that destruction by rogue gods, who commanded him to create chaos through the years in order to destroy the Mighty and the universes with them. (God Wars Series, First Ordinance Series)

Vogeffa II: A world which was nearly destroyed by climate change. All polar ice melted, leaving only one small continent for residents to live on. Drew a criminal element after a time, and became home to many who were considered mutants.

Vorina: Avii and wife of former Avii King Jurris. (First Ordinance Series)

Vrak: There are two, the original, conscripted by the Prophet, and an imposter placed by the Prophet to do his bidding and lead raiding parties to steal food and supplies from passing ships. (BlackWing Pirates Series)

Warlend Arden: Former King of Karathia. Abdicated in favor of his son, Wellend Arden. Now a member of the Avii race, through Zaria's efforts. Has red wings, denoting royalty of that race, along with retaining his warlock's skills. (First Ordinance Series)

Weldon Harper: Former Grand Master of the Werewolves on Old Earth. Member of the Saa Thalarr and of the Ba'Mirha—see Hierarchy of the Gods. (Blood Destiny Series)

Wellend Arden: Former King of Karathia. Attempt made on his life by his step-mother and her father, who wanted their natural grandson on the throne. Throne eventually taken by Wellend's half-brother, Wylend Arden. Father: Warlend Arden. Now a member of the Avii race, through Zaria's efforts. Has red wings, denoting royalty of that race, along with retaining his warlock skills. (First Ordinance Series)

Wib'burne: Homeworld of Zanfield Staggs.

Wilm Bedard: Noted journalist from Horlak (BlackWing Pirates Series)

Wimla: Avii and wife of former Avii King Jurris. Mother of young Liron. (First Ordinance Series)

Winkler: (William Wayne Winkler) werewolf and Former Dallas Packmaster on Old Earth. Mated to Queen Lissa, and serves as a Spawn Hunter for the Saa Thalarr. Member of the Ba'Mirha—see Hierarchy of the gods. (Blood Destiny Series)

Wisdom: One of the Mighty, aka Charles. (Blood Destiny Series, God Wars Series)

Woord'l: Campiaan Alliance world, home to Huyer Food Distribution, which was targeted by the prophet for theft of provisions (BlackWing Pirates Series)

Wyatt: See Garwin Wyatt San Gerxon.

Wyyld: Home of the Reth Alliance Founder, Ildevar Wyyld.

Yurik: Obsessed minion of the Prophet, placed in charge of getting his starship rebuilt. Yurik was out of his depth, however, and likely would have died sooner and at the Prophet's hand, had Le'Vestar Limn not known what he was doing (BlackWing Pirates Series)

Zanfield Staggs: Trillionaire from Felarku, Wib'burne. Loves to gamble and has a flair for the unusual or exotic. (BlackWing Pirates Series)

Zaria: Also known as Corinnelar the Vhanaraszh to the Larentii, and Corinne Watson on Old Earth. Zaria is a powerful enigma who holds the entire metal library, which contains information on everything in existence. Father: Wisdom. Mother: Unknown (R-D Series, First Ordinance Series, BlackWing Pirates Series)

www.ingramcontent.com/pod-product-compliance
Lightning Source LLC
Chambersburg PA
CBHW060943120726
47910CB00002B/463